Acclaim for Nicole Jacquelyn and Her Novels

"*Change of Heart* is sexy, emotional, and the perfect follow-up to *Unbreak My Heart*. Fans of Colleen Hoover, Jamie McGuire, and K.A. Tucker will enjoy *Change of Heart*."

—HarlequinJunkie.com

"This book is sure to stay in the minds of readers for a long time, just based off of the uniqueness of the protagonists alone. Gone [are] the shy, insecure female and the romantic male, two dominant figures who curse like sailors and like their sex fast and rough. The author also does a great job delving into the dynamics of adoption." —*RT Book Reviews* on *Change of Heart*

"*Unbreak My Heart* is a heartbreaking, heartwarming, heart-twisting love affair that proves love stands the test of time."

—Heidi McLaughlin, *New York Times* bestselling author

"Nicole Jacquelyn has penned an emotionally provocative story...I was hooked from page one as this amazing author put me through the wringer. It was a tumultuous ride that left this reader satisfied and craving more."

—NightOwlReviews.com on *Unbreak My Heart*

"*Unbreak My Heart* is a completely engaging, sweet, devastating, heartbreaking, and angst-filled story that captivated me from the beginning. Nicole Jacquelyn takes you on a roller-coaster ride of emotional ups and downs as a family has to find their way forward after a loss."

—HarlequinJunkie.com on *Unbreak My Heart*

HEART
of glass

ALSO BY NICOLE JACQUELYN

Unbreak My Heart
Change of Heart

HEART
of glass

NICOLE JACQUELYN

FOREVER

New York   Boston

Copyright © 2018 by Nicole Jacquelyn
Excerpt from *Unbreak My Heart* © 2016 by Nicole Jacquelyn
Cover design by FaceOut.
Cover photography © Jasmina007/Getty Images.
Cover copyright © 2018 by Hachette Book Group, Inc.

Forever
Hachette Book Group
1290 Avenue of the Americas, New York, NY 10104
forever-romance.com
twitter.com/foreverromance

First Edition: July 2018

Forever is an imprint of Grand Central Publishing. The Forever name and logo are trademarks of Hachette Book Group, Inc.

The publisher is not responsible for websites (or their content) that are not owned by the publisher.

The Hachette Speakers Bureau provides a wide range of authors for speaking events. To find out more, go to www.hachettespeakersbureau.com or call (866) 376-6591.

Library of Congress Cataloging-in-Publication Data
Names: Jacquelyn, Nicole, author.
Title: Heart of glass / Nicole Jacquelyn.
Description: First edition. | New York ; Boston : Forever, 2018. | Series: Fostering love ; 3
Identifiers: LCCN 2018004253| ISBN 9781538711859 (paperback) | ISBN 9781549169113 (audio download) | ISBN 9781538711842 (ebook)
Subjects: | BISAC: FICTION / Contemporary Women. | FICTION / Family Life. | FICTION / Romance / Contemporary.
Classification: LCC PS3610.A35684 H43 2018 | DDC 813/.54—dc23
LC record available at https://lccn.loc.gov/2018004253

ISBNs: 9781538711859 (paperback), 9781538711842 (ebook)

Printed in the United States of America

LSC-C

10 9 8 7 6 5 4 3 2 1

This one is for Clint,
for giving me the happily ever after I didn't
think existed outside of romance novels.

Acknowledgments

My Acknowledgments are always long and unruly, but I'm going to try to keep these short and sweet.

Thank you to my fella and our kiddos for being so great when mama had to write.

Thank you to my parents and Kristi for pitching in to keep my house running when I couldn't. Who knew that newborns were so much work?

Thank you to my agent and my editors, who were patient and understanding and have continuously cheered me on.

Thank you to Nikki for being my sounding board and giving me a swift kick in the ass when I needed it.

Thank you to Donna, as always, for being the first blogger to tell the world about my work.

Thank you to the readers. Without you, I wouldn't get to do what I love.

HEART
of glass

Prologue

Henry

I was never meant to be a dad. The thought ran continuously through my head as I stepped out into the afternoon sunshine. Hell, it had been running through there for months, but lately the words were like a hammer repeatedly slamming into my brain. I could barely think of anything else.

"Why don't you wait until Monday to run your mysterious errand?" my roommate asked, interrupting my inner demon as we walked out of work. "We're gonna head to the beach."

"Can't," I replied with a shrug.

Beach Fridays were a pretty common thing with the guys I hung out with. We usually got off work early on Friday, which gave us a few extra hours to enjoy the weekend. Traffic in San Diego sucked during the late afternoon, but if we knocked off early enough we'd just make it out to Imperial Beach before most people started their commute home.

I wasn't really going to miss anything that wouldn't happen again the next week.

"Well, if you get done with your mysterious errand soon, let me know," Rocklin joked over his shoulder as he walked toward his truck.

I waved him off as I pulled my truck keys from inside my pocket. There was a reason I wasn't broadcasting my plans to the entire fucking platoon. I didn't need my command all up in my shit over something that was a non-issue. I was headed over to legal now, before everyone over there got off work for the day. There was a good chance that they'd left early, too, but I was holding out hope that someone was there who could help me.

I tapped my fingers on the knee of my cammies as I waited in the uncomfortable chairs in the front part of the legal building. The place was mostly cleared out for the weekend, but thankfully it looked like someone was left in the back that I could talk to. I wasn't sure when I'd get another chance to meet with someone before I left for yet another training exercise next week, and the thought of leaving without getting everything squared away made me anxious as hell.

Leaning my head against the wall, I closed my eyes. Behind them, I pictured the little bald baby I'd seen just weeks ago. Morgan's baby.

Well, my baby, too, if I decided to think of her in biological terms.

My stomach rolled.

I didn't want to think of her that way.

When Morgan had let me know she was pregnant, I'd panicked and replied as if an abortion was the foregone conclusion. Almost two years later, I was still surprised that she hadn't punched me in the balls. Instead, she'd calmly told me that she was keeping the baby but she hadn't expected anything from me.

Relief had hit me first. Overwhelming, giddy, relief.

Then I'd questioned myself. Was I really that type of guy? Could I just walk away from my flesh and blood? I'd been raised in a family that took in kids that weren't even theirs. They prized family above all else, and there were so many times over the course of my life when I'd been part of a discussion about deadbeat dads and how horrible they were.

So, instead of running in the opposite direction, I'd tried to be present. I hadn't said a word to my family, preferring *not* to listen to their opinions and suffocating interference, but I'd kept in touch with Morgan as she'd carried the baby. Any relationship between us had been impossible at that point, but I'd still checked in just to make sure she was okay. I had no interest in going to doctor appointments, and when she'd revealed that she was having a girl, I'd felt nothing—but I'd still kept trying.

I didn't want to be the kind of man my parents made scathing comments about. I didn't want Morgan's daughter to grow up thinking there was something wrong with her or some shit like that and end up being a stripper with daddy issues.

Okay, I knew that last one was a sweeping generalization, but I couldn't help it. That was where my mind went. So, I'd tried.

I'd visited and I'd called and I'd made myself available for whatever Morgan needed, but eventually we'd both seen the writing on the wall. It just wasn't there. That feeling, the one I knew I was supposed to have, the one every parent had, even the shitty parents? I didn't feel it.

I wasn't curious about the baby. I didn't wonder if she was okay or worry about her. I didn't feel anything for her at all, beyond the normal concern over a tiny human. Would I jump in front of a bus for her? Sure. But I'd do that for any kid.

That's what she was to me—just a random kid.

There was something wrong with me, I was sure of that fact, but it wasn't something I could fix or change. I'd tried. Jesus. I'd been trying for a year to feel anything for her, and it didn't matter what I did or what awful scenario I pictured in my head trying to force some sort of reaction, I just didn't feel anything.

I tried to convince myself that I could fake it. I could just pretend to feel something until I actually did. No one would know. But after stopping by their place for her first birthday and watching this kid who looked like me eat her cake, and still feeling nothing beyond a little amusement and boredom, I knew pretending wasn't going to be an option.

There was something broken inside of me. Something I'd never realized I'd needed until that blank feeling was staring me right in the face, mocking my inability to connect.

"Harris?" a voice called from between two cubicles.

I stood up and slid my hand absently down the front of my uniform blouse, smoothing out the wrinkles as I walked forward.

"You're wanting to change the beneficiary for your death benefits?" the guy asked, glancing down at the papers he was holding as I followed him into the bowels of the legal department.

"Yes, sir," I replied.

I couldn't be her parent. I couldn't be the dad that taught her how to ride a bike or a surfboard. I wouldn't be there to scare her prom date, and I'd never bandage her knees after a hard fall at the playground.

But I could help from afar. I could make sure Morgan had the cash she needed to make sure the baby didn't go without. I could help in that way. And if something happened to me, I could make sure that they were taken care of. It was the least I could do.

And if someday the time came when Morgan and baby Etta received death benefits from me, I knew with absolute certainty that my family would find them.

They wouldn't be able to stay away.

Chapter 1

Trevor

Even months after his death, my little brother was still the first person I thought about when I woke up in the morning and my last thought before falling asleep at night. He was everywhere I looked, in every conversation I had even when his name wasn't mentioned. It was ironic, really, that he took up so much headspace when in the last few years before his death I could go days without thinking about him at all.

Henry had always been like that. He showed up at the least opportune moments, like the night I'd finally asked Kristen Preston out my junior year of high school and he'd plopped down beside us in the movie theater like I'd invited him along. When I should have been thinking about him and talking to him, we'd both been too busy to catch up, and now that he was gone and I'd do anything to erase that fact from my mind, he was all I could think about.

I missed him like hell. I was also so angry with him that I wanted to punch something.

I wondered if other siblings, ones who'd been born into the

same family by accident of birth, felt the same way toward each other as I did toward Henry. Did they get so angry that they wanted to shake sense into their little brothers, or was it easier to give up on someone they'd never had to fight for to begin with? When he'd come into our lives, Henry's placement had been temporary. It was months before we'd known that he might stay forever. As a boy who had watched numerous other children move in and out of our house, knowing that Henry would stay had been difficult for me. I'd had to make a conscious choice to think of him as family. Once that shift had been made, though, I'd known that nothing would ever sever that bond. Even after all of the things I'd found out about Henry after his death, I still felt myself fighting for the memory I had of him, searching for the answers that would show that his decisions in life had made any type of sense.

"Mom?" I called out as I pushed the door open without knocking. "You home?"

"I'm back here," she yelled back from somewhere in the bowels of the house I'd grown up in.

I followed the sound of her voice down the hallway and found her seated at the long table in her craft room, gluing little sheets of paper on to a scrapbook page.

"Hey, Trev," she said, lifting her head to smile at me. "Everything okay?"

Guilt hit me hard and fast. A few months ago, a random visit wouldn't have garnered that type of question, but my mom seemed to have aged by years in less than a few months. Losing Henry, a boy she'd raised as her own since he was only two, had been a blow she hadn't recovered from, but the revelation that he'd abandoned his own child seemed to have completely broken her.

"Just wanted to see you," I said, smiling back. I stepped into the room and looked over the scrapbook she was making. It was covered in photos of my cousin Kate and foster brother Shane's kids. It had been a few years, but I still couldn't believe that my foster brother and cousin had fallen in love. The page Mom was working on had snapshots of their four oldest running through a sprinkler. "Lookin' good."

"Thanks," she said, picking up a glue stick. "I swear, I can't keep up with the pictures. These are from last year."

I pulled up a chair from the side of the little room and spun it around, stretching out my long legs as I sat down beside her. My mom was so petite that I always felt like a giant when I was near her. From the time I was thirteen I'd been taller than she was, and we'd gotten a lot of speculating looks when she'd taken me into town for school clothes or other random shit, the small pale white woman bossing around the dark-skinned black kid who dwarfed her.

She'd never let those looks bother her, so I hadn't, either— at least not out loud. I'd just raised my chin a little and walked a step closer, making sure that any comments directed toward her would have to go through me first. When I was a kid, it had worked. People had backed off a bit, unwilling to cause problems. As I'd gotten older, though, it seemed to have become harder for the population just to accept shit as none of their business. I never knew if it had been the change in my appearance or the social changes that had risen up around us, forcing people to take a second look and choose which side they wanted to be on. As if there were fucking sides to begin with.

"Dad should be home in a little bit," Mom said, pulling my attention away from how her delicate hands placed small letters in an arch across the top of the page. "We're grilling burgers if you want to stay."

"Maybe," I replied. "I actually wanted to talk to you guys."

"About what?" She looked at me curiously.

"I think it's time I head down to California," I said quietly, watching her eyes flicker in barely disguised pain. "It's been a few months and we've all cooled off—"

"You know I don't think that's a good idea," she cut me off, her hands gone motionless on the table.

"Someone's gotta go down there, Mom."

"*I* should go," she replied stubbornly.

"No," I said with a swift shake of my head. I couldn't imagine my mom going very far from home to begin with, but I refused to imagine her going to California to see Henry's kid and getting shot down by the kid's mother, or, even worse, being manipulated in order to have a relationship with the baby. It would completely devastate her.

"Trevor," she said in warning, her back straightening away from her chair back. "I know you worry, son, but you have no idea how to handle situations like this. Birth mothers are—"

"Birth mothers?"

"Yes," she said patiently, reaching out to pat my knee. "They're protective."

"And adoptive mothers aren't?" I argued, clenching my jaw.

Mom laughed. "Please," she joked. "I'd fight a mountain lion for my sons."

"Then what are you—"

She stopped my sentence with a raised hand. "I should have said 'mothers,' okay?" she said with a small smile. "I meant all mothers. They're protective. And if you go down there, being abrasive and throwing your weight around, she's not going to want anything to do with us."

"When am I ever abrasive?" I argued.

"You mean other than right now?" she asked drily.

"I don't think it's a good idea for you to go down there, Ma," I said softly, unsure how to describe my reservations without insulting her.

"Agreed," my dad said from the doorway behind us. "You know how I feel about it, El."

"I'm not some piece of china," Mom said in exasperation, glaring at her husband.

"You don't know the woman—"

"I know her name. I know that she knew my boy—quite well if they had a child together. I know she's raising that child without the help of my son, and has apparently been doing that since before he died!" I followed my mom as she rose indignantly to her feet.

"Trevor can go down and introduce himself," my dad said, his eyes tightening at the corners and his voice deepening. "And you can be pissed all you want. I wanna meet Henry's child as much as you do, but *you* are my priority, sweetheart."

The worry in my dad's eyes must have hit a switch inside my mom, because one second she was standing rigidly in the middle of the room preparing for battle, and the next she'd softened and was walking slowly toward my dad, wrapping her arms around his middle as he stood with his arms braced on each side of the door frame.

"When you thinking about heading down?" Dad asked as his arms wound around Mom's shoulders.

"Next week," I replied, leaning my hip against the craft table. "I'm gonna drive down so I've got my truck."

"Shitty drive," Dad said in commiseration. "You gonna stay with Shane and Katie? Maybe they'd come with you to meet the baby."

"You're kidding, right?" I answered, my lips twitching. "I thought we didn't want to scare the mom off."

My dad guffawed as Mom shook her head.

"Everyone loves Kate," she said in admonishment. "If anything, she'd probably become best friends with the girl."

"Let's just wait and make sure she's worth being best friends with, huh?" I said as we moved out of the craft room and down the hallway toward the kitchen. "We don't know anything about her."

"Henry clearly liked her."

"Not necessarily," I said, embarrassment making heat race up the back of my neck. "We don't know if there was a relationship."

"Clearly not an important one if Hen didn't ever mention her," my dad said as he pulled food out of the fridge.

"What?" my mom asked, glancing between the two of us. "Are you saying she was a—*a one-night stand*?" She sounded so scandalized that my dad snorted out a laugh, while I wanted to sink through the floor. Having any conversation about sex with my mother ranked at about the same level of discomfort as having my balls waxed...actually, I'd rather be having my balls waxed.

"Not sure that Henry really had relationships," I muttered, when she continued to stare at me as if waiting for an answer.

"Well, that's just great," she barked as she stomped toward the kitchen sink. "And what about you?"

My eyes widened in horror as I stood there frozen, too afraid to move in case a sound would make her turn in my direction.

"Quit," Dad said, slapping my mom's hip lightly. "He doesn't want to talk about that shit with you, crazy woman."

"I thought I raised them to respect women," she replied as if I wasn't even in the room. "I thought I taught them that sex was a gift and shouldn't be taken lightly, but accepted with gratefulness."

"Now you're saying our sons should be grateful to women willing to have sex with them?" Dad asked dubiously as I looked around, frantically trying to figure out the best escape route.

"Well, aren't you grateful I have sex with you?" my mom snapped.

"Fair enough," Dad said in agreement.

Oh, fuck this. I needed to get the hell out of there.

"Trevor Raymond Harris, don't even think about it," Mom said without turning in my direction. I'd taken only one step backward.

"I need a beer," I said, inching my way toward the back door. My dad always kept his brews in a cooler out back so Mom had enough room in the fridge for food.

"You see what happens when you have sex willy-nilly?" Mom asked, spinning to stop my movement with a glare. "You see?"

"I've never gotten anyone pregnant," I said sharply, my shoulders snapping straight. "And I wouldn't."

"You can't know that for certain."

"I can damn sure do my best," I retorted, standing my ground. "I'm careful, always."

"Careful doesn't mean shit—"

"Ellie," Dad interrupted. "That's enough."

Mom's mouth snapped closed.

"It's not Trev you're mad at. Quit harping on him."

Mom's body practically quivered with suppressed anger, but she nodded shortly. "Go get your beer," she ordered, her voice softening a little. She left the room without another word.

"Jesus," I mumbled once she was out of earshot.

"She's dealing with a lot," Dad said, turning back to the onion he was slicing. "But you know that wasn't meant for you, right?"

"Yeah, I know."

"She's trying to understand what your brother was thinking, leaving that baby," he said without turning to look at me. "After all we've been through, those years of hoping and realizing that it just wasn't gonna happen for us, and then finding a different way to build our family...hell, I don't understand it, either."

"Just because it might've been a one-night stand," I said, shaking my head even though he couldn't see me. "That isn't a reason. Wouldn't be a reason for me."

"I know that, Trev," he said, looking over his shoulder at me and nodding. "I know you, son."

"I don't understand it either."

"You and Henry have never been the same person," Dad said, going back to his onion. "You and Shane and Henry have always been as different as chalk and cheese and steak, and that doesn't have nothing to do with how you look or when you came to live with us. Your personalities just couldn't be more different."

"I never would have thought that he'd do something like this," I said in disgust, stepping outside to grab a couple beers. When I stepped back inside, Dad was rinsing off his hands.

"I couldn't have imagined it either," Dad said, accepting his beer with a nod of thanks. "But shit. You're all grown men now. Gotta make your own decisions and live your own lives. I just keep telling myself that we've got no idea what the circumstances were around Henry leaving that baby."

"It's bullshit," I replied stubbornly.

Dad reached out and gave my shoulder a squeeze. "Remember one thing, Trev, while you're being pissed at your brother. He might not have taken care of his responsibilities the way we would've, but he still set up that life insurance to take care of them in case anything happened to him."

"You're not angry?" I asked as he picked up the platter of raw hamburgers.

Dad scoffed. "If he was here, I'd throttle the little asshole," he mumbled as he took the platter outside.

* * *

I rode my four-wheeler home late that night. I'd always enjoyed hanging out at my parents' place when I had the time. Even after my mom had lost her shit in the kitchen, I'd still stayed long after dinner bullshitting with the two of them. She'd seemed to have calmed down after a little time to herself, and I was thankful.

I'd always been really sensitive to my mom's moods. The moment I met her, I'd fallen in love with her. I'd been seven, standing on the front porch, surrounded by more trees than I'd ever seen in my life, with my social worker's hand on my shoulder and a ratty backpack strap hanging from my hand. And when the door had opened and the small white woman with her soft smile and pretty-smelling perfume invited us in, I'd felt like I'd hit the jackpot. I'd been in a lot of foster homes by then—more than I could remember or count—but for some reason I'd felt instantly like I'd found where I belonged.

I hadn't even minded much when her barrel-chested husband had come into the room and rubbed his hand over the small of her back in greeting. No, that was a lie. At first, I'd wanted Mike gone. The pretty lady who smelled like vanilla was mine, and I'd had a hard time watching him move around her and kiss her. I'd had few good experiences with men at that point, and the big man seemed like trouble.

As weeks had passed and I never witnessed Mike raise his voice, much less his hand, toward Ellie, he began to grow on me. I'd eventually even begun to spend time with him, tromping through the woods and fishing in the creek that ran through the property. Over time, our bond had strengthened into something that was lasting and irreplaceable.

But if I was honest with myself, even after I'd begun to call the two my parents, and even after Mike had wiped at his eyes during my adoption hearing—the first time I'd ever seen a grown man cry—my first love, and my biggest love, had always been Ellie. My mom.

So when Ellie cried, I felt it deep in my gut. When she was happy, it was like my entire body lightened until I felt like I could run for miles. I felt her emotions almost as if they were my own, and I'd spent a lifetime adjusting to her moods even though it drove her crazy. She'd never understand the way I felt about her. She couldn't.

She'd taken in a seven-year-old boy who'd never had a damn thing in his entire life, and she'd loved him. Her love hadn't been something I had to earn, and it had never been conditional. She loved me because I existed. It was that simple. And because it was so simple, I'd spent my life loving her back.

I think, somewhere in the recesses of my mind, my love for Mom was the reason why I couldn't forgive Henry. Beyond the fact that he'd gotten some woman pregnant and hadn't told me, his brother, and beyond the fact that he'd left that woman high and dry and had abandoned his child, I couldn't forgive him for the way Ellie's face had fallen when I'd given her the news. And I couldn't forget that he'd made me the bearer of that news by setting it up so that his will was given to me. The little asshole.

My house was dark and quiet as I stepped inside, and I wished for the millionth time that I had a dog. It would be nice to have someone to hang out with, someone who was waiting and happy to see me when I got home. But I just couldn't justify bringing a pup home when I was usually working late and it would be by itself all day.

I shoved out of my boots and pulled off my coat as I ambled into the living room and dropped onto the couch. Summer was coming, so there wasn't shit on TV, but I found a new action movie that I hadn't seen and threw my feet up on the coffee table. I needed a reprieve from the thoughts of Henry and my upcoming trip.

* * *

The next week passed in a blur of taking care of things that wouldn't wait at work and getting my house ready to close up for a while. I wasn't sure how long I'd be in California getting to know Henry's little girl and her mother, but I sure as hell didn't want to come back to a messy house and a fridge full of rotten food.

My house was built on my parents' property, so I knew it would be easy for them to run over and take care of things while I was gone, but I didn't want to bother them with it. I'd built my house on that piece of land partly because I couldn't imagine leaving the forest that had saved me when I was a kid and partly because I knew my parents would never leave, and eventually they'd need me close. Both my mom and dad were still young and getting around fine, but my dad had been a logger for thirty years before he'd partially retired, and I knew that the day was coming when he'd have trouble. Logging wasn't easy on a body. The pure physicality of the job would ensure that my dad's joints and bones wouldn't age gracefully, even if that same job had kept him fit well into his fifties.

My phone rang as I was cooking dinner with what was left in my fridge, and I answered it without picking it up off the counter.

"Hello?" I answered, barely paying attention.

"Trev?" Anita called. "Why can I barely hear you?"

"You're on speakerphone, what's up?" I asked, wrinkling my nose as I realized the broccoli I'd been ready to throw in the skillet was slimy on the bottom. Shit.

Ani was my cousin Bram's girlfriend, but she'd also been

one of the foster kids my uncle and aunt took in when we were teenagers, so I'd known her for half of my life. She was a little bit crude, made off-color jokes that were rarely appropriate, and never let you get away with anything. She was also one of my best friends. Ani was the type who'd fight with you until she was out of breath, then defend you to others as soon as she'd inhaled again.

"Me and Arielle are bored," she said. "Bram's working late, so we're coming over."

"You had dinner?" I asked, looking over my pitiful stir-fry.

"Yeah."

"All right," I said, nodding. "See you in a few."

"Actually, I'm outside the house."

I laughed and turned the burner down before heading to the front door. "Why didn't you just knock?"

"Well, I didn't want to just show up if you were beating the meat or something," she answered, disconnecting as I threw open the front door.

"You think I'd answer my phone if I was masturbating?" I asked as she carried her baby girl, Arielle, up the front steps.

"Hey," she scolded, covering Arielle's ear with her hand. "Watch the language!"

"Pretty sure with the amount of 'fuck's you use in a conversation, you can't bitch about other people's language," I replied, stealing Arielle as they reached me. "Hey, sweet thing."

I turned and led the way into my house, not bothering to wait for Ani as she kicked off her shoes at the front door. She could find her way to the kitchen just fine considering the amount of time she'd spent at my house, and she'd look at me like I was an alien if I tried to play host.

"Leaving tomorrow, huh?" she asked, as she entered the kitchen.

"That's the plan. I'm leaving early as hell so I can knock out most of the drive before noon."

"Good call," she said, glancing into my dinner pan and wrinkling her nose. "You're gonna stop for the night?"

"Yeah." I handed Arielle to her and went back to cooking. "I could probably make it by late tomorrow night, but there's no reason to rush."

"Dragging your feet a bit now that it's here?"

"Not at all," I argued. "But there's no reason to make myself miserable getting there when I don't have to."

"Word," she said, sitting down at the table. "Although, getting up just to drive another full day is going to suck."

"That whole drive blows. At least I'm not bringing any of the kids with me."

"True that," she said, nodding. "You'd have to stop every two hours so someone could pee."

"I'll just bring some plastic bottles."

"There's a visual I'd never hoped to have."

I laughed and dished up my dinner as she pulled out a toy for Arielle to play with and got more comfortable in her chair. As soon as I sat down across from her, she was staring at me closely.

"You ready for this?" she asked seriously, bouncing Arielle a little on her lap.

"I'll deal with that as it comes," I replied with a shrug. "Just hoping she's not a complete shit show."

"I doubt it," Ani said, shaking her head.

"What, like Hen ever picked normal chicks to go home with? The guy was a magnet for weirdos."

"Henry's a fuck," she replied. "Leaving his kid like he did...but I don't think he's a fuck that would leave his kid with a shitty parent."

"Hell, I feel like I didn't know him at all," I mumbled. "I have no idea what he would have done."

"He saw what shit parents did to kids when you were growing up—"

"Not firsthand," I argued.

"True," she conceded. "He got placed when he was so little I don't think he remembered his life before, thank God. But he still saw all those foster kids coming in and out of your house. Our family knows what that can do to a kid more than most."

"I'm just glad I'm going down there and my mom isn't," I said. "If the mom doesn't let us see the baby..."

"Yeah," Ani said softly.

"Where you guys at?" Bram called from the front door, letting himself in.

"Kitchen!" Ani yelled back, smiling.

"Come on in," I said drily as Bram strode into the room. "Make yourself at home."

"Always do," Bram replied, leaning down to give Ani a kiss and take Arielle from her lap. He looked at my plate and grimaced, glancing back at Ani. "Please tell me you didn't eat whatever that is."

"I didn't." She laughed.

"Tastes all right," I said, taking a bite. "Add enough spices and anything tastes okay."

"Did you put corn in that stir-fry?" he asked, pulling out a chair. I just shrugged. I'd used up the last of my perishables, so I considered it a win.

"Leaving in the morning?" Bram asked.

I looked at Ani and she rolled her eyes.

"Yeah," I answered. "I thought you were working late today."

"Nah," he said, kissing at the tiny hands trying to grab at his beard. "You got so much shit done this week, I didn't have much to do."

"Oh, shut it," Ani mumbled as I gave her a look. "We wanted to come see you before you left."

"You could've just said that."

"No, I couldn't. You would've said you were tired or something so we wouldn't come over."

"I am feeling pretty beat."

"Liar."

"Are you guys really that worried about it?"

"We just don't want you to go down there and run into a bunch of shit," Bram said seriously. "You should have one of us go with you."

"Pretty sure I can handle it," I said, shoving food into my mouth. The colder it got, the worse it tasted. I needed to finish it before it became completely disgusting.

"I don't like it," Ani said, leaning forward with her elbows on the table. "What if she's a complete bitch?"

"Then I'll deal with it. Jesus, you two act like I'm going to fight a kraken."

"At least Kate's down there," Ani mumbled.

"I haven't told her I'm coming down."

"I may have let it slip," Bram said so quietly I almost didn't hear him.

"Seriously?" I asked in irritation, giving up on the food in front of me. "You guys are seriously the most meddling people I've ever met."

"Look in the mirror," Ani retorted.

"I don't meddle. You come to me," I argued, getting up to dump the food in the garbage. "I let you figure out your own shit."

"He has a point," Bram said.

"Oh, boo hoo, Trevor," Ani snapped. "You have family in the town you're going to and they'll probably want to see you at some point. Poor baby."

"I told my parents I'd stay there but I was planning on getting a damn hotel. You know she's going to want to be in the middle of it all," I said, referring to Kate. "She's a problem solver and it's driving her insane that I asked her to stay away from that Morgan chick."

"Her name's Morgan?" Ani asked curiously.

"Yeah."

"What's the baby's name?"

"I have no idea," I said shortly. I turned to the sink and quickly washed my dishes while the kitchen grew quiet except for Arielle's gurgling.

"Come on, baby," Bram finally said as I finished up the last pan. "Trev's probably got a million things to do tonight."

I didn't turn around when they got up from the table, but I stopped what I was doing as Ani came up behind me and wrapped her arms around my waist.

"I love you," she said, laying her head against my back. "Let us know when you get to the hotel tomorrow, okay?"

"Sure," I replied, patting her hands with my wet ones.

"Keep us updated," Bram ordered as Ani let me go. "We all want to know what's happening, too."

I sighed and turned. "I know you do. I'll let you know what she says."

"I just hope she's open to letting us get to know them," Ani said with a shrug. "We don't have to be best friends, but I can't imagine having Hen's little girl out there somewhere and not knowing how she's doing."

"I'll do my best," I said, following them as they made their way to the front door.

The responsibility I'd taken on when I'd insisted on talking to the mother of Henry's child myself sat like a weight on my shoulders. I'd never had a hard time with people. Usually I could make them comfortable pretty quickly during conversation, and even though I didn't necessarily like that many people, most of them liked me. I was a generally likeable guy.

Meeting this woman would be different, though. I was Henry's brother. Henry, who'd apparently wanted nothing to do with his own child and had bailed before the woman had even given birth. I didn't know if Hen had been paying child support or not—I really hoped he'd at least done that much.

There was a good chance that Morgan Riley wouldn't want anything to do with me or our family. Unfortunately, if that was the case I couldn't really blame her. Henry had fucked her over in a big way, and if I was in her shoes, I didn't know if I would want anything to do with the family who would raise a man like that, either.

I locked the front door and turned off the lights as I made my way into my room. I still needed to pack my bag, and I wanted to get a decent night's sleep.

My room was boring as hell, much like the rest of my house. In the middle of the room I had a sweet king-size bed that

I'd splurged on, but the rest of my furniture was plain and mismatched stuff that had been passed on to me from various family members. I'd spent a lot of money building my house, making it exactly how I wanted it, but I'd never really cared about decorating the place. I'd always figured that when I got married my wife could do it up the way she liked.

Now that I was in my thirties, I was beginning to wonder if the whole wife thing would ever happen. I dated and I met plenty of women, but I'd never found one I wanted to spend more than a few months with. At first things would look promising, but inevitably I'd start questioning whether she was the person I wanted to see every day for the rest of my life and the answer was always no. I usually cut ties when I realized that. Four months seemed to be the magic number for me.

Pulling a duffel out of my closet, I briefly glanced at the box of Henry's stuff my parents had given me. Some of it was mementos from our childhood, and the rest were things the Marines had sent home from his barracks room. I hadn't been able to go through it yet, and I sure as hell wasn't about to open it tonight.

God, I missed my brother. He was a pain in the ass—selfish and egotistical and sure of himself in a way that few people were—but he was also the sweetest and funniest kid I'd ever met. I could still remember when he'd come to us. He was the youngest child my parents had ever fostered. My mom and dad had always chosen to take the harder cases and the older kids no one else wanted, but for some reason they'd agreed to take Henry, even though he'd completely upended their life in a way they weren't used to. Taking care of a two-year-old was very different from taking care of an older child, but they'd figured it out quickly.

I'd been leery of the tiny blond kid at first. I'd been nervous that I'd trip over him, or I'd accidentally leave my new pocketknife somewhere he could find it, or he'd choke on something and die while I was supposed to be keeping an eye on him. I hadn't been able to keep my distance for long, though. He'd just been so damn cute. His haircut was some ridiculous form of a mullet and one of his front teeth was missing because someone had knocked it out, but he'd had the biggest smile I'd ever seen and he talked a mile a minute in a language no one understood. For a long time I'd thought he was speaking Russian or something, but when I was older my mom had laughed and assured me that whatever he'd been saying for the first few months he was with us was complete gibberish.

It took less than two years before Henry became a permanent part of our family. By the time he left for kindergarten, his last name was Harris just like mine. And, just like me, he had an Iron Man backpack and a pair of high-top sneakers my parents could barely afford, and the same lines shaved into the sides of his fine blond hair. It didn't matter how different we looked; my little brother had wanted to be a mini version of me for his first few years of grade school.

I clenched my jaw and shook my head, trying to ignore the memories that would stop me from getting anything done except maybe lying on my bed and staring at the ceiling. I'd done enough of that already. For the first few weeks after Henry's death, I'd barely felt able to function. My brother had been away for years in the Marines, but at least I'd known he was somewhere in the world, laughing and using cheesy pickup lines that always seemed to work because the jackass was so damned good-looking. I'd known he was just a phone call or a plane ride away. Once he was gone, it was like a giant hole opened up inside me, and it sucked the air out of my lungs until I couldn't breathe without pain. Losing Henry had caused a physical ache in my chest that was so bad I'd gone to the doctor to have it checked.

I couldn't fall into that shit again. The nights of drinking until I passed out and days of hangovers on top of my misery were over. They had to be. I was a grown man with responsibilities and parents who'd already lost one son. I didn't have the luxury of wallowing, even though some days I wanted to. Hell, most days I considered calling in sick and starting the day with a bottle of whiskey, but I didn't.

I considered losing my brother the worst thing that ever happened to me, and, unlike Henry, I remembered my birth mother and the numerous shitty foster homes I'd been placed in before my parents took me in. I also remembered vividly being taken from the Harrises for over a month because of some bureaucratic bullshit when I was eight. The minute my social worker had led me out the front door had been one of the scariest and worst moments of my life. All of that paled in comparison to losing my baby brother. I would have gone through anything, lived through anything, if I could have been spared that loss.

Chapter 2
Morgan

I wasn't going to lie—I was struggling. To be fair, I didn't know many single moms who didn't struggle on some level. Even the ones who had plenty of money to spend and well-behaved children who never wrote on walls like the ones I was currently cleaning before work struggled. It was just a fact of life. Raising a human alone was a daunting task. When you added in the difficulty of supporting another person financially who couldn't even wipe their own ass yet and had to be monitored twenty-four hours a day, the struggle became very real.

I wasn't complaining. I really wasn't. Life was what you made of it—I'd learned that when I was young—but sometimes I just wanted to sit on my ass and not worry about the next bill that was due, or, in this instance, how I was going to get crayon off the walls of the house I was renting a room in for a fraction of what I knew it was worth. Since we'd moved in, I'd done my best not to mess anything up, which was nearly impossible with an active two-year-old. I knew my friend Max was doing us a massive favor by letting us live with him and watch the house while he was traveling on and off for work, and I didn't want him to regret it. Honestly, we'd be up shit creek if he changed his mind.

The job I had now paid more and had better hours than the shop I'd been working at in San Diego, but I still wasn't exactly bringing in the big bucks, and living in Southern California was ridiculously expensive. So far I'd managed to keep us afloat, but I wasn't sure how long I'd be able to juggle everything without asking for help.

I hated asking for help.

I had a safety net. I knew that. It wasn't as if me and my girl would ever go hungry or become homeless. My pop would never let that happen, and neither would my sister, Miranda. They offered to help out every time I talked to either of them on the phone, but neither of them lived close and I wasn't quite to the point when I'd accept moving home to mooch off of them. Besides, my sister was currently in college in Oregon and it wasn't as if we could move into her dorm room.

I just had to buckle down. Find a way to make some more cash so we weren't living paycheck to paycheck, and eventually find a place to live that was ours alone so I wasn't constantly worried that my roommate would decide we were too much trouble.

"Mama," Etta said, clapping her hands to get my attention. "Waynerot."

"I have no idea what you're saying to me," I replied conversationally. "But we don't write on walls."

"Me color."

"We only color on paper," I said for the fourteenth time in as many minutes.

"Me color."

"Right. Only color on paper," I said again. I was pretty sure she was hearing only what she wanted to hear, which was that she was going to get to color again at some point. If there was one thing my daughter got from her father beyond her looks, it was the fact that she picked and chose what she wanted to hear. I could tell her that we weren't having ice cream that day, and the only words she would focus on were "ice cream," and then she'd continue to ask about it all day long.

I hadn't been around a lot of babies in my life, so I wasn't sure if her selective hearing was normal, but it seemed like a personality trait to me. I had a feeling it was going to cause quite a ruckus as she got older. It drove me crazy, but a part of me couldn't help but find her singular focus a bit endearing—probably because she was my own kid and not someone else's.

"This will have to do for now," I said as I got to my feet, staring at the faded colors on the wall. "I have to go to work and you have to go to Carmen's house."

"Do for now," Etta said with a shrug, making me bite my cheek in an effort to keep from laughing. I couldn't let her see how entertaining I thought she was when she was being a pill or she'd continue to act that way.

"You ready to go to Carmen's?" I asked, picking her up and throwing the wet rag I'd been using in the sink.

"Carmen," she said, nodding with a small hum.

I was so glad she liked her babysitter. When we'd moved from San Diego to Anaheim, I'd had to put her in a new day care that we'd both hated. Thankfully, only a week later I'd met Carmen when she'd come into the new shop I worked at looking for her boyfriend. She was a stay-at-home mom with a newborn who had a hell of a time finding a sitter and was struggling without the income she usually made as a maid at a local hotel. Her boyfriend, Ray, was a tattoo artist and he made okay money, but they were still sinking.

Thankfully, she'd been so happy to have a little extra cash when we'd discussed her watching Etta for me, she didn't even ask for much. We had an understanding, Carmen and I. Both of us knew how hard it was to raise a baby on an income that barely paid the rent, so I paid her what I could and she never asked for more, because she trusted that I'd never pay less than I absolutely had to. Some weeks were good and I paid her more, some weeks were lean and I paid her less, but I was always fair and she was always happy for the money that let her stay home with her son. Honestly, I don't know how I would have managed without her.

The best part of the whole situation was that Etta loved Carmen and baby Sam. They went to the park, played in the backyard, and watched cartoons. It was pretty much a toddler's version of a vacation every day. The guilt of leaving my daughter to go to work six days a week was eased because I knew she was having an awesome time. It wasn't gone completely, oh no, especially not when Etta did something new that I missed, or fell down and didn't have me there to kiss her owies, but it was manageable.

Juggling my purse and Etta's diaper bag, I carried her outside into the warm morning. I loved the weather in Southern California. The perpetual sunshine always put a bounce in my step. It felt like nature's way of telling me to have a good day, and it never failed to improve my mood, at least fractionally.

I grabbed the mail from our mailbox as we left, and threw it onto the passenger seat of my old beat-up Focus as we headed across town. There was a ton of envelopes, mostly for Max, and I didn't even bother going through them yet. Nothing but bills ever came for me, and I wasn't looking forward to new past-due notices. I tried to keep up on everything, but some months it was just impossible. It was a game of roulette deciding which ones I'd pay and which ones I'd just have to wait to pay until the next paycheck. I hated it.

Choosing which bills to pay reminded me of when I was a kid and I'd have to go through the mail stacked on our kitchen counter, searching for the ones from the utility companies. I'd always nagged my mom to pay those first, because we could live with an eviction notice on our door but we couldn't live without power during an Oregon winter. My mother hadn't been horrible, but she hadn't been good, either. Absent most of the time, and hardly parental when she was there, I rarely thought about her now that I was grown. She'd had a penchant for shitty men, dead-end jobs, and hard drugs. In the end, the drugs had killed her and put me and my sister into the system. Thankfully, that had eventually led us to our dad.

I'd long ago come to terms with my mother's deficiencies as a parent and the way she'd died, but I was self-aware enough to know that I used her legacy as a guide to how I didn't want to live or raise my daughter. Etta would never have to worry about having enough food for dinner or her mom not coming home because she was off on a bender.

* * *

After I dropped Etta off and headed to work, I breathed a little sigh of relief. Leaving her for even a few hours always made me feel anxious, but once she was safely where she was supposed to be it got easier.

The shop I worked at wasn't far from Carmen's house, and for once in the entire time I'd been working there I was early. I sat back in my seat after glancing at the clock on my dash and shutting off the car. I had ten whole minutes to myself— it was like a freaking miracle.

Grabbing the mail off the passenger seat, I started leisurely flipping through the envelopes. Most of them were for Max, like I'd expected. There were only two bills—thank God—for me, and I shuffled them to the back of the stack so I didn't have to look at them and stuffed them all in the glove compartment. Something had come for me that I didn't recognize, but it looked official. I turned it over in my hands for a moment. New notifications were never a good thing in my experience, and I wanted to ignore it like I was doing with the other bills, but I knew that if I didn't see what it was, it was going to drive me crazy all day, like a bomb ticking away in my car.

My stomach clenched as I opened it up.

At first I didn't really understand what it said. The language was all very legal sounding and almost impossible to decipher.

Then suddenly what I was looking at became crystal fucking clear.

Life insurance paperwork.

Life insurance paperwork for the father of my child.

And if I was getting life insurance paperwork, that meant only one thing.

"Goddamn it, Henry," I whispered, dropping my head to rest on my steering wheel as tears flooded my eyes.

Chapter 3
Trevor

The address I had for Morgan Riley was in an apartment complex in Mira Mesa, one of the neighborhoods in San Diego. I only knew the neighborhood's name because I'd asked my foster brother Shane's opinion of the area on one of the many phone calls I'd received during my drive south. It seemed like an okay place, which settled my nerves a little.

I wasn't real comfortable in large cities. It seemed like the more crowded a place got, the rougher it looked. Mira Mesa wasn't bad, though. There were a lot of shopping centers and bars, but it didn't have the feel of people living on top of each other the way I knew a lot of other parts of San Diego did.

My stomach churned as I pulled into the apartment complex a little after five that evening. The parking lot was packed with cars as people came home from work, but I finally found a place half a block from the apartment I was looking for that would actually fit my four-door, long-bed truck. It stuck out like a sore thumb alongside the compact cars that filled the spaces on each side, and I tried to not let it bother me as I shook out the tension in my hands.

I'd forgotten what a nightmare the traffic was down here. I had no idea how Shane and Katie dealt with that bullshit every day. I'd lose my mind if I had to sit on a hot-as-shit freeway for hours just to get to work.

Morgan lived in a second-floor apartment, and I checked the address one last time before I mounted the stairs. I could hear music playing inside the apartment when I reached the door, and for a second I questioned why the hell I'd volunteered to be the one who made contact, but I forced myself to knock anyway.

The guy who answered the door was clearly military of some sort. He wasn't in uniform, but he had the same haircut, and tan lines around the sides of his head and right above his elbows that my brothers always had in the summer thanks to their uniforms.

"Hey man," he said, easily. "Can I help you with somethin'?"

"I'm looking for Morgan Riley," I said, automatically reaching out to shake the guy's hand. "I'm Trevor Harris."

His head cocked to the side as he took my measure, then he grasped my hand for a quick shake. "I'm Linc. Sorry, Morgan moved out about a month ago."

"She did?" I asked dumbly, my mind barely wrapping around the fact that I'd driven all that way for nothing.

"Yeah, she's up in Anaheim now."

"Shit." I reached up and ran a hand over my head in frustration.

"Why are you looking for her?" he asked, leaning against the door frame.

"She knew my brother Henry," I replied, clearing my throat. "He passed away not too long ago, so—"

"Aw, man. That sucks. Sorry to hear that."

"Yeah."

"Well, hey, I think I've got her address here somewhere," he said, turning to open a kitchen drawer near the door. "She left it in case we got any of her mail."

He rifled through the drawer for a minute, then lifted up a small sheet of paper and waved it from side to side. "Got it. You got a pen?"

For a split second I panicked because I didn't, in fact, have a pen. Then I realized that my phone was in my damn pocket.

Five minutes later, I was walking back toward my truck, both relieved and disappointed that I hadn't come face-to-face with my brother's ex. Half of me was glad that I had another day to psych myself up for the upcoming interaction, but the other half was frustrated that I hadn't gotten that first meet over with yet.

I called Katie as I pulled back on to the busy freeway.

"How'd it go?" she asked without preamble. "Is she nice? What does Henry's daughter look like? Is she going to let us see her?"

"Take a breath," I replied drily.

"I can't. This is huge."

"It's nothing, *yet*," I said. "She doesn't live there anymore."

"Oh no!"

"The guy who's in the apartment now gave me her address, though. She's up in Anaheim."

"Well, that was shitty of him. I mean, good for us, but

who freaking gives up info like that to some dude they don't know?" She paused, probably to inhale after her little rant. "What are you going to do now?"

"Go up there tomorrow, I guess. Can I stay at your place—"

"Yes!" she replied before I'd even gotten the words out.

"All right, I'll be there in a bit."

* * *

"Uncle Trev!" my nephews yelled as I climbed out of my truck an hour later. I threw Gavin up in the air, then hugged Keller against my side as I made my way slowly toward the front of the house. The drive between Morgan's old apartment and Shane and Kate's house wasn't far, but it had been such a fucking headache. Between the road construction and the sheer number of people getting home, I'd been mostly stopped in the stop-and-go traffic.

"You made it," Kate said happily as she ushered me into the house. "I know you're only here for the night, but I'm so glad we get to see you!"

"Me too," I murmured, leaning forward to kiss the top of her head. I still had Keller clinging to my side and Gavin in my arms. They were both built like little tanks, and their warm bodies pressing up against me were making me sweat even worse than I had been.

"You look like you need a beer," Shane called, laughing at the look on my face. "Or five."

"Just one would be great," I said, setting Gavin down as I moved toward the kitchen. "Where are the other kids?"

"Iris is sleeping, and Gunner and Sage are out back," Katie

said with a smile. "I didn't tell them you were here yet." She went to go get the kids as Shane handed me a beer.

"She moved?" he asked, leaning against the counter.

"Yeah, but I've got her address in Anaheim. Gonna head up there in the morning."

"There's a hotel up there that we stayed at when we took the kids to Disney for a weekend. I'll get you the info," he replied. "It's nice, cheap, and they do a full breakfast in the morning. Worth the price for just that."

"Yeah, eating fast food is getting old," I replied.

"When did you get here?" Sage called as she ran through the back door in a swimsuit. She was soaking wet, but I didn't stop her as she came barreling toward me.

"Just now," I answered as I leaned down to hug her. Half a second later, her arms and legs were wrapped around me as I lifted her off the floor. She was probably getting too big for her parents to carry around, but I was the fun uncle and as long as I could lift her I'd do it. "How's school going?"

"Good," she said, leaning back so she could see my face. "A couple weeks ago we had a new girl come to class, and I showed her around so now we're best friends."

"Funny how that happens, huh?"

"Yep. Auntie Kate says you never know what cool things will happen when you're nice to people."

"That's true," I replied, nodding.

"Time for a shower and pajamas, Sage," Kate said as she came inside with Gunner under her arm. "Then you can come back down and hang with Uncle Trev for a while."

A few minutes later, it was quiet in the kitchen as the kids got ready for bed upstairs.

"You sure you don't want me to come with you?" Shane asked as we got comfortable at the kitchen table. "Might be easier with me there."

"Nah." I shook my head. "It'll be bad enough when I show up."

"You think she'll react badly?"

"I have no idea," I replied honestly. "I figure it could go either way."

"Hopefully she believes that you're Hen's brother," he said with a small smile.

"I'm sure she'll see the resemblance," I joked with a shrug, thankful for the small humor that made my shoulders relax for the first time that day.

"Well, if you do need me, let me know."

"I will," I said with a nod, thankful for his support. Everyone had offered to help or go in my place, but Shane's offer was different. He didn't think he could handle it better than I would, and he wasn't worried that I'd fuck it up, he just wanted me to know that he had my back.

"I've got a sleepy boy for you," Kate said as she came back in the kitchen and handed Gunner to Shane. "If you let him sit on your lap, I have a feeling he'll be you-know-what in about five minutes."

We gathered around the table as the older kids trickled in, and spent the next hour listening to the kids tell me everything I'd missed since the last time I'd seen them. They were full of stories about school and the bus and weird things they'd found at the park. It was exactly what I'd needed to relax, and after driving for the last three days and barely sleeping, by eleven that night I'd fallen asleep fully dressed on the couch.

* * *

My good-byes the next morning were easy as the kids left for school, but it was always hard to leave Kate. We'd grown up next door to each other, played and fought and gotten into trouble like we were brother and sister. It felt weird to have her living so far away, even though she'd been living in San Diego for most of our adult lives.

The house Morgan had moved to wasn't nearly as nice as the apartments I'd been at the day before. It was stucco, like most of the houses in that part of California, but the walls were stained, and the grass in the front yard was completely dead and fried from the sun. From what I could see, the place looked clean like someone was taking care of it, but it still had the worn-down look of a house whose tenants didn't have much money for repairs.

I didn't even pause as I walked up the cracked sidewalk and knocked on the door. After going to the wrong place the day before, I think a part of me hadn't really expected an answer.

When she opened the door with her eyebrows raised like she didn't understand why anyone would knock, I almost swallowed my tongue. I knew immediately that I was looking at Morgan, but I couldn't for the life of me understand why I had the instant recognition.

"Can I help you?" she asked, not friendly, but not rude, either.

"Morgan?" I asked, cataloging her features. She was blond. Slim. No makeup, but she didn't really need it. Her eyebrows were darker than her hair. Gorgeous.

She didn't answer me.

"Morgan Riley?" I asked again, meeting her eyes in an effort to focus.

"Who are you?" she asked, closing the door a little and setting one foot behind it as if she was getting ready to slam it.

"I'm Trevor Harris," I replied slowly. "I think you knew my brother Henry."

I saw the recognition hit her swift and hard, but she didn't immediately respond. Instead, she looked me over. It wasn't assessing. It was more like the look you give someone when you haven't seen them in a long time and you're trying to pull up the memory of them so you can compare the present with the past.

Eventually, she swung the door open a little farther and motioned me inside.

"I thought I'd see you a lot sooner," she said easily as I walked into her living room.

There were toys scattered in front of the television and a few odds and ends around the room, but for the most part the place was tidy. None of the furniture was expensive, but you could tell the owner took care of it. I breathed a little sigh of relief. The place was cozy.

"What do you mean?" I asked as I met her eyes again.

"After—" She cleared her throat. "I figured someone would come eventually, once they contacted me about that franking insurance money."

"Franking?"

"I have a two-year-old," she said, sitting on the one chair in the room and gesturing for me to sit on the couch. "And, look, if I didn't have her, I'd give that money back. I wasn't expecting it and I don't particularly want it, but—"

"So you did get it?" I asked, my eyes wandering a little around the small house.

"Yeah," she said defensively. "It's put away for emergencies or Etta's college. We don't need it right now—"

"I'm not here about the money," I said, cutting her off with a wave of my hand. I'd gotten off track. What she did with that insurance money was none of my business.

"Well, why are you here then?" she asked, her shoulders visibly tensing.

I wiped my sweaty palms down the thighs of my shorts. I'd always been the calm one in my family. I'd always known what to say and how to say it, and I didn't even have to mince words most of the time. But right then, in that tiny living room, I wasn't quite sure what to say or how to say it. So many words played through my mind, and I shuffled through them quickly, trying to find the right ones. I hadn't expected her to let me in right away, and I'd known she'd be pretty but I hadn't imagined she'd be beautiful. I was feeling a bit off-kilter.

"First," I said slowly, pausing my fidgeting hands, "I want to apologize."

"For what?" she said with a scoff.

"For my brother." I let that sink in as her mouth snapped shut. "I don't know what you guys had, if it was a one-time thing or a relationship." Jesus, I hoped it wasn't a relationship. "But whatever it was...he wasn't raised to run out on his responsibilities."

"Let me stop you right there," she said with a soft smile. "Because I think you might be confused about some stuff."

I watched her closely as she settled more firmly into her chair, her body relaxing fractionally.

"I've never been angry with Henry," she said, shrugging one shoulder. "We didn't plan to get pregnant. Honestly, we took every precaution there was, but ship happens, you know?"

My mouth twitched at her alternative word for *shit*.

"But Henry didn't want kids. It wasn't just a 'for now' thing, and it wasn't about me. He never wanted kids."

That was news to me.

"I could've made him step up," she continued. "I could have forced it. But it was my decision to go through with the pregnancy, not his."

"That's a pretty forgiving way to look at it," I said, surprise coloring my voice. A small voice inside my head wondered if the reason Henry didn't have a relationship with his daughter was because Morgan hadn't allowed it, and that was why she was so forgiving, but I quickly silenced it. Even if Morgan had made Henry's life a living hell, there hadn't been any excuse for what he'd done.

She shrugged again.

"His good days as a parent wouldn't have been as good as my worst days," she said gently, her voice filled with understanding that I hadn't afforded my brother since the minute I'd learned of his daughter's existence. "He just wasn't equipped for it, and she deserves better than that."

I swallowed the lump in my throat, a little bit in awe of the calm woman in front of me. I couldn't understand how she was just okay with the way Henry had bailed on her. What she was saying made sense intellectually, but emotionally I was still grappling with her words. Part of me, a big part, wondered if she was full of shit. Something didn't feel right.

"Is that all you wanted?" she asked after I'd been quiet too long.

"No," I said, swallowing hard again. "We—me and my family—we'd like to get to know you. You and the baby, I mean." I stumbled over the words. "No pressure, whatever you're comfortable with. We were just hoping that we could meet her, maybe, or—"

"I'm cool with that," she said, saving me from my word vomit.

"You are?" I asked, watching her closely. Now would be the time she would state her demands.

"Sure." She nodded, surprising the hell out of me. "A kid can't have enough family."

"Well, she's got a big one," I replied idiotically as I tried to figure out why this was going so smoothly.

"I know."

I nodded, then paused. "Wait, what? Did Henry talk about us?"

She laughed a little and tilted her head to the side.

"You don't recognize me, do you?" she asked, smiling.

I stared at her, but recognition was just out of reach. "Should I?"

"When you knew me, I was about six inches shorter and about fifteen pounds heavier," she said. "And my last name was Harlan."

"Morgan Harlan," I said out loud.

"I was fostered at your house for about two months when I was thirteen," she said, and just like that, recognition dawned.

"Holy shit," I breathed, looking her over again.

"That's what Henry said when I ran into him at a bar," she said, laughing. "*He* recognized me, though."

"I'm sorry," I said, my voice still a little bit high with surprise. I wondered if she'd been this beautiful when we were kids and I just hadn't noticed. Thirteen-year-old girls weren't on my radar back then.

"No worries." She waved her hand from side to side. "I look different than I did ten years ago, and you were too old to pay any attention to me when we were kids anyway."

"Hen had the biggest crush on you," I remembered out loud before I could catch myself.

"I know," she said, still laughing a little. "But he was such a scrawny thing back then, I didn't even care."

"Damn," I said, shaking my head a little as memories, one after another, played through my mind. She'd come to us just as school was letting out for the summer, and she'd spent those two months with us running wild all over the property with the rest of the kids. I'd been too old to spend my days playing in the creek—by then I'd already started working with my dad at the logging company—but I still remembered sitting down to dinner with all the muddy, sunburned, disheveled kids each night.

"What happened after you left?" I asked. I'd always wondered what happened to the kids who stayed with us after they were gone, but beyond the few who had stayed in contact with my parents, I'd never had the chance to ask.

"That's a long story," she said, still smiling. "But eventually, my dad got out of prison and got us back."

"Prison, huh?" I tried to keep the judgment out of my voice.

"A marijuana charge," she murmured, rolling her eyes. "Pretty much bullship."

"Didn't you have a little sister?" I asked, changing the subject since it seemed like a sore one.

"Yeah, Miranda," she said, happily. "They put us back together after I left your house."

"I always felt like shit when kids came to us without their siblings," I said with a small shake of my head. "I didn't understand why they did that."

"Sometimes it just worked out that way," she said pragmatically. "Your parents were some of the good ones, though. They made that summer bearable."

"We had a full house then," I remembered out loud. "I was surprised when you got placed with us."

A sound from somewhere in the house made me freeze, and seconds later a small voice called out.

"Hold that thought," Morgan said, standing up. "I'll be right back."

It took everything in me not to pull out my phone the minute she walked away. I couldn't believe how well things were going. The best-case scenario I'd imagined hadn't even come close to what I was actually dealing with.

"You hungry?" Morgan asked, coming up behind me. Her tone made it clear she wasn't addressing me, but I turned around anyway.

There she was. Henry's blond-haired, brown-eyed little girl. Shit, she was cute.

"This is Etta," Morgan said, bouncing the baby on her hip. "And her hair is a mess when she wakes up from a nap."

I smiled as Etta said, "Mess," and threw her hands into the air.

"Hi, Etta," I said, getting to my feet.

"That's Trevor," Morgan told her, pointing at me. "Wanna say hi?"

"Hi!" Etta gave a little wave, and a lump settled in my throat.

She looked like my brother when he'd first come to live with us. The cheeks were the same, and the shape of her nose and eyes were pretty much identical to Hen's. Her mouth was all Morgan, though, especially when she smiled.

"I gotta get her some lunch," Morgan said. "You're welcome to stay, but it's nothing fancy—"

"I'd love to stay," I said quickly, ignoring the little voice in my head that warned me to be careful.

"Okay."

"I just need to make a phone call."

When Morgan carried Etta into the kitchen, I stepped outside the front door, pulled my phone out of my pocket, and scrolled through my contacts. Inhaling deeply through my nose in an effort to calm my excitement, I called my mother.

"Mom?" I said as soon as she'd answered. "She looks just like Henry."

Chapter 4

Morgan

Did you have a good sleep?" I asked calmly, trying to keep the nervousness from my voice as I sat Etta in her booster seat at the table.

I zoned out as she answered me, going on and on about her nap using language that only she understood. There were usually a few words I recognized mixed into her long sentences—both in English and Spanish thanks to Carmen's tutelage—but for the most part I just let her go on and on describing who-knew-what.

I smiled and nodded as her rambling continued, but my heart was thumping hard as I moved around the kitchen, waiting for Trevor to come back inside. I hadn't been lying when I'd said that I'd expected someone from Henry's family to show up. The life insurance policy he'd left us was no joke—it was a huge amount of money, and I knew that would raise some questions. However, I hadn't really expected them to want anything to do with us.

The Harris family *was* kind of incredible, though. I'd

realized that during the summer I'd lived with them. They were kind and funny and inclusive, and they were the best foster family I'd ever been placed with. But along with those attributes, they were also fiercely protective of their own. It wasn't a bad thing—far from it. If anything, it was another point in their favor. But learning that one of their kids had a child they'd never met probably didn't paint me in a very favorable light.

"Sorry about that," Trevor said as he walked slowly into the kitchen behind me. His deep voice was tentative, like he was afraid I was going to kick him out of my house at any moment.

"No worries," I replied, swallowing hard as I glanced over my shoulder. He had no idea how badly I'd needed those few moments of privacy to get my shit together. "Sandwiches and bananas for lunch, if you're hungry."

"Sure," he said, his kind stare focused on Etta as she pushed her disheveled hair out of her face. The blond strands were so fine that I had a hard time keeping it pulled back, and every time she brushed it out of her eyes it slowly moved right back to where it was to begin with.

"She looks a lot like Henry," Trevor said, glancing at me quickly with a grimace.

"It's fine," I assured him with a small shake of my head and a smile. "She knows who her dad is—was. And yeah, she does look a lot like him."

"Henwyetta," Etta said, pointing to herself. "Me Henwyetta."

"That's a very pretty name," Trevor said seriously, and I got the feeling that he was avoiding my gaze on purpose as he sat down in one of the kitchen chairs.

"It's weird, right?" I said, turning back toward the counter to finish the sandwiches. It *was* weird, and my family had tried to talk me out of it. I shrugged, even though I wasn't sure if he was looking. "She has my last name, so I just figured that, I don't know, she should have something of his, too."

"No, no, not at all," Trevor argued. "It's cool of you."

"Well, it's hers for life now," I joked uncomfortably. "So..."

"You never know," he replied, his voice light. "Maybe she'll change it to something else when she's older. *The Artist Formerly Known As* or something."

"You like Prince?" I asked, relieved to find a way to change the direction of the conversation. This was by far the most uncomfortable situation I'd ever been in, and that included the day I'd had to tell Hen I was pregnant.

"Everyone likes Prince," Trevor replied.

Then it was nothing but silence. Even Etta was quiet as she waited for her food, which was pretty unusual for her. I had a feeling that she was too busy looking over the stranger sitting at our kitchen table to bother with her normal commentary.

Finally, Trevor spoke again. "I'm actually more partial to country music," he said, filling the silence.

"Really?" I scrunched my nose as I turned my head to look at him.

"What? That surprises you?" he joked, glancing down at himself.

"I'm surprised when anyone says they prefer country music," I said drily, taking the time to look him over. "Did your girl run off with your dog and leave you with the trailer-house mortgage?"

Trevor scoffed as I placed sandwiches and bananas on plates.

"It's not all about runaway women and dogs," he replied. "Some of it is about cheating, too."

"I stand corrected." I passed out the plates and grabbed Etta's juice from the fridge before sitting down across from Trevor at the table. "Small bites," I warned Etta as she picked up a quarter of her sandwich.

"I stopped by your old place," Trevor said as he picked up his banana. "You, uh, might want to tell that guy not to give out your information to people. Not that I think you have anyone looking for you, or whatever, I mean—"

I laughed as he tried to backpedal, his face tightening in mortification.

"No, I get it," I cut him off, raising a hand to stop him. "That's Craig. He's my old roommate's boyfriend. He's actually not the idiot that he seems, and he wouldn't just give out my address to anyone."

"He was pretty free with the information," Trevor said cautiously. "I thought he said his name was Linc."

"Craig *Lincoln*," I replied, taking a bite of my food. "And you said the magic word—Henry."

"You were really expecting one of us to show up, huh?" he said softly.

"I was reasonably sure someone would, yes," I answered, leaving out the fact that I'd be dreading it for over a month. "We'd already moved when I got the news." I took a deep breath, remembering the way that life insurance letter had completely blindsided me. "I think it took a while for things to be forwarded. Anyway, I called them and let them know that someone might come looking."

"Thank you."

"Tanks!" Etta said, as if Trevor's words had reminded her that she should have used her manners when I'd given her lunch.

"You're welcome," I said, smiling at the peanut butter and jelly smeared across her cheeks. "Is it good?"

"Mmm," she hummed, nodding. *"Bueno."*

We finished up lunch and Trevor got to watch as I wiped Etta down from hairline to neckline, and cleaned her hands from fingertips to elbows while she whined. It never failed—she couldn't keep her mess to a minimum, but she couldn't stand the cleanup afterward and she made sure I knew it.

"There," I said, raising my hands in the air above my head like a calf roper in a rodeo. "All clean."

"Down!" Etta demanded, not willing to forgive me just yet. "Me down!"

"Good grief," I mumbled, rolling my eyes as I teased in a singsong voice. "You're such a baby."

"Me no baby!"

"Hey," I said, glancing at Trevor in embarrassment. "Mama was teasing. Stop it."

"Me no baby," she said again, her lips puckered in a mutinous pout.

"Are you a lady?"

"No!"

"Are you a woman?"

"No!"

"Well, what are you, then?" I asked as I unbuckled her from her seat.

"Me a big girl," she said, popping her thumb into her mouth as I gave her a cuddle.

"You're Mama's big girl," I said, rocking her from side to side. I knew I shouldn't have baited her, but sometimes I couldn't help it. Maybe it made me a shitty mother, but God, sometimes it was just funny to annoy her. Lately, though, she'd been a little more sensitive to the whole baby/big girl thing. I was pretty sure it was because she was getting more teeth and everything made her more emotional when she wasn't feeling good.

I set her on the floor and let her wander off as I grabbed the washcloth and started wiping up her place at the table. I wasn't quite sure what to say to my unexpected guest now that he wasn't occupied with my lame attempt at a meal.

"Uh, I should probably get going," Trevor said, standing up. "I didn't mean to stay so long."

"Oh." I looked up in surprise and nodded. He'd been kind of quiet, and we'd run out of awkward conversation, but his announcement still seemed a little abrupt.

I followed him to the front of the house and watched as he crouched down in front of Etta, who ignored him as she sat on the floor playing. He seemed so massive in our small living room as he said his good-byes to my daughter, but everything about him screamed gentle. That was what I remembered most about him from when we were young: his kindness. He never seemed like a pushover, but out of the entire group of Harris and Evans kids, he'd been the most levelheaded and calm one.

"I'm staying at a hotel with a pretty nice P-O-O-L," he said. I was thankful he spelled the last word. It was smoothly done and I wondered if he had any kids of his own, but I didn't feel comfortable asking. "If you ladies feel up to it, later or tomorrow, or whenever."

"Okay, maybe." I nodded briefly. "How long are you staying in town?"

"My plans are kind of up in the air at the moment." He raised his hands in an *I don't know* gesture.

We stood there looking at each other, and I laughed a little when he didn't say anything else. "Uh, we should probably exchange numbers or something?"

"Oh, right!" He made a noise in his throat as he searched for his phone, finally pulling it out of one of his pockets and shaking it side to side.

The minute I'd given him my number he was out the door, leaving me standing there unsure what to do with myself.

Someone had finally showed up, just like I'd known they would, but it hadn't been nearly as painful as I'd been imagining. Awkward, yes. Uncomfortable, yes. But not painful. He'd been nice. Polite even. I really hoped it wasn't all an act to gain my trust.

With my mind whirling I glanced at Etta, then jogged down the hall to my room, pulled my phone from the charger, and added Trevor to my contacts. Then I dialed my sister.

"Ranna," I said the minute she answered. "Henry's brother just left my house."

"Oh, shit," she blurted in response. "Hold on a second."

I waited for her to finish whatever she was doing while I walked back into the living room and dropped to the couch.

"Okay, I'm back." The noise around her had quieted. "So what happened?"

"He just showed up at my door," I said, keeping my voice quiet even though Trevor was long gone. "I think he wanted to get a good look at Etta."

"Are they pissed about the money?"

"Oddly, no."

"Oh, come on." She snorted in disbelief.

"No, really," I replied, my own disbelief coming to the forefront again. "He didn't even want to talk about it. He actually apologized."

"For what?"

"For Henry."

My baby sister was quiet for a moment. "That's really weird."

"I kind of thought so, too. But he seemed pretty pissed that Henry wasn't around."

"Well, the guy *is* dead."

"Miranda," I snapped.

"Oh, you know what I mean."

"Yeah." My little sister didn't really have any connection to Henry beyond knowing that he was Etta's dad and that he'd bailed on us. His death hadn't affected her in any way that mattered, and sometimes she was really insensitive when he was brought up in conversation. I couldn't really blame her. I would have felt the same way if the shoe was on the other foot.

"So, what? He just stopped by to say hello?" she asked.

"I think he wanted to get a good look at me and Etta."

"Morgan," she said in warning.

"It wasn't like that."

"You don't know that for sure."

We'd discussed how Henry's family would handle knowing that he had a daughter numerous times since I'd found out about his death. While I knew logically that they didn't have any grounds to try to take her, the thought still made me nervous. Miranda, too. We'd seen how the system worked, and it wasn't always in the best interest of the child or the parent, no matter how well-intentioned child advocates were. There were just so many kids who fell under their care that it was impossible to do the right thing for every single one, no matter how hard they tried. We'd lived that firsthand, and while everything had worked out in the end for us, it had taken a long time before we'd felt secure again.

"He said they'd like to get to know us," I said, watching as Etta lined up her dolls on the floor. "I think they're just curious."

"You don't know these people," she argued, her voice hardening. "You might remember them as good, but it's been ten years."

"I'll be careful," I promised, smiling at Etta as she handed me her least favorite doll to play with.

"Good. So, what's the brother like?" she asked.

"Nice. Kind of quiet. Nervous. Older than us."

"That tells me exactly nothing." She laughed. "Does he look like Henry? Yum."

I snorted and made Etta's doll dance when she glanced over her shoulder at me.

"No, they're adopted, remember?"

"Oh, yeah."

"He's still hot, though," I conceded.

"Yes!"

"You're a train wreck," I joked.

"Yeah, yeah. So what's he look like?"

"Black," I said, picturing Trevor in my mind. "Gorgeous.

Big brown eyes, crazy thick eyelashes, huge smile, broad shoulders—"

"How's his ass?"

"I didn't—"

"Don't lie to me, sister!"

"You could bounce a franking quarter off of it, okay?"

Miranda laughed. "I knew you checked."

"Of course I did, I'm not blind. But it's a non-issue. Don't be weird about it."

"Hey, this is a purely academic conversation," she argued. "I'm not saying you have to bang the guy."

"Oh, God," I mumbled, my cheeks growing warm at just the thought of it. It had been a long time since I'd been with anyone, and no one, including the father of my child, had been as appealing to me as Trevor Harris. He was really good-looking, that was undeniable, but there was something else that just seemed to do it for me. I wasn't sure what it was—the way he held himself, or the courteous way he tried to make me comfortable, or something I couldn't even pinpoint—but hell, he did it for me in a big way.

"Oh, shit," Miranda said, cackling. "You totally want the brother!"

"I do not!" I snapped back.

"Yes, you do! I can tell!"

"You are *never* meeting him," I mumbled, just imagining how that conversation would go.

"I could," she said, her laughter dying down. "You never know."

"He said the family would like to get to know us," I replied, biting at my lip in anxiety.

"Hey," Miranda said soothingly, hearing the way my tone had changed. "As long as they're on the up-and-up, that's a good thing, right? We talked about this."

"You can't have enough family," I replied, not surprised that the minute I sounded nervous she tried to calm me down.

"Exactly. If something happened to me and you—"

"Don't say that."

"If she needed them for some reason, it's good that they want to be around."

"You're right," I said, sliding down on the couch until I was flat on my back. "I know you're right."

"Hard to let people into the circle of trust, though," she said understandingly.

"Seriously."

"Can we please get back to the hot brother now?" she whispered, like it was a secret.

I giggled and rolled to my side to watch Etta play. "Well...did I tell you he has a franking beard?"

"Oh, God," my sister replied, dragging out the last word like a moan.

"He asked us to go swimming at his hotel while he's here," I whispered so Etta wouldn't hear me.

"Are you going to do it?"

"I don't know. I'm thinking about it, though. It seems like it would be less weird than having him come to the house again."

"And you could see him in a pair of swim trunks."

"Right, because *that* is what's most important."

"Well, it's not unimportant, either," she replied. I could just imagine her shrugging her shoulders like perving on my daughter's uncle was a totally reasonable thing to do.

Just as I was about to reply I noticed Etta's face scrunched up in concentration and I quickly pushed myself off the couch.

"I gotta go," I told Miranda as I grabbed Etta by the hand. "I need to bring Etta to the bathroom."

"No bathwoom!" Etta argued, trying to pull her hand from mine.

"Love you."

"Love you, too," she said, laughing.

I disconnected and got Etta to the bathroom just in time for her to look at me triumphantly.

Oh, yeah. Trevor's good looks were super important, I thought as I brought Etta into our bedroom to change her diaper. Almost as important as somehow convincing my daughter that pooping on the toilet was fun.

Chapter 5
Trevor

As soon as I stepped into my hotel room and realized that I had absolutely nothing to do except sit there and wonder how in God's name my little brother had left those two females without a backward glance, I wished I hadn't left Morgan's house. Even the awkward silences and the feeling of being a weird spectator in their life had been better than the thoughts racing through my head now.

My throat tightened with emotion as I remembered my mom's excitement and the sound of her tearful laugh when I'd called her. She'd wanted to know everything all at once, and her questions had been so rapid that I hadn't had a chance to answer all of them. Knowing that a little piece of Henry was still out there in the world had been a small comfort once we'd moved past the circumstances of her existence. However, not knowing if his child was happy and safe had been like a dark cloud of worry hanging over all of us. It was a huge relief to know that not only was she okay, but that her mom was some-one my parents had known. The fact that Morgan had been with our family for just a short while, and over a decade ago, didn't dim that relief.

I'd hoped that Morgan would be a good mom. I'd prayed for it, actually, and I wasn't a man who prayed very often. But what I'd seen while I was sitting in her little house was way better than what I'd been willing to accept. She was great.

I knew a lot of mothers. I'd spent my life around all different types: the bad ones, the good ones, the distracted ones, and every kind along the spectrum. I knew how to spot the bad apples. She wasn't one. If anything, she reminded me of my cousin Kate in the way she parented, and that was a huge compliment.

I dropped down onto the edge of my bed with a sigh.

I'd ignored it for as long as I could, but now that I was alone I let myself think of how gorgeous Morgan was. I'd been so concerned with watching how she treated Etta that I'd been surprised by the punch of attraction that had hit me out of nowhere. Damn, Morgan was fine. She didn't seem to realize it, either. I mean, she moved like a woman who knew she had it going on, but she didn't capitalize on what she had with skimpy clothes or makeup. It seemed like she just took her good looks for granted, which was even more appealing. Too bad she was completely off-limits.

I needed to stay focused on what was important— Henrietta. If I'd thought that I could meet my niece once and then head back home, I'd been kidding myself. I hadn't had nearly enough time with her. Honestly, I wasn't sure any amount of time would feel like enough.

God, she was really something. She'd been pretty quiet,

maybe a little shy, but she hadn't seemed to care very much that I was there. She'd just taken it in stride, neither disinterested nor interested in me, just sort of accepting that I was going to hang with them for a while.

Two-year-olds were hard to read—catch them at a bad time and they seemed like complete lunatics or catch them at a good time and they seemed like angels. Right after nap time seemed to be the sweet spot for Etta, because she'd definitely fit into the angel category. She'd seemed confident in her surroundings. She was also easily riled, which was probably a trait she'd gotten from Morgan. Henry had been totally mellow from the moment he'd come to live with us, even though that was pretty uncommon for a toddler who'd had to switch homes over and over during his short life.

Henrietta. I shook my head in disbelief. Morgan had actually named her baby girl after Henry, the man who had deserted them. Even though I couldn't understand it, I still loved that she'd done that. My mom was going to love it, too. She felt really strongly about names and the meaning behind them, probably because her kids already had them by the time they came to her. I asked her once why she hadn't changed Hen's name when he was little. She could have chosen anything she wanted, and he wouldn't have known the difference. Mom had just shook her head and smiled. She'd said that she didn't want to change our histories, and our names were a part of that.

Goddammit, I was angry with my brother. Even knowing how selfish Henry could be, more interested in showing off and charming people than in making real connections, I still couldn't believe what he'd done. I didn't understand how he could've left that sweet baby without a backward glance. Early on, after I'd read everything the military was willing to send me about the training accident where he'd died and had gone through all of Hen's paperwork, I'd been so angry that it had scared me. I wasn't that man. I didn't rage. But knowing what I knew, and understanding just how selfish my baby brother had been? I'd felt myself turning into someone I didn't recognize. After a particularly toxic conversation with Ani that left her in tears, I'd realized that I needed to lock it down, so I did. I pushed back all of that anger and rage until I could barely see it past the grief. Unfortunately, now, after I'd seen his child, I could feel that anger bubbling to the surface again.

Taking a deep breath, I squeezed my hands around a soft hotel pillow until the joints in my fingers ached. Closing my eyes, I pictured Etta's face until the anger disappeared like smoke from a cigarette. Lingering, but invisible.

My phone rang as I slipped off my flip-flops and lay down on the bed.

"Hello?" I answered.

"Well?" my cousin Kate asked, her voice high and excited. "How did it go?"

"At least say hello, Kate," Ani mumbled, surprising me.

"Did you guys seriously just group-call me?" I asked in disbelief.

"Well, yeah," Kate replied. "We wanted to know what happened. Two birds with one stone, dude."

"It was her idea," Ani clarified. "I just went along with this middle-school three-way call."

"Wah, wah. You didn't exactly argue," Kate snapped back. Then her tone changed. "How did it go, Trev?"

I took a deep breath and smiled. "Best possible scenario," I replied.

"Yes!" Kate practically yelled.

"Oh, thank Christ," Ani said.

"Morgan's cool. Seems to have her shit together and from what I could see in the hour I was there, she's a good mom," I told them, relief making my voice light. "Plus, she's totally open to letting everyone meet Etta."

"Etta's the baby's name?" Ani asked as I heard Kate sniffle.

"Yeah, *Henrietta*."

"No fucking way," Ani muttered in happy disbelief.

"Yep."

"That's *so* cool," Kate said, her voice wobbly.

"It was a trip," I said, trying to find the right words to explain the experience I'd just had. "She was super cool about everything, invited me to have lunch with them, talked about Hen like she had no hard feelings whatsoever, said she'd be open to Etta knowing this side of the family."

"Sounds fishy," Ani said.

"What's she look like?" Kate asked at the same time.

I frowned a little in confusion at her question, but answered anyway. "Blond. Brown eyes. She's taller than Ani, but probably shorter than you—"

I stopped my description as Ani started to guffaw.

"Not the mom," she chuckled. "She was asking about the *baby*."

"Oh."

"I'm guessing the mom is pretty," Kate joked. She was laughing, too.

"You're both assholes," I muttered. "Etta looks like Henry.

Pull out one of Mom's old photo albums from when Henry first moved in with us, and that's almost exactly what Etta looks like."

"Awesome," Kate said happily.

Ani was still chuckling. "Hopefully without the mullet," she mused.

"Nah, her hair is still pretty thin, but it's not a mullet. She brushes it out of her face constantly, though," I said, smiling. "Like she's totally irritated with the whole mess."

"What's she like?" Kate asked. "Was she shy, or did she like you right away?"

"Not shy," I said, picturing Etta as she said hi to me. "But she wasn't super impressed with me." I laughed.

"That's okay, we aren't either," Ani quipped.

"Is she talking a lot?" Kate asked, not through with her questioning.

"Not a lot," I replied. "But some. She isn't talking in full sentences the way Sage was at that age, but she makes her wishes known. Mostly a lot of gibberish with some recognizable words thrown in."

"That's normal," Kate assured me. "Sage was an anomaly. That one's a total brainiac."

"She seemed good. Healthy and happy."

"God, that's such a relief," Ani said. "I've been having fucking nightmares about all the potential horrors she could be living with since we found out about her."

"Tell me about it," I replied in commiseration.

"Did she say when we could meet Etta?" Kate asked. "We're not busy this week. I mean, Shane has to work, but beyond that, we're free."

"Slow down, turbo," I replied. "We didn't make any plans or anything like that."

"You didn't?" Ani asked.

"I didn't want to overwhelm her," I replied defensively. "I was just glad she was okay with making contact."

"That's fair," Kate chimed in quickly.

"You want to know the weirdest thing I found out today?" I paused for effect. "Morgan was actually one of our foster kids back in the day."

"No shit?" Ani said in surprise.

"Yeah, about ten years ago, just for a couple months during the summer."

"I don't remember any Morgan Riley," Kate said dubiously.

"She's a year younger than Henry, I think," I replied. "Blond hair? She only stayed for about two months, and her last name was Harlan."

"Huh," Kate said. "I think I remember her, but I had a summer job by then so I wasn't around much. Do you know anything else?"

"Not really," I said, trying to think of anything descriptive I could use to jog Kate's memory without pointing out how gorgeous Morgan was. I didn't need to flame that fire after the ribbing I'd already gotten. "Hen had a huge crush on her, though. I remember that much. He followed her around like a puppy."

"Wait," Kate said, drawing the word out. "Didn't she have a really bad haircut?"

"How the fuck should I know?" I asked in bewilderment.

"You're such a guy," she snickered. "I think I do remember her! She was nice. Kind of quiet, but she got along with everyone."

"I'm just pissed that Hen was so fickle," Ani joked. "I thought he saved his unrequited love for yours truly."

"Don't worry, sis, he loved you best," Kate said soothingly, her voice choked with laughter.

I fucking loved that we could finally joke about him again without feeling the need to clarify or hide our amusement. There had been a time, right after Hen died, when we'd all felt a little uncomfortable making jokes. It had seemed weird for a while, laughing when our hearts felt like they'd been torn out. Slowly, my family was healing. Thank God.

My phone started to beep, so I pulled it away from my ear to check the call-waiting.

"Shit." I fumbled, trying to put it back against my ear. "I gotta go."

"What? Why?" Kate asked in confusion

"She's calling me."

"Morgan's calling you?" Ani asked.

"That's what I said," I replied. "Gotta go."

Then I hung up on them without a second thought. I'd call them both back later, preferably separately so I didn't have to hear them talking over each other again.

"Hello?" I said, crossing my fingers that Morgan hadn't hung up yet.

"Hey," she said, sounding a little nervous. "So, I have to work for the next few days."

"Oh, uh, okay," I replied dumbly.

"I was thinking if you were serious about the swimming, we could do that today? Or not. Whatever. We just won't have time tomorrow. It's really no problem if you're busy—"

"Morgan," I said, cutting off her chattering. "I'm not busy. I came down here to see Etta."

"Oh. Right."

"So, yeah. Come whenever you want. I'll be here all day."

"Cool," she said, her voice calmer now. "Then I'll just pack her up and we can head that way. Where are you staying?"

* * *

I'm not going to lie, I started to get nervous the second I hung up the phone. It was embarrassing, even if no one was there to see it. My palms were kind of clammy and I stood in the middle of the room, looking around like a lunatic. I didn't even know what I was looking for.

I'd been less nervous when I'd knocked on their door earlier. At least then I'd felt like I had a purpose. I was there for a specific reason, and I'd gone into the situation with a plan.

I didn't have a plan now.

No, now I was just going to spend time with a niece I'd just met and a woman I didn't know. Normally I was cool around people I'd just met, but this situation was out of my comfort zone. I was seriously attracted to this woman, and it made me feel all sorts of guilty and freaked out, and that wasn't even the worst part. It was really important for Morgan to like me and trust me. I had to make sure she did. The stakes were so fucking high.

Striding to my bag, I tried to remember if I'd packed a pair of swim trunks. I hadn't exactly planned on acting like I was on vacation while I was in California. I pulled everything out of my duffel and swore as I searched. I hadn't brought any. Why had I invited them to go fucking swimming of all things? We were in Anaheim, for Christ's sake. I could have taken them to Disneyland fully dressed.

The only pair of shorts I had that even resembled something I'd wear swimming were some black board shorts. They'd have to do. I didn't have time to go shopping for something better, and the hotel's amenities didn't include more than snack food.

I looked down at myself after I'd changed into the shorts and swore again. "Fuck!" I'd slid them on bare-assed, and they were practically indecent. There was no way I would be climbing into a body of water in those things the way they were unless I wanted everyone in the pool to know that I was circumcised. Grimacing, I took them back off and pulled on a pair of boxer briefs to wear underneath.

I wondered what Henry would say if he could see me stressing about my meet-up with what should have been his family. Would he have been pissed at how attracted I was to Morgan? Proud of Etta? Jealous that I was getting to spend time with them? Regretful? Would he have even cared at all?

Twenty minutes later as I was pacing in front of the hotel like an idiot, I saw Morgan walking toward me, wrestling with a huge bag as she tried to lead Etta across the parking lot. The baby was interested in everything, and I couldn't help but laugh as they made it to a little landscaped area and she tried to sit down so she could look at some rocks.

"You could help, ya know," Morgan called, laughing as she tried to shoo Etta along. She said something I couldn't hear, and then they were moving again.

Chastised, I met them halfway and took the heavy bag off of Morgan's shoulder. "Good Lord, woman," I mumbled, pretending to stumble. "What's in this thing?"

"Clothes," she said, lifting Etta into her arms. "Snacks, diapers, wipes, blankie, a stuffed animal, towels, some arm-floaty things, and some bricks."

Her face didn't change expression, making me snicker.

"Not sure if the arm-floaties are going to work if you're planning on adding the bricks."

"The bricks are for me," she deadpanned as I held the lobby door open for them. "I need the cardio."

"No you don't," I said without thinking as she passed me. Jesus, what was wrong with me?

The back of my neck heated as she snorted in response.

"Pool's this way." I pointed and tried to pretend that I hadn't just low-key hit on her without conscious thought. Thankfully, Morgan was the type to let things go and followed me with nothing but a nod.

"You want to go swimming?" she asked Etta as we walked inside the humid pool room. The place was pretty deserted since it was the middle of the day midweek. I'd seen families leaving on the shuttle that stopped in front of the hotel that morning, and I guessed most of them were probably out at the theme parks around the city doing their thing.

I stripped off my shirt and stepped out of my sandals as Morgan got Etta ready to swim. Both of them were wearing one-piece suits, but that was pretty much the only resemblance between the two pieces of clothing. Morgan's suit had cutouts in very strategic places and I had to clench my jaw to keep it from dropping. The woman had some gorgeous tattoos, or maybe it was just one tattoo but it was huge. It spread from the top of her thigh, up her side, and ended on her shoulder, leaving her arm bare. I could see only parts of it, but it looked like bright, vibrant flowers connected by tangled vines. I would have given up a year of my life to see the parts hidden by her suit.

Etta's skin was the opposite—so flawless and pale that I was thankful for the indoor pool. I wasn't sure how even sunblock could keep that delicate skin from burning. Her little suit was black with tiny red flowers and looked like a replica of a 1940s pinup's swimsuit. It was freaking adorable, and it reminded me of something Ani would put on my niece Arielle.

"Me swimmin'," Etta told me, toddling over to where I was standing. "Me swimmin' suit." She pointed to her chest. "Me swimmin' pannies." She pointed to her hip.

"Don't be telling people about your swimming panties," Morgan scolded jokingly, laughing as she swooped down and lifted Etta into the air.

"Memaids," Etta informed me with a nod, pointing to her hip again.

Morgan met my gaze and rolled her eyes, laughing. "Mermaids," she clarified. "We're still working on acceptable conversation topics."

"Mine are just boring black swimming panties," I told Etta, grimacing as I realized how creepy the word sounded coming out of my mouth. I quickly pointed to the waistband of my boxers that were peeking out the top of my shorts in an effort to move the conversation along. "Boooring."

"Bowing," Etta said, pursing her lips in commiseration.

Morgan laughed as she carried Etta to the steps of the pool and set her down so they could walk into it together.

"Crap," she mumbled. "Hold on, babycakes. I forgot your floaties."

"I can grab them," I assured her, holding my hand up as Etta started to fuss about getting pulled back out of the pool.

"They're right in the top of the bag," Morgan replied, giving me permission to touch her stuff.

"Cool floaties," I called to Etta when I found them under a couple of beach towels. It was really more of a life-jacket-type thing than the floaties we'd used as kids. I handed it to Morgan and watched as she threaded Etta's arms through the little armholes so that the poofy life-jacket part was across her chest, then buckled the entire contraption at her back.

"They work really well," Morgan told me as I slid into the pool. "Go ahead, baby," she said to Etta. "Get your swim on."

My heart practically stopped as Etta jumped off the stair she was on and disappeared under the water, just to pop back up again with a squeal. The water wasn't deep, maybe about three feet, but there was no way she could touch the bottom.

"I keep a close eye on her," Morgan told me in reassurance as she sat down on the pool stairs. "But she likes to swim around on her own."

"She's got no fear," I said, swallowing hard as Etta arched her back until she was floating, her face pointed toward the ceiling. Her head kept dipping farther into the water as she tried to lift her feet higher. My hands were fidgeting with the need to go spot her.

"Nah, why should she?" Morgan asked, cool as a cucumber. "She knows I'm right here."

"Good mama," I murmured, still watching Etta closely as she rolled over and started to doggie-paddle across the pool. That was better. She seemed a bit more steady when she was moving.

"Eh," Morgan said easily. "I try."

It took me a second to know what she was talking about, I'd been so focused on Etta. "I know a lot of kids older than her who freak out in the water," I said, finally turning my head to look at her as I leaned against the edge of the pool.

"I think that probably comes from the parents' nervousness," Morgan replied with a nod. "Kids pick up on that stuff. My mom was scared to death of roller coasters, and I still won't go near one even though logically I know they're safe."

"You live in Southern California and you don't go on roller coasters?" I asked as Etta made her way toward me.

"There's more than amusement parks down here," Morgan chided with a little laugh. "But to be clear, I'll go on rides, I just won't go on those open-air roller coasters."

"So, you're cool with the baby rides, then."

"Whatever." She laughed and splashed water in my direction.

"No 'plashin'!" Etta scolded as she reached me.

"Sorry," Morgan replied. "You're right, no splashing."

"You don't like water in your face?" I asked, crouching down so that I was eye-to-eye with the tiny swimmer. "Me either."

She said something that I couldn't understand, but by the look on her face and her tone, it sounded like a diatribe about the evils of splashing water.

"She doesn't like when water gets in her eyes," Morgan translated as Etta turned away and started paddling around again. "Washing her hair is a franking nightmare. She swims like a fish, though, and the irony is not lost on me."

"I have a nephew that was the same way," I replied. "Not the swimming part, but the hair-washing aversion."

"Do you have a lot of nieces and nephews?"

"Six," I answered. "Well, Etta makes seven."

"That's awesome," Morgan replied, smiling as we watched Etta swim. "My sister doesn't have any kids yet, so Etta's the only grandchild."

"Yeah, Shane—my foster brother, you never met him, I don't think—and my cousin Kate have five. Then my cousin Bram has one."

"I remember Bram. He's a twin, right?"

"Right."

"He was the pissy one?"

"Right again." I laughed. "His twin's name is Alex."

"Alex was the cute one," she said, her lips twitching as she hummed a little.

"If you say so." Discussing how cute Alex was might have been in the top ten things I'd never want to discuss with the woman sitting next to me.

"Everyone said so," she replied with a laugh.

"Anyway," I murmured, changing the subject. "Etta's got a lot of cousins to play with."

"That's awesome," Morgan said.

"Do you—" I cleared my throat and started again. "Do you think you'd be cool with meeting them? There's a lot of us, but maybe they could come in waves or something."

Morgan's laugh sounded almost like a bark, and her hand flew up to cover her mouth.

"Come in *waves?*" she asked, her eyes crinkled in the corners as she tried to hold back laughter.

"I don't want you to feel overwhelmed—"

"Trevor, I was shuffled around foster homes for two years as a teenager. Your family isn't going to overwhelm me."

"Well, that's good," I said, pausing as Etta jumped off the pool stairs again. "Because they all want to meet you guys."

"Sounds good to me," she replied, looking away. "We'll make it happen."

"Yeah, kind of hard with my parents in Oregon," I said, picking up on the hesitant tone of her words. "But Shane and Kate and the kids live down here, outside San Diego."

"No shit?" Morgan said.

"Yeah. She's been bugging me to come see you guys since we found out about you."

"She can come see us." Morgan shrugged. "I mean, I have to work and stuff, so it'll depend on our schedule."

"I'll let her know," I replied, deciding then and there that I'd give it a few days before I told Kate any such thing.

Morgan was being really cool about letting Etta see our side of the family. She'd been kind and welcoming to me from the minute she saw me on her front step, and she'd even agreed to bring Etta to hang out with me, but I could tell by the way her body had tensed just now that she was feeling a little cornered. I didn't want her to feel like that. If she was going to have a relationship with us, she needed to know that we weren't going to try to push her around or take over her life. At least that's what I repeated over and over in my mind. If I was honest with myself, a small part of me wanted to force the issue, even though I knew that would be an asshole move.

"So, what do you do for a living?" I asked, redirecting our conversation.

"What do *you* do for a living?" she shot back.

"I run the family logging company," I answered easily. "Me and Bram pretty much run the show now that our dads are semiretired."

"Interesting," she said. Her hands skimmed the surface of the water, back and forth in a hypnotizing pattern. They were delicate, just like the rest of her, and she wore a thin gold band on the pinky of her right hand.

"Plumber?" I guessed jokingly. "Construction worker? Flagger? Underwater demolition expert?"

"What, you think I couldn't do those things?" she asked accusingly.

"Hell, I bet you could do any of them," I replied, quickly realizing my mistake. "But you don't have the tan for construction or flagging, I've never actually met an underwater demo expert, but I'm pretty sure they're rolling in it and your house is kind of small—"

"Hey!"

"—and I just can't imagine you plunging other people's shit every day."

"Maybe I just take really good care of my skin," she argued, grinning.

"There's no way," I laughed. "I mean, I'm sure you do. But it's impossible to stand out in the sun all day, even with sunblock, and not get some sort of tan."

"I am a bit vampirish looking."

"Surprising, considering where you live."

"I really do take good care of my skin," she whispered conspiratorially, before raising her voice to a normal level again. "But you're right. I don't work outside. I actually work at a tattoo shop."

"Oh yeah?" I glanced at the tattoo on her shoulder, not letting my eyes wander any farther south even though I really wanted to.

"Yeah, I do piercings, though."

"Cool." I nodded. I didn't have any piercings, I'd never even gotten my ears pierced, but I knew plenty of people who did. Ani had a couple different ones, always adding to them when she felt the urge, and currently had a septum ring. "You ever have to pierce any interesting places?"

"I've pierced everything," she replied, with a roll of her eyes. "Etta," she called, "come back this way, baby."

She waited until Etta was a little closer to us, then relaxed again against the steps. "I'll just say, women generally whine a whole lot less than men. Higher pain tolerance."

"Seriously?"

"Oh, yeah. You wouldn't believe the amount of guys that come in, planning on getting their dicks pierced on a dare, and then completely punk out once they see the needle. It was worse in San Diego, though. Half the idiots would come in with a little liquid courage and we'd have to turn them away. No piercings or tattoos if you're drunk."

"Yeah, piercing my junk has never been an aspiration of mine," I mumbled, cringing at the thought. I covertly slid my hands away from my junk when I realized that I'd cupped them in front of me in an instinctual protective move.

"Different strokes," she said with a shrug. "Women usually come in because they actually want the piercing, and they just want to get it over with before they lose their courage."

"I'd imagine it hurts like a—" I stopped talking and glanced at Etta before *motherfucker* came out of my mouth.

"I don't know. Tattoos take a lot longer, and a lot more people have those. Sit in a chair for hours while someone pricks you over and over, or take five minutes and be done, you know?"

"I'll take your word for it," I said, just as Etta decided to grace me with her presence again.

"You name?" she asked.

"My name's Trevor, remember?"

"Twevo."

"Yep."

"Twevo," she said my name and then continued to speak, but I had no clue what she was trying to tell me. I listened for a word that could give me a clue, but I didn't hear a single one that sounded even vaguely familiar.

"You want us to swim with you?" Morgan asked.

"Twevo," Etta clarified.

"Hey, what about me?" Morgan acted affronted. "I'm your best friend!"

Etta sighed like she was really put out, then giggled as Morgan dipped underneath the water and swam toward where we were sitting.

Morgan popped up just inches from Etta and the shriek the little girl let out practically shook the walls as she scrambled to swim away. Shooting me a grin, Morgan dipped back under the water as Etta yelled in excitement, thrashing her way across the shallow end of the pool. Once again, as soon as Etta paused to try to find her mom under the water, Morgan popped up and startled her, making her scream in laughter.

I'd been holding it together up to that point, but watching them play almost knocked me to my knees. I had never seen anything more beautiful in my life. Etta started splashing her mom just as I dipped down to swim toward them, my heart in my throat.

"Hey, I thought there was no splashing," I said roughly as I slowly made my way in their direction.

"Oh, that's just for us," Morgan replied jokingly, sputtering as she wiggled her fingers at Etta like she was going to "get" her. "The no-splashing rule doesn't apply to Miss Henrietta.

"Oh, no, Etta!" Morgan warned as I dipped lower in the water. "Trevor's gonna get ya!"

I dipped below the water just in time to see Etta's little legs going a million miles an hour as she tried to swim around me. Her movements were spastic and seemed like they'd get her nowhere, but she moved pretty quickly across the pool as I followed her, finally popping up when I ran out of air. As soon as I'd sucked in a bit of oxygen, my face was completely submerged again in the sheet of water that Etta had somehow sent my way.

"No, Twevo!" Etta yelled, but she was laughing so hard that she could barely catch her breath.

I let her move away from me and watched as she realized that she could no longer see her mom where she'd left her before. Her eyes grew wide as she searched the pool, then slammed shut when she squealed as Morgan popped up next to her.

We took turns following Etta around the pool for over an hour, letting her wear herself out as she tried to swim away from us over and over. Morgan and I weren't even breathing heavily, but by the time we decided to get out of the pool, Etta was completely worn out. She didn't even fuss when Morgan told her it was time to go.

"Twevo," Etta called out as she approached the steps and clumsily reached for me. "Up."

I glanced at Morgan, who seemed unconcerned, then lifted Etta into my arms. She was so light it was kind of unbelievable. Like I'd told Morgan, I had a lot of nieces and nephews, but Etta was built far smaller than any of them, and it was really noticeable once I held her. I smiled as Etta's eyes met mine. It was kind of amazing how someone so light could also feel so incredibly heavy. Jesus, I missed my brother.

Etta dropped her head to my shoulder as I carried her toward the chairs where we'd left our stuff, and instinctively I raised my hand to rub her back softly. The girl was a character, there was no doubt about that. She was sassy and demanding and a little bit spoiled, but, God, was she sweet.

I unclipped the floaty and pulled it off of her as Morgan followed us from the pool. The floaty thing was dripping wet and heavy, and I wasn't sure where to put it.

"Just drop it on the floor," Morgan said, grabbing a towel and wrapping it around herself. "I brought a garbage bag to put it in until we get home."

I nodded, then let Morgan wrap a towel around Etta and tuck it in between us.

"I'd just leave her in the swimsuit until we got home, but I'm pretty sure she's going to pass out in the car," Morgan said, looking around the room. "Do you know where the bathrooms are?"

"You can change her in my room if you want." I met her eyes as her brows rose in surprise.

Shit. Inviting her to my room was weird, wasn't it? She barely knew me. I held back a grimace as I waited for her answer.

Chapter 6

Morgan

Being with Trevor was easy. I hadn't expected that.

While I'd already realized that he was a nice guy, I hadn't yet figured out that he was going to be someone I felt comfortable with right off the bat. It was true, though. The longer we hung out, the more comfortable I felt, and it wasn't even because of any specific thing he did. He was just—there. Quick with a comeback, funny, easygoing.

I followed him and Etta up to his hotel room while she sleepily mumbled nonsense against his shoulder, and I knew that I wasn't making the smartest decision of my life. I mean, sure, I wasn't getting any weird vibes from him, but he was still someone I'd just met. Knowing each other as kids wasn't really an endorsement. I'd once known a guy during my childhood; we'd played together because our dads were friends, and I would have considered him someone I "knew" relatively well—until I'd heard that he'd been arrested for drugging and raping a girl.

People were funny that way. You never really knew them until they were comfortable enough to show their true colors.

Sometimes if you were lucky someone opened up right off the bat; other times you never saw the real person beyond the façade.

My sister is going to lose her mind, I thought as I followed Trevor into his room. It gave me enough pause that I discreetly pressed the slide lock between the door and the frame so that it didn't close all the way and there was an inch of hallway visible through the gap. Trevor glanced over his shoulder at me and clearly noticed what I'd done but just gave a little smile, like it didn't bother him in the least.

"Down," Etta demanded, lifting her head. As soon as her feet hit the floor she was off exploring the room.

I pulled out a diaper and some clothes as she opened drawers and checked out the mini fridge under the counter, fascinated.

"I'm gonna change in the bathroom," Trevor said, lifting a duffel off the counter. "Give you ladies some privacy. Just knock when it's safe to come out."

"Thanks," I said as he stepped into the bathroom and closed the door behind him. Vaguely, I wondered how long he'd stay in there if I didn't knock. The bed I'd dropped our bag onto seemed way softer than the one I had at home, and it was looking pretty inviting after our long day.

I needed to get the hell out of there before I got any more comfortable. If I was really thinking about how inviting a strange man's hotel bed looked, I needed to get my ass home. I didn't have any time for that kind of crap in my life, especially not the kind that came with the baggage Trevor would be carrying.

"Henrietta," I sang softly, ignoring the urge to run. "Henrietta, come to Mama, it's time to get dressed."

I sang the little ditty to a tune I'd made up when she was just a baby. She'd always loved when I sang to her softly, but back then I hadn't known a single children's song. In the middle of those early nights when nothing seemed to calm her down and I was three levels past exhaustion, I'd never been able to remember any songs at all.

"Henwyetta," she sang back, as she toddled toward me.

I stripped off her swimsuit and swim diaper as I continued to sing, occasionally glancing at the bathroom door to make sure Trevor was still closed inside. "Henrietta, you're all wet, what in the world have you been doing? Henrietta, let's get you dressed, so you can be nice and cozy."

She hummed along as I snapped the sides of her diaper and pulled a sundress over her head. I let her roam the room again as I quickly got dressed in a sundress of my own and threw my hair into a bun at the top of my head. I'd deal with the tangled mess later when I had some conditioner and could actually brush through it.

"Want to go knock on the door?" I asked, standing awkwardly at the foot of the bed. I was beginning to get uncomfortable, and kind of wished that we could just leave without saying our good-byes. "Go see if Trevor's done?"

I smiled as she ran across the room and started knocking—and then didn't stop. She hadn't realized yet that a few knocks would do, so she just knocked and knocked and knocked until the door opened slightly.

"Is this my signal?" Trevor asked, not even peeking through the door.

"Yeah."

The door opened wider, and he stood there in a pair of shorts and a white T-shirt, grinning. "I wasn't sure if it was a false alarm or not," he said, glancing down at Etta.

"I let her knock," I replied dumbly. I was pretty sure I was staring, but damn. That shirt did all sorts of things for his shoulders and chest. I'd just been looking at him shirtless for hours, but that white T-shirt was somehow pushing all of my buttons at once.

"I see that," he said, crouching down in front of Etta. "Good job, peanut."

"Job, 'Eanut," Etta copied, bouncing a little up and down.

"Were you singing?" he asked, glancing up at me.

An embarrassed smile pulled at my lips, but I tried really hard to play it cool. "You heard that, huh?"

"Just the tone," he replied.

"Wed pannies," Etta interrupted, leaning sideways until he couldn't see anything but her. "Wed pannies." Then she lifted up her dress to show Trevor her diaper, making me snort with laughter.

"Oh God," I rasped, covering my face with my hand. "I'm in so much trouble with her."

"Cool red panties," Trevor replied to Etta, his smile growing. "You like the color red?"

"Yes." She nodded resolutely, then got bored with the conversation and turned away to play with the mini fridge again.

"Is that a cloth diaper?" Trevor asked, rising to his feet.

"Yep. We've used them since she was little." I smiled a little, but I couldn't interpret the look on his face. I wanted to get out of there, but I had no idea how to extricate myself without looking like a jerk. Women in movies always had some easy-breezy way of saying that they needed to leave, but it didn't happen like that in real life. I'd never found a non-awkward way to tell someone that I had to go. Usually it just came across as rude.

"If you're using cloth diapers because you need money and don't want to tap into that insurance payout," he said slowly, stopping my thoughts short. His eyes were nothing but kind. "I can—"

"Lord," I said, cutting him off. "You're too nice. Seriously, how the *shell* are you so nice?" Now I felt even worse for wanting to bail. Was this guy for real?

"Shell," he mumbled, shaking his head at my tweaked swear word. "Seriously, Morgan."

"Oh, I know you're serious," I said, my lips curving up at the sides. "But we're totally fine."

"Are you sure?"

"Positive," I replied. "We do okay."

"I'm sorry. I just thought—" He didn't finish his sentence as he gestured vaguely toward Etta in her cloth diaper.

"Cloth diapers are actually pretty expensive," I informed him. "At least at first. She's had those same ones for over a year, so the cost is low now, but when I was building her stash, it got pretty steep."

"Really?"

"Yep. Anywhere from ten to thirty-five dollars a diaper, usually." Those diapers had come slowly to us. I'd had to save here and there, putting away five-dollar bills when I had them until I had enough for each one.

"Jesus."

"Cool thing about those, though, is that they're one size, so she's been using them for a long time. I won't have to get any more, she'll just wear them until she potty trains."

"Why, uh, why did you decide to do that?" he asked. "If that's not a rude question."

I laughed. "Not at all." Etta came toward me, and I sat down, pulling her onto my lap. I grabbed her blankie and stuffed animal from our bag. As soon as she was holding them, she popped her thumb into her mouth and her body relaxed against mine. "So, when she was tiny we were pretty strapped," I smiled ruefully, remembering just how *strapped* we'd been. "And I somehow saw this chat room with all these moms who were cloth diapering and loved it. At first I just grabbed what I could, secondhand waterproof covers, flat old-fashioned diapers made out of towels, stuff like that. Crazily, it worked better than I'd expected. Eventually, I got some more expensive and easier-to-use diapers whenever I had a little extra cash, and now she's all stocked up."

"Huh," Trevor said contemplatively.

"Plus, she's not filling the landfills with her poo," I pointed out, complete with my finger pointed in the air. "All green, baby."

"Always a plus," Trevor said, laughing. "I wouldn't want to be cleaning poo off diapers, but no judgment."

I rolled my eyes in amusement. "When it's your kid, it's different. Plus, you know how many times she pooped through her disposable diapers? *That* was nasty. I had to clean her from the neck down *and* I still had to clean poo off clothes, so..."

"Point taken," Trevor said, raising his hands in surrender. He was leaning casually against the counter on the other edge of the room, with his bare feet crossed at the ankles.

"And the diapers she wears now don't have any chemicals rubbing against her skin all day—"

"You win," Trevor interrupted, his smile huge. "You're a genius and I'm just a lowly disposable-diaper supporter."

"Still?"

"Cloth diapers all the way, now," he said teasingly. "I've been converted."

"I always knew I'd make a difference in the world," I joked wistfully, making him laugh.

"Looks like she's down for the count," he replied, nodding toward Etta.

I nodded without looking down at her. I'd felt her body go limp the moment she fell asleep. "I should probably get her home," I said, making sure I hadn't left anything on the bed before getting to my feet. Finally, I had a legit reason for leaving.

"I'll get that for you," Trevor insisted as he pulled our bag from my hand. "I can walk you down."

We were quiet as we made our way to my car. It wasn't an awkward silence, like we'd dealt with before, but felt more like neither of us knew what to say because we had no idea when we'd see each other again. He lived in Oregon and I wasn't sure how long he'd be visiting, but I had to work for the next six days and there was no way I'd be able to make time for him to see Etta. By the time I got home from work every day, Etta and I were both completely beat.

"Thanks for letting me see her," Trevor said after I'd buckled a still-sleeping Etta into her car seat. "Really. Thank you."

"Of course," I replied with a small smile. As much as I wanted to keep Etta all to myself and was afraid of what the

Harris family showing up in her life might mean, I wasn't a monster.

"So, I'll get in touch with you about visits and stuff?"

"Sounds good." I nodded. In the back of my mind I knew that I could always blow them off if I needed to, especially with them living in a different state.

"It was really nice to meet you . . . again."

"You too," I replied, and I meant it.

One awkward hug later and I was in my car and headed home. It had been such a weird day, my emotions were out of control. I couldn't wait to get home so I could curl up in a ball with a cup of coffee and try to make sense of the impact that the Harris family would have on our lives.

* * *

Late that night, I was wrapped in a blanket on the couch watching TV when my phone dinged with a new message. My eyes widened when Trevor's name popped up on the screen.

I wanted to thank you again for today. I can't even explain what it felt like to see a little bit of Henry in Etta.

I smiled and swallowed the lump in my throat. I understood how Trevor felt. I got to look into the little copy of Henry's face every day. I was sure at some point I wouldn't think of him as often as I did, but as of now, it was hard to ignore their resemblance.

Henry and I hadn't been close. He'd been kind of impossible to get close to, and I'd never tried very hard. Our relationship, for lack of a better word, had been nothing more than a way to let off steam. We'd hung out for a couple of months, usually with a group of his friends, and more often than not had ended up naked together by the end of the night. Henry had been a lot of fun, but even if I'd been searching for my forever, I'd known early on that he wasn't someone I wanted to be with long term. He was a nice guy, though, and I'd considered him a friend, even after he'd made it clear that he couldn't be Etta's dad. The guy'd had a lot of problems that he hid well from the world, and I couldn't fault him for that. I told myself that we all had things that we tried to deal with as best we could. No one was perfect, especially not me.

I clicked on the message and sat with my thumbs poised over the phone screen, unsure how I wanted to reply.

You're welcome, I finally typed. *I'm glad that Etta has family that wants to know her. I was nervous about all that.*

His reply was almost instantaneous. *Nervous?*

How did I explain all of the fears that had been plaguing me since Etta was born? Part of me had felt relieved when Henry had decided to completely distance himself from us. I worried about how Etta would feel about his decision as she got older, but I'd also felt a sense of comfort knowing that she was all mine. I was sure that made me a horrible person, but I couldn't help it.

I would have never made that decision for Henry, could have never taken away his rights if he'd wanted them. However, knowing that he didn't want a relationship with Etta had made me feel more secure. When I was a kid, my mom had taken us away from my dad for no reason and moved us from Central California to Oregon. I'd never forgiven her for that, and I would never have done that to Etta. The flip side of that had been the constant fear that Henry would change his mind and try to take our daughter from me.

Having a child was scary, period. Having a child with someone you didn't share your life with made it infinitely scarier in a variety of ways. The loneliness had been horrible in the beginning, and when it was mixed with the fear of sharing my baby with someone who didn't seem to want any solid part in her life? Well, that had been damn near devastating to think about.

I just wasn't sure what your family would do, I replied. *You always hear horror stories about stuff like that.*

Henry's family scared me more because they had a history of taking in kids that weren't theirs. It was admirable, the way they'd taken in foster kids. I wasn't sure how they'd been able to do that. I was pretty sure I didn't have the strength to raise kids like my own knowing I'd probably have to give them back. But that also meant that they had the knowledge and contacts to be able to take Etta.

It wasn't logical. I knew that. Etta was safe and happy and cared for, and the courts usually favored mothers in situations like that. My fears weren't rational; they were the outcome of a life lived in a series of hotels with my mother and then multiple foster homes while my dad fought to get me and my sister back. I'd learned the hard way that the courts didn't always work the way they were supposed to.

My heart raced a little as I waited for Trevor to text me back. I hoped I hadn't offended him, but I was trying to be honest. Well, as honest as I was willing to be, considering the fact that I was still pretty freaked out that he'd shown up at all.

Lucky for both of us, my family's pretty great.

How are they doing? I asked, curious about them. I remembered his parents fondly, even though they scared the shit out of me. It couldn't have been easy losing one of their boys. *I can't imagine losing a child.*

They're okay. Mostly. Still dealing. My mom is taking things the hardest, but she's hanging in.

Henry was the baby, right?

Yep. He's the youngest.

Are you the oldest?

How could you tell? My distinguished good looks?

Process of elimination. Aren't there only two of you? ;)

Beeeeep. Wrong. There's three. Shane is in the middle of us. Just a little younger than me.

I don't remember him.

He was a foster, he might have come after you were there? Not sure. He was pretty old when he moved in, but he was one of the kids who stayed. He ended up marrying my cousin Kate.

Incestuous, much? I grinned.

Ha! Maybe if he'd grown up with us. Honestly, we all knew it would happen eventually, but it took them forever to figure their shit out.

Wait, are they the ones with all the kids?

Right. Sage, Keller, Gavin, Gunner and Iris. The first four are from Shane's first marriage. Long ass story, don't ask.

That's a LOT of kids.

No shit. They make it work though.

What about you? Any kids?

Smooth, Morgan. Nice transition. Jesus, why was I still talking to the guy? Nothing good would come of striking up a friendship with Trevor Harris.

Nope. No kids for me yet. I haven't found someone I wanted to be with for longer than a few months, so...

Me either. I joked.

Shit, I didn't mean it that way.

No worries. Etta was the best surprise I've ever gotten. Like Christmas and my birthday all rolled into one.

I bet. She's awesome.

When I didn't reply right away, he texted again.

Let me pull this foot out of my mouth. I've always been really sure of the fact that I don't want to be a part-time dad. I want to be there for everything. So, I haven't planned any kids, and there haven't been any unplanned either. That's not to say that I wouldn't be happy with any child, no matter if I was with their mother or not.

His attempts to backpedal were admirable, and I couldn't help but snicker. He hadn't offended me. I knew the way Etta had been conceived wouldn't have been the ideal situation for most people. I'd just been glad she was, so I tried not to think about it.

I get it. LOL

I do want kids, though. Eventually.

Clock's ticking.

You just told me to be patient!

Not too patient.

Now you sound like my mom.

Ouch.

Nah, I love my mom so that's a good thing.

Mama's boy, huh?

And not ashamed to admit it.

I grinned at his response. Our texts had been flying back and forth so fast that I hadn't realized my show was over and my coffee had grown cold. Yeah, I was one of those people who drank coffee at night. It was more of a comfort thing for me than a caffeine fix. My dad always drank black coffee and it reminded me of home the way other people said hot chocolate gave them similar comfort. I didn't have any little-kid hot-chocolate memories.

I know you're working all week so I think I'm going to head home tomorrow.

The smile fell off my face even though I knew it was definitely a good thing that Trevor was leaving so Etta and I could get back to our normal lives.

I'll come back down to visit as soon as I can—maybe I could bring my mom and we could plan it so you have some days off?

Sure, sounds good.

I'll text you.

I didn't bother with a reply. I could already feel myself shutting down and shutting him out. It wasn't anything he'd done or hadn't done. I'd just always had the habit of fitting people into their little boxes. I'd developed the habit as I'd shifted in and out of foster homes. Being able to leave people behind, the good ones and the bad ones, and not think of them again had been the only way I'd survived the moves. If Trevor was leaving the next day it was time to put his box on the shelf until I had to deal with it again. It was easier that way. Besides, I'd known the minute he'd shown up at my door—his expression a mixture of nervousness and hope—that I wouldn't let Trevor Harris upend our lives.

Chapter 7
Trevor

Mom," I groaned in exasperation. "I hear you. I told you she hadn't texted back yet, and she still hasn't. I'll tell you when I know anything."

I'd been home for a little over two weeks and my mom was already itching to take a trip to California to see little Etta. I understood her impatience, but there wasn't really anything I could do to speed things up.

Morgan and I had texted a little after the day we'd met, but that contact had tapered off pretty quickly. I wasn't sure if she'd just been humoring me for a while, or if she was crazy busy now, but she wasn't returning my texts with any sort of efficiency. She wasn't completely ignoring them, sometimes writing back a day later, sometimes not until two days later, but I could tell she didn't want to talk to me.

I was surprised. I'd gotten the impression that we'd gotten along pretty well. I thought she'd liked me. However, I wasn't about to tell my mom, who was waiting on pins and needles, that Morgan had decided that she didn't want anything to do with me but seemed too polite to ignore me completely.

Morgan had agreed to let my parents get to know Etta, and she hadn't told me she'd changed her mind. That was the important thing, no matter how she seemed to be acting toward me now.

"I'm just anxious," my mom said with a shrug as she cooked dinner. "And excited, too. You should have taken more pictures."

"I didn't want to come off as creepy," I told her for the hundredth time. I'd been able to get two photos of Etta, one when she was playing on the floor in their house and one when she was stepping into the pool in her swimsuit, but I hadn't taken any more. Morgan had seemed pretty laid-back, but honestly, those two photos had made me feel like a creeper because I hadn't asked to take them. I wasn't sure how the mama bear would feel about that if she knew.

"She looks just like Hen," Mom said, repeating herself. "I can't believe how much. Her mom must not have very strong genes."

"She's blond, too," I reminded her as I pulled some plates down and started to set the table. "She doesn't look like Hen, but she's not his opposite, either."

"I wouldn't have cared either way," Mom said quietly. "But it's nice, don't you think?"

"Yeah, it's pretty cool." I thought about how beautiful Morgan was. Etta definitely wouldn't have lost anything if she'd looked more like her mother. Henry and Morgan must have looked like a couple of movie stars when they'd been out together. The thought made my stomach sour.

"What's pretty cool?" my aunt asked as she and my uncle let themselves in the back door.

"How much Henry's baby looks like him," my mom answered, grinning. "It's uncanny."

"No kidding," my aunt replied, setting a dish filled with something that smelled like heaven on the counter. She'd seen the photos dozens of times, too. She and my mom had studied and scrutinized them over and over, talking about how happy and healthy the baby looked, what her body language might have meant, and what dolls she seemed to prefer based on the toys in the photo.

It was like they'd turned into private detectives, body language experts, and child psychologists overnight. And if I was being honest, it was getting a little annoying. They talked about Etta a lot, but they didn't mention her mom much. I knew it wasn't deliberate because they had no frame of reference, but I'd seen her. I'd seen why Etta was so happy. Why she seemed fearless in the pool and perfectly happy playing by herself on the floor. That was all Morgan's doing. She was raising that fearless, happy kid.

Whenever my mom mentioned how Henry was fearless at that age—he wasn't—or how he played by himself—he didn't—I'd had to grit my teeth against the need to argue. My mom was still grieving. She was remembering Henry the way she wanted to, as the happy and confident kid he'd become later, after years of living in a stable home with loving parents. Why would I take that away from her? I wouldn't. Not in a million years.

"Have no fear, Arielle is here!" Ani called as she carried Arie into the kitchen *Lion King*–style, the baby squealing in delight as Ani held her high. "And we're starving."

"I brought beer," Bram said, exhaustion clear in his voice. "I'll put it in the cooler."

He shuffled past me with nothing but a head nod. From what I'd gathered when I'd seen him at work, Arielle wasn't sleeping at night. Ani and the baby were able to catch up on some of that rest during the day while he was at work, but he'd been pretty much falling asleep at his desk all week. It didn't look like he'd gotten much rest over the weekend, either.

"I'm crossing my fingers that she sleeps this week," Ani announced, putting Arielle into one of the high chairs next to the dining room table. "At some point, she'll get tired enough to sleep, right?"

"She's still giving you trouble, huh?" Aunt Liz asked, smoothing down Arielle's hair as she moved around the table.

"Yeah. Her pediatrician said this phase is normal, but holy shit. I'm about to drop."

"You?" Bram asked with a huff. "You're napping during the day."

"Barely," Ani snapped. "If you think that I'm sleeping all day, your head is so far up your—"

"Children," my dad said in warning, shutting them both up. "Know you're both tired, know you're both grumpy, but hell if I'm gonna listen to it. Figure it out at your own house."

I chuckled, then grunted as Ani elbowed me in the side as she strode past. My dad and uncle had both made it perfectly clear that they didn't want to deal with any of the kids' relationship problems during family dinners. It wasn't a new thing.

Any other day of the week and the older men were ready and willing to listen and offer up advice. All of the older generation were like that. However, at dinner on Friday, you were expected to leave all of that nonsense at home. Even when we were kids, we hadn't been allowed to argue at the table.

We were sitting around the table discussing anything and everything that happened lately when my phone chimed in my pocket. If I'd thought about it, I would have silenced the stupid thing.

When the phone beeped, my mom's head shot up like a bloodhound's.

"No phones at the table," Ani griped, stuffing food into her mouth. Damn, that woman needed to get some sleep. She'd come in trying to hide it, but the longer she sat there, the more convinced I was that at any moment she was going to faceplant into her mashed potatoes.

"Is it her?" my mom asked as I cut up the meat on my plate. "Trevor, is that her?"

"I don't know," I said calmly. "I'm eating." I lifted my fork and knife like they were evidence.

"Well, check it," she said, annoyed.

I knew she was anxious and waiting for news, but it still drove me crazy that I was fishing my phone out of my pocket in the middle of dinner so that I could tell my mom who was contacting me. I kind of hoped it was someone from work, but I knew it wasn't. Those guys might text me later in the night to invite me out with them, but they wouldn't text the boss—me—right after work on Friday.

Hey, Trevor. Sorry, I haven't texted back, I've been crazy busy. Yeah, you guys can visit, but we're actually moving, so it'll have to wait a bit.

Moving? Where the hell were they going, and why? The thought made my stomach churn. I knew where they were now. I knew how to find them. If Morgan moved and changed her number, they could pretty much disappear. Was that what she was doing? Son of a bitch. I glanced at my mom and stood up from the table.

"She said you could visit," I said, giving my mom a small smile as she clapped her hands together once in happiness. "I'll be right back."

I strode outside and hit Morgan's contact before the door had even shut behind me.

"Hello?" she answered. I was a little surprised.

"You're moving?" I asked.

"Nice greeting," she said drily. "Yes, we're moving."

"Why?"

She sighed and I snapped my mouth shut, swallowing against the need to interrogate her. I was being kind of an ass. A nosy ass.

"Not that it's any of your business," she said, not unkindly, "But I lost my franking job, so we're headed up to stay with my dad in Sacramento for a while."

"You lost your job?"

"It's like I'm talking to a parrot."

"I'm sorry," I mumbled, shaking my head. "That sucks, what happened?"

"I took the job under the conditions that I'd pitch in if someone else didn't show up," she said, sounding frustrated. "Which was fine, because no one ever really did that. Pretty much everyone in the shop needed the money, so we always showed up for our shifts. But then the owner hired his franking cousin or something, who never showed up, and they had to keep asking me to come in."

She went silent.

"And you can't just drop everything and go in," I said in understanding. Those motherfuckers.

"I make it a point *not* to drop my kid," she joked miserably. "I took some of the shifts, but Carmen's got a life, too, and she couldn't watch Etta every time they called."

"They fired you for that?" I asked, assuming that Carmen was her babysitter.

"Well, they hemmed and hawed, but yeah. Which is crazy. Now they're down a piercer and that cousin is still working there and never showing up for his shifts. Someone needs to go to franking business school. Idiots."

"Idiots!" Etta yelled in the background.

"Etta, don't say 'idiots,'" Morgan replied.

"Idiots!"

"This is what my life looks like right now," Morgan said into the phone while Etta sang the word over and over. "No joke, this is my life."

"Shit, that sucks." I leaned against the railing of the porch as Morgan sighed into the phone. The people she was working for must have had their heads up their asses.

"It is what it is. Not the end of the world, you know? But damn, it's frustrating. All my clientele are down here, and I'm going to have to start from scratch in Sacramento."

"You're staying with your dad, huh?" I tried to sound nonchalant, but it was hard not to completely interrogate her.

"Yeah. He's totally stoked that we're moving in with him. Me? Not so much." She laughed a little, but the noise was forced.

"You have a rainy day fund," I reminded her quietly. "If you really don't want to move—"

"No," she cut me off. "That's for emergencies and hopefully I won't ever have to use it and Etta can have it for college."

"Morgan, that's for *life*," I argued. "That's for when you need it."

"But I don't *need* it," she said. "Not right now. I have enough cash to move us and get settled. This isn't an emergency. It's just a franking speed bump."

"I can help."

"Nope," she said, huffing in annoyance. "Absolutely not."

"Why not?"

"Because I take care of my own ship," she said. It took me a minute to remember that "ship" was her word for shit. "This really isn't a crisis, Trevor. It's just a frustration."

"Well, what about the move?" I asked, picturing her driving a truck with Etta riding shotgun. "Do you need help with driving or any of that?"

"Hell no," she said, and somehow I knew she was smiling. "I've got Etta's babysitter Carmen and her man coming over to help pack us up, and I can drive a moving truck like a boss."

"You seem very proud of that."

"Heck yes, I am," she said with a small laugh. "It's a good life skill to have. I can also change a tire, check and change the oil in my car, and shoot a pistol *and* a rifle."

"Well, look at you," I replied, grinning. My body relaxed as I realized that whatever had been going on with Morgan didn't really have anything to do with me. She was back to the same funny, easygoing woman I'd met, and she wasn't talking to me like she couldn't wait to get off the phone. She was . . . chatting.

Like we were friends. It was a complete 180-degree change from the text responses I'd been getting.

I didn't take the time to question why she ran so hot and cold. I probably should have.

"So, yeah. My landlord is being super cool about all of it, so if I move out before the end of the month I don't have to pay next month's rent," she said. "Me and Etta are packing like crazy."

"Damn, you only have a few days," I replied. "You sure you don't need any help?" If I helped her move I'd know exactly where she was headed. It wasn't as if I could ask for her dad's address without sounding like a stalker.

"Nope, we're all set. Most of the stuff in this house isn't ours, so I'm just packing up the bedroom and bathroom, really. Piece of cake." I wasn't sure what she was doing, but she sounded a little out of breath.

"I should probably let you get back to it," I said reluctantly, glancing at the front door of my parents' house. "Let me know how the move goes."

"I will," she replied.

We hung up, and I stood outside for a few minutes more. Damn, I liked her. Part of me knew that it was a good thing, but another part of me, the more realistic part, knew that I was sliding quickly into forbidden territory. I *really* liked her. More than I should have.

Beyond the fact that she was fucking gorgeous, because I'd been with gorgeous women before, she just—seemed to fit me, which was not something I should even be thinking about. It was just so easy to talk to her, even when I was nervous. I liked hearing about what she was doing and I liked listening to her talk to Etta. Hell, I even liked the way she moved, all efficient and quick.

And I was thrilled as hell that she was moving closer to me, even though she was still an entire day's drive away.

I needed to get my head on straight. Quick. Even thinking about Morgan made my stomach flip in a mixture of lust and guilt. So much fucking guilt.

"Everything okay?" my dad asked, stepping out the front door. I knew my mom had sent him to investigate, but I couldn't even be mad about it.

"Yeah." I nodded and scratched at my beard. It needed a trim. "Morgan and Etta are moving, so I was just calling to get some details."

"Moving?" he asked, coming farther onto the porch. "She tell you about that before?" I understood the suspicion in his voice. It mirrored my own.

"She lost her job—"

"Well, that's no good."

I listened closely for judgment in his tone, but there wasn't any. Damn, I was on edge. Of course he wasn't judging her. My dad was one of the most easygoing and accepting people I'd ever met.

"No shit. She and the baby are moving up with her dad for a while, I guess."

"You know where that is?"

"Sacramento," I answered, turning to face him as he sat down on one of the rocking chairs that lined the porch. "She's cool with a visit, but she asked that we wait until they're settled."

"Mom's not gonna be thrilled about that," he said with a

sigh. "She's been damn near counting the days to a date that hasn't even been set yet."

"I know."

I wasn't looking forward to telling her she was going to have to wait even longer. She'd been looking at flights since the day I got home and showed her the photos of Etta. I knew she was trying to keep her excitement in check, but it was clear to anyone who knew her how anxious she was.

It killed me that she was so fixated on my niece. I understood it, to a degree, but I worried about how it would all play out once she'd met Etta. The sweet baby girl wasn't her father, and treating her as a stand-in wasn't right. It wasn't that I thought my mom was doing it on purpose—I didn't even think she realized what she was doing—but it still worried me.

"I'll let her know after everyone leaves," my dad said, giving me a small nod. "If you don't want the interrogation, you might have to leave the rest of your dinner."

I chuckled a little, but nodded back. If I went back inside, I'd never be able to leave without telling everyone at the table exactly what my phone call had entailed. Unfortunately, I'd only gotten halfway through my dinner, but the rest of it wasn't worth the headache.

I gave my dad a hug, holding him for an extra few seconds as I remembered the first time I'd willingly touched him—nearly two years after I'd moved in—and left. The man had been watching out for me in small ways and big ways since before I'd even acknowledged his presence, and as I rode home through the woods, I wondered if I'd ever get to step into that role for someone else.

* * *

A few hours later, after eating half a package of Oreos and ignoring calls from pretty much everyone in my family, I got a picture message from Morgan. It was kind of dark, but I could still see Etta curled up on her side, with her thumb in her mouth, halfway inside a moving box that was tipped on its side. The caption read, "Finally figured out a way to keep her occupied...then she fell asleep ten minutes later. Fail or win? You decide."

I laughed out loud and saved the photo on my phone, making it my screen saver before I texted back.

She was occupied for ten minutes AND put herself to sleep for the night. Definite WIN.

I swear to God, she unpacked half of the stuff I packed today. LOL. I need to start taping the boxes right away instead of waiting until I have the tape handy.

I smiled and muted my TV so that I wasn't distracted.

Still don't need my help?

Nope! I'll pack more while she's sleeping. I'll be done with everything by the time she wakes up in the morning.

Damn. Pulling an all-nighter huh? You're going to be tired tomorrow.

I'll be okay. It should only take a few more hours.

I glanced at the clock and grimaced. It was almost eleven o'clock already.

When are you getting the moving truck? And what are you going to do with your car?

Tomorrow, and pull it behind me. LOL. I can't leave her behind, she's been a loyal transporter. Plus, I'll need wheels when we get to Sac. My dad rides a Harley—no room for a car seat on one of those.

Keep me posted on the move? I knew that the question sounded like a good-bye, and I didn't text anything more. I didn't want to stop talking to her, but hell if I was going to interrupt her packing when she was already going to have to be up all night.

Sure. We should be there by late tomorrow night…and then I'm going to have a drink. A big one. LOL

I didn't text back, but I didn't turn up the volume on my TV, either. I hated the idea of her driving a moving truck all the way to Sacramento on only a few hours of sleep. I believed her when she said she was fully capable—it didn't have anything to do with that—it just went against every instinct I had to watch her do it alone. The women in my family were as strong and capable as the men in every way that mattered. I'd known that from the beginning, and had been reminded of that fact my entire life. But the men in my family would never sit idly by while the women moved/hauled/unpacked their house alone. Hell, Ani was one of the most independent people I'd ever met—man or woman—and we still went over to her house to help her fix it up. I'd painted and sanded more things in her place than in my own.

For about an hour I sat there, wondering if there was any way that I could get Morgan to change her mind and wait one more day so that I could fly down and help her. An entire hour.

When I finally realized what an idiot I was being, I stood up and stretched as if that would make the rationalizations in my head disappear. I was being an idiot. A nosy, pushy, idiot— even if it was only in my own head. Acting like that worked for some men, my cousins and brother in particular, but that wasn't me. I stepped in when I was needed, but I didn't try to make decisions for other people or convince them that I was right. Besides, I'd barely talked to Morgan since I'd left California. She wasn't my responsibility by any stretch of the imagination.

I pulled up my cousin's contact and pushed CALL.

"Why the hell are you calling so late?" Kate asked, her voice scratchy.

"Did I wake you up?"

"No," she groaned. "I was laying on the couch watching TV. Shane's gone this week doing training. What's up?"

"She's moving," I blurted. Yeah, so I guess I *couldn't* just let it go. "To Sacramento. And she's doing it by herself."

"Wait, who?" Kate asked in confusion.

"Morgan."

"Morgan, Henry's baby-mama?"

"Yeah. Don't call her that, it's demeaning or something."

"It's not demeaning," she scoffed. "But okay. I'll refer to her as Etta's mother from now on."

"Good." Hearing Morgan referred to as Henry's *anything* made me want to punch something.

"Trev, I love you, but I still have no idea why you're calling me at midnight."

"She's moving all her stuff and the baby from Anaheim to Sacramento all by herself," I explained.

"And?" she still sounded confused, but after a few seconds she made a noise of understanding. "Having a hard time not butting in?" she asked in amusement.

"She's driving a fucking moving truck tomorrow. With a two-year-old."

"Is she a bad driver?"

"Not that I know of."

"Is she nervous?"

"Not at all. Overconfident, if anything," I grumbled as I made my way through the house, turning off lights and opening windows to let in the cool night air. "She can even change a tire."

"That's good to know," Kate mumbled. "So can I."

"It's not like you've ever needed to," I replied.

"But I could if I did," she argued. "Trev, it sounds like you're getting all worked up about nothing. What's your deal?"

"Nothing," I answered defensively, "I just don't like that she's doing it by herself. None of you would have to do it by yourself. The boys would step in to help."

"One of us . . ." her voice trailed off. "Trev, does she want our help? Because if she does, we can drive up there tomorrow after Shane gets home and help her."

"No. She's leaving in the morning anyway." I sighed. "She says she doesn't need any help."

"Then I don't see the issue." There were a bunch of muffled sounds, like she was moving, then her voice came through clearer. "Are we worrying about Morgan because she's Henry's—Etta's mother," she said, switching how she referred to Morgan midsentence. "Or are we worrying because you've got some unresolved something going on with her that you're not telling us about?"

"There's no unresolved anything," I shot back.

"Really? Because you've been acting weird since you got home, and you're awfully protective of a woman that we've had minimal contact with."

"And on that note, I'm done."

"Don't get defensive, you ass," Kate snapped. "I'm not accusing you of anything. I'm just trying to figure out what the fuck is going on."

"Nothing, all right?" I replied, anxious to get off the phone. "She's a nice woman, and she's the mother of our niece. She's family."

"Okay," Kate said dubiously.

"I don't know why I called you," I mumbled as I got ready for bed.

"Because you wanted to talk shit out," Kate replied. "You feel any better?"

"No."

She laughed. "Well, call me in the morning and we can talk it over some more. I need to get some sleep."

"Fine. Love you."

"Love you, too, Trev."

She hung up and I tossed my phone onto the bed in frustration.

Jesus, I was a basket case. I needed to get my shit together and nip whatever shit I was feeling for Morgan in the bud. She was a non-issue. Etta was who I needed to be concerned with, not her mother. I couldn't even list all the ways my attraction to Morgan was fucked up. It was something I needed to get a handle on fast.

I told myself all of this as I stripped down and got into bed, but as I closed my eyes, I still had a nasty feeling in my gut about Morgan driving that moving truck on the interstate all day.

Chapter 8

Morgan

I'll call you when we get there," I told Carmen, hugging her one last time.

The truck was loaded and Etta was strapped into her car seat. All I had left to do was go. It was harder than I thought it would be.

We hadn't made a ton of friends in Anaheim—we'd only been there a few months—but it already felt like home. Now we had to move yet again. It sucked. When we'd left San Diego, I'd mistakenly thought I was making the right decision. Little did I know that change would eventually mean I'd be headed back to Sacramento to live with my dad.

I liked my dad. I loved him, of course, but I liked him, too. He was a good guy. Funny, mellow, took everything as it came and didn't worry much about the future. He was a good friend to have, plain and simple, but he was a pain in the ass as a roommate. The guy never cleaned up after himself, rarely grocery shopped, and left greasy motorcycle parts all over the house. Bringing a two-year-old to live with him sounded like torture. Except I knew he'd try his best. He loved us and he doted on Etta, and if there was any way he could make our lives easier, he'd do it. He'd spoiled me and my sister rotten when he'd finally gotten us back. We'd rarely had money for extra stuff, but he'd given us whatever he could, whenever he could.

I climbed into the truck and smiled at Etta, who was kicking her feet excitedly, her thumb in her mouth and little blond wisps of hair flying in every direction.

"You ready, Freddy?" I asked, reaching over to roll up her window. God, I hoped the air conditioner in this thing worked. I really didn't want to deal with the wind coming through the windows as we drove seventy on the freeway.

"Weddy," she replied.

I pulled my phone out of my pocket and took a quick photo of her and sent it off to Trevor. He'd appreciate the tired-but-thrilled look on her face. Immediately regretting the message, I tucked the phone away without waiting for a response. Trevor wasn't my friend. I needed to stop treating him like one and tuck him into his neat little box with other unimportant people.

"We're off like a herd of turtles," I mumbled, the same old saying my dad would use anytime it took Miranda and me a long time to leave the house. I hadn't even started driving yet and I was already exhausted just thinking about it. I waved at Carmen and carefully pulled on to the street, getting a feel for the truck I was driving.

I may have been overstating my confidence when I'd talked to Trevor the day before. I'd driven a moving truck before. Once. But this was the first time I was pulling a car behind me. It was nerve-racking as hell. The entire contraption was just so freaking long. I was afraid I would take a corner too sharp or something similar and hit someone.

My hands were sore and throbbing from gripping the steering wheel by the time I got on the freeway. As soon as I was in the slowest lane I felt like I could relax a little. At least on the freeway I didn't have to make any corners or deal with any cross-traffic. I didn't even have to switch lanes if I didn't want to. It wasn't like the truck could go fast anyway. The entire thing felt like it was groaning every time it switched gears.

I dreaded the moment Etta told me she was hungry or needed her diaper changed and I had to take an off-ramp in this thing. I was just hoping that by the time that happened, I was feeling far more comfortable driving the beast.

* * *

Etta made it three hours before she started fussing to get out of her seat, and by that time I was so impressed that she'd lasted such a long time that I wasn't even frustrated or worried about how I'd exit the freeway. I pulled off at the first exit I could see with some fast-food restaurants, then very carefully parked in a lot filled with big rigs. So far so good. I was feeling pretty proud of myself.

I unbuckled Etta's seat so she could climb out of it, then checked my phone. Normally I wasn't such a stickler about texting and driving, but I sure as shit wasn't going to try and check messages when I was driving this behemoth—at least that was what I'd told myself. I'd also been forcing myself not to check if I'd gotten a response from Trevor.

I had one message from my dad telling me to give him up-
dates as I drove—he was stuck at work and hadn't been able
to help with the move—and four texts from Trevor. The first
was a reply to the picture message I'd sent, but the others were
variations of the same theme, to let him know where I was
and how the drive was going. I wasn't sure if he'd kept texting
because I wasn't replying, or if he was just *that* worried, so I
just gave in and called him, ignoring the thrill that ran up my
spine when I heard his deep voice.

"Trevor," I said, the minute he answered. "It's illegal to text
while I'm driving."

He laughed a little but it didn't sound genuine. "How's it
going?" he asked. "Easy as you thought?"

"Not too bad," I replied, gathering up the diaper bag and
my purse as Etta climbed onto the seat next to me. "It was
kind of hard at first, but I think I've got the hang of it. We
just stopped for some food and a diaper change."

"How's Etta doing?"

"Surprisingly well. I think she's enjoying being in the front
seat and sitting so high. She's been waving at God-knows-
what all day."

"Other drivers?"

"Uh, no." I snorted out a laugh. "We're sticking to the slow
lane, so there's no one on her side of the truck."

Trevor laughed. "Probably a good idea. Takes a lot of prac-
tice to switch lanes with a rig that long."

"That's what she said," I quipped, making him chuckle
again. "Hey, I better get going. I need to get her cleaned up so
we can get back on the road."

"All right. Let me know when you're on the road again?"

"Jesus, you're a worrier, aren't you?" I teased, not surprised, really, but a little—flattered? I wasn't sure what I was feeling, but whatever it was made my stomach flip.

"Not usually," Trevor murmured. "Text me."

I agreed, then said good-bye as I threw the door open and stepped down. The fast-food place I planned on grabbing our early lunch from was across the street, but it was a quick walk and it only took a few minutes before I was changing Etta in their nasty bathroom.

It probably would have been more sanitary to change her in the truck, but I refused to do it. If there was one thing my dad taught me, it was that I should always be aware of my surroundings. I wasn't about to leave my back toward the outside as I tried to change my squirmy kid on the truck seat. That was just asking to get mugged or worse.

I'd found that truckers weren't nearly as bad as people made them out to be; my dad had plenty of friends who took to the road to feed their families, but there were bad apples in every bunch. A woman alone and distracted by a toddler was easy pickings, and I didn't plan on making myself a target.

"Fwies?" Etta asked as we walked into the restaurant. "Me want fwies."

"You can totally have french fries," I replied, glancing around the crowded room. "How about some apples, too?"

"Yoguwt," she argued, skipping along beside me.

"Yogurt works." I smiled and gave her hand a small squeeze. "You're my favorite road-trip partner, you know that?"

"Know dat," she agreed, nodding.

Half an hour later, we were pulling back on to the freeway.

I didn't text Trevor that we were on our way, choosing to pretend that I'd forgotten. It was nice to know that he cared, but I didn't want to get into the habit of constantly checking in with him. At least that was what I told myself.

* * *

Dear God, I was tired. After an entire day on the road my ass was numb, my legs were cramping, and I had a tension headache that was quickly turning into a migraine. The only time I'd been happier to see my dad's place was the day he'd gotten us out of foster care.

"My babies," my dad called, coming out to greet us as I pulled to a stop. "Finally."

"I'm not even attempting to park this thing," I replied, throwing the truck into park and setting the brake. I opened the door and jumped down, waving him toward the driver's seat. "She's all yours."

My dad chuckled, his deep voice instantly soothing me. "I'll get her parked. Baby sleeping?"

"Yeah, thank God. She started whining about an hour ago, and I couldn't distract her anymore."

"Long trip," he mused in understanding.

I stepped onto his front lawn and lifted my arms in a huge stretch as he climbed into the truck and expertly parallel-parked it along the curb. By the time he climbed down from the cab with Etta in his arms, I felt marginally better.

"You need anything outta here tonight?"

"Just the diaper bag," I replied, walking tiredly to the passenger side to get it.

"That's my girl," Dad said, waiting for me on the sidewalk. "Packing light."

I glanced at the packed truck and scoffed. "I packed a toothbrush and a spare set of clothes for Etta in the diaper bag, but I'm too tired to go searching for anything else."

"I'll get the boys to unload in the morning," he said, throwing an arm over my shoulder as he led me toward the front door. "You can sleep in if ya want."

"Beyond the fact that Etta's going to be up at seven and bouncing off the walls, no way am I letting any of your friends unload my shit without supervising," I replied, bumping him with my hip. "Sweet offer, though."

"Such a priss." He grinned and kissed my forehead. "Good to have you back, sweetheart."

My dad had changed his sheets in preparation for our arrival, thank God, and his room was all ready for me and Etta to crash in. Our stuff would be unpacked into the spare bedroom the next day, and we'd be able to sleep in our own beds once we'd set them up, but thankfully he'd thought ahead and knew we wouldn't both fit on the couch for the first night.

The house smelled so familiar that I smiled as I inhaled deeply. The scent was a mixture of wood, grease, and Brut aftershave that I'd always associate with my dad. I wasn't even sure why he smelled like the Brut—he hadn't shaved his face for as long as I'd been alive—but he must have worn it like cologne or something. That familiar scent was the first thing I remember noticing the day he'd picked me and Miranda up.

"You know where everything is," Dad said quietly as he laid Etta down on the bed. "You want a cup of coffee, or are you ready to hit the sack?"

"Coffee," I replied with a nod. "I'll just get her tucked in and then I'll be out."

"I'll start a pot."

"You mean you didn't have it waiting?" I scolded playfully.

"Wasn't sure how tired you'd be," he grumbled, swatting at me as he left the room.

I changed Etta and tucked her in, laughing quietly to myself as she slept right through it, then pulled my phone out of my pocket.

I didn't have any new texts from Trevor, but I'd been texting with him throughout the day whenever we stopped. After the first stop when I'd pretended to forget to text him, I'd felt like such a jerk that I'd given in and replied to the rest of the messages he sent. Even though I tried to be irritated about his long-distance hovering, he cracked me up with his worrying and asking me to text him whenever I stopped or got on the road. I was surprised he hadn't asked me to send him my exact location every time we'd stopped at a truck stop.

Got to my dad's. Etta's passed out and I'm visiting before I crawl in with her.

His response was immediate.

Glad you guys got there safe. Sleep well.

I sent a smiley face back, then left my phone on the bed when I left the room. Dad was sitting at the kitchen table with two cups of coffee. He slid one toward me as I sat down across from him.

"Let it percolate right into the cups," he said with a grin, lifting his mug in a salute.

"God, your coffee always tastes better than mine," I groaned after I took my first sip.

"That's 'cause you make it so damn weak," he replied. "Shit tastes like water."

"It does not."

"Does too. Stay away from my coffeepot."

"Fine with me." I leaned back and kicked off my shoes, propping my feet on an empty chair. "I'm not going to complain about someone else making my coffee."

Dad laughed. "I bet not. How you been doing, princess?"

I sighed. "Fine. Pissed I lost that job over something so stupid, but fine."

"Ranna says Etta's other family's been sniffing around." He raised his eyebrows as he sipped his coffee. "How's that going?"

"Okay." Damn, my whole body was sore. I set my coffee down and stretched my arms toward the ceiling. "The only one who's been around so far is her uncle, and he's been cool."

"Yeah?"

"Overprotective, maybe? But nice. He's been asking if Etta's grandmother and grandfather can come visit, but I put them off until we're more settled here."

"You worried about it?"

"Not really." I shrugged. "Maybe a little. They were cool when I was a kid, but I don't really know them anymore."

My dad knew that I'd been fostered with Henry's parents. It was hard to keep that kind of thing a secret when I was trying to explain to him why he shouldn't kill the absent father of my child. Dad didn't understand what would possess a father to abandon his children—Miranda and I were the most important things in his life—but he did understand demons, and how they could ruin a person's life and force them to make decisions that didn't make sense to anyone else.

"Good thing for baby girl to have family," Dad said, pulling off his glasses to rub at his eyes. "Scary for you, though, I bet."

"A little," I conceded, wrapping my hands around my coffee mug. "Dealing with Henry was one thing; dealing with his entire family is a little bit much."

"You're a good mama," Dad replied, understanding the words I wasn't saying. "You don't need to worry."

"We'll see."

"Sometimes I could strangle your mother," he said tiredly. "For making you and your sister's lives so damn hard."

"Well, she's dead," I said soothingly, patting his hand. "So I'm not sure what good it would do."

"Give me some satisfaction," he said under his breath, making my lips twitch.

We'd had the same conversation a hundred times, and I was sure we'd have it a hundred more. When my mom had taken off with us, my dad had looked for us, but he'd eventually stopped, assuming that Miranda or I would contact him if we needed him. He hadn't had any idea about the life we were living in Oregon, and he hadn't known when my mom overdosed and we'd been placed in foster care. He'd been in prison when he'd eventually found out that Miranda and I weren't with our mom or each other, and as soon as he was free it had been an uphill battle to get us back.

He was bitter about it, and I didn't blame him one bit.

After a while of drinking our coffee in companionable silence, I stood from the table and stretched again. "I'm gonna get some sleep," I told him as I put my cup in the sink. "I'm beat."

"Okay, princess. You let me know if you get too hot and

want me to open that window in the bedroom. It sticks like hell."

"I will. Love you, Dad," I said, kissing the top of his head as I passed him.

"Love you too," he said as I walked away. "Glad to have you home."

* * *

"Frances, you drop that box and I'll shave off half your beard while you're sleeping," I warned as one of my childhood friends carried two too many boxes toward the house. "I'm not joking."

"Call me Frances again, and I'll drop-kick it across the yard," he shot back, kicking out his leg just to irritate me.

"Sorry, Frank," I sang, walking up the ramp into the hot truck.

We were halfway through moving my stuff into the house, and it was already so hot that I had sweat stains on my T-shirt. It was a good thing I had absolutely no intention of trying to impress the guys who'd shown up that morning to help.

After I'd hugged both of them hello, I'd pointed them in the direction of the truck and we'd started to unload. Dad kept an eye on Etta and built our beds as we moved the boxes in, but none of us let him carry anything heavy. A few years ago he broke his back when some bitch in a Honda ran a stop sign and slammed into his motorcycle, and he'd been having problems ever since. I wasn't about to have him mess himself up more by carrying a box of my books into the house.

Sometimes, when I was away from home for a long time,

I began to feel like the life I'd left behind didn't matter. It seemed so far away that I let myself forget the connections I had in Central California. But the minute I was home, I began to remember why I'd felt so safe and comfortable in that little town outside Sacramento.

My dad's friends were really more like a family. When he'd brought Miranda and me down from Oregon, they'd seemed big and scary, but after only a few hours, my sister and I had both known that we'd found our tribe. The men and their wives were rough around the edges. They smoked and drank and partied all night. They also loved their kids, went to every school event, and looked out for each other like no one I'd ever met before or since. Their kids were even better. It was like, from the moment they'd met us—two petite blond-haired girls who were suspicious of everyone and everything—they'd adopted us as their own.

Frank was the oldest son of my dad's closest friend, and one of the few of us kids who'd stuck around once we were grown. He had two younger brothers named Reggie and Olly, but only Olly had stayed in the area. He was helping unpack, too.

"Girl, you look hot as hell," a raspy voice called out behind me. "And I don't mean attractive."

"Thanks, old man," I replied, laughing as I turned to face my honorary uncle. "You look old, but that's not surprising."

"I'm in the prime of my life," he argued, his big barrel chest shaking as he laughed. "Come give your uncle Danny a hug."

"Missed you," I said as I wrapped my arms around his waist.

"Same. You home for good?"

"Home for now," I answered, leaning back to meet his eyes.

"Always on the move," he said, shaking his head. "You and that sister of yours."

"What can I say?" I shrugged as I stepped back. "I've got places to go and people to see."

"Yeah, yeah," he replied, reaching out to give my ponytail a yank. "Where are my pain-in-the-ass sons? They helping you?"

"Your pain-in-the-ass sons have been here for two hours," Frank said, walking toward us. "Where you been, old man?"

"In bed with my wife," Danny replied, wiggling his eyebrows and grinning.

"That's my mother you're talking about," Frank bitched, shaking his head as he hopped into the truck, not bothering with the ramp.

"So sensitive," Danny said quietly to me, shaking his head as his eyes twinkled.

"Move," Frank ordered as he carried boxes down the ramp. "Don't want to be doing this shit all day."

"Nobody made you come," I sniped back, shifting out of his way. "You're in such a pissy mood."

"You know I love ya," he called back over his shoulder. "But it's already hot as fuck out here."

I rolled my eyes and grabbed a box, taking a minute to get my balance with the extra weight before following him toward the house. I wasn't about to stand around chatting while other people unloaded my stuff.

"You going to be here for a while?" I asked as Danny carried a couple of boxes behind me.

"Yeah, got nothing else planned. We'll catch up later," he huffed, out of breath.

It was hard seeing my dad and the uncles aging. Every time I came back, I was surprised to see how they'd changed. None of them were really old, but living the life they'd lived and working the jobs that were so hard on a person's body took its toll on each of them. They were slowing down, no doubt about it, and it was tough to watch.

Less than an hour later, I stood staring into the small bedroom that I used to share with my baby sister, wondering how in the heck I was going to find a place for all of our stuff. My bed and Etta's crib were built and ready for linens, but I wasn't sure where we'd put them. There were plastic bins and boxes lining the walls almost to the ceiling.

"I draw the line at unpacking," Frank said, laying a hand on my shoulder as he came up behind me.

"I'm not even sure where I'll put everything," I confessed, grimacing. I hadn't thought that Etta and I had very much stuff until we'd unpacked it into the small room. We'd been spoiled with space at our old place.

"Just leave everything in boxes and spend twenty minutes searching through them whenever you need something," Olly chimed in, grinning as he came down the short hall. "That's what Frank's been doing for two years."

"Ew," I replied. "Seriously?"

"Apartment's temporary," Frank mumbled. "Just until I can get the old house sold."

"Gotta get the ex-wife out before you can sell it," Olly said helpfully. "And I don't see that happening."

"Still?" I asked, shaking my head. I'd never really liked Frank's wife, but I'd made an effort whenever I saw her. It didn't matter. Her snotty comments when we'd visited made it clear that she hadn't liked me or Miranda. I couldn't exactly blame her, though. Miranda and Frank had this never-ending relationship that wasn't good for either of them. They got together and broke up so many times that most of us stopped paying attention to their ups and downs until Frank came home from Vegas with a wife, effectively ending things with Miranda for good. I'd always wondered if Frank was the reason Miranda had chosen the college in Oregon, but I'd never asked. My sister would never have admitted that he had anything to do with her decisions.

"My ex is none of your business," Frank mumbled. He kissed the side of my head. "I'm out of here. Call if you need anything."

"You shouldn't have said anything," I chastised quietly as Olly and I watched him leave.

"Someone's gotta say something," he replied. "Or he's never going to get off his ass and fix it."

"Not your call," I reminded him as I caught sight of the plastic garbage bag that held our linens half hidden behind a cardboard box. I ripped the bag open and tossed him the sheets to my bed. "It just pisses him off."

"He'll get over it," Olly said as he rounded the bed and started helping me make it.

* * *

Later that night, my dad, Danny and his wife, Lorraine, Olly, and I were sitting around the table playing dice and catching up. Etta had fallen asleep on my dad's lap and was snuggled against his chest, not even flinching when the dice rolled loudly on the wood table. It felt like old times, when I was a kid and we'd all get together for a barbeque or whatever, and the kids would sleep where they landed and the adults would stay up visiting long into the night. I loved it.

My phone rang in the middle of a game and my dad's eyebrows shot up. "Know that ain't your sister, since she's usually in bed by nine."

I laughed a little and glanced at my phone, smiling a little as I saw Trevor's name on the screen. We hadn't talked all day, but I'd texted him a photo of Etta drooling with her head resting on the table about an hour before.

"I'll be back," I told everyone. "Skip my turn."

Ignoring the good-natured grumbling, I left the room and answered before Trevor could hang up.

"Hey!"

"Hey," Trevor replied, sounding surprised at my excited greeting. "How'd the unpacking go?"

"Good." I stepped into my room and closed the door behind me. "I mean, the only things that made it out of boxes are our clothes and sheets, but I call that a win."

"Definitely," he agreed. "That was a long drive yesterday. You've got time to put everything where you want it."

"You're never going to let that *long drive* go, are you?" I joked, sitting down on the edge of my bed.

"Hey, I thought I was pretty cool about it."

I snorted.

"Wish you would have let me help, but you got there and everything's all good," he clarified, chuckling a little.

"I really appreciated the offer," I said, getting more comfortable on the bed. "But I had it covered."

"Clearly," he replied. "Now that you're there, you gonna let us come visit?"

I opened my mouth, then paused. Was I? Much to my chagrin, I'd grown lax at keeping my distance from Trevor. He was just so...likeable. I tried to tell myself that it was good that I was forming a relationship with Etta's uncle, but I knew, deep down, that Etta wasn't the only reason why his texts were the highlight of my day.

"I know you just got there," he continued. "But I'm having some serious withdrawals here."

I felt my cheeks heat at his tone, then shook my head to clear it. He meant Etta. He missed *Etta*. Jesus, I needed to get my head on straight.

"We can plan for something soon," I finally replied, clearing my throat. "I know you're anxious to see Etta again."

"I'm—" He stopped short, then dropped the bomb that would change everything. "It's both of you."

Sometimes a million things can run through your head in the space of just a few seconds, reasons for something, reasons against something, recriminations and memories, pros and cons, denial and acceptance. It happened to me then, the barrage of thoughts that raced past almost too fast for me to fully comprehend them.

Before I could open my mouth I was startled by loud knocking on my bedroom door.

"Look at you," Olly teased. "Pretty sure I found you talking to your boyfriend when you were seventeen in that exact same spot, all dreamy eyed and blushing."

"I have to go," I mumbled into the phone, my eyes widening in horror as Olly came closer. "I'll text you tomorrow."

I didn't wait for a reply before ending the call and sticking my phone down my shirt where I knew Olly wouldn't reach for it. When he and his brothers had decided that Miranda and I were family, they'd *really* decided it, and that came with every annoying-older-brother trait imaginable, including but not limited to embarrassing the hell out of us as often as possible.

"Oh, come on," Olly complained.

"You know, when you knock you're supposed to wait for the person to answer before you open the door," I snapped, climbing off the bed.

"Who was that? Thought your dad said you were single?"

"It was Etta's uncle," I replied, pushing past him.

"Whoa," he replied, frowning as he grabbed my arm. "Etta's dad ran like his ass was on fire and now you're going for the brother?"

"I'm not going for anyone."

"Girl, I just saw you," he argued. "You're definitely doing something."

"No, I'm not." I shook my head. "That would be weird, right?" I tried to laugh, but the noise got stuck in my throat. Oh, crap.

Olly tilted his head as he looked at me like he was reading my mind. "No, I guess not," he finally said, giving my arm a squeeze. "From what I've heard, you weren't ever serious with Etta's dad. And it's not like it's gonna cause trouble with the brothers, since one of them's dead."

"Still," I muttered, wincing at the abrupt way he'd spelled it out. I glanced quickly down the hall to make sure no one was eavesdropping. "If something did happen, then I'd be screwed when we stopped. I don't want to mess anything up for Etta."

Why was I even thinking about that shit? If something *did* happen? I needed my freaking head examined. Nothing was going to happen. Nothing could happen. Even if it was technically acceptable, it was still wrong in a lot of ways. I'd been burned in the past and I'd brushed myself off and kept moving, but this was Etta's family we were talking about. There would be no escaping that aftermath.

"Aw, come on," he said consolingly, throwing an arm around my shoulder so he could lead me back toward the kitchen. "If the guy stopped wanting to see Etta just because you broke up, he wouldn't be worth the trouble anyway. Plus, you need to get laid. Your shoulders are all tense."

I elbowed him hard in the side as we reached our parents, and ignored the surprised *oomph* as I sat back down in my chair. He was a jackass, and he made a little bit of sense, but I wasn't going there. Besides, I could barely focus on his words when a deeper voice was saying *both of you* over and over in my mind.

Chapter 9

Trevor

I was such an idiot. The minute Morgan hung up on me, I threw my phone across the room like it was a poisonous snake and watched it bounce across the carpet and slide under my recliner. Good. It could stay there until I figured out what the hell I was going to do now.

I knew I shouldn't have said anything. I knew that making any kind of mention about how much I wanted to see her again would backfire. *I knew it*, and yet I still opened my big mouth and let it slip out.

Two seconds later I'd heard a guy's voice in the background and Morgan had ended our call in a hurry.

God, if I fucked up my family's chance for a relationship with Etta I was going to start wearing a hair shirt under my clothes. I'd never understood that method of penance—it seemed pretty weird—but I was starting to understand it now. The constant reminder of my stupidity would help me be smarter in the future.

Hell, maybe I should order one online just in case.

Flirting was halfway acceptable. Some men flirted with anything that walked on two legs—it didn't mean anything. But saying something like that? Telling her I was having withdrawals from her? That crossed the line, big time.

Unable to stay in the house where the walls seemed to be closing in, I threw on my coat and headed outside. A ride would clear my head and I'd just changed the oil in my four-wheeler, so she was ready for a trip. I started the engine and then glanced at the house, wondering for a split second if I should go back for my phone, but decided against it. I needed to unplug for an hour or six. Maybe if I didn't have the thing with me I'd be able to put some figurative distance between me and Morgan.

I rode through the woods and over wide fields of waist-deep grass, up massive hills and down into canyons. My parents' land butted up against my uncle and aunt's, the lines so blurry that we'd always considered it one big piece of property, and I knew every foot of it like the back of my hand. Sometimes I ambled along, and sometimes I practically flew, but I didn't stop. I rode by the light of the moon and a single headlight until I was out of gas, filled up with the extra gas can I carried on the back, and finally headed home.

By the time I got to my house I was covered in mud, soaking wet, had scratches all over my hands from blackberry bushes and a pretty nasty-looking scratch on my calf where a stick had pierced through my jeans. On the bright side, my head was clear and I'd stopped chastising myself for a comment that Morgan may not have even heard or cared about.

Sometimes I found myself fixating on things I should have or shouldn't have done. It didn't happen often anymore. It had been worse when I was a kid and worried constantly that I was doing the right thing, the thing that would make me the most friends or convince some family to like me. The panicky sensation of saying the wrong thing had mostly disappeared after the first year with my adoptive parents, but occasionally I fixated on a certain specific sentence or phrase that I wished I hadn't said. I hated feeling that way, so I always made sure to think my words through before I spoke.

The problem was, I *had* thought about those words before I'd said them to Morgan. I'd run them over in my head twice before I'd even opened my mouth. It hadn't changed the fact that I really shouldn't have said them, and the response I'd gotten had made me instantly regret them.

It was the middle of the night by the time I kicked my boots against the side of my porch to knock off the mud and shrugged as if knocking off the last bit of my panic. The words were said and the damage was done. They hadn't been that bad, and if I was honest I knew that I could spin them any way I wanted. If Morgan started acting strange or uncomfortable, I'd get us onto solid ground again. There wasn't any other option.

Checking my phone as soon as I'd walked inside seemed like playing into my panic, so I ignored it. After a shower and downing an entire bottle of water, I finally allowed myself to grab it from under the recliner. There were two messages waiting for me, and both were from Morgan.

The first was a photo of Etta in her crib. She was sleeping with one hand hanging out between the rails and the other flung out above her head, wearing nothing but a T-shirt that had a motorcycle rally logo on it and a hot-pink diaper. The next was a text message.

Sorry about that. My dad has people over. I'll text you in the morning.

Once I read the message, the photo seemed a little like a peace offering. I wasn't sure why she felt like she needed one, but I wasn't going to complain. Checking the time stamp, I huffed when I realized she must have sent it less than a half an hour after I'd left the house. She was probably asleep by now, so I didn't bother replying. I should probably keep my mouth—or in this case, my typing fingers—to myself anyway.

I climbed in bed and stared at the ceiling.

Never in my life had I worried so much about what a woman besides my mother, aunt, or cousins thought. I'd never really cared enough. Sure, I was careful with women's feelings and I treated them well, but I'd never worried that something I said would make them bail.

If I was being honest with myself, my worries about Morgan cutting contact went far deeper than her allowing Etta to get to know us. That was a concern, always, but in the time I'd known them, Morgan had become just as important. I craved her like I'd never craved anything in my life, even knowing how wrong it was. I wanted them both, and that scared the shit out of me.

* * *

"Monday morning," my cousin Alex yelled through the phone as soon as I'd answered the next day. "I just love a Monday morning!"

"Are you drunk?" I asked tiredly, contemplating hanging up as I strode toward my office. "Some of us are working."

"I've been at work for hours," he replied. "I'm just so glad it's Monday."

"What do you want?"

"Just calling to say hello. Shoot the shit. Chat. See how it's going with Etta and the hot mom."

"Who told you she's hot?" I asked, coming to an abrupt stop.

"No one." He started chuckling. "But Kate said you had a thing with her, and by your tone, our dear Katherine was correct."

"Oh, fuck you," I muttered, continuing to my desk so I could sit down and put my feet up. After riding half the night, and tossing and turning the other half while I waited for an acceptable time to text Morgan back, my entire body was aching and I was so tired my eyes were burning.

"I gotta say," he continued as if I hadn't spoken. "This development surprises me. You and Hen never had the same type."

"She's everyone's type," I snapped back, lacking my usual finesse. "Fuck, I didn't mean that. Forget I said it."

"That pretty, huh?"

"Is there a point to this conversation?"

"Not really," Alex said sunnily. "Just checking in with you. We haven't talked in over a month."

"Sorry, man," I murmured, feeling instantly guilty. I hadn't been very good at returning calls, even though part of me was anxious to talk to everyone daily just in case something happened. I'd rarely talked to my brother while he was away and then suddenly I didn't have any more chances. I didn't want that to happen ever again.

"No worries," Alex said. "Just figured it was time."

"Yeah, you're right," I said, thankful that the discussion had veered away from Morgan. "How you been?"

"Good. Just working a lot."

Something in his tone was off.

"And?" I asked.

"Met someone," he said, his voice a bit more serious.

"Oh, yeah?" I wasn't sure what to say. Alex had always been more of a playboy than anything else. I didn't remember him ever bringing up a woman in conversation.

"She's great, Trev. Seriously. Not sure she likes me all that much, though." He chuckled a little uncomfortably.

"No fucking way." I laughed. Even Morgan had reminded me how attractive the fairer sex found my cousin. I'd never once heard him complain about striking out or even coming close.

"She's...serious. About everything, man. I can barely get her to laugh." He sighed. "When she does, though, it's like Christmas."

"Oh, Jesus," I mumbled, making him laugh.

"I know, I know. I sound like a dumbass."

"Slightly." He did sound like a jackass, but what really bothered me was the easy way he spoke about the woman. I was so jealous of him I could barely see straight.

"She's great, man. Really. I think you'll like her."

"I'm going to meet her?"

"Eventually, if all goes well, yeah."

My mouth nearly dropped open in surprise. He was actually serious.

"Whoa."

"Yeah. *Whoa.*"

We were both silent for a long moment.

"So, am I gonna meet Morgan?" he asked finally. "That's her name, right?"

"You've already met her," I replied. "Surprised no one has shared that little tidbit of information with you."

"What?"

I spent the next twenty minutes explaining to him how Morgan had lived with us as a kid, and trying to describe what she looked like without comparing her to Christmas the way he'd done with his new girl. Even without flowery descriptions, though, I was pretty sure he saw right through me. Thankfully, he didn't give me too much shit about it, and eventually we got off the phone, agreeing that we'd make a point to talk more often.

I actually felt better after our conversation. My infatuation with Morgan seemed less and less obscene the more she came up in conversation, even though I really didn't want to be discussing her with anyone. Knowing that neither Alex nor Kate seemed angry about my little infatuation made the entire situation more palatable, I guess. They made me feel like less of a creep for slobbering after my little brother's ex. The guilt, though, was still there, slithering underneath my skin.

I set my phone on my desk, then swore and picked it back up, deciding to text Morgan a reply to the photo she'd sent instead of replying to her apology.

Did she even move in her sleep? She looks completely exhausted.

A few minutes later, she texted back.

That's what happens when you're spoiled rotten all day. She's not used to all these people doting on her. ☺

Well, she better get used to it. She's got about twenty more people waiting in the wings to do just that, I replied.

Yeah, about that.

I waited, watching the little dots on the screen for what seemed like a very long time.

You guys can visit whenever. I think we're as settled as we're going to be and I'm sure your mom is going crazy waiting.

I huffed in surprise. As much as I wanted to take Morgan at her word, she'd been so dodgy that I hadn't really expected her to invite us down there—especially after my slipup the night before.

I breathed a sigh of relief and decided to call her instead of texting.

"Hey," she answered.

"Hey." My voice came out all weird and garbly, and I quietly hit the heel of my hand against my forehead in irritation. Yeah, apparently my anxiety wasn't completely gone.

"Trevor, you called me," she said, laughing a little at my awkward silence.

"Right." I wiped a hand over my face, trying to get my act together. "I just thought it would be easier to talk instead of text. You're serious about us visiting whenever? Because the minute I tell my mom, she's gonna want to start driving south." I may have been exaggerating, but it wasn't by much. I wouldn't have been surprised if my mom was already halfway packed in anticipation.

Morgan laughed nervously. "Yeah, I'm sure. Come whenever. I have to start looking for a job tomorrow, but other than that we're pretty free."

"Are—"

"So—"

We both spoke at the same moment, then stopped.

"So, I can't wait to see you, either," she said finally, her voice a little tentative.

"Jesus, woman," I muttered, glancing at the open door to my office and wishing I'd closed it. "You made me wait for that one." What the hell was I doing? I wasn't even falling down the rabbit hole, I was fucking jumping. I just couldn't seem to stop myself.

"I know," she replied. "Sorry."

"I'm—" Someone paused in my doorway, and I stuttered to a stop. Hell, I knew I shouldn't try talking to her at the office.

"Brought doughnuts," Bram said grumpily. It looked like he still wasn't getting much sleep. "Get one if you want." Then he stomped away without waiting for a reply.

"Shit, are you at work?" Morgan asked.

"I'm the one who called you," I replied with a smile. "Remember?"

"Oh, right. Dang, you're slacking."

"I'm part owner, so I do what I want," I boasted.

"No you don't!" Bram yelled from the other room, making me regret again that I hadn't shut my office door.

"Shut it, Bram," I yelled back, trying to cover the microphone on my phone.

"I'll just talk to you later," Morgan said, laughing. "Let me know what your mom says."

"All right," I replied, almost calling her "beautiful" but stopping myself at the last second. I needed to stop this train before it completely left the station. "I'll call you tonight."

I set my phone down on my desk as soon as we'd said good-bye and hopped to my feet, barely refraining from punching the air in celebration like some nineties sitcom hero. I was a mix of jumbled emotions: guilt and worry, a little bit of fear, and a whole hell of a lot of excitement. I was going to see her, and not only that, I was going to introduce my parents to Etta. I had what my mom liked to call "ants in my pants" and there was no way I was going to be able to stay at my desk. Instead, I walked to Bram's office to give him shit.

"Still not sleeping?" I asked cheerfully, smiling when he flipped me off.

"I don't think she needs it," he answered seriously, lifting his hands in supplication. "Honest to God, I don't think my child requires sleep."

"Sure she does."

"No, I'm completely serious. She's up like twenty hours a day. It's insane."

"How's Ani?" I asked, leaning against the door frame.

"She's in a pissy mood and pretty much hates everything except Arielle."

"So what you're saying is she's being mean to you," I said with blatantly fake sympathy.

"Man, I just want to sleep with my woman," he grumbled. "And when I say sleep, I mean sleep. I doubt I could even do more than that at this point."

Bram wasn't much of a talker, and was even less so when something was bothering him, so I instantly grew serious at his words. It was kind of funny that Arielle was keeping them up so much, but I could see the toll it was taking on him, and it wasn't a small one.

"Why don't you guys leave her with me tonight?" I asked, still thrumming after my conversation with Morgan with an energy that made staying up all night with an infant seem like an okay idea.

"Are you serious?" he asked, his face sagging with relief. "Please be serious right now."

"Yeah." I nodded. "Give Ani a call and let me know."

"Oh, I'm telling you yes right now," he said firmly. "Ani can argue all she wants."

"Cool." I pushed myself away from the door frame and stretched. "Let me know later when you want to drop her off. I'm headed out for the day."

"What?" he asked, his head jerking back in surprise. "Where you going?"

"I'm the boss," I joked. "I'm going wherever I want."

I walked away with the sound of his curses ringing in my ears. I felt for him—Monday was always super busy for us and it was going to suck trying to get everything done while I was gone, but there was no way I was going to be able to work. My mind was too cluttered with Morgan and Etta and the trip I needed to plan so I could get down to see them.

I left the office and drove straight to my parents' house. I'd been avoiding my mom since Morgan had put off any visiting, and I was anxious to tell her she could finally make some plans. I just hoped I could tamp down my excitement enough that she didn't see right through me.

"Hey, Ma?" I called as I opened the front door. "Where you at?"

"She's out back," my dad replied, coming down the hallway. "What are you doing here at eight in the morning?"

"Took the day off," I said, laughing a little at the surprised look on his face.

I wasn't someone who took random days off. I planned and let them know in advance if I wouldn't be in the office, and I didn't even do that very often. If there was one thing my dad had taught me, it was the value of a good work ethic. My career in the family business hadn't dampened that; if anything, it made me work harder. As one of the owner's sons, I set the example, and I didn't want it to be a shitty one. We were building something that was going to last, hopefully for generations. I wouldn't jeopardize that by half-assing my job.

"Well," he said with a shrug. "You wanna spend your rare day off with your mama, you be my guest," he teased.

"Can't think of better company," I replied.

We walked out back to where my mom was planting flowers in little pots, and I sat down on the porch steps to watch her work.

"Trevor," she said happily. "What are you doing here?" I guessed I'd surprised both of them.

"I got a call from Morgan today," I said easily, leaning back against the porch. "She said whenever we want to visit, we're welcome."

"Really?" Mom asked, pausing with her hands still wrist deep in the soil. "God, that's a relief."

"I told you she just wanted to settle first," I reminded her.

"Well, yes," she replied, her hands moving in the soil once again. "But I thought that just might be to put us off, you know? A lot can change in ten years—we don't really know this woman. She could have any number of things running through her head. I'm just glad she'll let us see little Henrietta."

"You'll like her, Mom," I said, watching her closely as my dad sat down in a lawn chair near us. "And she already likes you."

"I never said I didn't like her," she argued. "What I remember, anyway. She was a sweet girl. Good manners, though I have no idea where she picked those up, considering her parents."

"She still has good manners," I replied, a little bothered by my mom's comment. From what Morgan had said, her dad was a stand-up guy. Sure, he'd had trouble in the past, but from what I could tell, he was a good father. Besides, if she really judged by where a person came from, her view of me and my brothers couldn't be very high.

"When did she say we could go visit?" my dad asked.

"She said whenever," I replied, trying hard not to open my mouth and ask my mom exactly what she'd meant about Morgan's parents. "So, as soon as we decide to go, we'll go."

"Good, I'll go put my shoes on," my mom joked. I forced a smile.

"I told her that was a possibility," I confessed.

"Oh, yeah? What else have you told her?" Mom asked.

"That you're great," I replied, my smile coming more easily at her teasing tone. It was hard to stay mad at my mom for any length of time. "That you can't wait to meet them. That we all consider them part of our family."

"Oh, good," my mom said. "I've clearly raised an intelligent man."

"Was that ever in question?"

"Well," my dad said, drawing out the word and making my mom laugh.

"We can go whenever you're ready, Mom," I said, my voice a little quieter as I watched her wind down from excitement to nervousness. This was the Mom I knew, the worrier. Not the woman who ranted about her sons' sex lives and insinuated that someone with bad parents was somehow less.

"I was ready months ago," she said, giving me a sad smile. "I was ready the minute I knew about her."

"I don't know about that," my dad said. "Pretty sure you weren't ready for anything but a fainting couch at that point."

"I've never fainted," my mom argued, rolling her eyes.

"First time for everything," my dad muttered.

"How about Friday?" my mom asked, glancing at me. "Is that too soon?"

"Nah, Friday's good. I'll let Morgan know."

"You seem like you're pretty good friends with her now," Mom said, her voice curious in a way that was almost insinuating. The calm that had been settling back over me was gone again in an instant.

"We get along pretty well," I replied cautiously, not knowing where the conversation was headed. "She's a cool girl."

"Woman," my dad corrected.

"Woman," I clarified.

My phone started ringing and I answered it quickly before my mom could continue her questioning.

"Bless you," Ani said before I could even say hello. "Bless you, bless you, bless you."

"I didn't sneeze," I joked.

"I owe you huge," she replied. "Thank you so much."

"Excited to finally get some sleep?" I asked, then whispered Ani's name to my mom, who was staring questioningly at me.

"Dude, you have no idea. None. I was actually wondering if you could pick Arie up tonight because I'm too nervous to drive this tired."

"Sure," I said immediately. I didn't want her driving tired and it was easy enough to buckle Arie's car seat into my truck.

"What time?"

"Seven. No, five. No, six. Does six work?"

"Yeah, six is fine," I replied. "I'll bring dinner."

I laughed and hung up as she started scratchily singing "Wind Beneath My Wings."

"I'm keeping Arielle for the night," I told my parents as I stuffed my phone back into my pocket. "They need to get some sleep."

"That's sweet of you," my mom said.

"You're going to regret that," my dad said at the same time, laughing.

"Probably," I said ruefully. "But it's one night, and I'm pretty sure Bram couldn't make it one more day with no sleep."

"Ani, either," my mom said. "I stopped by there yesterday so she could take a little break, and the poor girl had so many energy drinks in her system she was shaking like an addict and couldn't even nap."

"Now, why can she call Ani a girl, and you say nothing?" I asked my dad, just to rile him.

"Your mother can call her a girl," he responded, leaning back in his chair. "Because she's twice as old as Anita and watched her grow up." He raised one eyebrow. "When you're our age, you can do the same. But when you're speaking about a woman who's the same age as you, you show her the respect she deserves by calling her the correct title."

"You're a feminist," I replied, still egging him on.

"If you call respecting women *feminism*, then I suppose I am," he said, refusing to take the bait. Usually he went on a long diatribe about how he disliked labels and always had, finally winding around to admitting that he did consider himself a feminist, "whatever that meant."

"Why do you poke at him?" my mom asked in amusement, shaking her head. "You know he sees right through it."

"Yeah, but usually he gets riled up anyway," I replied.

"I'm still sitting right here," my dad said, leaning down to pick a pinecone off the ground to throw at my head with unsurprising accuracy.

I barely ducked in time to dodge it.

"I'm out of here," I said, climbing to my feet. "I'll tell Morgan to plan on seeing us Saturday?"

"Yes," my mom said, glancing at my dad for confirmation.

"Are we driving or flying?" I asked, wondering what my bank account looked like. I usually didn't worry about it, knowing I had plenty. Although I should probably check it after my trip to California earlier in the month.

"Driving," my dad said. He hated to fly. "We'll take our rig."

I hesitated for a minute, wondering if I'd need my truck while we were there. I hoped so.

"Sounds good," I replied, unable to think of a reason to take two vehicles. "I can help drive."

"Good," my mom said. "That way I can read the whole way down."

"Over forty years of marriage and I still have no idea how you can do that," my dad said as I kissed my mom good-bye.

"It's easy," Mom replied to him as she gave me a quick squeeze around my waist. "You look at the letters. They form words."

"Smart-ass," my dad said as he gave me a little wave good-bye.

* * *

"Arielle," I murmured late that night as I rubbed her back in little circles. "Uncle Trev is tired. Aren't you tired?"

We were sitting on the couch watching a documentary on World War II, and she was showing no signs of sleeping. Thankfully, she wasn't crawling around the house or trying to open every cupboard in the kitchen anymore, but she was still wide awake as she sat on my lap. I'd done everything I could to tire her out, thinking, like an idiot, that *I'd* be the one to get her to sleep.

How very wrong I'd been. I'd taken her to the park, to a fast-food place that had a massive play area, and finally on a nature walk to the creek and back. It didn't seem to faze her. It was like the kid was a robot. If you looked underneath her skin you'd find a metal case with batteries that were still fully charged.

My phone rang, and I realized instantly that I'd completely forgotten to call Morgan like I'd told her I would.

"I'm sorry," I answered, not bothering with a hello. "I'm watching my niece tonight and I completely forgot to call."

"No problem," she replied. "Which niece?"

"Arielle," I said, smiling at the pretty little girl as she glanced at me after hearing her name. "She's Bram and Ani's. All the others live in San Diego."

"Oh, right. You told me that before, I think."

"Yeah, probably. It's hard to keep track, though. There's a lot of us."

"Do you babysit a lot?" she asked curiously.

"Not really," I confessed. "Not that I wouldn't, they just don't really ask me. Between my mom and aunt they usually have it covered."

"Lucky," she said with a laugh.

"Oh, yeah. They're all about the babysitting. I offered to keep Arie tonight, though, so her parents could get some sleep."

"Grandmas aren't willing to do the overnights, huh?" Morgan joked.

"Actually they are," I replied, not wanting to give her the wrong impression. I got more comfortable on the couch and got Arielle situated against my chest before continuing. "I think Ani and Bram have been refusing their help because they didn't want the oldies to have to stay up all night."

"All night?"

"That's what I hear," I said, glancing down at Arielle, who was still watching the documentary, even though there was no way she understood anything they were saying. "She's getting about two hours, give or take a few minutes."

"Oh, that sucks," Morgan said. "How old is she?"

"Eight months." I wasn't sure of that, but I acted like I was. I knew my guess was pretty close.

"I had to deal with that shit with Etta for only about a week when she was teething, and I honestly thought I might die from sleep deprivation."

"Shit, huh?" I asked, surprised at her language.

"Ugh," she sighed. "My dad's a bad influence."

"How's that going?" I asked curiously. She'd seemed really reluctant to move back in with her dad, but she seemed happy to be there. I wondered what he was like. She seemed to put the guy on a pedestal.

"It's actually kind of great," she said ruefully. "There's always a pot of coffee waiting for me in the morning, and it's been really nice to spend some time with the old man."

"Damn," I said, taking a deep breath. "The coffee thing sounds nice."

"I know, right?" she said, sighing happily. "His coffee is way better than mine, too."

"I know what you mean. Coffee always tastes better at my parents' house, too. Sometimes I go over on the weekends, just for that."

"Do you spend a lot of time at your parents' house?" she asked. I laughed a little at the question. What constituted "a lot" in her mind? I spent a lot more time with my parents than my brothers did, but I'd always lived close. I wasn't sure what would be considered a normal amount.

"I live really close to them," I finally said. "I built a house on our family property."

"Oh."

"But it's not next door or anything," I rushed to clarify. I really didn't want her to think I was living with my parents. I wasn't that guy. "We have a lot of property, so when it was time to build or buy a house I decided to do it here.

Eventually they'll get to the point where they'll need my help getting around and I didn't want to be too far away."

"That's sweet of you."

"Plus, it cut way down on my mortgage," I confessed.

"Yeah, I can understand that logic," she said jokingly. "My dad won't let me pay anything until I get a job, so I've been leaving money around the house in the hopes that he would find it and assume it's his."

I laughed loudly and startled Arielle, making her entire body tense.

"Sorry, sweet thing," I murmured, kissing the top of her head. "Is it working?" I asked Morgan.

"I'm not sure," she replied. "But I found a twenty in my jeans yesterday, and I know I didn't put it there."

"He's giving it back?"

"Probably," she grumbled.

"Your dad sounds like a good guy."

"He is," she said. "The best."

"I'm looking forward to meeting him."

"When's that happening?" she asked. "I told him today that you guys would be visiting pretty soon."

"My mom wants to drive down Friday."

There was a long pause before she replied. "She's not wasting any time."

"I told you," I reminded her, trying not to get defensive at her tone. "We'll get settled and then I was hoping we could see you on Saturday?"

"Sure, we don't have anything planned this weekend. Do you know how long you're staying?" The question sounded a little strained.

"I didn't ask, but I'm guessing only a few days. I have to get back to work, so we can't stay too long."

"Work? What's that?" she teased.

Even though I'd heard the anxiety in her voice when we discussed the visit, Morgan and I still talked for almost two hours while Arie sat wide awake on my lap. It got later and later, and I knew I should let her get some sleep, but I couldn't make myself get off the phone. I was learning things about her that I wouldn't have known if we'd been getting to know each other any other way. Talking with her long distance changed the way we interacted. There were no barriers to the things we shared, no embarrassment. It was as if the distance between us gave us a free pass to actually be ourselves instead of the polished versions we showed the world. The only thing we didn't discuss—that we never discussed—was Henry.

I'd been around her in person only for a single day, but as I got off the phone that night, I realized that I missed her.

Oh, and my voice eventually soothed Arielle to sleep.

Chapter 10
Morgan

W hy are you so damn nervous?" my dad asked me on Saturday morning, mimicking me by flapping his arms while he spun in a circle. "They're the ones who should be nervous. You hold all the power here, kiddo."

I knew that. It sure didn't feel like I had any power, though.

The night before when Trevor texted that they'd arrived safely, I'd almost called and asked him to come over. Instead, I'd chickened out and called my baby sister so I could listen to her chatter for over an hour. When I'd gone to bed with her positive affirmations in my head, I'd felt calm.

As soon as I'd woken up in the morning, though, all that calm was gone. I was a jittery mess. Thank God my dad had no idea that most of my nerves came from the fact that I was about to see Trevor again. Trevor, who was built like a tank and had the biggest smile I'd ever seen. Trevor, who'd confessed to me that his mom was his absolute favorite person on the planet even though he was pretty sure that made him a mama's boy. Trevor, who I knew was off-limits but I couldn't stop thinking about.

"Twevo," Etta said for the hundredth time that morning. "Twevo coming."

"Yep," I answered, glancing around the house to make sure nothing was out of place.

My dad's house was small, and old, and it showed. But the man had always taken pride in the place, and that showed, too. He'd bought it as soon as he'd had a down payment, about six months after we'd moved in with him, and he'd worked his fingers to the bone to pay it off. There were manicured flowers in the front yard, and slightly browned but neatly trimmed grass in the back, and even though he was a bachelor and didn't keep it as clean as I would've, the inside was functional and clearly taken care of.

"Twevo, Mama!" Etta yelled, staring out the front window from where she stood on the couch. "Twevo, here!"

"Showtime," my dad teased, laughing when I glared at him.

I moved slowly to the front door and waited two seconds after the knock to open the door, even though Etta was making an impatient ruckus beside me. There was no need to show my nervousness, after all. I held the power.

I hung on to that sentiment as I met Ellie Harris's eyes.

"Hi," I said, barely glancing at her husband and Trevor as I reached down and pulled Etta up onto my hip. "Come on in."

I held the power. I held the power. I held the power.

"Hi," she breathed back, taking a step forward as I moved backward into the house to let them in. She seemed mesmerized for a moment as her eyes landed on Etta, then shook her head with a small laugh and looked back at me. "Thank you so much for having us."

"Of course."

"It's nice to see you again after all this time," she said, shifting her purse on her shoulder. "I remembered exactly who you were as soon as Trevor mentioned you'd lived with us."

"It's nice to see you, too," I said. "Did Trevor also mention that he *didn't* remember me?"

I chuckled as she threw a look over her shoulder at her son.

"Oh, come on," he groaned, grinning. "I was too old to pay attention to the kids that summer."

"Your house was the best one I was placed in," I told Ellie seriously. "Thank you."

"I'll second that," my dad said, joining the fray. "Thanks for taking care of my girl when I couldn't."

"You're very welcome," Ellie said, obviously sizing my pop up, even though she tried to disguise it. "We loved having a house full of kids, right, Mike?"

Trevor's dad stepped forward, and I was startled for a moment. I barely remembered him from when I'd lived with them. Even though he'd always made it home for dinner, he'd usually been gone working all day and I hadn't had much reason to interact with him.

If I had remembered him, the resemblance between him and his adoptive sons wouldn't have been so freaking startling.

It wasn't their looks. Clearly. Henry had been all blond and lean, and Trevor was dark and built, while Mike was just an ordinary dark-haired white guy, thickening a little around the middle. It was the way they held themselves that was so uncanny. Their straight backs, the way their heads tilted just so, how they moved and stood, the firm set of their mouths, and the little grins they gave that made their eyes crinkle.

I hadn't noticed the similarities between Henry and Trevor,

but now that I'd seen their dad, it was impossible to miss. The thought made me a little nauseous.

Mike reached out to shake my dad's hand. "I remember your daughter, too," he said, shooting me a smile. "She was a sweetheart."

"Still is," my dad said, almost boastful. "Come on in, no reason to stand here in the entryway."

Etta squirmed to be let down, so I set her on her feet. She instantly ran to my dad and grabbed his hand so she could be in the middle of the commotion as the oldies, as Trevor called them, moved more fully into the living room. I had stepped forward to follow them when a light hand on my hip made me freeze.

"Hey, stranger," Trevor said quietly into my ear.

"Hey." I glanced over my shoulder at him and felt my cheeks heat at the way he was looking at me. We'd been borderline flirting in our texts and phone conversations, even though I kind of assumed that we both knew nothing could come of it. But having him there, in my dad's house, magnified whatever it was between us to a level that was nearly impossible to ignore. I was in so much trouble.

"It's good to see you," he murmured simply, giving my hip a squeeze.

Then we were following the parents into the room and finding seats. It all happened in less than five seconds, but I could've sworn his mom was looking at us strangely from the moment we sat down.

"Can I get anyone drinks?" I asked, trying to play hostess, even though I could still feel the press of Trevor's hand on my hip.

"Me Henwyetta," Etta interrupted, climbing off my dad's lap. He'd tried to contain her but clearly hadn't succeeded. I tried hard not to laugh. "Me two."

"You're two?" Ellie asked, leaning forward in her seat so that she was closer to Etta's height. "Wow."

"Me wearin' bwue pannies." Etta started pulling on her romper to show them the blue panties she was talking about.

"Etta," I scolded, trying and failing to hide my embarrassment. "Remember what we talked about?"

She looked at me blankly.

"We don't show people our panties," I whispered.

"What, Mama?"

"We don't show people our panties," I whispered again, wishing the floor would open up and swallow us both.

"What, Mama?" Etta asked again, making Trevor start to chuckle.

"We don't show people our panties," I finally said at a normal level.

"Oh," Etta replied, completely unfazed.

The room went silent for a moment.

"Good advice," Mike finally said, nodding.

My dad started to guffaw, and I slapped a hand over my face in mortification.

"Mine are white," Ellie said, glancing at me with an understanding smile before looking back to Etta. "Boring." It was almost the exact same thing Trevor had said on the day we'd met him.

"I wouldn't go that far," Mike murmured about Ellie's underwear, making my dad laugh even harder.

"*Oh, come on,*" Trevor grumbled.

Then we were all laughing, and the ice had been broken.

* * *

"Trevor said you're searching for a job?" Ellie asked later that day while she helped me make lunch. They'd been at our house for a few hours already and didn't show any signs of leaving. I was strangely okay with it. Ellie doted on Etta, which hadn't surprised me. It was Mike who I'd watched curiously all morning. He seemed enthralled with my little drama queen, even though he was less obvious about it than his wife.

"Yeah," I replied. "I haven't had any luck so far."

"And you do tattoos?"

I glanced at her quickly, but she wasn't looking at me.

"Actually," I said, looking back at the fruit I was cutting, "I do piercings."

"Really," she said, drawing out the word like she was intrigued. "Do you pierce *anything?*"

Her insinuation was clear, and I giggled. "Your son asked me the same thing."

"Which son?"

"Well—" I paused. "Both of them, actually."

"I'm not surprised," she said drily, making me smile. "They both like to think they're open-minded, but I can imagine their shudders."

Before I could confirm her impression, she spoke again. "If I'm wrong," she said, lifting a hand like a stop signal, "don't tell me."

"No." I chuckled. "You're right. Both of them cringed."

"My nieces have both had piercings," she said, wiggling her head from side to side. "I know some people don't like them, but I always thought they looked pretty. Though I could do without the bull-ring hanging from Ani's nose. A little nostril piercing, I think that's the way to go."

"It's called a septum ring," I said, smiling still. "And if you ever want your nostril done, I can do it."

"Oh, I don't know about that," she mused, finishing up on the sandwiches she was making. "Mike would probably have a conniption."

"He doesn't like them?"

"He's never really said so, but I have a feeling he'd have an opinion if I were to put an extra hole anywhere."

"I don't have any piercings, either," I replied. I'd learned quite differently about spousal reactions depending on the location of the piercing, but I wasn't about to touch that conversation with a ten-foot pole. "Well, besides my ears. I got those done when I was a baby."

"See too many of them?" she asked.

"I think they're beautiful, I've just never really felt the urge." I shrugged. "I have a tattoo, though."

Before she could ask me where it was, the guys came in from the backyard with a soaking-wet Etta.

"She wanted me to spray her with the hose," my dad explained as Trevor carried my girl out in front of him in an attempt to stay dry.

"Oh, man," I said, rinsing off my hands. "Come here, princess."

"Me wet," she told me as I took her from Trevor. "Me 'plashin'."

"I can see that." I met Trevor's eyes as he laughed. "She likes splashing," I said inanely.

"Yeah, I remember. Just not when someone else is doing it, right?" His voice was nonchalant, but his eyes said so much more. They said that he remembered everything about that day, and he was currently remembering very clearly what I looked like in my swimsuit.

"Lunch is ready," Ellie said, interrupting the silent conversation going on between me and her son.

"I'll be right back," I blurted, uncomfortably.

"Wight back," Etta repeated.

"You're soaked," I murmured as I brought Etta into our room. "Are you having fun?"

"Yes." She nodded while I stripped off her romper and diaper.

"It's nice having them visit, huh?" I grabbed a sundress and a clean diaper and tossed her gently onto the bed, making her giggle. "You like them?"

"Me wike Twevo," she replied.

"What about Ellie and Mike?"

"Funny," she said, her little face serious.

"They are pretty funny." I got her dressed as she squirmed to get away. "They like you. I can tell."

"Me funny."

"Yeah, you're funny, too."

She replied with some long string of words that I didn't understand, but I nodded along, knowing that she thought she was making perfect sense.

When we got back into the kitchen, everyone was already seated at the small kitchen table and my dad had pulled his computer chair from the living room so I'd have a place to sit.

"Little crowded," my dad said unnecessarily.

"Just the way we like it," I replied, smiling. I wasn't joking. If it was up to my dad, we'd always have people over. I was a little less of a social butterfly, but I felt the same way when it came to people we were close to. I didn't remember how many times we'd had Danny and his family over for dinner and cards, or the whole huge group of my dad's friends over for a barbeque out back. I loved having the people I cared about around me, joking and laughing and having a good time. It made me feel a part of something bigger, and reminded me that I'd come a long way from the girl who'd had no one but her little sister when the state had come to take us away.

"What do you do, Stan?" Mike asked.

"Body work," my dad replied, lifting a hand to cover the way he spoke with food in his mouth. "Cars mostly, some bikes. Slowin' down, lately, though."

"He's good," I chimed in, nodding. "I've seen some of the work he's done."

"It's mostly just repairs," my dad clarified, smiling at me. "But every once in a while I get something cool to work on. Retirees coming in to get their hot rods prettied up."

"Oh yeah?" Mike said, clearly interested.

I sat back while they carried the conversation, and, like a moth to a flame, my eyes moved to Trevor.

He was already looking at me. His movements didn't pause while he ate his sandwich and the watermelon I'd sliced, but his eyes never left mine. They stayed constant, full of promises and heat. I'd never met anyone before who could say so much with just a look.

My stomach fluttered as I looked away, but I couldn't help

but glance back at him, over and over, while we sat around the table. Something was going to happen. Soon. There was no way he was leaving California without making good on all the things he was imagining. I was thrilled and terrified in equal measure.

"Mama," Etta said, breaking the tension that I was sure no one else at the table felt but me. "Me done."

"Are you sure?" I asked, leaning over to brush the hair out of her face. "You didn't eat much."

I started to rise from my seat, but Ellie stopped me.

"I can get her cleaned up," she offered.

As soon as I'd nodded my agreement, she was out of her chair and helping Etta, leaving me with nothing to do except look at Trevor again. The dads were completely consumed with their conversation about old cars, not paying any attention to us whatsoever when Trevor's lips turned up at the corners.

"You're gorgeous," he mouthed.

"Stop," I mouthed back, widening my eyes.

I wasn't sure what was happening between us, but whatever it was absolutely couldn't happen in front of our parents. Especially not *his* parents.

"Can't," he mouthed back.

I rolled my eyes but couldn't stop grinning.

"Trevor," Ellie said, surprising me enough to make me jump. "Do you remember when Henry was this age? I swear, if you cut Etta's hair into a mullet they could pass for twins."

Henry's name was like a bucket of ice water dumped over my head. At first I was startled, and then I had trouble even drawing in a breath.

From the moment the Harrises had walked through our front door, no one had said a word about Etta's dad. He was the reason they were visiting. Without him, I wouldn't have Etta. All of us knew that—it was like the elephant in the room. But I'd mistakenly assumed that they weren't speaking about him for a reason, so I hadn't brought him up, either, and my dad had followed my lead.

Having Ellie bring him up so casually after hours of visiting seemed almost like she was making a point. Unfortunately, I had no idea what point she was trying to make.

"There's definitely a resemblance," Trevor replied, not missing a beat. "She's got Morgan's smile, though."

"Yeah, she does," my dad said, proudly. "My younger daughter Miranda's smile is just the same."

"Oh," Mike said in surprise. "I didn't know you had another daughter."

"She's two years younger than me," I replied, feeling uncomfortable but not sure why. "She lives up in Bend."

"Going to school up there," my dad boasted. "She's gonna be a psychologist."

"She wants to be a caseworker," I clarified. "She's majoring in psychology."

"Well," Mike said, nodding. "We definitely need more of those."

"Good ones," I mumbled.

"I've never met a bad one," Ellie replied.

I couldn't pinpoint where it was coming from, and I didn't know when it had started, but suddenly I felt very uncomfortable. I didn't know what it was. There wasn't anything in Ellie's tone that indicated that she was upset, and her expression was completely relaxed, but I could feel the change in her regard. There was something about the way her head was tilted, a sharpness in her eyes that hadn't been there before. She was judging me. Judging and finding me lacking in some way.

My palms grew sweaty.

"Lunch was great," Mike said, sighing happily as he stood up. "Thank you."

"You're welcome," I said, standing, too. I was acting weird and I knew it, but I couldn't be casual. The entire energy in the room had changed, and I didn't know why or how to fix it.

Etta began to whine about something, and my dad, God bless him, stood up.

"It's about nap time, I think," he said kindly, reaching for Etta. "You getting sleepy, princess?"

"No," Etta said, curling into him anyway.

"We should probably get back to the hotel for a while," Mike murmured. "I think I need a nap, too."

Trevor was the last one to move from his spot at the table. He was watching everything play out with an expression I didn't recognize but thankfully didn't say anything. He barely glanced at me long enough to say good-bye.

It only took a few minutes for the Harris family to leave, but they were some of the longest minutes I could remember. The moment the door shut behind them, my dad turned to me with a frown.

"Don't know what the hell that was," he murmured as he handed Etta to me, then he wrapped his arms across his chest and mock shivered.

"I'm going to lay her down," I replied, ignoring his comment.

I needed a moment to process what the heck had just happened. The visit had gone well. Actually, it had gone great. At least for a while. I just couldn't figure out how it had all changed so quickly, and I was now left with a huge ball of anxiety in my chest at the thought of seeing Etta's grandparents again.

* * *

An hour later, I was sitting on the back porch with a beer, still trying to pinpoint exactly what had made my spidey-senses go so haywire, when I got a text from Trevor.

You busy?

I glanced at my shorts, bikini top, and the beer in my hand before answering. Etta was still asleep, and my dad had gone to a friend's house. Did I give him the truth? I wasn't sure if I was up for a chat.

Not really, I replied after a few minutes of internal debate. His reply was instant.

Good. I'm out front.

"Shit," I mumbled, scrambling to my feet.

Hurrying through the house, I threw open the front door before he could ring the bell and wake Etta.

I probably should have taken the time to throw on a shirt.

"Oh, Jesus," he said, taking a small step back as soon as he got a good look at me. "You're trying to kill me."

"I didn't know you were coming over," I replied.

"I just told you."

"Yeah, that you were *here*."

"Tomato, tomahto."

"I'm sorry," I replied, acting like I was going to leave him standing there on the front stoop. "We don't need our carpets cleaned."

Trevor laughed. "Do those salesmen still go door to door?" He moved closer.

"I don't know. I don't answer the door when strange men come knocking."

"Sure you do." He grinned. "You let me in."

"Momentary lapse," I teased. I took a step back and he took another step forward. Oh, God. Were we really doing this?

"You going to make that mistake again?" he asked softly.

I tilted my head to the side, like I was trying to decide on my answer, and that's when he made his move. *The* move.

One long finger slid between my breasts and snagged the string that held my bikini top around my rib cage, just as his head dropped toward mine until our lips were millimeters apart.

"Let me in?" he asked, his breath minty and cool against my lips.

"I don't know," I whispered, still playing the game. "I'm not supposed to let people in when my dad isn't home."

Trevor groaned as his lips descended on mine.

The kiss was explosive. I knew no other word to describe it. I'd been kissed hundreds of times before, but I'd never felt it all the way to my toes the way I felt it then. The lips I'd watched smile widely, and grin secretly, pressed against mine until there was no space between us.

When his tongue slid against mine, questioning yet

completely confident, my knees threatened to buckle. He tasted the way he smelled, like mint and something unique to Trevor.

Without a word, he wrapped his arms around my waist and lifted me off my feet so he could carry me fully into the house. As soon as the door shut behind him, all pretense of civility was gone. I couldn't have described the thoughts that ran through my head if I'd tried. We were greedy and almost desperate as we tore at each other's clothes. His shirt dropped to the floor first. My shorts followed. Then his shoes, and his shorts.

Somehow, we maneuvered ourselves to the kitchen table, and I yelped as my ass hit the edge, but neither of us paused. My hands slid into the back of his boxer briefs as his fingers untied the bikini straps at my neck. His mouth tore from mine, but before I could protest, his lips were wrapped around my nipple and he was sliding the bikini bottoms down my legs.

"Fuck," he muttered as he moved his mouth to my sternum. "Do you want me to stop?"

I jerked in surprise, and tilted my head down to look at him, wondering if he was teasing me. What I found in his expression was completely the opposite of what I'd expected. He was serious. His breath was coming in huge gulps and his body was practically radiating with tension, but he was absolutely still.

It was the moment of truth, the split second of sanity when I could have stopped everything.

"No," I said quietly, catching his hands and setting them back on my hips when he misunderstood me. "I don't want you to stop."

"I'm not trying to rush you," he said in relief, pressing his face between my breasts, before turning his head and sucking hard enough to leave a mark. "We haven't talked about this or—"

His words cut off as I ran my hand along the side of his face, relishing the scruff of his beard against my palm. Groaning, his mouth moved lower, nipping and sucking at the skin of my belly. When he urged me to turn with the press of his hands, I spun unsteadily to face the table, my hands banging loudly on the top as I felt his mouth move to the curve of my ass.

"I'm—" he murmured against my skin. "You're—" He didn't finish his thoughts, instead, he hummed against my skin as his hands moved up the insides of my thighs. My legs began to shake as his fingers moved along my skin, and by the time they'd reached my center, I was bracing my forearms against the table in an attempt to stay standing.

"Trevor," I mumbled, as one of his hands kneaded my ass and the other swept back and forth lightly against my clit. "Oh, shit."

"Feel good?" he asked quietly.

I nodded, swallowing hard as I tried to keep myself from making too much noise. My hips instinctively rocked back toward him and my head dropped forward as his hands slid away and his erection pressed against me through his boxers.

"Yeah?" he asked, gently nudging me from behind.

"Yes," I mumbled, reaching back to pull at his boxers.

His body moved away from me, and I sighed in defeat, thinking he'd changed his mind. Then, just seconds later, before I could even push myself up from the table, he was back.

"Condom," he said, running a hand gently down my spine.

He slid inside me with no hesitation whatsoever. Any reluctance or second thoughts were gone. All we could do was feel, his fingers interlaced with mine on the table and his muscular body pressing and retreating over and over as I followed his movements with my own.

It didn't matter how we were positioned, or that we were in the middle of my dad's house, or that my child was sleeping peacefully in her crib. Nothing outside the way his skin slid against mine, and his dark fingers gripped my palms, and his breath trembled against my throat, mattered. It was the best sex, hands down, that I'd ever had.

But once the orgasms had waned and our skin cooled and I stood upright again, recriminations and doubt began circling in my mind with the force of a tornado. What in God's name had I done?

"You are the most beautiful woman I've ever seen," Trevor said softly, brushing his hands against my cheeks as I stood there, naked and regretful.

"I need to get dressed," I replied numbly, almost wincing at the change in his expression.

I slid out of his arms and awkwardly bent at the knees to retrieve my swimsuit bottoms. Unfortunately, that put me at eye level with his cock, which was still semi-hard and covered in a condom. A very full condom. Dear God.

I snapped back up and almost hit my head on his chin. He hadn't moved an inch as he'd watched me fumble and stare.

"Morgan?" he asked as I stepped away, covering my breasts with my arm.

"Etta's going to be up soon," I said, avoiding eye contact and snatching my bikini top from the table.

"You serious right now?" he questioned. He didn't reach for me, but his entire body shifted as he tried to get me to look at him.

"I'm sorry," I mumbled, walking toward the entryway, where my shorts were lying in a heap.

"I've still got a condom hanging off my dick," he said incredulously.

"There's paper towels on the counter," I replied, deliberately ignoring his tone.

I didn't watch, but I could hear him as he moved farther into the kitchen. Scrambling, I barely got my top back on before he was in my peripheral vision again.

"Am I missing something here?" he asked as he jerkily pulled his boxers up his thick thighs. "'Cause I was pretty sure you were on board with all that."

I didn't answer. I had absolutely no clue what to say.

"Morgan," he said again sharply, making my head lurch up in surprise. "Please tell me that I didn't get my signals crossed here."

The look on his face and the way he held his body made my stomach twist in remorse.

"You didn't," I said scratchily, shaking my head. "I told you yes." I cleared my throat. "More than once."

"Then what the fuck, baby?" he asked softly, taking a step forward.

"We shouldn't have done this," I said, retreating back a few steps. "This was such a bad idea."

His head flew back like I'd slapped him.

"I disagree."

"I'm sorry," I replied, wrapping my arms around my waist. I

really wished I was wearing more clothes. I'd have done damn near anything for a freaking robe.

"Yeah." He made a sound in his throat and looked at the floor, rubbing a hand down his face. "Me too."

We were silent as he put his clothes back on. I tried to keep my eyes averted to give him some privacy, but couldn't help but glance over a few times, marveling at the way his muscles flexed as he moved. I knew it was a bad idea, and I was nauseous with guilt, but I still wanted him so badly that my heart was racing.

"Bye," he said awkwardly, giving me a shallow nod before walking calmly out the front door and closing it quietly behind him.

"Oh shit," I said, once he was gone. "Oh, God. Oh, shit. Oh, fuck. Fuck. *Fuck.*"

I stood there in the entryway, replaying every single moment since he'd come to the door, with the heels of my hands pressed against my stinging eyes, until I heard Etta calling for me.

Chapter 11

Trevor

I'd done a lot of stupid things in my life. I'd let my cousin Kate cut my hair into a Mohawk. I'd raced my car when I was sixteen to earn extra cash. I'd sold the only thing I had left from my birth parents, a watch I'd been told was my grandfather's, because I was angry. But I'd never, in my entire life, done something as stupid as bending Morgan over her kitchen table and fucking her like I hadn't had a woman in years.

I was shaking as I drove back to my hotel.

I'd really messed up this time.

As soon as I threw my parents' SUV into park, I quickly dragged my phone out of the pocket of my shorts.

Within seconds, I was blurting, "I need to talk to you."

My cousin Ani didn't miss a beat. "Hit me," she shot back.

"I need you to listen and I need you to keep your mouth shut and then I need you to tell me what the fuck to do."

"Oh, shit, Trev," she said, clearly understanding the gravity of my words. "Give me a sec."

She put me on hold while I fidgeted and slammed my head back against the headrest, then came back on the line.

"Tell me what happened."

"I like her. I'm fucking crazy about her," I said quickly. "I've been thinking about her since the minute we met. It's not getting any better. If anything, it's getting worse. The more I see her, the more I want to see her."

"We're talking about Morgan?" she asked.

"I told you not to speak."

"Sorry. Continue," she said, clearly amused.

"So, we've been talking. Flirting, kind of. She's into me, I know that much. The chemistry is through the roof. I swear to God, it's enough to burn a fucking house down." I rubbed at the headache growing right above my eyes. "I'm never wrong about this shit, Ani. Never."

I paused, but she'd taken my directions to heart and didn't reply.

"I had sex with her," I blurted, unable to stem the flow of words. "It was incredible. I sound like an idiot, I know that, okay? But it was the best sex of my life. What the hell is wrong with me?"

"Oh, *shit*," Ani murmured, her surprise obvious. "What is it with the people in this family boning inappropriate partners?"

At any other time, I would have laughed at the truth in her words. My cousin Kate had gotten pregnant with her dead best friend's husband, my foster brother Shane, and Anita had started a secret relationship with her foster brother Abraham. Neither of those situations had started out very well, but everyone ended up happy.

I didn't see that happening for Morgan and me.

"Everything was great," I said, shaking my head, then wincing at the way the movement made my head pound. "But then the second we were finished, she got weird."

"Weird, how?"

"She got jittery—started getting dressed as fast as she could and told me it was a mistake."

"Oh," Ani muttered.

"What does that mean, 'oh'?" I replied, panicky. "What?"

"I don't know her, Trev," Ani said soothingly, trying to calm my ass down. "I'm not sure—"

"Just tell me."

"It sounds like she was having some buyer's remorse," she admitted apologetically.

"You think?" I asked sarcastically. "Tell me what to do."

"Take a step back," she said instantly. "Trev, take *two* steps back."

"I don't even know if that's possible."

"It has to be," she argued. "You have to look at this from all angles, dude. She's Etta's *mother*."

"I know that!"

"Then you know that what I'm saying isn't bullshit," she snapped. "This chick is going to be around. She has to be if we're going to see Henry's kid. Don't fucking scare her away."

I inhaled sharply at the idea that Morgan would use what happened as a way to distance herself and Etta from my family.

"She wouldn't do that," I said, refusing even to contemplate it. I couldn't imagine that scenario without losing my fucking mind. It was hard enough having any respect for myself after banging my brother's ex, but if I ruined our chance at having a relationship with Etta I wouldn't be able to live with myself.

"You don't know that," Ani said, not unkindly. "You don't know her very well, Trev. You guys have been talking, I know, but you've only been around her a couple of times."

"I know her," I argued.

"If you knew her, you would have seen that she wasn't ready to have sex with you."

I felt like I'd been punched in the chest. "Is that what you think of me?" I asked in bewilderment. "Seriously?"

"Trev, no," she argued. "That's not what I meant. You're taking my words wrong."

"They were pretty fucking clear."

"I have no doubt that she was willing," Ani said quickly. "Don't be an idiot."

"Of course she was," I practically yelled.

"I'm just saying that maybe she wasn't ready yet, asshole," Ani shot back, her voice rising, too. "You guys barely know each other, and you're Henry's brother."

Inhaling through my nose, I made an effort to calm myself down. I was reacting instinctively without thinking about what I was saying, and it was beginning to make me feel even more anxious.

I always thought things through. Always. So why had I gone off half cocked and done something so idiotic?

"Just give her some space, Trev," Ani said gently, while I continued to breathe slowly, in through my nose and out through my mouth. "That's the best advice I can give you."

"I'm sorry I yelled," I replied. I wasn't someone who argued or spoke to people angrily. I thought things through and replied calmly and rationally—always.

"No worries," Anita replied. "It was kind of mind-blowing listening to you lose your cool. You *are* human."

"Funny," I muttered.

"It'll work out, dude."

"Thanks for the talk," I said.

"Anytime. You know that."

We got off the phone, but I didn't move. I couldn't.

Anita had *just* told me to give Morgan space, and I knew that it was solid advice, but I couldn't stand leaving things the way they were. I wrote and rewrote the text message four times before I finally pressed SEND.

I don't think it was a mistake.

Simple and direct.

I stayed where I was for half an hour, staring out the window while the car idled. She didn't text me back.

* * *

"I just think that maybe we could get to know them better if they came to our place for a visit," my mom said the next morning at breakfast. We were eating at the hotel before we went over to Morgan's again, and my mom was trying to convince my dad that it was a good idea to invite Morgan and Etta to Oregon. "Her dad monopolizes the conversation and Morgan can't seem to get a word in edgewise."

"I didn't notice that," my dad replied, clearly not agreeing with her.

I didn't agree with my mom's opinion, either. If anything,

Morgan's dad had seemed hesitant to speak, unless he felt like his daughter needed him to step in. The man was a pro at redirecting conversation, and he did so whenever Morgan began to look uncomfortable or unsure. I respected him a lot for that. He'd clearly let his daughter take the lead, even though anyone could see how protective he was.

"There's no hurt in asking," Dad said, reaching out to pat Mom's hand. "But they're just getting settled down here, so I doubt she'll say yes."

He had no idea how right he was about what Morgan would think in regard to visiting Oregon. She'd never texted me back the day before, and I'd had a long time to think about what that meant and how I planned on responding.

There was only one thing I could do to salvage the situation. It felt wrong, and it killed me to do it, but I had to step back, like Ani had advised. If there was any chance of getting Morgan back to the point where she was comfortable with me again, I had to find a way to go back to being her friend, nothing more. When I'd come to the decision early that morning, I'd thought I'd feel better about it. I'd been wrong. I felt worse as I sat there listening to my parents, knowing that I had to keep my distance from the woman they were discussing.

"I bet she will," my mom argued, snapping me back to the subject at hand. "Her sister lives in Bend. I bet we could use that as incentive."

"You sound like a used-car salesman," I replied, shaking my head. "Why don't you just ask and let Morgan decide without using anything else to lure her?"

"I'm not trying to lure her," Mom said, tilting her chin up. "I'm just trying to—"

"Lure her," my dad cut in, laughing. He leaned over and kissed the side of Mom's head. "Let's just see what she says."

Half an hour later, we were in the SUV on our way to Morgan's dad's house. Even though I'd assured Ani that she'd never keep Etta from us, I was still a little surprised that she hadn't called to cancel. If I was feeling nervous about seeing her today, I couldn't even imagine how she felt.

I didn't regret having sex with Morgan, regardless of how the interlude had ended. I was disappointed about how she'd acted afterward and I'd felt like shit all night trying to figure out exactly how it had all gone wrong, but I couldn't make myself regret it. I'd dream about her smooth skin, trembling muscles, and quiet sounds of pleasure for the rest of my life. It was a cross I would willingly bear.

"Have you talked to Kate lately?" my mom asked, dragging my attention from the scenery out my window. "She mentioned meeting us while we were here, but I haven't heard anything about it since."

"No," I replied, shaking my head. "She didn't say anything to me."

"I should have called her this morning," my mom mumbled, digging in her purse.

"We're leaving tomorrow," my dad reminded her. "If Kate didn't show up last night, she's not coming."

I quietly pulled out my phone and texted my cousin while they argued about her plans.

You coming to Sacramento?

Gavin's puking, so no. Sorry I didn't let you know yesterday. Super disappointed.

"Gavin's sick," I said, interrupting my parents. "That's why she didn't call you yesterday."

Inwardly, I breathed a sigh of relief. I was sorry that little Gavin was throwing up, but enormously thankful that Kate wouldn't be anywhere near the situation I'd landed myself in. Unlike my parents, who wouldn't suspect a thing, Kate would have taken one good look at me and known something was up. Then she probably would have meddled and made everything worse. I loved my cousin, but it was impossible for her to keep her nose out of other people's business.

"Stan's here again," my mom said quietly as we pulled up to the house.

"I like him," my dad replied with a shrug.

"Not surprising," she said, smoothing down her hair. "You're living vicariously through his car stories."

"The man has good stories," Dad said, climbing out of the driver's seat.

I listened to them talk, their conversation moving to other things as we made our way up the sidewalk, but I barely noticed a word they said. I was too busy preparing myself to act casual when I came face-to-face with the woman who'd rejected me so spectacularly the day before.

The front door opened, and the first thing I saw was Etta, scrambling outside like she couldn't wait a second longer to see us.

"Twevo!" she yelled, making my dad laugh as she bypassed them as if they didn't exist.

"Hey, sweetheart," I greeted as I lifted her high in the air.

As I lowered her to sit on my arm, my eyes met Morgan's over her head, and my breath caught. Etta was chattering in her normal gibberish, but all I could see was her mother. Morgan was wearing a pale purple sundress and her hair was in a messy knot on top of her head. She was barefoot...and nervous. I hated that she was nervous.

"Hey guys," she said, trying to hide the discomfort with an easy smile. "Come on in."

"Thanks for having us over again," my mom said as she started into the house.

"Of course," Morgan replied, waving my dad into the house. "You should get as much time in as you can before you have to head north."

She was being welcoming without a hint of hesitation, and I inhaled a huge sigh of relief. I was rarely wrong about people, and clearly Morgan was no exception. She wasn't going to punish my parents for something they had no control over, and I shouldn't have doubted her.

"Hey," I said, giving her a small smile as I carried Etta inside.

She was obviously taken aback by my casual greeting, but after her initial reaction, she hid her surprise behind a small smile of her own.

The door closed behind me as I set Etta on her feet, and the second I stood back up I knew it wasn't going to be easy to pretend that my feelings for Morgan had disappeared. I was standing in the exact spot where she'd torn off my shirt the day before, and the memory made my heart pound.

"Does anyone want coffee?" Morgan asked, moving across the room. Her voice wobbled only a little, but it was enough for me to realize that she'd been thinking about the same thing as me.

"I'd love a cup," my dad said, sitting down on the couch.

"Lucky for you, my dad started it before he jumped in the shower," Morgan replied with a little laugh. "My coffee is pretty bad."

"You probably just don't put enough grounds in," my dad said, nodding. He took his coffee seriously. "That's usually the problem."

"You might be right," Morgan conceded.

I stepped into the living room and sat on a chair just as my mom chimed in.

"I put enough grounds in, Mike," she said in exasperation as she sat down on the floor with Etta and accepted a doll with a smile. "You're just too picky."

Morgan laughed and I felt it in my stomach. I didn't turn to look at her, though. If I had any chance of making my plan work, I needed to look at her as little as possible. Everything about her called to me, and I needed to keep my distance.

* * *

My mom and Etta played on the floor for over an hour while the rest of us talked about nothing significant. On the surface, the group seemed easy and relaxed around each other, but I could feel the tension in the room. The longer we spent in that small house, the more it seemed like my mom was desperate to soak up as much time with Etta as she could.

I wasn't sure if Morgan and Stan noticed the way she'd completely checked out of our conversation, but one look at my dad told me that he'd seen the change happen, too. It was almost as if she was deliberately ignoring the fact that we were in the room in an attempt to focus solely on her only grandchild. I understood it, to an extent, but it also made me nervous for reasons I couldn't really explain.

My mom had taken it so hard when Henry was killed. She'd raised him from the time he was little, so fierce in her attempts to protect him after the abuse he'd suffered as a baby that I sometimes wondered if his death had triggered some sense of failure in her. She hadn't been able to protect him in the end; she hadn't even had the opportunity.

"Me hungwy," Etta said, getting to her feet to toddle toward Morgan. "Mama, Etta hungwy."

"Okay," Morgan said, lifting the baby onto her lap.

My mom jerked as if someone had poked her in the side, and my gaze shot to my dad, who was watching my mom intently.

"Does anyone else want something to eat?" Morgan asked, unaware of the strange undercurrents.

"I'm good," I said, quickly turning to face her.

It was a mistake. She was standing too close. I could smell the lotion she wore and my mouth began to water.

I carefully left my expression blank as everyone else told her that they didn't want anything, either.

"Get on up off the floor," my dad said casually, reaching a hand out to my mom.

It was clear that Stan hadn't noticed anything different, but I had to hold back a wince as my mom slowly nodded and lifted herself up off her knees. She was surrounded by dolls in different stages of undress, which made her disappointment even more depressing to watch.

It scared me.

It had taken my mom a long time to drag herself out of the pit of depression after Henry's death, and she still wasn't on solid ground. I didn't know if she could ever fully come back from something like that, but she'd at least been making headway at functioning again. After watching her this morning, I was really afraid she'd slide back down once we left Sacramento.

We were leaving for home in less than twenty-four hours, and I had no idea when we'd be able to see Etta again. She was one of ours, yes, but her life was here, with her mom. This little girl didn't belong to Kate or Anita, who would both go out of their way to make sure she had a relationship with my mom. Etta belonged to Morgan, a woman my parents barely knew. She had no sense of loyalty or dedication to us; she had her own family.

"Me wike bananas," Etta said as she came sauntering back into the room, her blond hair floating back and forth as she walked. She had a banana in her hand and a shit-eating grin on her face.

"Henrietta," Morgan called sternly, making her daughter pause. "Come back in here."

Etta glanced behind her, and I could see with absolute clarity the moment when she decided to completely ignore her mother's order. My mom shifted on the couch, but before she could stand up, I was out of my seat and lifting Etta into my arms. I hadn't been sure what my mom's plan was, but could only imagine her playing the doting grandma by ignoring Morgan's wishes.

"You're supposed to be at the table," Stan said to Etta, tilting his head like he was disappointed.

"No table," Etta replied, her body stiffening.

"Come on," I said softly, ignoring her attempt to get down as I walked her into the kitchen. "Your mama wants you to eat that in here."

"No table," Etta screeched, kicking me in the side.

"Henrietta," Morgan said warningly, her voice stern. "Knock it off."

The mom voice didn't seem to faze my niece in the slightest. She continued to struggle as I handed her to Morgan.

Just as I made the handoff, Etta threw her half-eaten banana on the floor and completely lost it in a temper tantrum that was so loud I was pretty sure my ears popped.

"I'm so sorry," Morgan said, her voice barely audible beyond Etta's screams. "Jesus."

"What happened?" my mom asked, coming around the corner out of breath like she'd been running.

"She's okay," Morgan said, embarrassment making her cheeks a deep red.

She moved around us and hurried down the hall while Etta shoved and pushed at her shoulders.

"What happened?" my mom asked again, clearly freaked out.

"Nothing," I said, shaking my head. "She's throwing a fit."

"That wasn't a fit. Children don't scream like that unless they're hurt. Something is clearly wrong."

Even though I thought she was overreacting, I tried to keep my voice even when I replied. "She didn't want to sit and eat," I said, picking up Etta's banana off the floor.

"That wasn't a normal fit," my mom argued. "Kids don't just—"

"Yes," I interrupted. "They do. I've seen Keller do the same damn thing."

"Keller also lost his mother," my mom snapped, not willing to let the conversation go.

"I watched him do it before Rachel died," I snapped, tossing the banana in the garbage. "You're looking for something that isn't there."

"Oh, because you know so well what goes on in this house?" Mom hissed, making me freeze in surprise.

"What exactly are you insinuating?" I asked, my voice barely audible.

My mom scoffed and left the room without another word while I grabbed a paper towel to wipe the banana residue off the floor. I was still crouched low when I realized that Morgan had walked back into the room and was silently watching me.

"Thanks," she said quietly.

"No problem." I was irritated but trying not to let it show in my voice or body language.

"What's she looking for?" she asked, her voice still just as quiet.

"What?"

"Your mom. What's she looking for?"

I looked up to find that Morgan had wrapped her arms around her waist and was shifting her weight almost imperceptibly from one foot to the other.

"She's just overprotective," I replied vaguely, getting to my feet again. "Too many years taking care of troubled kids."

"She thinks Etta is troubled?" she asked, her spine stiffening.

"No." I shook my head as I tossed the paper towel in the trash. "I just mean she's oversensitive."

"What, does she think I hurt her?" Morgan asked, her voice getting higher. "That something's wrong with her?"

"No," I said, shaking my head again in denial. I had no idea what was going on in my mom's mind, but I knew with absolute certainty that if she spooked Morgan now, we'd probably never be welcome to see Etta again. "No. Morgan."

"Do you think that? You've barely even looked at me today."

"You know that doesn't have anything to do with what's going on today," I replied, lowering my voice.

"I don't know anything," she said, her eyes wide. "Was this all your plan? Did you come here to check me out? Try to find me doing something wrong?"

"What are you—"

"Like having sex while my kid's asleep in the next room," she said drily, shaking her head slowly from side to side.

I wanted to snap at her that she was being ridiculous, because she was, but as I took a closer look at her face, my stomach dropped. She was genuinely terrified. I didn't know what had triggered the fear, but it was clear as day.

"I think you're an awesome mom," I said quietly, taking a small step forward.

"Your mother doesn't," she replied, glancing toward the living room. "Kids throw fits, okay? Especially kids who are dramatic on a good day."

She was shaking.

"I know that."

"It doesn't mean that I'm a shitty parent."

"Morgan," I said, trying to find the words to calm her down. "No one thinks you're a bad parent."

"Think they're leaving," Stan said, ambling into the kitchen. I wasn't sure how much he'd heard, but it was enough to make him stand closer than usual to his daughter.

"It sounds like Etta's done," Morgan said, swallowing hard. "I'll go get her so she can say good-bye."

She spun and left the room, and I watched her disappear down the hall until Stan's voice got my attention.

"Not sure what you people are doing here," he said, shaking his head. He lifted his hand to stop me when I opened my mouth to reply. "But she don't give no second chances, so you may want to watch yourself."

"My parents just wanted to meet their granddaughter," I said when he'd finished.

"Well, they've done that," he said with a hum.

He walked away and I went to where my parents were standing in the entryway, waiting for me. They didn't look like they were in a hurry to leave, but the decision to go had clearly already been made.

"All better," Morgan said with forced brightness as she carried Etta toward us. "Sometimes we have a hard time when we have to do things we don't want to do, right, Etta?"

"Don't we all," my dad said jokingly. "Thanks again for having us."

"My pleasure," Morgan said, trying and failing to hide how uncomfortable she was.

My mom moved forward and kissed Etta on the top of her head, then smiled thinly at Morgan.

"Mike and I were wondering if you and Etta would like to come and visit us soon," she said. "Just think about it, and we can talk later."

Mom smiled again and then followed Dad out of the house, leaving Morgan and me standing there dumbfounded. How my mom had thought it was appropriate to ask Morgan to visit after the last few minutes was completely beyond me, and I could tell that Morgan was confused, too.

"I'll talk to her," I said quietly, meeting Morgan's eyes.

"Thanks for coming to visit the munchkin," she said kindly, dismissing me. "She had an awesome time."

I nodded and tickled Etta's side gently, then left the house. That was that.

* * *

We left Sacramento the next morning. I spent the entire drive home trying to tune out my mom and dad while they talked about Morgan and Etta, the trip, and the proposed visit. I had no idea why they thought Morgan would agree to come to Oregon after they'd made things so uncomfortable for her the day before, but I didn't say a word. I wasn't about to start an argument when we'd be stuck in the car for hours. They barely shut up, but thankfully we were home by dinnertime.

I'd made the decision to take a step back from my relationship with Morgan, but as each month passed, it got harder to keep my distance. I'd spent the early years of my life trying everything I could to make people like me and welcome me into their lives, and I refused to do that as an adult. Frankly, I had too much respect for myself ever to go down that road again.

Life slowly went back to how it had been before my first trip to Anaheim. I went to work, hung out with my cousins, and debated getting a dog. It was as if nothing had changed, even though, for me, everything had.

I didn't expect to hear from Morgan again.

Chapter 12

Morgan

Charity will ring you up," I said, grinning at the eighteen-year-old girls who'd come in to get matching nose rings and were currently beaming with happiness at their new hardware. "Jesse?" I called into the little waiting room. "You're up, man!"

My fears of leaving all of my regular customers and their referrals behind had been for nothing. The new shop I'd found, with a little help from Olly, was busy all on its own. Their reputation was so solid the customers coming in didn't even care which piercer they ended up with. They knew they were in good hands, and I was making a steady income on commission. We hadn't had any slow days since I'd started.

Thank God, life was finally getting back into a somewhat normal routine again. Etta was staying with my aunt Lorraine while I worked and she wouldn't even let me pay her, so I was building up a pretty sweet little nest egg. Everything was working out far better than I'd envisioned.

There was only one snag in my happy ending, and it was

shaped like a muscly logger with a beard that I could still feel in my palms if I was daydreaming hard enough. I ignored the voice in my head begging me to call and apologize for the shitty way I'd treated him.

I'd handled that situation badly and I was too much of a coward to do anything about it. I just kept remembering the look on his face when I'd said it was a mistake. Jesus. I may as well have kicked him in the balls.

It didn't help that his mom had been so weird the next day. If anything, her behavior had only confirmed my opinion at the time. It was only later, after I'd cooled down and stopped freaking out and I'd received the first of many friendly texts from Ellie, that I'd realized how badly I'd messed up.

I knew I was too worried about what people would think. I hadn't always been that way. For a long time, I'd done whatever the hell I'd wanted and damned other people's opinions. However, as soon as I'd had Etta, all of that had changed.

Old fears had risen to the surface with the birth of my daughter. I knew how lives could be turned upside down due to prejudices. I'd seen it during the long year when my dad had fought to get us back.

There wasn't any part of me that thought Trevor would sit idly by if his mom decided to cause problems for me. However, I couldn't be *sure*. He was a self-admitted mama's boy.

So instead of calling or even texting, I completely cut contact.

To my surprise, I really missed him. I missed the texts throughout the day and the random phone calls at night. I missed being able to send photos of Etta doing something funny to someone other than my sister. I also missed the sex.

Even though it had happened only once, and I'd gone a long time without before, it was as if my body was constantly primed for it now.

After finishing up Jesse's bridge piercing with a barbell that sat right between his eyes, I sent him off to pay and cleaned my station from top to bottom. He was my last client and I was looking forward to picking Etta up and grabbing some dinner. I loved what I did, but my back ached like crazy from leaning over people all day.

I said good-bye and left the shop with a little bounce in my step. Sure, I was still debating what to do about Trevor, and I'd been fielding texts and calls from his mom all week, but life was still looking up. I wasn't sure what I was going to do about Etta's visiting her grandparents, but so far Ellie seemed to be giving me a little space to figure it out. Most of the contact we'd had revolved around how Etta and I were doing. She didn't pressure me to choose a time when we could see them again, but the question was always there, right beneath the surface conversation. No matter how kind Ellie was to me now, I couldn't get past the way she'd looked at me and the comments she'd made to Trevor when they'd come to visit. I wasn't sure when I'd be ready to spend any real time with her again. Thankfully, I didn't have to make any decisions about that tonight.

As I debated between the sushi place near our house and delivery pizza, my phone rang in my purse.

I almost ignored it. If Etta had been with me, I would have. Thank God I didn't.

When I answered, my sister's voice came through the line and my stomach twisted.

"Morgan," she rasped, hiccupping like she couldn't catch her breath. "I think I did something stupid."

"Are you okay?" I asked in alarm. "Ranna? *Are you okay?*"

"I don't know," she replied, her voice wobbling.

I gritted my teeth as I quickly opened my door and climbed inside.

"Are you hurt? Where are you?" Throwing my car into reverse, I held my phone with my shoulder and backed out of my parking space.

"I'm not hurt," she said, sniffling. "I don't think I'm hurt."

"What do you mean, *you don't think you're hurt?*" I snapped frantically as I raced toward my aunt and uncle's house.

"Can you come to Bend?" she asked, not clarifying. "I'm sorry. I know you just started that new job and—"

"Of course," I said, not thinking it through. "I'm on my way."

She started to cry and my eyes filled with tears. I'd never been able to stay calm when my sister was upset. Ever since we were little kids, I'd felt her pain almost as acutely as my own.

I had no idea what was going on and no idea why she needed me, but it didn't matter. She'd never asked me to come to her before. Sure, there had been times when her homesickness had made it almost impossible for her to stay in Oregon at college, and two years before, she'd broken up with her boyfriend and had called every night because she was so lonesome, but she'd never asked me to come to Oregon. Not once.

"I'm on my way home from work," I said soothingly as she cried. "I just have to get Etta and pack and then we'll be on our way."

"Don't tell Dad," she said frantically, her words garbled and nasally.

"Ranna, I have to tell him we're leaving," I argued as I pulled onto my aunt's street. "We live with him."

"Don't tell him why. *Please*, Mor."

The sick feeling in my belly turned into something else as I pulled to a stop and stared out the windshield. Whatever had happened to Ranna must have been ugly if she didn't want our dad to know. We told him almost everything. When Miranda had called to tell me that she was having a bad high from some weed she'd scored off a friend, I'd called my dad to pick her up. When I'd found out I was pregnant from a guy I knew I didn't have a future with, I'd called my dad as soon as I'd hung up with Miranda. We kept personal things to ourselves, but we didn't keep secrets in our family. Not without reason. And the only reason I could think of that Miranda would refuse to tell our dad that she was upset was if she thought he'd do something that would land him back in prison.

"Okay," I said finally. "I won't tell him why."

"You promise?"

"I promise."

I glanced at the house and saw Etta waving excitedly in the front window.

"I'm at Danny and Lorraine's," I told Miranda. "I'm going to go in and get Etta. I'll let you know as soon as I'm on the road."

"Okay."

As I climbed out of the car, I realized that she'd never answered one of my questions.

"Where are you?" I asked, jerking to a stop.

"In my dorm."

"You're safe?"

"Yeah."

I ground my teeth at her short answers.

"Lock your door and stay there," I ordered.

"I'm okay, Mor," she said, her breath hitching as the crying stopped.

"No you're not," I argued, my nose stinging. "But I'll be there soon, okay?"

Once we were off the phone, I hurried to get Etta. It was a nightmare trying to leave my aunt in any kind of rush. Usually I stayed for coffee and visited for a few minutes, but I could barely carry a conversation with the questions and fears running through my head.

The two hours it took between Miranda's phone call and the minute we started north in my car were some of the longest of my life. I'd succeeded in convincing my dad that I had a few days off for a surprise visit to see my sister, and barely talked him out of riding along, but after that I'd still had to pack, feed Etta dinner, and grab some energy drinks at the corner store before we could get on the road.

By the time we started north on Interstate 5, the sun was starting to set and Etta was getting drowsy in the backseat. I was thankful that she was such an easy kid to travel with, because we'd be driving all night in order to reach my sister as quickly as possible.

I hated that I had to bring Etta with me, but the alternative wasn't an option. We'd never been apart for more than nine hours while I worked, and that wasn't going to change anytime soon. She was still too little to be without me overnight. I guessed if she had another parent it would be different, but it was just me and her. Where I went, she went.

I called my sister once from the road to make sure she was okay, but left her alone after that. She seemed really tired and I was hoping she could get a little rest even if she didn't actually sleep. Besides, keeping my tired eyes on the road and my foot from pushing the gas pedal all the way to the floorboard took all of my energy anyway.

At three in the morning, after Etta had fallen asleep and we'd stopped for gas twice, I finally reached Miranda's college campus. It was quieter than I expected. Prettier, too. There were ornamental trees everywhere, and lots of grass, and even the parking lots filled with inexpensive cars were clear of trash and yard debris.

The campus was obviously well taken care of. I wasn't sure why that mattered to me, but it did. It was kind of comforting knowing that my sister lived and went to school in a nice place. There'd been years where I'd lived in complete dumps while I tried to figure out my life, so I was glad she was figuring hers out in a place that looked like this.

Finding her building was pretty easy since the campus was quiet and I could drive as slowly as I needed in order to read the well-placed signs on every corner. Finding a parking spot that didn't have a reserved sign on it was a little harder, but I managed. By that time I was so antsy to get out of the car and find my sister I'd have parked on the manicured grass if I hadn't found something pretty quickly.

I lugged sleeping Etta and our bag into Ranna's building using the code she'd texted to open the front door, then followed even more well-placed signs to her room on the second floor.

And then I just stopped, frozen. I needed to get to her, to

touch her and make sure she was okay, but a part of me was dreading the moment she opened that door and I had to face whatever it was that had made her need me there.

Finally, I lifted my hand and knocked using the rhythm we'd used as kids that let her know it was safe to open the door. I hadn't had to use it in more years than I could even remember. It took her almost a minute to come to the door and when she opened it, surprise and relief made me sway a little on my feet.

She was wearing a pair of my dad's old pajama pants and an oversized hoodie, and her hair was sticking up at all angles, but she looked fine. Haggard and sad, but physically I couldn't see anything wrong with her. Her hands were tucked into the sleeves of the hoodie and her long toes with chipped blue polish were peeking out of the hem of the pajamas, curled into the ugly brown carpet in a way that had always reminded me of a baby monkey. Everything seemed almost normal. It wasn't until she opened her mouth that every horrible thought that had run through my head in almost seven hours of driving was confirmed.

"Sissy," she whispered, her entire body seeming to sag in relief as her sad eyes met mine.

"What happened?" I asked, pushing inside the room.

I laid Etta down on the bed so I could wrap my arms around my sister.

"I don't know," she replied, her forehead resting against the side of my neck.

My arms tightened and I rocked her a little from side to side, the same way I did with Etta when she was upset.

"I don't know what happened. I woke up and I didn't remember anything."

My head began to pound.

"I went out. I'm always careful when I go out." Her body shuddered. "I'm a fucking senior. I'm not an idiot. I'm *always* careful."

"Okay," I said, unsure how to respond. "Okay. Who were you with when you went out?" She wasn't letting go of me so I didn't let go, either. I'd stand there in that spot all night if I had to, my muscles so tensed that I was practically vibrating.

"I went by myself."

I cringed, but didn't respond. Miranda had always been independent. She'd never needed a large group of friends or a posse to feel comfortable. She was just fine going to a restaurant or a movie on her own; if anything, I think she preferred it.

"And where did you go?" I asked when she didn't say anything else.

Her chest heaved against mine, and if it hadn't been silent in the room and I hadn't been listening intently, I wouldn't have heard her whispered "I don't remember."

I held her even tighter as the implications of her words set in. She'd gone out by herself and woken up alone in her room, but she had no idea where she'd been or what had happened. Hours and hours of her life just *gone*.

I swallowed hard and smoothed a hand down the back of her short hair.

"Were you sick when you woke up?" I asked, my voice trembling. "Do you hurt anywhere?"

Miranda was silent for a long moment.

"No," she replied.

Relief hit me first. Overwhelming, full-body relief. But

crashing on top of that, with the power of a sledgehammer, was the knowledge that my baby sister was lying. I wasn't sure if she was lying to both of us or just me, but I knew deep in my bones that she wasn't telling the truth.

"Thank you for coming," she said, lifting her head from my shoulder.

"Shut up," I replied, trying to lighten the mood, just a little. "I needed a break anyway."

We both knew that was a lie, too. I'd barely just started my new job after weeks of not working. I wasn't even sure if I was going to have a job to go back to. It didn't matter, though. Family trumped everything.

"I'm so tired," she said, dropping to the only chair in the room.

"Climb in with Etta," I ordered, stepping over to scoot Etta over against the wall. "She doesn't take up much space."

"No," Miranda argued quietly. "You've been driving all night. You sleep there. I'll—"

"Ranna," I murmured in warning, my big-sister voice coming out to play. "Get in bed."

And just like when we were little and she knew that I was in charge, my sister nodded and climbed into bed next to my daughter, curling around her with a sigh. I pulled Etta's blanket out of our bag and tucked it around their shoulders, swallowing the bile that rose in my throat as I wondered who'd done the same thing the night before.

The bed was tainted, I knew that much. I sat down in the chair across from them and beat back the need to pull them both up and burn the entire thing.

Who the hell had brought my sister home the night before?

Who had left her with no memory of what had happened and scared the shit out of her?

My mind raced as I sat there, listening as Miranda's breathing evened out. I was so angry I could barely see straight, and as the night wore on I went over and over possible scenarios. Someone must have seen her. She lived in a dorm, for Christ's sake. People were in and out of the hallways all the time. It had to be nearly impossible for someone to carry Miranda's passed-out body into her room without someone noticing.

Right?

I wanted to weep. I wanted to scream when Miranda jerked awake twice and then tried to hide the fact that she'd had a nightmare. I wanted to pull every sleeping college student in that building out of their beds and make them tell me where they'd been and what they'd been doing the night before. I wanted to pound on the walls and trash the tiny room.

I wanted to go back and teach Miranda that there was safety in numbers. I wanted to tell her that the college she'd chosen sounded awful and she should pick another. I wanted to have come to visit a week earlier so she wouldn't have been out alone.

By seven in the morning, I could hear people moving around outside Miranda's door as they got ready for the day, and that made me even angrier. Someone must have heard something. Someone had to have noticed *something*.

I left a note for Miranda on her desk and stepped outside the room, my eyes roving over every person I saw. Guys and girls were moving from place to place, not making eye contact or interacting at all as they stared at their phones and started their days. A sense of futility settled around my shoulders like a heavy blanket. Those people wouldn't have noticed if I'd come out of Miranda's room covered in blood and reeking like a sewer.

My hands shook as I pulled out my phone and scrolled through my contacts, finally settling on one. The only person I could stomach talking to. The man I'd treated like crap and had been ignoring for weeks.

Chapter 13

Trevor

I'd been up half the night with the black Lab puppy I'd finally broken down and adopted, so when my phone rang I didn't even bother to look to see who it was before answering it.

"You got Trevor Harris," I grumbled, assuming it was a work call as I walked toward my truck.

"Hey, Trevor Harris," a familiar voice replied, making me stumble to a stop and check the caller ID.

"Morgan Riley," I said, unable to hide the surprise in my voice.

I knew I'd see her at some point, since she'd been in contact with my mom and had agreed to visit again sometime, but I hadn't expected her ever to call me again. No, I pretty much figured I'd have to ignore the way she'd avoid me at any family function she brought Etta to, just to keep things civil.

"How've you been?" she asked.

I almost laughed, the question was so asinine. I'd gone from missing her like crazy to thinking that I may have made the wrong decision when I'd backed off, and I'd finally landed on being pissed at how she'd handled things and even more pissed at myself for getting into that situation in the first place. Why the hell was she calling me?

"I'm good," I answered flatly. I climbed into my truck and started her up without another word. I sure as hell wasn't going to carry the conversation. She was the one who'd called me.

"That's good," she said, the last word kind of fading to nothing at the end.

It was then that I noticed that her voice was off. Something was different. Something was wrong.

"Is Etta okay?" I asked.

"Yeah, she's fine," Morgan replied instantly. "She's good."

Then silence again. Not a single word that gave any kind of indication as to why she'd called me or what she needed. She just sat there on the phone, like it was completely normal.

We both broke the silence at the same time.

"What do you—"

"I think someone drugged my sister."

"Say what?" I snapped, my hand tightening on the steering wheel.

"I think someone drugged her," she said again, sounding completely baffled.

"You gotta give me some context here," I replied, trying to stay focused on the road. "Who drugged her?"

"I don't know," Morgan ground out. "I have no idea. She told me she can't even remember where she went and then she woke up in her dorm room."

"She's still in Oregon?" I asked, turning into the parking lot at work. "Do you need me to go over there?"

I couldn't imagine something like that happening to Kate or Ani while I was in a completely different state. The thought of being unable to get to them made me livid.

"No," Morgan replied. "No, I'm here."

"You're where?"

"I'm in Bend. I'm with my sister."

"You were with her?" I barked, my breath catching.

"She called me after," she clarified. "I drove up last night."

"Where's Etta?"

"She's with me," she answered, like it was the most normal thing in the world.

"Jesus Christ," I mumbled, throwing my truck into park as soon as I'd reached my parking spot. "Is your sister okay? Is she hurt? Are you okay? What do you need?" The words tumbled out before I could think them through.

"I'm okay," Morgan said, her voice wobbling. "I don't need anything."

"Are you sure?" After all the time that had passed and her absolute rejection, there had to be a reason for her call. At that point, I didn't even care what it was. I just wanted to give her whatever she needed.

Maybe that made me a sucker. I didn't care. If there was ever something in my power to give that Morgan needed, I was pretty sure I'd do my best to give it to her.

"I guess I just needed to hear your voice," she said quietly.

I felt those words in my chest.

"You can hear my voice whenever you want," I reminded her. It had never been my decision to stop talking—that had been all her doing.

"I know," she replied. "I screwed up." Her voice got high,

and I knew, even though I'd never heard that tone before, that she was crying.

"Hey," I said gently. "Hey, it's okay."

"She's really freaked out," Morgan said, sniffling. "She lost hours, Trevor. Poof. She has no idea what happened."

"Did she report it?" I asked, shaking my head as Bram started toward my truck. He spun on his heel and went inside the building instead. "Has she talked to anyone?"

"I don't think so. She called and asked me to come, so we drove up here last night. She said she didn't think she was hurt, but—"

I grimaced and consciously unwrapped my fist from where I'd been gripping the steering wheel. There were few things in my life that could make me completely lose it, and violence directed at women was one of them.

I didn't understand it, I didn't want to understand it, and just the thought of it made me see red.

"She needs to report it," I said, opening my truck door when it began to feel like there was no air left in the cab. "She needs to go today."

"I don't know if she will," Morgan mumbled after clearing her throat.

"What? Why?"

"Because," Morgan snapped, then sighed heavily. "Just because."

I shook my head in confusion but didn't argue. Even if I thought she was doing the wrong thing, her sister's decisions weren't my business. I didn't know Miranda. I'd heard plenty about her, but I hadn't ever actually met her.

"I better go back inside," Morgan said. "I don't want them to wake up when I'm not there."

"Okay." I scrubbed a hand over my face, not sure what to do. "Call if you need anything."

"Okay."

"Seriously, Morgan," I said. "If you need *anything*. I'm only a couple hours away."

As soon as she hung up, I hopped out of my truck and stood for a minute in the cool morning air, trying to calm down.

Was it shitty that I was glad Morgan had called, even though I hated the reason for it? The fact that she and Etta were only a couple hours away made me almost jittery.

"What's going on?" Bram called, walking out of the building as soon as he saw that I was off the phone.

I debated blowing him off, but only for a second.

"I was talking to Morgan."

"Really?" he asked dubiously. "What'd she have to say?"

All of the cousins knew something had gone down between us, but I was pretty sure Ani hadn't given them the details. Bram was her other half, though. I knew he'd heard the entire story.

"She's in Bend," I replied, nodding when his eyebrows shot up. "Something happened with her sister."

"She broke her leg or she's in a coma?" Bram asked, asking in his own ass-backwards way how bad the situation was.

"She woke up not remembering the night before," I said quietly through my teeth.

"Oh, fuck," he replied, instantly growing serious. "We need to go down there?"

"They have no idea what happened," I answered, shaking my head.

"Did she report it?" His question didn't surprise me, but I

did find it a little ironic that reporting it was the first thought in both of our minds, while Morgan and her sister felt exactly the opposite.

"She's not going to."

"Why?" Bram asked, completely baffled.

"I've got no clue." I started toward the front door but stopped before I made it to the sidewalk in front of the building.

"Man, why wouldn't you report shit like that?" Bram asked, coming up beside me. "That makes no sense."

"Agreed." I flexed my hands, wishing I could hit something.

I couldn't go inside. I couldn't work all day wondering what was happening on that college campus. I couldn't stay where I was, hours away from Morgan, knowing that she was with her sister who'd just been attacked.

Not only was she shouldering that responsibility alone, but she also had a two-year-old with her, and God only knew who had drugged her little sister.

"You heading over there?" Bram asked, reading my mind.

"She's probably going to be pissed."

"Who fucking cares," Bram replied with a shrug. "At least you'll be there if she needs ya."

I paused and met his eyes.

"Hey, man," he said, lifting his hands out in front of him. "No judgment. I kept going back after Anita dropped my ass. I know it's not always as simple as it looks. *She* called you."

"Ani told me to back off."

"If I'd backed off, me and my woman wouldn't be where we're at now," Bram said easily.

I nodded. "I'll call you later."

"I'll do your job for you," he called out as I walked back to the truck. "Just like fucking always."

I flipped him off over my shoulder and left without another word.

Three hours later, I was checking into a hotel in Bend.

* * *

"What do you mean, you're here?" Morgan asked tiredly when I called to find out exactly where they were.

"I'm in Bend."

"Oh."

When she didn't say anything else, I got worried.

"Morgan?"

"You didn't have to come here," she said slowly. "I'm pretty sure my sister's going to be pissed if she knows you did."

"I'm here for you," I said simply. "Where are you?"

"But *I'm* here for my sister," she said, not quite an argument, but close enough.

"Morgan, where are you?"

Surprisingly, she didn't hesitate when she rattled off her sister's building name and room number, and as soon as I got off the phone I headed in that direction. Bend is a growing town, but it isn't very big. However, it's pretty spread out. It took me about twenty minutes to get to the university's campus, but only five to find Miranda's building and charm my way inside.

Their security was shit. All I'd had to do was ask someone to hold the door for me as I'd pretended to look for something in my pockets, and I'd been let inside without a thought. I knew most colleges were that way. I'd visited Kate at school years ago and it had been the same in her dorm building, and it had bothered me then just as much as it bothered me now.

I found Miranda's room easily, and before I'd even knocked I could hear Etta chattering inside.

"Who are you?" a girl who looked almost exactly like Morgan asked as soon as she answered the door. Her hair was cut short on the sides and she had an eyebrow ring. She also had puffy dark half-circles under her eyes.

"Twevo!" Etta yelled, running past Miranda. "You heah!"

"Hey, baby girl," I responded, swinging her up as she reached me. "I missed you."

"Me missed you!" she tightened her arms around my neck and pressed her cheek to mine as I met Miranda's eyes.

"I should have known she'd call you," she said in resignation. "Come on in."

The room was small, but tidy. There was a desk and chair, a bed, and a tall dresser, but nothing that shouted someone with a personality actually lived there. Everything was— blank. Like a clean slate.

"I'm not much of a decorator," Miranda said with a shrug when she noticed my perusal.

"Me either," I confessed. "But I'm pretty sure I'm better at it than you."

Miranda smiled, but I didn't get the chuckle I was hoping for. Instead, she glanced at the woman lying with her back to us, her body wrapped in a sweater on top of a bare mattress.

"Morgan just finally passed out," she said quietly. "She was up all night."

"Did you get some sleep?" I asked gently, staying where I was by the door.

I was a big man, and I'd been a big man since I was about sixteen years old. And in that small dorm room, with a girl who'd just been terrorized and couldn't even remember it, I probably seemed even bigger. I wasn't about to move any closer.

"I got some," she answered, smiling wanly. "Probably still dealing with some aftereffects."

She said it so calmly that I had a hard time controlling my expression.

"You should tell someone," I said, leaning over to set Etta on the floor when she started to wiggle.

"Who?" Miranda asked, shrugging one shoulder. "The police? I don't know anything. I can't even remember what happened after I walked out that door." She pointed to the door at my back. "I'm pretty sure I waited too long for any blood test to tell us what I took, and I'm sure as hell not letting any doctor feel me up in the off chance that they'll find a hair that's not mine."

"You have a pretty cynical view of the system," I replied calmly.

"Oh, come on, man," she replied with a scoff. "You know it's true. Plus, you know what everyone will think. That girl shouldn't have gone out alone. She should have been more careful. Why does she think we can help her, when she doesn't have any fucking clue what happened? Maybe she's making it up. Maybe she drank too much and now she's trying to play it off like she doesn't remember."

"Bullshit," I said, finally cutting off her diatribe. "I haven't thought a single one of those things."

"You're not a cop."

"Why the fuck does that matter?"

"Because, it does," she ground out. "Cops look at women like me, and they see trash."

"No one could look at you and see trash," I countered, shaking my head. "Not a single person."

"Oh, yeah?" she said. "You know how many times my social worker looked the other way when I was in the system? Do you know how many times I called the cops that year and *they* looked the other way?"

"Cops are just like any other group of people," I argued. I knew that as much as anyone. It sucked but it was the truth. "You've got bad ones and good ones. Shitbags and heroes."

"It doesn't even matter," she said, her voice strained. "It happened and now it's over. Someone drugged me and I lost a few hours of time that I can't get back. The end."

"Is that all they did?" I asked gently, absently jiggling my toes up and down as Etta sat on my foot, bouncing her up and down on the floor.

"Yes," Miranda answered flatly.

"It's none of my business," I said.

"No it's not."

"But if anything else happened—"

"It didn't."

"You need to go to a clinic," I continued, ignoring her denial. "You need to get checked and you need a morning-after pill, and anything else they can give you."

"Nothing happened," she said again.

"Okay," I replied, tipping my head down in concession. "But if you're not sure, you need to go in."

"I'm sure."

"Okay," I said again.

"I have to pee," she said, ending the conversation. "And you can come out of the doorway."

She walked to the connected bathroom and shut herself inside, but I didn't move. Something had happened that she wasn't willing to admit, but it wasn't my job to make her face it. What had happened was something I'd never deal with or be able to understand.

"Thank you," Morgan whispered as she rolled over, tears running down her cheeks as she faced me. "I didn't even think of that." She shuddered with a silent sob. "She needs to see a doctor."

"Don't know if she'll agree to it," I murmured back, keeping my voice low.

"She will," Morgan said, wiping at her face as she sat up. "She's been listening to me since she was born—that's not stopping today."

My lips twitched, but I didn't reply. Miranda seemed pretty fucking similar to her older sister, and I couldn't imagine anyone talking either of them into doing something they didn't want. I guessed if anyone could make Miranda do something, though, it would be Morgan, and vice versa.

I watched the woman I'd been thinking of and missing get up off the bed and straighten her shoulders before smiling widely at Etta. Then, as she stepped toward me and wrapped her arms around my waist, resting her forehead against my chest, I knew with absolute certainty that I loved her.

Just like that, I knew. I loved her like I'd never loved anyone else. I loved her in a way that I knew wouldn't go away.

I loved her strength and her compassion and her understanding. I loved the way she became a lioness when it came to her family. I loved the way she could muster up a smile for her baby even in the tensest circumstances. I loved that she'd apologized when she knew she'd done something wrong. I loved that she was stubborn and a little guarded. I loved the way her fine hair got stuck in my beard, and the feeling as she pulled away and the strands tickled my chin. I loved the way she fit me. And more than anything, I loved that when she'd needed me, she'd called, trusting that I'd be there even after the way shit had ended the last time we'd seen each other.

But Jesus, what a terrible time to realize that I was in love with her.

The door opened, and as soon as Morgan spun out of my arms, Miranda walked out, her hands raised in surrender.

"You're right," she said, moving slowly toward her dresser. "I need to go to a doctor."

"I'll go with you," Morgan said, grabbing her bag off the floor. "Just let me get changed and I'll make an appointment."

"Do I need one?" Morgan asked, pausing with her hands inside one of her dresser drawers.

"It doesn't matter," Morgan answered reassuringly. "I'll get you in to see someone today."

Miranda's relief at her sister's words was almost a physical presence in the room. It was clear that she trusted Morgan's word implicitly. If her older sister said she'd do something, she would. End of story.

Henry had felt that way about me. He'd trusted Shane, too, but their relationship had been very different. I'd been Henry's protector. I'd been the one to double-knot his shoes before school and give him a piggy-back ride when he fell and hurt himself. I'd been the one to keep the monsters at bay when he hadn't wanted to wake our parents up after a nightmare. I had no fucking clue why he hadn't felt comfortable telling me about Etta, but goddamn it broke my heart.

I quietly played with Etta while Miranda got dressed and Morgan called the local women's clinic. I was pretty sure that the campus had their own clinic, but according to Morgan's mumbling, they were useless. I didn't bother to ask why. The woman was on a mission and within fifteen minutes she had an appointment made for her little sister.

"I'm not sure how—" Morgan said to me, her words sliding to a halt as she grimaced.

"How about I just ride with you?" I said, wishing I could reach out and slide my hand over her hair, but knowing, as she fidgeted and paced, that it wasn't the right time for that. "I'll keep Etta while you ladies go in."

"*Ladies* is a stretch," Miranda said drily as she came out of the bathroom. She was still wearing the shirt she'd had on before, but had pulled on a different hoodie and pair of jeans.

"Is that okay with you?" Morgan asked her as she picked up Etta's diaper bag. "If Trevor comes along?"

"Fine with me," Miranda replied with a shrug.

I stepped into the hallway first. Morgan had Etta in her arms and was close behind me. But it took only a few seconds to realize that Miranda hadn't followed.

We both looked back to see what the holdup was, and my entire body grew tight as I witnessed Miranda's eyes fill with terror. She froze. Her entire body, from her eyelashes to her fingertips, went completely still as she reached the threshold to her room.

"Ranna?" Morgan called softly.

Miranda's chest started to heave visibly beneath her baggy sweatshirt, and I took a slight step forward because I wasn't completely sure that she was going to stay upright.

"Need a second," Miranda rasped, trying to control her breathing.

"Take as long as you want," Morgan replied instantly.

We stood there watching Miranda calm herself down until I couldn't take another second of her clenched teeth and fisted hands.

"Miranda," I murmured, taking another step forward.

"What?" she said quickly, her embarrassment clear.

"I'm a big guy, yeah?"

"So?"

"You want to come out of there," I said, nodding to her bedroom. "You can. No one's going to even look at you while I'm here."

She glanced down the hallway in both directions, but still didn't step through the door. Etta chattered to Morgan and wriggled a little to get down, but Miranda still didn't move. My phone chimed with an incoming text message that I ignored, but still Miranda didn't even twitch.

Then, without warning, she stepped forward and pulled the door closed behind her. Moving swiftly, she came close to my side, then flinched when I moved to put my arm around her shoulders.

"Don't," she blurted. "Don't touch me, okay?"

"No problem," I said easily, but inside I was trying not to completely lose it.

Miranda and I followed Morgan downstairs, side by side but

carefully not touching. It was sprinkling rain outside, and we hurried to Morgan's car as Miranda pulled her hood up over her head.

"I'll sit in the back," Miranda said, climbing in before I could protest.

I wasn't sure how I'd fit in the back of that car, but I would have at least offered to. I watched as Morgan buckled Etta into her seat, reaching past her to touch Miranda's knee before leaning back out of the car.

"Can you drive?" Morgan asked, speaking up for the first time since we'd stood waiting for Miranda to leave her room. "I'll navigate."

"Sure." I walked around the car and met her at the back, but the minute I reached for her she shook her head.

"If you touch me, I'll lose it," she said shakily, tossing me her keys. "I'm hanging on by a thread here."

"You're doing good," I replied, holding her gaze.

"I'm trying. *Fuck*."

"Sometimes a real curse word goes a long way, huh?" I replied, a little relieved when my comment made her lips twitch, just a fraction.

"Sometimes," she agreed.

It took us only fifteen minutes to reach the clinic, but Miranda's appointment lasted two hours. By the time Morgan led her pale-faced sister outside to meet us, Etta was fussing and I was pacing the small patch of grass we'd commandeered as our own. I had no idea what would take so long, but knew it wasn't anything good.

"Let's go," Morgan said, ushering her sister straight to the car.

"Come on, sweet thing," I said to Etta, picking up our stuff as I hurried after her mother.

Without any direction, I drove us back to Miranda's dorm building. The two women in the car were completely silent until I put the car in park. Then, when I was about to climb out of the driver's seat, Miranda finally spoke.

"I'm not going back in there," she said firmly, staring out her window in the backseat.

I let my hand fall from the keys in the ignition and waited for Morgan to respond.

"Okay," she said, slowly. "Okay."

We sat there in silence for a few more minutes. I kept my mouth shut as they contemplated our next move, and barely moved as Morgan's hand settled on mine.

"I'll go grab your stuff," she said, turning toward the backseat. "You have garbage bags?"

"In the bottom of the can," Miranda replied dully.

"Okay, I'll be right back."

My hand tightened on Morgan's as she tried to pull away.

"I'll come with you."

When neither sister argued, I nodded and climbed out of the car. We waited until Miranda had locked the doors behind us, then trudged inside the building. I didn't know how Morgan felt, but after Miranda's long-ass doctor appointment, her dorm room seemed almost sinister. I'd known something bad had gone down there, but now that my thoughts had been confirmed, the place made my skin crawl.

I could barely restrain myself from stopping every guy I saw, just to look closely at his face. Was that guy the one? The dude in the blue sweatshirt? What about the gray jacket? Was he the douche bag?

I was looking at every face, searching for guilt.

"My sister doesn't have much stuff," Morgan said as she pushed resolutely into the small room.

She went straight to the garbage can in the corner and pulled the trash bag out of it. Underneath were four more unused bags that she tossed onto the bed.

"I'm going to do her clothes first, then the desk."

"I can do the desk," I replied, grabbing a trash bag. "Should I leave anything?"

"No." She cleared her throat. "No, she's not coming back."

I stopped and watched as Morgan angrily opened the top drawer, almost pulling it completely out of the dresser.

"She's never coming back to this place," she hissed, snatching out handfuls of clothes and stuffing them into the garbage bag in her other hand.

"Sweetheart," I said softly, trying to calm her.

"I can't," she said, shaking her head and refusing to turn toward me. "I need to get her stuff out of here. *I* need to get out of here."

"Okay," I replied, clenching my jaw. I wanted to wrap my arms around her and force her to take a second, but I didn't. Instead, I turned toward the desk and quickly removed the notebooks, pens, and random school shit. It ended up being really heavy and I had to double-bag it, but thankfully Miranda really didn't have much.

All of her personal items filled only three garbage bags.

"Just a sec," Morgan said, walking into the bathroom. She came out only a few seconds later with a small makeup bag in her hand. "I'll replace the rest of it," she murmured, shaking her head.

Then I was lifting the bags from the floor and following her out of the room. A few people watched as we moved through the common areas, but no one said a word as we carried Miranda's things out of the dorm. Not one person asked who we were or why we were stealing bags of shit from one of their schoolmates. It was the weirdest fucking thing.

"Trunk," Morgan said, opening it up so I could put Miranda's things back there. As soon as I'd dropped them in, her head drooped forward. "Jesus."

I wasn't sure if it was a prayer or an exclamation. Maybe it was both.

"Let's get the fuck out of here," I said, reaching up to cup the side of her face.

"I don't even know where to go," she said with a watery laugh. "I need to get a hotel room or something."

"I've got one," I replied, sliding my hand down to squeeze the back of her neck gently. She seemed so brittle, standing there, that I was afraid to touch her anywhere else.

"Okay. Where are you parked?"

We agreed that she'd follow me back to my hotel, and I left as soon as she'd climbed into the driver's seat. As I passed the car, I glanced inside the backseat and saw Miranda leaned against Etta's seat. The baby was sleeping peacefully, and Miranda was holding her hand. It was as if she'd needed that connection, even though Etta was completely passed out beside her.

When I climbed into my truck, my phone chimed again.

The message I'd ignored earlier was from Katie, and I ignored it again. The most recent message was from Morgan.

Hotel won't work. Miranda refuses to stay anywhere near here. Thanks anyway.

I sighed and brushed a hand over my face, smoothing down my beard.

Makes sense. My house?

I sent the text, not expecting an agreement, so when the reply came, I was shocked.

I checked my rearview mirror at least fifty times as I drove home. Every time, the Riley women were still following right behind me.

Chapter 14

Morgan

Going to Trevor's house wasn't my smartest idea. I knew that. However, when I'd made the suggestion to Miranda and she'd agreed, I hadn't had the heart to refuse. At that point, I would have done anything to make her feel safe.

Trevor seemed to do that for her. I'd seen her glance out the tinted windows of the doctor's office more than once and watch as Trevor had played with Etta in the grass. For some reason, he seemed to help her. Maybe it was from his "I'm big and strong" speech when we were standing in the hallway, or the inherent kindness that seemed to ooze out of him. I think a part of her may have been reminded a little of the day our dad had come to get us from our caseworker's office. Whatever it was, I wasn't willing to take it away.

She'd been through enough.

I refused to let myself think about the things that had gone down in that doctor's office. Miranda had let me stay only after I'd promised not to go crazy. She'd known even before they'd called us back that it wasn't going to be pretty. There'd been a lot hidden under the baggy clothes she was wearing. Things that I couldn't bear to think about. Not yet.

"This is it," Trevor announced as I climbed out of my car. "I'll get everything opened up, and you guys can make yourselves at home."

I nodded as he nervously headed toward his front door. I wasn't sure what he was nervous about—*we* were the ones who were intruding on his space. As soon as he disappeared into the house, I turned to where my sister was gingerly climbing out of the car. The long drive must have made her achy because she winced as she stretched.

"He lives in the middle of nowhere," she said, her voice scratchy after the hours of silence.

"Like a serial killer," I replied.

"Or a hermit," she shot back with a shrug.

"Is that better?"

Before she could answer, Trevor's garage door rolled open and he strode out, carrying a wriggling black puppy.

"Jesus," Miranda mumbled. "It's like a freaking lumberjack calendar."

"Sorry," Trevor said sheepishly as he set the puppy down. "I let him out this morning, but my cousin hasn't been here yet to let him out again."

"You have a puppy," I said dumbly. He'd told me during our long conversations that he wanted one, but I hadn't known he'd actually gotten one.

"Oh, hey," Miranda said softly as the puppy went straight to her. "You're freaking adorable. What's your name?" She crouched down, and I inhaled sharply at the grimace she tried to hide.

"He doesn't have one yet," Trevor replied, striding toward us.

"You haven't named him?" I asked as the puppy jumped around Miranda like she was the best thing he'd ever seen.

"Any ideas?" Trevor asked.

"He looks like a bear," Miranda said, getting slowly to her feet as the puppy went to look for the perfect spot to pee.

"Koda," I said softly, watching as the little furball sniffed every tree and bush.

"*Brother Bear*," Miranda said, her lips curving a little bit.

"Good choice," Trevor replied. "I haven't seen that movie in years."

"Etta likes it," I mumbled, shrugging.

"Henry liked it, too," Trevor said nonchalantly. "He used to watch it even when he was a teenager."

"That's because Henry was a lost boy," Miranda said.

I stiffened. I'd heard her use that phrase before.

"Lost boy?" Trevor asked.

"Yeah." Miranda wasn't looking at us, and I gritted my teeth because there was no way to stop her from saying whatever insulting thing was about to come out of her mouth. "He never grew up."

Trevor made a choking noise in his throat.

"Jesus, Ranna," I hissed, shaking my head in embarrassment.

"No," Trevor said slowly. "That's a pretty good description."

My gaze shot to his, and I was surprised to find understanding there.

"I'll never pretend he was perfect," Trevor said, loud enough for Miranda to hear. "But he was my baby brother and I love him."

"That's how I feel about my little sister," I replied through my teeth, glancing at Miranda. "Even when she's unkind."

"Sorry," Miranda said, leaning against the side of the car. "It's been a long day."

"No worries," Trevor replied before I could chastise her again. "You guys want to come in before it starts raining?"

My little sister started toward the house without another word. We watched her walk slowly inside, and I took a deep breath. It looked like we were definitely staying. Why was I so anxious about going into that house?

"Want me to grab Etta?" Trevor asked, resting his hand on my back as he passed me.

Oh, yeah. Now I remembered why I was so damn jumpy. Just that small touch, and my skin felt like it was on fire.

* * *

After a tour of the house and bathroom stops for all of us, I stood in the kitchen with Etta, unsure what to do. Miranda had closed herself into a bedroom the minute she'd seen it, and I was trying to give her a little while alone before I intruded. My normally chatty sister was anything but, and I had a feeling that she needed the quiet.

I wasn't going to leave her alone for long, though, especially after the things I'd seen during that doctor's exam earlier. This wasn't the first time I'd watched Miranda retreat into her shell, but it was the first time since we'd reached adulthood. Whether it had been the luck of the draw, or the fact that she'd been younger than I was, she'd dealt with far more abuse when we were in the system than I had. I'd been placed with families who were mostly like the Harrises, but Miranda hadn't been so lucky. When we'd reunited I'd barely recognized the sister I'd been separated from. It had taken years for our relationship to go back to what it once was. I'd always felt guilty for that.

"Are you guys hungry?" Trevor asked, coming in from whatever he'd been doing outside.

"Twevo!"

"Hey, sweet thing," Trevor said, grinning at Etta. "Did you have a good nap?"

"Me no nap," Etta argued, wrinkling her nose.

"Oh, sorry," Trevor conceded, lifting his hands in mock surrender.

"Me hungwy."

"I'm okay," I cut in with a small shake of my head. I wasn't sure how I'd choke anything down, my stomach was still so upset.

"I'll just grab Etta something, then," he said, watching for my nod before he moved toward the fridge. "I've got some apple slices in here."

"Apples!" Etta said, kicking her legs to get down.

I set her on her feet and moved to the counter, practically collapsing onto the bar stool there. Man, I was exhausted. I hadn't really slept since the night before last and now that the adrenaline was wearing off I was beginning to feel the effects.

"You have presliced apples?" I asked, leaning my elbows on the counter as Trevor crouched down to hand Etta the small package.

"Yeah. It's wasteful," he said sheepishly. "But I don't like eating apples whole."

"They taste different when they're sliced?" I asked, sort of joking, but mostly confused.

"No." Trevor smiled up at me. "I just don't like biting into them. The skin gets stuck in my front teeth."

"I feel that way about corn on the cob."

"What?" He shook his head in disappointment. "You don't like corn on the cob? That's just wrong."

"I never said I didn't like it," I murmured, resting my head on my arms. "I just always cut it off the cob instead of eating it like a savage."

"Sabbage," Etta said dramatically, chomping into an apple slice.

"You're so ferocious," Trevor replied, poking her gently in the side.

"No, Me is sabbage," Etta growled, baring her teeth and half the apple in her mouth.

"She's something," I mumbled with a snort.

"Hey," Trevor said quietly, coming to his feet. "Why don't you lay down for a while?"

"I'm okay," I argued, straightening. I was tired, but it wasn't like I was about to drop. I still had things to do. I needed to check on Miranda. Etta was peeking inside all the kitchen cabinets she could reach, and I had to make sure she didn't get into anything she wasn't supposed to. At some point, I needed to call my dad and tell him where we were, without telling him why we were there. I couldn't just go to sleep, I had to keep an eye on everything and everyone. That was my job.

"Well, I can keep an eye on the little miss," Trevor said, replying to the words I hadn't realized I'd muttered under my breath. Maybe I was more tired than I thought. "Why don't you go in and check on your sister? Your dad can wait."

I looked at him, then at Etta, then back at him again. I trusted him. I wouldn't be in his house if I didn't. However, leaving my child in someone else's care had never been easy for me, and his muscular shoulders and beautiful smile didn't change that.

"We'll stay in the house," he promised, lifting Etta into his arms. "Watch a movie. Maybe go get the P-U-P-P-Y out of his kennel for a little playtime."

I shook my head. "I'm okay—"

"Let me do this for you," Trevor said firmly, cutting me off. "Let me help."

"You've already helped," I replied, waving a hand through the air at his clean but oddly impersonal house.

"Then let me help some more."

We stared at each other for a long time before I finally conceded with a small nod. I rose wearily from my seat and ran a hand down my ponytail, glancing around to make sure there wasn't anything else I needed to do before I went in to Miranda.

"We're good," Trevor said, coming around the counter. "Go."

"Mama's going to take a nap," I told Etta. "You want to hang with Trevor for a while?"

"Twevo," she mumbled around her mouth full of apple, nodding happily.

"Be careful," I warned him. "Make sure she chews it up really good."

"I will," he said, resting a hand on my back for just a second before giving me a gentle shove. "This isn't my first rodeo."

"Yeah, yeah. She has a sippy cup and diapers in the diaper bag. There's also a change of clothes. Not sure why she'd need them, but—"

"Morgan," Trevor mumbled in amusement. "Go."

"Fine."

I walked down the hallway and knocked quietly on my sister's door but didn't wait for her to answer it before I pushed my way inside. She was lying on the bed on top of the linens, but she'd pulled the sides of the comforter up until she was wrapped like a burrito, and she was fast asleep.

I breathed a sigh of relief and climbed in next to her, careful not to touch her. We'd always been able to cuddle up when we shared a bed—it wouldn't be anything new, but I didn't want to chance it. She'd seemed okay when I'd touched her earlier in the day, but after she'd shied away from Trevor, I wasn't sure if I should make contact, especially when she was sleeping.

The pillow was thinner than I liked, so I gingerly folded it in half and stuffed it under my head, careful not to jostle the bed. Then I just lay there, staring at my baby sister's face. The lines between her brows were furrowed, and the dark half-moons under her eyes were still there, but for the first time since I'd walked into her dorm room she looked almost peaceful. It eased the tightness in my chest, just a little, but I knew it wouldn't last. Eventually, I fell into a deep sleep.

* * *

"Sis, you better wake up," Miranda said, shaking my shoulder sometime later that night.

When I opened my eyes, what little sun we'd had was

gone and it was almost completely dark outside the window. I wasn't sure how long I'd slept, but it wasn't nearly long enough. I still felt like crap.

"What's wrong?" I asked, searching her face. "Are you okay?"

"I'm fine," she replied. "You snore."

"No I don't."

"You really do."

"Is that why you woke me up?" I asked in irritation, scrubbing a hand down my face.

"No, I woke you up because someone's here. A woman."

"What?" I sat straight up in bed and turned my head toward the door.

"She got here a few minutes ago," Miranda said, unwrapping herself from the blanket. "Trevor sounded annoyed that she was here, but I couldn't hear what they were saying."

"Shit." Considering the fact that Trevor lived on his parents' property, I shouldn't have been surprised that someone had stopped by. I just hadn't thought about it because I was too worried about other things. I swung my legs off the bed and paused to let the dizziness pass. Ugh, I hated when I got up too quickly and felt like I was going to topple over. "Stay here," I ordered as soon as I had my land legs again.

"Bullshit," Miranda countered, following me to the doorway. "You're not leaving me in here."

As soon as I opened the door, I could hear Trevor's voice. He clearly wasn't annoyed any longer as he chuckled at something the woman said. My stomach twisted. I knew I shouldn't have taken a nap.

As soon as we reached the end of the hallway, Etta came into view. She was sitting in the middle of the living room with a bunch of coloring books spread out around her, calmly coloring something with a marker.

"I really hope that's not permanent," I said stupidly. It was the first thing that had popped into my head.

"It's not," Trevor said, standing up from the couch. "They're washable."

I turned to look at him, but didn't say anything else as our eyes met. I registered that there was a woman *and* a man sitting around the room, but I didn't acknowledge them while I waited for Trevor to explain what the heck they were doing in his house.

"I forgot to call and let them know they didn't have to take care of Koda tonight," he said sheepishly. "Sorry. I know you guys weren't up for visitors." He looked at Miranda, who was standing slightly behind me, and gave her an apologetic smile. "But once they knew you were here, they wouldn't franking leave."

"Jesus, you have him saying it now?" Miranda mumbled.

I didn't bother to reply, just continued to stare at Trevor, my blood boiling. I'd trusted him to take care of Etta while I was in the next room. I'd let my guard down, and this was how he'd repaid me?

"She's probably wondering who the hell we are," the woman said to Trevor, like she thought he was an idiot.

Huh. Maybe I liked her. It was too soon to tell, but the odds were good.

Trevor made an annoyed sound, then swept his hand toward the couple in the room. "This is Anita and Abraham, and their baby, Arielle."

My eyebrows rose as I glanced over and finally noticed the car seat with the sleeping baby on the floor.

"We're his cousins," Anita said, getting to her feet. "And you can call me Ani."

I shot one more look at Trevor, then stepped forward. "I'm Morgan," I said, reaching out to shake Ani's hand. "This is my sister, Miranda."

"Nice to meet you," Ani said. She shook my hand, but only gave Miranda a head nod. Abraham waved from the couch.

"Mama," Etta said, diverting my attention. "Baby!" She pointed to the car seat, then lifted a finger to her lips. "Her sleepin'."

"I see that," I said quietly, moving around the adults so I could kneel down in front of Etta. "What are you doing?"

"Me colorin'."

"Only on the paper, right?"

"Wight." She held up the book and proudly displayed the scribbled-on page.

"Nice work," I said, nodding. "I think that should go on the fridge."

"I'm sorry we just barged in," Ani said as soon as Etta was consumed with her task again. "We're kind of used to bugging Trev whenever we want."

"And she's nosy," Abraham cut in. "Once she knew you were here, I would've had to drag her out."

"It's okay," I said slowly, looking over at Miranda. She was still standing outside the living room area, but she didn't look uncomfortable. She'd leaned easily against the wall and seemed to be enjoying the show.

"Etta looks a lot like Henry," Ani said.

"I know," I replied. God, it was awkward. My hair was a mess from my nap, I was pretty sure my eyes had little crusties on them from sleeping, and I was in a strange house with a bunch of people I didn't know. There was no way I could make a good impression.

"Jesus," Ani said, shaking her head. "I know you do." She laughed at herself, and I couldn't help but admit that the sound eased my tension a little. "I'm no good at meeting new people. Swear to God, it's like my mind goes completely blank and I have no idea what to say."

"Just give her a minute," Trevor teased. "She'll figure it out pretty quick."

"Shut it, Trev," Ani said, shooting him a mock glare. "It's just that I heard Etta looked like my cousin, but it didn't really sink in how much until I'd actually seen her in person, you know?"

"Yeah," I replied, glancing at Etta. "She's pretty much all Hen."

"She's got your mouth, though," Trevor argued. When we glanced at him in surprise, he cleared his throat and looked at Miranda. "Miranda does, too."

"Oh, yeah," Ani said. "I can totally see that. It's the lips."

"And the smile," Trevor said, unwilling to let it go. "Same smile."

"Yeah, yeah," Miranda said jokingly. "We get it, man."

Abraham chuckled then, and I was pretty sure it startled Miranda and Etta as much as me. His laugh was infectious, and completely at odds with the strong, silent vibe he was giving off.

"I was going to start dinner," Trevor said uncomfortably in a clear attempt to change the subject. "Anyone else hungry?"

"Me hungwy," Etta replied, not bothering to lift her gaze from the coloring book.

"You're always hungry," Trevor teased. "Anyone else?"

"Actual food?" Abraham asked. "You're not going mad scientist again, are you?"

"Fridge is fully stocked," Trevor replied flatly.

"I'm hungry," Ani said, shrugging.

"Same," my sister chimed in.

"Sure," I mumbled, when everyone's eyes focused on me.

An hour later, I knew so much more about Trevor than I'd thought possible. There was something so different about watching someone in their natural habitat. I'd known he was funny and quick witted, but I hadn't realized how dry his sense of humor could be. That side of him came out when he was around his cousins, bantering back and forth. He was more sarcastic with them, his quips coming easily.

I'd known that he was good with Etta, but his affinity for kids was even more apparent when Arielle woke up and he was the first one to grab her out of her car seat. He held her while he moved around the kitchen, and only reluctantly gave her up when it was time for him to pull the taco casserole out of the oven.

His skill in the kitchen was something I remembered in vivid detail, but he was also a really good cook, which I hadn't even thought about. I'd watched quietly while he and Ani had moved around each other, cutting and browning and generally throwing things together like they'd been doing it for years—which they clearly had—but Trevor was the one who was in charge. Ani deferred to him, asking questions and looking for his approval. In the end, the dinner they'd thrown together was phenomenal, and even my sister had eaten a large helping.

I caught Miranda's eyes more than once, and while I

couldn't overlook the dullness in her expression as she tried to contribute a little to the conversation, I also noticed that she was intrigued by the dynamics, too. When Trevor had introduced his cousins, he'd made it seem like he hadn't had any choice about letting them inside the house, but dinner that night made it clear that wasn't the case. It hadn't been out of his hands; he'd just been unwilling to turn them away. I couldn't decide how I felt about that.

On one hand, I liked that he cared about their feelings. On the other, it really bothered me that he'd put their wishes before mine. It was silly. I knew that. They were his family. But somewhere, deep in my subconscious, I'd expected him to put me first and the fact that he hadn't hit me harder than I'd expected.

"You do piercings?" Ani asked, yanking me out of my silent contemplation.

"Yeah." I nodded. "For about four years now."

"Cool," she replied, grinning. "I've been thinking about getting another one. I always get bored and let them close up, and then a year later miss them and have to have them repierced again."

"A lot of people do that," I said. "Or they start working somewhere they aren't allowed to have them, and then come back to be repierced when they switch jobs."

"I'm a stay-at-home mom, now," she said, shrugging. "So that's not really a deal breaker for me anymore."

"That sounds nice," I replied, unsure what the common response was. I couldn't imagine being able to stay home with Etta. Would I like to? Maybe. I'd just never been in a position where money came without a shit-load of hard work.

"It's been an adjustment," Ani said conspiratorially. "But honestly, I love it. It was really hard leaving her all day."

"Yeah, I know that feeling," I agreed.

"At some point, I may want to go back—"

"No you won't," Abraham cut in with a smile, clearly teasing. "You'll just want to add a couple more."

"He's probably right," Ani grumbled. "I can't help it. Give me all the babies."

The entire group laughed.

"I'd like to have more at some point," I said, once it was relatively quiet again. "But Etta's a handful as it is."

"Me no handful," Etta said absentmindedly, stuffing ground-beef pieces into her mouth. "Me Etta."

"Right," I agreed drily.

"I'm just going to watch everyone else have them, enjoy them while I'm around, and go home to my quiet house when I'm done," my sister chimed in, lifting her drink into the air like she was saluting us.

"I was pretty sure that would be my future, too," Ani said quietly, looking at Abraham in a way that made me feel like I was intruding by witnessing it. "But life takes some crazy turns."

"Amen to that," Trevor said, speaking up for the first time in a while.

"I can't have kids," Ani said matter-of-factly. "Arielle's adopted."

"No, really?" my sister said in mock surprise, making me nearly choke on my drink. I glanced at the happy baby on her dad's lap. She had much darker skin than both her parents, but I never would have even thought about it until Ani threw the fact into our conversation.

"I know, right?" Ani said, laughing a little. "She's way too pretty to come from us."

"You're gorgeous," Abraham said, leaning back in his chair. "Shut up."

"I know, but you're practically a gargoyle," Ani shot back, making a face at him.

I smiled behind my glass. Abraham was many things, but he was about as far from one of those ugly statues as any man I'd ever seen. The guy could be a model.

"Good thing I'm fantastic in bed."

"And that's where I stop this conversation," Trevor said, setting his napkin on top of his plate. "I don't want to hear about any of that."

"I'd be willing to listen," my sister joked.

The smile on her face was worth every moment I'd spent with the unwelcome visitors. It was worth the disappointment I'd felt when I realized Trevor had introduced my daughter to people I didn't know. That small smile was a glimpse at the sister I knew, the one who breezed through life. My breath caught in my throat and I tried really hard not to let myself show any reaction.

Half an hour later the kitchen was clean, my sister was back in her room with a sleepy Etta, and Anita, Bram, and Arielle had left after a friendly round of hugs. The visit hadn't been as bad as I'd expected, but I was still worn out. It had been such a long day.

I was on the front porch sitting in a lawn chair when Trevor found me.

"How you holding up?" he asked as he carried Koda onto the porch and set him down to investigate the area.

"Fine," I murmured, staring out at the trees. His driveway was long and winding, and even when I tried I couldn't see the main road from the house. I couldn't see any other houses, either, which was kind of surprising since I knew both his parents' house and his uncle and aunt's house weren't very far away. The place was totally secluded.

"You mad?" He sat down on the top step and leaned against the railing, his long legs stretched out in front of him.

"Should I be?"

"Come on, Morgan," he said quietly. "Let's not play that game, all right?"

"What game?" My shoulders grew tense as I continued to look into the woods.

"The game where you shut me out and refuse to talk about anything? That one? You remember it?"

"Please," I scoffed, crossing my arms over my chest.

I really didn't want to have the conversation we were having. I didn't want to talk anything out or even acknowledge that there was a problem. I wanted to stew. I wanted to sit there in the quiet and decide for myself how I felt about everything that had happened. I fucking hated confrontation of any kind. It made my skin crawl and my heart race.

"I forgot to call them," he said, getting more comfortable in his spot. "I couldn't just make them leave after they'd driven out here to help me out."

"That's exactly what you could have done," I said so quietly I wasn't sure at first that he'd heard me.

"You *are* mad," he replied.

"It's fine."

"Clearly, it's not, or you wouldn't be having an attitude."

"I'm not having an attitude," I said, my face devoid of emotion when I met his gaze.

"Is this going to happen every time you're pissed?" he snapped. "You're acting like a—"

He didn't finish his sentence and I immediately sat forward in my chair.

"A what?" I asked, cocking my head to the side. "A bitch?"

"No."

"Oh, come on, Trevor," I wheedled. "Say what you were going to say."

"I wasn't going to call you a bitch," he said softly.

"Sure you were."

"No, I wasn't."

"Right," I said sarcastically. I pushed myself to my feet, ready to leave him there on the porch, but before I could take a single step he was standing as well.

"I was going to call you a child," he said with a sigh, standing between me and the door. "I was going to say that you were *acting like a child*."

"Then why didn't you just say it?" I snapped back.

"Because," he said, standing straighter, "I don't use words to hurt people."

My head jerked back in surprise. The words were so simple, but as he stood there, his gaze never leaving mine, I knew that the meaning behind them wasn't. I had no idea how to respond.

"I'm sorry about how that all played out," he said softly. "I know you wanted to be in control of how Etta met my family."

"It's not just that," I ground out. I wanted to yell in frustration, but his previous comment had taken the wind out of my sails. "My sister," I choked out. "We came here so she could feel safe. How do you think she felt, having to deal with strangers after the last couple of days? How do you think *I* felt?"

"I know." He nodded somberly. "I know. I'm sorry."

"I'm—" I shook my head, refusing to finish my thought as all the emotions of the past couple of days made my throat feel like it was closing up. This was why I didn't want to discuss anything. This was why I preferred to stew on my anger until it eventually faded away. And I knew it would fade; it always did. Even if it never went away completely, it became manageable.

"What?" Trevor asked, reaching for me. "You're what?"

"I'm angry," I gritted out through my teeth, unable to keep the tears from filling my eyes. "I'm so angry."

He wrapped his arms around me, but I was too busy trying to hold myself together to reciprocate the embrace. I was shaking as his hand started to rub my back soothingly, up and down in long sweeps.

"They *bit* her," I said, unable to keep the disbelief from my voice. "They burned her and they bit her and then they put her in her bed like it was nothing."

Trevor made a pained sound in his throat, but didn't speak.

"How does someone do that to another human being? How do you leave marks on someone with no remorse?"

"I don't know," he said.

"The doctor said she was lucky that there was no sign of a rape," I whispered. "*Lucky.* Can you believe that?"

Trevor didn't respond. He just continued to hold me while I shook with suppressed rage. It was too much. All of it was too fucking much. My sister and I had lived through so much crap when we were kids, first when we'd lived with our train wreck of a mother and later with a series of foster families, that it was time for us to have it easy. Wasn't it? I mean, was that too much to ask?

Why in the hell did certain people have such easy lives when the rest of us had to fight for every piece of happiness we could grasp? And then, when life was ready to give us something good, why was it so hard for the have-nots just to accept it?

Why was I standing in the arms of a man I cared about, one who'd forgiven me for treating him like crap, and I couldn't even hug him back? I couldn't force myself to do it. I just stood there, letting him attempt to soothe me, and the entire time I berated myself and my life and every person who'd let me down.

"What do you need?" he asked, holding me tighter. "Tell me what you need from me."

His words only made me angrier. I didn't know what I needed. Couldn't he see that? Couldn't he see that I had no idea what to fucking do?

"I don't need anything," I said dully after a few moments of silence.

"Yes, you do."

"No. I'm fine."

"No, you're not."

"I am."

"Morgan," he said stubbornly. "Tell me what you need from me."

"I don't need anything from you," I replied, my own stubbornness more than a match for his. I pulled away but refused to meet his gaze.

"I can see it on your face, baby," he said. "You called me for a reason."

"You're the only person I know who lives close."

"Bullshit," he replied before I'd even finished my sentence.

"What do you want me to say?" I practically shouted, throwing my hands into the air in frustration.

"Tell me what you need!" he replied. His tone was just as frustrated, but he never raised his voice.

I stared at him silently.

Trevor sighed and used one hand to rub his eyes like he was tired. He took one step back, but before either of us could leave the porch, we were distracted by the sound of a car coming down his gravel driveway.

Chapter 15

Trevor

It had felt like we were almost there, like we were almost to the point where she could force herself to go beyond the superficial and tell me something real. I was beginning to realize that it was easier for Morgan to ask for help when she wasn't the one in need, but the minute her needs came into the equation, she completely shut down.

Now, though, any type of breakthrough was completely off the table. Morgan was motionless beside me as my mom pulled to a stop and climbed out of her car.

"Morgan?" Mom said in surprise, her eyebrows nearly reaching her hairline as she stopped short of the porch. "What are you doing here?"

It wasn't the tone of her voice that got to me, and it wasn't her body language or the fact that someone must have told her I had guests before she'd arrived. It was the words she'd used. She didn't say, "I didn't know you were visiting," or "When did you get here?" She specifically asked why Morgan was at my house, and that didn't set well with me at all.

"What are you doing here, Mom?" I asked easily, turning the question back on her.

"Oh, I was out and about," she replied lamely, making some weird motion with her hands. "I wanted to meet that new puppy of yours."

I turned to look for Koda, who I'd been completely ignoring during my talk with Morgan, and found him passed out on the welcome mat.

"He's right here," I said, lifting him into my arms.

I walked down the steps before my mom could come any closer and handed her the sleepy puppy.

"Oh, he's cute," she said, pulling him against her chest. "Did you get him from the Mallorys?"

"Yeah, the last litter," I replied. I didn't understand why we were making small talk when we both know Koda wasn't why she'd come, but I let it slide. The longer I watched her the more I could sense her nervousness, and I didn't want to make it worse.

When the screen door creaked behind me, Mom's head shot up to look over my shoulder. "Is Etta here, too?" she asked Morgan, halting her escape.

"Yeah," Morgan replied. Her voice was hoarse, but any emotional remnants of our previous conversation were gone.

"Can she come out for a few minutes?" Mom asked hopefully, giving Morgan a small smile.

"She's asleep," Morgan replied quickly.

As irritating as my mother was, the disappointment on her face was still hard for me to see. Before I thought it through, I turned to Morgan.

"Maybe she hasn't crashed yet," I said.

I immediately knew I'd fucked up, but I didn't fix my mistake. I'd never been able to watch something upset my mom without trying to fix it. So, like an idiot, I met Morgan's gaze and waited for a response.

"I can check," she replied.

She turned and walked into the house without another word.

"Why's she here, Trevor?" my mom asked as soon as Morgan had disappeared. "You didn't tell me she was coming to Oregon."

"She's not here for a visit, Mom."

"Well, she's visiting you," she replied, annoyed. "You could have at least let me know."

"She didn't want you to know," I said, instantly regretting my words when I realized how they'd come across. "I just mean that she's headed home soon, Ma. She came up to get her sister—"

"Why? Isn't it the middle of the semester?" she cut in.

I hadn't had a chance to climb out of the pit I'd dug for myself when Morgan came back outside without Etta.

"Sorry," she said uncomfortably. "She's asleep."

My mom sniffed only loud enough for me to hear but nodded in understanding. "Well, okay then," she said.

I hated that she was upset. I knew it must be killing her to be so close to her granddaughter without being able to see her, and, honestly, I didn't understand why Morgan didn't just wake the baby up. It wasn't like my family had many chances to see Etta. Waking her up once so that she could have a little visit wasn't going to do any kind of damage to her schedule. Hell, I wasn't even sure Etta had a schedule.

"Maybe next time," Morgan said kindly.

"Sure," my mom replied, her lips wobbling a little as she smiled back. "I'll call tomorrow and see if we can work something out then."

She stiffly handed Koda to me, and kissed my cheek when I leaned down to offer it. Then she climbed back into her car and drove away.

"Morgan," I called, trying to catch her as she went back inside the house.

"I'm going to bed," she said over her shoulder, not slowing down for a second.

"Let me put the dog in his room and then—"

The quiet sound of a bedroom door closing interrupted my words.

* * *

Early the next morning I woke up to the sounds of people walking around my house. It was a scenario that had never happened before, and I lay there for a while enjoying the sound before I got up. I liked having people in the house. Every once in a while Shane and Kate came to visit, but they'd never stayed overnight at my place. It was just easier for them to stay with the oldies so the grandparents could have as much time as possible with the kids.

"'Morning, Trevor," Miranda said as I made my way toward the coffeepot. "Thanks for letting us stay last night."

"Of course," I replied, giving her a smile.

Morgan's little sister was still looking pale, and she held herself in a way I'd seen a lot of foster kids hold themselves when they'd come to stay with my parents, but she looked better rested than she had the day before. I couldn't imagine the pain she must be in, both physical and emotional, but I hoped she'd gotten some sleep.

"You guys want to do anything today?" I asked, taking a sip of weak-as-hell coffee and trying not to grimace at how disgusting it was. "I've got all the movie channels if you just want to hang on the couch, but there's also a lot of trails on the property if you feel like taking a walk."

Miranda lifted her hand to stop my chatter. "I think we're actually heading home soon," she said apologetically.

"Oh." My mouth snapped shut and I looked down the hallway toward where I knew Morgan and Etta were.

"It's probably time I went to see my dad," Miranda said. "He must be wondering why Morgan hauled ass to Oregon and if we don't tell him something soon, he'll be on his way here."

"You could call him," I replied, pouring my coffee down the sink.

"I think he'd probably rather have that conversation in person," she said quietly. "Don't you?"

I paused with my hands on top of the coffeepot. "Yeah." I turned and nodded my understanding. "You're right."

"But thank you," Miranda said again. "For everything you did yesterday and for letting us crash at your house."

"You're welcome here anytime," I told her, completely serious. "You ever want to come visit, hang out in the woods or go fishing or just escape for a while—you've got a place here."

"You're good people," she replied, cocking her head to the side. "You know that?"

"I try."

Morgan came down the hallway carrying Etta and their bag, and my conversation with Miranda was suddenly over.

"Twevo!" Etta said happily, kicking her legs to get down. As soon as she was standing on her own two feet, she ran to me and wrapped her little arms around my leg. "Koda?"

"He's out in his dog run," I replied, running my hand over her silky hair. "You want to go see him?"

"We need to go pretty soon," Morgan said, readjusting the bag hanging on her shoulder. When our eyes met, though, she relented. "But you can go see him for a few minutes," she told Etta. "*Only* a few minutes."

I nodded in understanding and led Etta out the back door to where Koda's temporary setup was. At night he slept in the mud room on a huge dog bed that I figured he'd eventually grow into, but during the day he had a fenced-in area with a house and some toys to play with. At some point he'd be old enough to roam as he pleased, but while he was young I wasn't taking any chances that he'd get lost or killed by a predator in the woods.

Etta rambled on and on in her little gibberish as soon as I let Koda out to play with her, however, my attention was quickly divided between her and the open kitchen window when I heard the women inside start to speak. They must not have known the window was right by Koda's pen. I was the subject of their conversation, so I didn't feel an ounce of remorse for eavesdropping.

"Why are we leaving now?" Miranda asked.

"Because Dad's going to lose his mind—"

"He has no idea what's going on, Mor. I'm pretty sure he could wait a couple more days to find out."

"We can't just stay here."

"Why not? He freaking invited us."

"Just leave it, Ranna, okay?"

"No. This is crap. I like it here, and I'm not in a hurry to go tell Dad why I'm dropping out of school."

"You know he'll understand. You can finish up at a school in Sacramento."

"That's not the point and you know it."

"I'm sorry that you don't want to go home yet," Morgan said. "But I don't want to stay here anymore. Maybe we can find a hotel on the way down and stop for a couple days or something."

"Why don't you want to stay here? God, you're so annoying. Trevor practically worships you—"

"No, he doesn't," Morgan cut in flatly.

"And we don't have the cash to just hang out in a hotel," Miranda continued like her sister hadn't spoken.

"Just let it go, please."

"This is bullshit," Miranda mumbled so quietly I almost didn't hear her. "You're treating that guy like crap."

"No, I'm not."

"Yeah, Morgan," she snapped. "You are."

Everything went silent then.

"Twevo," Etta called. "Twevo, Koda potty."

"Oh, yeah," I replied, walking over to pick her up so she wouldn't follow the peeing puppy. "He's not very good at it yet."

We watched as he peed all over himself, refusing to stop in his exploration of the side of the house long enough to pause and lift his leg.

"I think he needs a bath," I told Etta.

"Koda no like baths."

"I'm pretty sure he will. Don't you like baths?"

"Me no like baths," Etta replied, shaking her head.

"Let's put him back in his pen for now," I said, my lips twitching.

We spent the next few minutes calling and cajoling Koda over to the fence, and a few after that praising him for listening. Then, before I was ready, Morgan came out the back door to get Etta.

"Time to go, baby," she said.

"Me no go," Etta argued.

"Don't you want to see Grandpa?"

"No."

Morgan sighed. "Sorry, toots. We have to go home."

"No," Etta said, scrunching up her face in annoyance.

"Yep," Morgan replied, coming over to pull an unhappy Etta from my arm. "But Auntie Ranna is coming with us. Maybe we can get some snacks, what do you think?"

"No," Etta said again, though a little less adamantly this time.

"Can you say good-bye to Uncle Trevor?" Morgan asked.

I was startled, but I didn't let it show. She'd never referred to me as "uncle" before.

"Bye," Etta said mutinously.

"Bye, Henrietta," I replied, I leaned forward and gave her cheek a kiss, making sure that my beard tickled along her jawline.

Etta giggled, giving me the response I was hoping for.

"I'll walk you out front," I told Morgan.

So many things ran through my head as we made our way around the side of the house. I wanted to ask her why she was in such a rush to leave. I wanted to know if I would hear from her or if my phone was going to go silent once again, if the fact that she'd called when she'd needed me had actually meant anything. I wanted to tell her that I was sorry for siding with my mom the night before, that I knew I'd messed up, that I loved her, that I missed her already and she hadn't even left yet, that I could no longer imagine my life without her and Etta in it.

Instead, I walked her to the car and opened Etta's door so Morgan could buckle her into her seat. I rested my knuckles against Miranda's window in a silent good-bye, and smiled when she fist-bumped me through the glass. Finally, as Morgan climbed into her car, I said the only thing I could. The only thing that was safe. Two words that I hoped encompassed everything I was feeling and everything I knew she wasn't ready to hear.

"Drive safe," I ordered, stepping back from the car.

With a nod, she threw the car into reverse and turned around, leaving me standing there in the driveway.

* * *

"Has she called?" Bram asked at Friday night dinner a week later.

"No," I replied shortly. "Not since she texted to let me know that they made it safely."

"Well at least she did that."

"I guess."

"Man, you need to figure that shit out," he said, shaking his head in disappointment.

"You think I'm not trying?" I spit back. "I feel like I'm walking on eggshells."

"Well," he said, like it was the easiest thing in the world. "Just step on them."

"What?"

"If you feel like you're pussyfooting around her, stop doing it."

"There's more to it than that," I ground out, popping the top of my beer. I took a long swallow and leaned against my parents' back porch railing. "If I play it wrong, she disappears and it's my fault that we can't see Etta."

"Oh, come on, Trev," he replied. "That's weak."

"No, it's practical."

"No. It's weak." He shook his head at me. "Trev, if she was like that? You wouldn't be all strung out over her. You're using that as an excuse, man. A lame one."

"She's been pretty clear on how she feels."

"Has she?" he asked. "Really? Because what I saw was her calling you when she was upset, and then hiding out at your house for the night. I saw her watching you while we were hanging out. She wasn't saying much, but damn, she was *watching*."

"She bailed," I ground out, shrugging my shoulders in an attempt to hide how much that bothered me. "She doesn't want to be with me."

"Or maybe you don't want to be with her," Bram countered, shaking his head. "Looks to me like you're both too fucking stubborn to figure it out."

I opened my mouth to argue, but he lifted his hand in a gesture to be quiet.

"We can play this game all night, but I'm not a fucking woman, and I don't want to talk about your feelings," he said bluntly. "What's that saying? *Would you rather be right or be happy?* I guess that's the question. You want to stay here secure in the fact that she left and you're the injured party, or you want to go and make the first move to fix it? Up to you."

He walked back into the house, but I stayed outside for a little while, thinking over what he'd said. I'd spent most of my life trying to make sure the people around me were comfortable. At that point, it was so ingrained in my personality that I wasn't sure I could change it. When Morgan had left, I hadn't argued. That was what she'd wanted, so I'd let her go. It had made things easier on me, if I was being fully honest with myself. If Morgan was making that decision, then I didn't have to deal with the guilt that loving her caused me. I didn't have to worry about my parents' reaction or how our relationship would look to everyone else.

As time passed, though, I realized what a cop-out my "letting her go" excuse was. There was a difference between being overbearing and showing someone that you cared about them. I'd been so concerned about the former that I was beginning to think I'd neglected the latter.

When my dad poked his head out the door to let me know dinner was ready, I turned and walked into the house still mulling things over.

"We should start having dinner at your house again," my mom told my aunt as we dug into our food. "I know you were trying to make things easier on me for a while, but we're cramped around this table."

"Fine with me," Aunt Liz replied, grinning. "I think Kate's bringing the kids up soon and we'll need the extra space."

"Oh yeah?" My mom smiled back, but it didn't reach her eyes. "That'll be nice. Shane hasn't said a word about it."

"I think they just decided today," Aunt Liz said. "I'm sure he'll call you tonight."

"Probably."

Ani elbowed me in the side. "If Shane even knows it's happening," she mumbled to me under her breath. "The last I heard, he was training most of the month, so I doubt he'll come."

"It's nice that Katie's so good about bringing the kids for visits," my mom said. "And that she lets you see the kids when she's here." She popped a piece of food into her mouth with a roll of her eyes, and the muscles in my back and neck instantly tightened as I waited to see where she was going with her comments.

"Why wouldn't she?" Aunt Liz asked.

"Exactly," my mom replied. "It seems like, if you were in the neighborhood, you'd at least let your kids visit their grandparents."

"That was ridiculous," my aunt said, shaking her head in disgust. "Especially when she was on the property."

"She has a name," I said coolly. "It's Morgan."

"Trevor," Ani said quietly, trying to calm me.

"We know Morgan's name," Mom replied.

"Well, then why don't you use it?" I asked, my words a little more clipped.

"What has you all balled up?" Mom asked, scrunching her nose in confusion. "*You* got to see Henrietta while she was here."

"Don't do it," Ani warned under her breath, tapping her foot against mine under the table.

"It would be a little hard *not* to see her when she was staying at my house."

"Yeah, what was that about?" Aunt Liz asked.

"Not our business, Lizzie," my uncle Dan said in an undertone as he reached out to press his hand over my aunt's on the table.

"What's not your business?" my mom asked, looking around the table. "What am I missing here?"

She looked at my dad, but he didn't say a word.

"What?" she finally asked me directly. "Is this about whatever is going on with you two?"

I didn't reply. I couldn't. I didn't even know if there was anything between Morgan and me anymore. I wasn't about to get into it with my mom over something that may or may not even happen.

"You obviously realized that was a bad idea," my mom said, scoffing. "I could tell by the way she stopped popping up in conversation."

I really tried to keep my mouth shut. I clenched my teeth and fisted my palms on my thighs in an effort to let her observation go. In the end, though, I just couldn't stop myself.

"Actually," I said, taking a deep breath. "If anyone decided that, it was her. If it was up to me, she'd have my ring on her finger."

The table went completely silent for about two seconds, and

then all hell broke loose. Bram started laughing, Ani dropped her head into her hands like she couldn't believe what I'd said, my mother and aunt were talking over each other wondering what the hell I was thinking, and Uncle Dan was trying to shush my aunt. But when I glanced over at my dad, he wasn't fazed at all. His lips were pulled up just slightly on one side as he looked at me, and his eyes showed not an ounce of surprise.

I knew the words would be explosive. I also knew that they were very premature. I'd have to get the woman to actually talk to me if I was ever going to propose marriage. However, I didn't know of any other way to make the seriousness of my position any clearer. If it was up to me, Morgan and I would be together. We'd be a family.

"That woman," my mom began.

"Careful now," Dad warned, his chin jerking up.

"Mike," my mom said in surprise.

I watched anxiously as my dad swallowed and set his fork down on the table.

"The boy's made his intentions more than clear," Dad said quietly, his gaze never leaving my mom. "And I didn't raise him to let any woman be disrespected in his hearing, especially not the woman he cares about. I know you're upset, Eleanor, but you be careful about what you say."

My mom's cheeks reddened and her mouth tightened in anger.

"Why on earth would you think that this is even remotely appropriate?" she asked my dad in disgust.

"Why would you think it wasn't?" Dad countered. Everything went silent after his words of acceptance, and I felt like I could take a deep breath for the first time in months.

My parents rarely fought. Sometimes, when I was a kid, I'd hear them arguing quietly after all the kids were in bed, but by the next morning everything was usually cleared up. They didn't hold grudges, and normally they didn't disagree on anything that was important. I'd never seen them argue in front of others.

"Enough," I said, barely raising my voice. As much as I loved my dad sticking up for me, I couldn't watch it any longer.

My mom and dad both turned to me in surprise.

"I appreciate it," I said to my dad with a nod. "But this isn't up for discussion."

My mom started to sputter, and I just shook my head.

"I care about your opinion," I said, meeting the beautiful blue eyes that I'd loved since the moment I saw them. "But in this case, it's not your call."

"She was your brother's girlfr—"

"She wasn't his anything," I interrupted through gritted teeth, unwilling to let her use that argument. Anger rose up in me like a tidal wave. "And he left her and their daughter high and dry."

"You have no idea what happened between the two of them," she replied stubbornly.

"I know more than you do," I countered. "I know enough."

"Enough to make you think it's okay to—"

"Mom," I said, cutting her off. "Henry fucking left her!" My hands were clammy and the back of my neck felt hot. My stomach was churning with nausea, but I couldn't stop the words flowing from my mouth. "If I'm supposed to show some sort of loyalty to Hen by *not* loving the mother of his child, then I guess I'm a shitty brother. I'd like to say that if Hen was here, I'd tell him the same thing, but let's all be honest. If Hen was here, we wouldn't even *know* about Etta or Morgan."

"How dare you talk about your brother that way," my mom hissed, tears filling her eyes. "You get out of my house." My head jerked back at the venom in her words.

"Eleanor," my dad thundered.

"Okay," I said, completely shattered and still practically vibrating with anger. I slowly pushed my chair back from the table and rose to my feet. "Let me know when I'm welcome again."

My dad called my name as I walked toward the front door, but I didn't pause. I couldn't stop. The minute I got outside, I vomited everything I'd eaten that day into the hydrangea bushes lining the front porch. Shaking, I climbed onto my four-wheeler and started for my house. By the time I got there, I had two text messages on my phone.

Ani: *Let me know if you need to talk.*

Bram: *About fucking time.*

* * *

"Okay," Ani announced, pushing through my front door without knocking Sunday afternoon. "I gave you all day Saturday to stew."

"Thanks," I grumbled, leaning back against the couch as I tucked a sleeping Koda more firmly against my side. "Good of you."

"This isn't you," she snapped, throwing her cell phone at

me. I dodged it just in time and it hit the couch arm beside me. "I've called you four times."

"Didn't feel like talking."

"You're done."

"Say what?"

She came to a stop between me and the coffee table and put her hands on her hips, looking a bit like a pissed-off fairy about to take flight.

"You," she said firmly, "are going to get off your ass, take a fucking shower, and pack a fucking bag."

I ignored the order as I took another sip of my beer.

"You've been so fucking worried about what everyone would think," she said, kicking my bare foot with her boot. "Well, the cat's out of the bag now. You don't have any more excuses. Pack your shit and head south."

"You're forgetting a little detail," I argued. "Morgan's not interested."

She kicked my other foot in frustration, making me yelp.

"Shut it," she replied. "That woman's totally gone for you. Grow a pair and go get her."

"You've been spending too much time with Bram."

"You're right, I have," she said smugly. "Because he kept coming back even when shit got hard. And now look at us, we're the picture of domestic goddamn bliss."

"Oh, yeah," I snickered. "You guys are practically the Waltons."

"Trevor," she said in warning. "If you don't get up and shower off the stink clinging to you, I'm going to drag the hose in here."

"I'm going," I replied, getting to my feet. "Can you put the pup in his kennel so he doesn't shit in the house while I'm in there?"

"Don't bother trying to lock me out," she said, scooping the puppy up. "I've got a key."

"I knew that was a bad idea," I mumbled under my breath as I shuffled toward my bathroom.

I'd been sitting in the house, not answering any calls or texts, since I'd left my parents' house Friday night. My family meant well, but I just hadn't had the energy or the inclination to talk to them afterward. I was sure that the family rumor mill had been running rampant, and I wasn't really interested in fueling it.

If my mom had called, I would have answered. She hadn't.

I took a deep breath as I stepped into the shower and turned on the spray. She was pissed, clearly, but I didn't know how to fix it, and I wasn't even sure if I wanted to. Not yet. I'd spent my whole life trying to please her, but I couldn't budge on this subject and it was tearing me up. I felt like I was being pulled in two opposite directions. If I went one way, I could potentially get everything I'd wanted for my entire adult life. If I chose the other direction, I could repair the rift between me and the woman who'd been my champion since I was seven years old. The decision seemed impossible.

I let the water run over my head and down my chest as I thought about Morgan. She'd been radio silent since she'd been back in Sacramento. I hoped that it was because she was too busy helping her sister settle in, but I was pretty sure that wasn't the case.

If there was one thing I'd learned about relationships in my lifetime, it was that you made time for the people you cared about. It didn't matter what was happening in your life—if you had a spare second, you made contact. I hadn't gotten that from Morgan.

Now, Bram and Ani were pushing me to go after her, and I was pretty sure that would be a mistake. At what point did chasing her make me a fucking stalker?

By the time I was out of the shower I still hadn't come to a decision.

"I packed your bag," Ani announced as I walked out of the bathroom with a towel around my hips. "Jesus, cover up, would you?"

"You're in *my* bedroom," I replied flatly, grabbing some boxers and a pair of jeans from the top of my dresser. "Leave so I can get dressed."

She walked out the door but left it cracked a little so I could still hear her.

"If you leave now, you can be there by morning," she said. "I'll take care of the pup."

"I'm a shitty driver when I'm tired."

"Then it's a good thing you've been just laying around since Friday night," she shot back. "Plus, the adrenaline will keep you wide awake."

"Why are you so invested in this?" I asked, opening the door as soon as I was dressed. "Why are you pushing so hard?"

Ani looked startled for a moment before shrugging her shoulders. "I want you to be happy," she said simply. "It's your turn."

"It may not be the happy ending you're hoping for," I replied, throwing my arm around her shoulders.

"*Happy ending*," she snickered, elbowing me in the side.

Then she sobered. "If you come back all heartbroken, I'll have Liz babysit Arie, and Bram and I will come over and get shit-faced drunk with you. How's that?"

"Sounds good," I replied. When we reached the front of the house I found a packed suitcase sitting on the couch.

"I put every piece of summer shit I could find in there," Ani said easily. "Not sure if any of it matches, but you won't die of heatstroke."

"Thanks."

I looked around the house, contemplating all the things I needed to do before I left. The kitchen was a mess, most of the windows were open, and my living room looked like a tornado of chips and soda had hit.

"I'll clean up," Ani said, shoving my suitcase at me.

"You don't have to do that."

"It's a one-time-only offer, so enjoy it," she shot back. "Go, before you lose your nerve."

Within minutes I'd said good-bye to Koda and I was driving away from the house. It was weird, but with every mile farther from my house and closer to Morgan, instead of grow-ing nervous, I became more and more sure that I was making the right move.

Chapter 16

Morgan

Are you franking kidding me, Ranna?" I hissed, looking around the living room where she'd been storing her stuff. Everything was gone, her clothes, her school stuff, all of it. "I'm going to kill you," I muttered under my breath.

I stomped into the kitchen and snatched my phone off the table, calling her for the fifth time since I'd woken up twenty minutes ago and realized she was gone. I'd known that she was feeling hemmed in since she'd gotten to Dad's house, but I hadn't imagined that she'd just take off without a word. She was an adult, I knew that, but she had to know Dad and I would be worried about her.

"Miranda," I gritted through my teeth when I got her voicemail again. "Where the hell are you? If you don't call me back I'm going to call the boys and tell them to start looking for you." I hung up with a vicious push of the END button and slammed my phone back onto the table. If it was anyone else, I would have said I'd call the police, but I couldn't do that to my sister. Telling her that I was going to send my dad's group of friends after her would have to be enough.

Life at Dad's had taken on a completely different tone since I'd arrived with Miranda in tow. Etta and I had been happy before, almost carefree as we'd settled in and I'd been able to find a good job so quickly. Once Miranda was added to the equation, though, things had become a lot more difficult. I'd been so worried about her lately that she'd accused me of suffocating her. She was moody and sullen, and while I understood it completely, her moods had still set all of us on edge.

Dad had been livid when she'd explained what happened to her, and he'd practically closed himself up with us when he wasn't working instead of hanging with his friends like he normally would. Since I'd lost my position at the shop because I'd bailed with no warning, that meant we were all in the same place. Constantly.

We'd started to bicker and fight about stupid shit. Etta felt the tension and was more difficult than normal, her thumb rarely leaving her mouth. Frankly, I hadn't been sure how long all of us living together could last.

I hadn't imagined for a second that Miranda would just take off, though. I had no clue how she'd even left, considering she didn't have a car. Turning in a circle, I tried to see if she'd stashed her things somewhere in the house, but I hadn't found anything by the time I heard Etta talking in her crib ten minutes later.

"You're awake," I said cheerfully to Etta even though I was silently fuming. "Did you sleep good?"

"Yeah," Etta replied, laying her head on my shoulder as I lifted her out of her crib.

"Good grief," I teased. "You're getting too big to lift."

"No me not," she argued, wrapping her legs around my hips.

That was another thing I'd begun to notice. Instead of Etta insisting that she was a big girl all the time, she'd begun to hint at the opposite. Sometimes I had to have my dad distract her just so I could have a few minutes to myself on the back patio.

"You're right," I said softly, kissing her head. "You're still my baby."

There was no argument from my sassy two-year-old.

I changed her diaper and threw the messy one into the full diaper pail while holding my breath. I wasn't sure why, but I was getting even less done around the house than when I'd been working full time. Everything was messy, the diapers needed to be washed, and I was pretty sure I hadn't had a shower in three days.

"Auntie Wanna?" Etta asked as I carried her into the kitchen.

"I'm not sure where Auntie Ranna is," I replied, forcing myself to keep it cheerful. "Maybe she went to the store."

I was getting Etta some cereal when my phone rang. I answered it before it could ring again.

"Hello?"

"Don't freak out," Olly said, not even bothering with a greeting.

"Why would I freak out?" I asked slowly, glancing over my shoulder at Etta. She was watching me, her mouth slightly parted and her thumb stuck in her cheek.

"Got a call from Frank this morning—"

I knew what he was going to say before he'd even finished his sentence, but I could still barely believe it.

"He said he wasn't comin' in this week 'cause he was takin' a trip up the coast."

"Son of a bitch," I murmured, staring at the sink full of messy dishes. "Miranda's with him, isn't she?"

"That's what he said," Olly replied. "I figured you didn't know, since your pops hadn't mentioned it."

"Nope," I said, smiling at Etta as I passed her on my way out of the kitchen. As soon as I made it far enough down the hallway, I continued. "She left without a fucking word."

"Well, at least you know she's with Frank."

"That doesn't exactly fill me with comfort," I snapped back.

I trusted Frank with my life. He was practically family, and I knew he'd never intentionally let anything happen to Miranda. However, their story was a fucking shit show, and I couldn't think of anything worse for her at the moment than to be snuggled up on the back of his bike for days.

"He'll take care of her," Olly said.

"Oh, yeah," I spit back sarcastically. "I'm sure he will."

Olly laughed. "Calm down, mama bear," he said. "I'm sure she'll be fine."

He didn't have any idea what had happened to Miranda in Oregon. None of our extended family did. It was how she'd wanted it, so my dad and I had respected her decision. I was regretting that now.

"I gotta go," I replied, not bothering to argue with him. "If you talk to Frances, tell him to call me."

"I'll make sure to let him know you called him Frances, too."

"I don't give a fuck," I mumbled back before hanging up the phone.

I debated calling my dad while I gave Etta her breakfast, but decided against it. The longer I thought about it the less I wanted to throttle my sister and Frank. She'd had something bad happen to her, but if I took a step back and looked at it from the outside, I really didn't have any say in what she did or who she chose to spend her time with. She was an adult.

While I knew that emotionally she was setting herself up for a fall, I also knew that physically she would be okay with Frank. I'd have to be okay with that, even if I hated it. I just really hoped that when she got back from whatever the hell they were doing, she wasn't worse off than when she left.

Sometimes my family was completely exhausting. I couldn't imagine having to deal with more people than just my dad and sister. How did people with big families do it?

I drank lukewarm coffee while Etta finished her breakfast, and went about cleaning up the kitchen. I hoped a clean house would help soften the blow when my dad came home to find his youngest had flown the coop.

* * *

Two hours later, I was sweaty, dirty, and had something sticky in my hair when the doorbell rang. Etta and I had been cleaning the house and dancing to Disney music since she'd finished breakfast, and she didn't look any better. I was pretty sure the sticky substance in our hair was the aftermath of a bag of fruit snacks we'd shared after cleaning the floors.

"Why would someone bother us?" I asked Etta, throwing my hands in the air. "We're busy!"

"Busy!" she yelled back in annoyance, drool dripping down her bare chest. At some point I'd stripped her down and she was in nothing but a leopard-print diaper and a pair of princess slippers. I was biased, but still pretty sure she was the cutest kid in the universe.

"We need to send them away," I said, still using an overly exasperated voice as I climbed off the floor.

"Can I help you?" I asked with a flourish as I swung open the door. My jaw dropped when I saw Trevor standing on the front stoop, a stuffed animal and some flowers in his hands. "Oh, shit."

"Oh, shit!" Etta parroted, running toward the door. "Oh, shit! Twevo!"

"You're clearly happy to see me," Trevor joked, his lips twitching in amusement.

"Twevo!" Etta yelled again, throwing herself at him.

My heart skipped a beat as I tried to catch her, but thankfully Trevor was already there, dropping the stuffed animal so he could sweep her up against his chest before she tripped over the threshold.

"Hey, sweet thing," he said happily as Etta's grimy arms wrapped around his neck. "I missed you."

"God, I'm sorry," I muttered as I picked the stuffed giraffe off the ground. "Uh, here." I tried to hand him the toy, but he didn't reach for it.

"Cool music," he said instead, settling Etta more firmly on his arm. "One of my favorites." He stared at me for a long moment, then swallowed hard. "You going to let me in?"

I remembered vividly the last time he'd said those words to me, but I didn't reply the way I had before. My tongue felt glued to the roof of my mouth as I stepped back from the doorway so he could come inside the house. There were cleaning supplies all over the place, the music was still blaring, and I could feel a bead of sweat rolling down my back beneath my T-shirt. I wanted to sink through the floor in mortification.

"Mama cleanin'," Etta said proudly. "Me helpin'."

"I see that," he replied, his eyes twinkling. "It looks like you were eating candy, too."

"Fruit snacks," I clarified, my cheeks heating as I tried to push my messy hair back toward my ponytail.

"You need any help?"

"No," I blurted quickly. "No, that's okay. We were almost done."

Etta started rambling, probably trying to tell Trevor what we'd been doing when he showed up, but neither of us paid very much attention. We were stuck, staring at each other.

I wasn't sure why he was there. We hadn't talked since I'd left his house, and he was the last person I would have thought was at the door. Clearly, I was an idiot, because he was standing right in front of me. His T-shirt and shorts looked clean, but wrinkled, and he smelled good like he'd just taken a shower.

"I missed you," he said softly as Etta squirmed to get down.

"What are you doing here?" I asked as he set Etta on her feet.

"I missed you," he repeated, his gaze meeting mine as he rose back to his full height.

"But—" I shook my head in confusion, but I couldn't look away from him.

I'd done a very good job of blocking thoughts of him since I'd been home. Between dealing with Miranda and trying to keep my dad from completely losing it, I hadn't really had a moment to myself to wallow. I hadn't let my mind wander in his direction because, honestly, I'd had too much on my plate already. Now that he was standing just two feet away, ignoring him was impossible and I couldn't believe I'd been able to do it in the first place.

"I haven't heard from you," he said gently.

"You could have called," I replied, lifting my hands and letting them fall back to my sides.

"Would you have answered?"

"Yes."

"Really?"

"Maybe," I confessed sheepishly.

He nodded in understanding but didn't look away. "How's Miranda?"

"Better." I glanced over to see Etta lying on the floor on top of a couch cushion. "She actually went on a trip this morning with an old family friend."

"Oh yeah?"

"Mm-hmm."

I brushed my hair out of my face again, barely holding back a grimace. I was pretty sure I stank. The T-shirt I was wearing was my dad's, the basketball shorts were from God knew where, and my toenail polish was so chipped it looked hideous. He'd shown up at the worst possible moment.

"Morgan," Trevor said, moving my hand away from my hair. "It's fine."

"I need a shower," I replied ruefully. "I wasn't exactly expecting company."

"You look beautiful."

"No, I'm disgusting."

"Stop," he muttered, the tone one I'd never heard from him before. "Stop fidgeting."

He took a deep breath and ran a hand over his beard.

"Put Etta in her crib," he ordered, startling me a little.

I turned to look at her as I began to argue, but my mouth snapped shut when I realized that she'd fallen asleep on the floor. It was the first time in a week I hadn't had to listen to her whine about her nap for a half hour before she fell asleep. Without a word, I moved around him and scooped her up. It took only a few minutes to get her settled in our room, and when I came out and closed the door behind me, Trevor was waiting in the hall.

"I thought it was probably a mistake, coming down here," he said quietly, stepping into my space. "Hadn't heard from you in a while and I wasn't sure what kind of reception I'd get."

My eyes widened as he backed me up against the wall. I didn't protest, even though I was gross and pretty sure he was going to notice it soon. If anything, my body softened at his advance, the tension in my shoulders and neck dissipating.

"Went back and forth, the whole drive down," he said, his hand coming up to rest at the side of my neck. "Is she going to tell me to leave her the fuck alone? Not answer the door? Try and let me down easy? Does she miss me?"

He grinned and my heart started to race. I wasn't sure if it was panic or euphoria.

"I should have trusted my instincts from the beginning," he said conversationally. "I was so worried about stepping on your toes, though."

His fingers began to play with the hair at the nape of my neck, and I shivered.

"Your instincts?" I croaked, frozen as his fingers drifted back and forth against my neck.

"You want me," he said easily, his hand tightening fractionally. "You've wanted me from the start."

I started to argue that it wasn't so simple as that, but he cut off my words with a few of his own.

"You wanted me when you were staring at my chest in the pool," he said softly. "You wanted me when you invited me in here." He tipped his head to the side as his knee notched between my thighs, letting me know that the *here* he described wasn't the house. "You wanted me when you kicked my ass out. You still wanted me when you called from your sister's dorm."

"What made you come to that conclusion?" I rasped, tipping my chin up a little in defiance. The words he said were true, but the delivery was given in a way that was totally foreign from the Trevor I'd come to know.

"The way you look at me," he replied.

It was the simplicity in his answer that stopped any argument I could have made.

"I look at you the same way," he said sweetly, his head dropping down so that his mouth was just millimeters from my ear. "Like I've been swimming under water and I've finally come up for air."

My head fell back against the wall with a thump as his lips

met the skin just below my ear. "Like I'm looking at the present I've been asking for all year under the Christmas tree."

His lips drifted across the front of my throat and dipped into the notch of my collarbone. "Like I can't believe how lucky I am that I finally found you."

"Were you looking for me?" I asked dumbly, the words tumbling from my lips before I could hold them back. I froze as soon as I'd realized what I'd said.

"Baby, I've been looking for you my entire life," he replied, raising his head until our foreheads were pressed together. "You might not be there yet," he breathed. "But I've never been more sure."

My eyes watered, but I held tears back by sheer force of will.

"I need to shower," I replied. It was quite possibly the worst and most truthful thing I could have said.

Trevor stiffened for a moment, his eyes hard on mine, but before I could apologize, or do anything, really, his whole body began to shake with laughter. With one hand braced against the wall and the other still wrapped around the side of my neck, Trevor leaned against me, his face in my throat as he laughed like a lunatic.

When he was done, he lifted his face and kissed me so quickly I didn't even have a chance to pucker up.

"I got into it with my mom," he said, his smile gone.

"Oh, no," I murmured. Maybe that was why he'd come to see me. I knew how close he and his mom were. He must have been pretty upset if he'd driven all the way to Sacramento. "Do you want to talk about it?"

Trevor huffed in amusement and barely shook his head from side to side.

"I told her I'm going to put a ring on your finger," he said bluntly.

Intellectually, I understood the words he was saying. However, logically, I couldn't wrap my mind around the meaning.

"You *what*?" I blurted, trying to figure out if he was joking.

"I made it clear that you and I were something they'd have to get used to."

"Jesus," I mumbled, pushing distractedly at his chest. I completely ignored what he'd just said as I moved out of his arms. "I'm sweaty and I need a shower like you would not believe."

I left him standing in the hallway as I stepped into the bathroom. He could handle himself while I cleaned up really quick. It wasn't like it was his first time at our house.

I was in the shower for less than five minutes when his voice on the other side of the shower scared the crap out of me.

"I can't figure out if you do it on purpose," he said, "or if you just have no idea."

"I don't know what you're talking about," I snapped, my heart still beating like it was going to jump out of my chest. "Can I take a shower in peace?"

"Probably not," he replied, stepping in next to me.

I wanted to be pissed. I really did. But oh, my God, all that dark skin was on full display and he showed absolutely no sign of self-consciousness.

"I'm in the shower," I muttered.

"Me too," he replied in amusement.

"I know." I continued to stare until he began to chuckle. "Why?"

"Because I knew you weren't going to be able to focus until

you took a shower," he replied, reaching for my shampoo. "But I didn't want to wait that long."

I let him lather my hair without a peep. Half of me was relishing what we were doing, but the other half was completely freaking out. Why was he here? Why was he making a move now, when he'd backed off before? What was his endgame? And why in God's name had he told his mom he wanted to marry me? Had he been joking about that? She must have freaked out.

"I can see the wheels turning," he said as he tilted my head back to rinse the shampoo out. "You want to share your thoughts with the class?"

"No," I replied, sputtering when soap ran down my face.

"Whoops," he said easily, wiping the residue away. "Why don't you feel like sharing?"

"Maybe I'm not the sharing type," I replied.

"Sure you are," he argued, gently moving my hands back to my sides before reaching for my body wash. "You just don't want to share anything about *yourself*."

"What are you doing?" I asked as he knelt in the shower.

"Washing you."

"I can wash myself," I replied, taking a tiny step backward.

"I know," he said, tilting his head to look at me, even though it made water splash into his face. "But I'd like to do it."

I cocked my head to the side, wondering what I was missing in his enigmatic answers, but stepped forward again, giving him permission.

He started with my feet and moved upward, not exactly rushing, but not taking his time, either. He didn't miss a single spot, but he didn't linger. By the time he reached my hips, I was almost vibrating with need, but he moved past any erogenous zones as he made his way over my back and torso.

"You don't like asking for help," Trevor said as he massaged soap onto my hand. "You don't like talking about your feelings or getting in too deep."

I opened my mouth to reply, but shut it again when he shook his head in warning.

"I'm talking now, you'll get your chance," he said, moving farther up my arm. "At first, it threw me for a loop. You were so welcoming when I showed up that first time. So easy. I took that for granted."

"Easy?" I asked, ignoring his glare.

"You know what I mean," he replied. "Stop interrupting."

I closed my mouth and raised one eyebrow. I couldn't wait until it was my turn to speak. Why the hell was I letting him boss me around, anyway? He was in my house and he'd interrupted my damn shower.

"So when you went all cold on me, I had no idea how to respond." He shrugged his shoulders and smiled ruefully. "It was such a change from how you'd been in the beginning that I instantly backed off."

I wanted so badly to speak, but I didn't. His hands moved to my shoulder and armpit, and he didn't hesitate for a second even though I hadn't shaved in days. I willed myself not to blush.

"I hadn't realized yet, that's what you do." He paused on my collarbone, then kept moving. "You shy away from anything personal, even the aftermath of sex."

"That's not true," I argued, unable to keep silent any longer. "I've talked to you about a ton of personal shit."

"You've texted sometimes," he conceded, nodding. "But in person? No way."

"Wrong," I replied.

"Name once." His hands never stopped moving as he cleaned my other arm, this time starting at my shoulder.

"We talked about personal things the first time you showed up!"

"We talked about *Henry*," he corrected. "We didn't talk about you."

"Yes we did."

"No," he said seriously. "We didn't. You brushed off how Henry had hurt you, and that was that."

"He didn't hurt me."

"Didn't he?"

"No."

"It didn't bother you at all that he walked away from you?"

"No," I said emphatically.

"It didn't hurt you that he walked away from Etta?"

"I think I'm clean," I said bluntly, pulling my hand from his. I turned and flipped the shower knob off. "I'll get you a towel."

I stepped out of the shower but didn't even get to the towels under the sink before he was spinning me around to look at him.

"This is what I'm talking about," he said. "You refuse to talk about anything personal."

"Sure," I replied, refusing to back down even though we were both dripping all over the floor. "It bugs me that he didn't care about Etta. Of course it did."

"Then why pretend it doesn't?"

"Because it doesn't change anything," I shot back. "Me whining about it doesn't change a goddamn thing!"

"It's okay to be mad."

"I'm not mad!"

"Then what are you?" he asked softly.

"I'm sad," I gritted through my teeth. "Okay? It makes me so goddamn sad for her."

"It's okay to be sad about it."

"I know that," I shot back.

"It's okay to talk about."

"Why in the hell would I want to do that?"

"Because I need you to," he replied, his eyes steady on mine.

"Why?"

"Because I want to take care of you."

I scoffed. I couldn't help it. I'd been taking care of myself for as long as I could remember. Did my dad and sister have my back? Without question. Did I ask them for anything? Never.

"I take care of myself."

"Letting me in doesn't make you weak," Trevor continued.

"I never said it did."

I twisted to grab us some towels, then brought mine to my face, blocking him out. This whole conversation was making my stomach twist with anxiety.

"Look at me," he ordered. "Now, Morgan."

I dropped the towel so I could meet his eyes. What I saw there wasn't what I'd expected.

"I'm in love with you."

"No, you're not."

"You're so damn willing to help everybody. I tell you I got

into an argument with my mom, and you instantly go soft and ask if I want to talk about it, but the minute I tell you how I feel about you, you stiffen and change the subject."

"Those are two completely different situations."

"I realize that," he said easily, drying himself off. "Your reactions are constant, though."

"Why are we even talking about this?" I asked in annoyance, reaching for the door handle.

"Because," he hissed, his hand flying out to grip my wrist, "you won't let me help you. You deflect the minute I get too close."

"I don't need your help."

"Jesus Christ, Morgan," he spat, his other hand slapping loudly on the countertop. "Maybe *I* fucking need to help you."

"What?" I said, surprise making my voice higher than normal.

"I'm in love with you," he said again, his voice loud in the small bathroom. "All right?"

"Okay," I replied almost inaudibly.

"Finally," he told the ceiling. "I'm getting through."

"That's not funny," I retorted.

"No," he said, shaking his head. "It's not."

He let me leave the bathroom, and I walked without a word to my bedroom and closed the door behind me. Etta was still sleeping as I got dressed, but I checked on her anyway, just to stall for time. I wasn't quite sure how I was supposed to respond to anything Trevor had said.

Did I love him? I wasn't sure. I could picture myself with him. I missed him like crazy when he wasn't with me, and I wondered constantly what he was doing. I hated the thought of him with someone else, and imagining him hurt or upset made my chest ache with sadness. I would put his happiness before my own. Was that love? I'd never been in love, so I couldn't be sure. It didn't feel like the way I loved my family.

I cared about him, though. I knew that much.

"I don't want to fight with you," I said meekly when I found him in the kitchen a few minutes later.

"Baby," he sighed, turning to look at me. "We weren't fighting."

"It felt like fighting."

"It wasn't." He walked toward me and slid his hand down the back of my hair, kissing my forehead. He took my hand and led me to the couch, pulling me down beside him when we got there. "I don't understand why you do it," he began, tucking me in against his side. "But for some reason, you have a very easy time helping others but deflect anytime someone wants to know how you're doing."

"It just rubs me the wrong way," I replied. It was easier to talk with him when we weren't making eye contact. It felt safer somehow. More impersonal.

"Okay," he said, pausing for a moment. "But I need you to let me in."

"I don't know what you're talking about."

"I'm beginning to understand that," he said with a sigh.

"Honestly," I said, staring at the picture of me and Miranda across the room. "I have no idea what you want from me."

"A few answers?" he asked.

I swallowed as I stared at that photo of me and my sister, then finally nodded.

"Are you glad I'm here?" he asked.

I nodded again. That question was easy. No matter the circumstances or where we were, I was always glad when he was near.

"Did you miss me?"

I nodded again. Even when I'd deliberately thought of something else in order to function, I'd always missed him. I didn't have to be thinking about him to miss him; it was just a constant, like breathing.

"Do you love me?"

That question was harder. In fact, in that moment, it may have been the hardest question anyone had ever asked me. I wasn't even sure in a practical sense what romantic love was.

"I don't know," I said softly.

Trevor stiffened beside me.

"I care about you," I continued. "I hate the thought of either of us being with anyone else and I think about you constantly—but that just seems like jealousy and lust to me."

Trevor huffed in relief, and his body lost a little of the tension. "Seems like a pretty good start," he said finally.

He leaned down and just like the first time he'd kissed me, the entire world fell away as his lips met mine. His mouth was wider than mine, and he usually controlled the kiss, but I couldn't stop from pulling his full bottom lip between my teeth so that I could run my tongue along the soft inner edge. He tasted like mint, and the outer edge of his lips were slightly chapped, so they rasped against mine as he pulled away and then came back for more.

Where we'd been frantic the first time we'd kissed, this time we took our time exploring, slowly and leisurely mapping each other's dips and hollows. His tongue ran along the roof of my mouth and I shivered. My teeth nipped at his lips again and he groaned.

I was leaning back, relishing the way his weight began to press me into the couch, when we heard the front door open. Both of us sat up quickly as my dad came into the house, and Trevor's hand on my shoulder was the only thing that kept me from jumping off the couch like a guilty teenager.

"Trevor," my dad said in surprise, stopping short.

"Hey, Stan," Trevor replied easily, leaving his arm draped over my shoulder.

"You here for a visit?" my dad asked, closing the front door as he got over his surprise.

"Yeah," Trevor answered. "Took a few days off and decided to come see everyone."

I squirmed as my dad took off his boots, but for some reason froze when he tilted his head up to look us over. His eyes missed nothing as they ran over the way Trevor and I sat on the couch, but he didn't comment on it. "Missed my pretty mug, did ya?" he joked, rising back up.

"Like you wouldn't believe," Trevor joked back, his body relaxing even further.

"You staying for a bit? I need to take a shower, but I won't say good-bye if you'll be here when I get out."

"I'll be here," Trevor replied.

My dad nodded and headed toward the hallway, but paused when Trevor called his name.

"There's some water on the floor I forgot to clean up," he said. "Sorry about that."

"Don't wanna know why you were in my shower," my dad

said with a wave of his hand, not bothering to look at us. "I'll be out in a bit."

"Was that necessary?" I asked as soon as my dad disappeared. "Really?"

"I didn't want him to fall and break a hip," he replied.

"Why didn't you just clean up the water?"

"Because I was too busy trying to figure out if you were going to give me the freeze again," he said, seeming almost embarrassed. "I completely forgot."

I laughed.

Chapter 17

Trevor

I'd gone back and forth at least a thousand times as I drove south to see Morgan and Etta, but by the time I'd made it to Sacramento I'd been sure I was doing the right thing. When Bram had accused me of making excuses about why I hadn't gone after Morgan, I'd denied it, but once I'd taken a good long look in the mirror, I'd known the truth. I'd been too much of a chickenshit to go after what I was dying to have. I'd been too worried about what people would think and how my mother would react, and terrified that Morgan would laugh in my face.

My fears were ridiculous. I'd known that since the minute she opened the door, sweaty and dirty, and had looked at me like a piece of chocolate cake she wanted to take a big bite of. I knew in that moment that there wasn't a goddamn thing on earth that would make me give up that look, not my mom or anyone else. I didn't care what they thought.

I have no idea how I'd been so ignorant for so long, but in the hour I'd been at Morgan's I'd realized so many things.

She hadn't been indifferent. She hadn't tried to push me away. I honestly didn't believe that she'd even consciously done it.

The woman I was in love with just didn't have any idea how to let someone love her. She didn't have any good friends, and as far as I knew she'd never had a steady boyfriend. Morgan was stunted, for lack of a better word. Stuck in a place where she was unable to let anyone outside her family get close to her.

It was going to be hard, loving someone like that. Not the feeling—I knew that the feeling wouldn't go away. It was the action of loving someone like Morgan that would be difficult. She didn't accept it graciously. She didn't assume it was her due. Morgan actively distanced herself from caring gestures and intimacy; it was like she didn't trust anyone's motives when they were trying to be kind.

"I wasn't going to freeze you out," she said, rolling her eyes as she flopped backward on the couch. She laid her legs over my lap and got comfortable, and I missed the warmth of her against my side. "I was just thinking."

"That usually doesn't go well for me," I joked, squeezing her foot.

"I don't think I can give you what you want," she said, looking at my face but not making eye contact. "I'm never going to be the needy girl who asks you to fix all her problems."

"Good," I replied, surprising her enough that her gaze finally met mine. "I want a woman, and I don't want one who can't stand on her own feet."

"But—"

"Just as long as she lets me know what the problems are, so I can listen. Maybe give some advice if it's needed."

"That's not true," she argued. "You just made this whole big deal about how I never ask for help, blah."

I was so frustrated that I wanted to shake her, but I didn't let any of that show in my voice when I replied. "I want you to include me," I said. "Just let me in."

Our conversation was interrupted as her dad came out of the bathroom. The man had taken the shortest shower in the history of running water, yet he was obviously clean and he'd already pulled his hair back into a neat ponytail. I was a little impressed, even though I would have been happier with a few more minutes alone.

"I hear your sister ran off with Frank," he said to Morgan as he made his way into the small kitchen. "You know about that?"

Morgan froze and then climbed off the couch to follow him.

"Not in advance," she replied as soon as she'd reached the kitchen. I followed slowly, unsure whether I was intruding or not. "Olly called me this morning to let me know."

"Yeah, he's the one who gave me a heads-up, too." Stan said. He looked at me and lifted the coffee carafe in his hand. "Coffee, Trevor?"

"No thanks," I replied. I glanced between him and Morgan, wondering what I was missing. Earlier Morgan had nonchalantly said that Miranda was on a trip with a family friend, but the minute her dad had brought it up, she'd gone stiff as a board.

"She was here when I left for the shop," Stan said, sitting down at the table with a sigh. "She must have left right after."

"It was a shitty thing to do," Morgan replied, sitting down across from him in front of a second mug of coffee.

"Needed to feel the wind on her face," Stan said contemplatively. He gave Morgan a small smile. "Been there a time or two myself."

"She could have at least said something." Morgan crossed her arms over her chest, her face scrunched up in annoyance. "And what the hell did she do with all of her stuff?"

"Hell, I don't know. Maybe she took it to Frank's." Stan sighed. "Would you have let her leave?"

I sat down at the table so I wasn't looming over them, but kept my mouth shut. I wasn't a part of this particular conversation, and I really didn't want to overstep. Besides, the fact that I was keeping quiet was probably why they felt so free to talk about it in front of me.

"It's not like I would have tackled her and locked her in," Morgan grumbled, taking a sip of her coffee. "I just would have pointed out what a horrible idea it was."

Etta started crying in the other room and Morgan sighed, setting down her mug as she stood from the table.

"I'll be right back," she said quietly, leaving the room.

It didn't take long before Stan's focus moved to me, and I forced myself not to fidget under his close regard.

"I don't think she realizes what a force she is when she sets her mind to something," Stan told me, his lips tipping up in the corners. "She mighta been surprised when Miranda snuck off, but I've seen it coming."

"Has it happened before?" I asked, glancing toward the quiet hallway.

"Not so much the sneaking," Stan replied. "But Miranda's had itchy feet for as long as she's had the space to run. I just never curbed it the way Morgan would've."

I nodded in understanding. Henry and Shane were the same way. They'd just gone about it differently, choosing to join the military instead of riding off on the back of a motorcycle.

"Haven't had a chance to thank you for what you did up in Oregon," he said, giving me a nod. "Stepped in and helped my girls the way you did."

"You don't have to thank me," I replied.

"Doing it anyhow," he shot back. "Not sure how it all came about, but Ranna was sure thankful that you let them camp out at your place."

"They're welcome anytime," I said with a shrug of my shoulders. "You too."

"Ah well, I appreciate it," he said with a chuckle. "Can't think of a reason I'd be up in that tiny town you call home, though."

"Hopefully there'll be a couple reasons," I said, glancing over my shoulder again.

"It's like that, is it?" Stan asked knowingly. "I had a feeling."

"Not sure I can convince her," I confessed, meeting his eyes.

"I had a feeling about that, too." He took a long sip of his coffee, then set it down on the table, lacing his fingers as he leaned forward on his elbows like he was about to tell me a secret. "My daughters didn't have an easy time of it," he said quietly. "Living with their mother and then getting shuffled around in the foster care system."

"I've gotten the impression it was pretty bad," I replied. I hated that they'd had bad experiences, but I knew it wasn't unheard of. I'd been in some pretty bad homes before I'd ended up with Ellie and Mike, and I imagined that it was much worse for two pretty little girls.

"They don't talk about it much," Stan said, staring at the table. "But they're both still dealing with the aftereffects, I think. Miranda's a runner, takes off when she's upset. Morgan's a fixer. My oldest takes care of everyone, but wouldn't let you know if she was on fire."

"I've noticed," I said wryly.

"I'll tell you the secret to dealing with her," he said, chuckling a little. "You watch. Watch her and when you see something, you help without asking." He shrugged. "That's the key. She'll never ask for it, no sirree. But if you step in and do it, she'll accept it."

"That's it?" I asked, staring at him in confusion. It wasn't exactly the big revelation I was hoping for.

"That's it," he confirmed. "If you're looking to change her, you won't. At this point, it's ingrained in her very nature."

I stared at him dumbfounded. How did you live with a person who refused to let you in? How did he do that with his own daughter? I had no idea what to even say.

"She loves ya," he said. "I know my daughter better than anyone, and that's clear as day."

"She's not so sure," I replied with a scoff.

"It's like you're not hearing a word I say." He lifted up a fist and tapped it against the side of his head. "She's not going to ask for anything, kid."

He looked at me expectantly, then scoffed when I continued to watch him in complete confusion.

"Telling someone you love them? It's nothing but asking them to love you back. Otherwise, the words would go unsaid, bud. You'd show it, but you wouldn't have to say it."

I slumped back in my chair as he stood from the table and

set his empty mug in the sink. Without a word, he went out the back door and I heard the faint sound of the garage door opening once he was outside. He'd dropped his words of wisdom and left, like some kind of wizard from a damn fantasy novel.

I sat in that kitchen chair for a while, going over his advice and trying to understand his perspective on love. In my family, love had always been something freely given. The words were thrown out like confetti. When you said good-bye, you told the person you loved them. When you were happy, or sad, or sitting quietly together, saying I love you was commonplace. They were words that had never come with any strings attached.

When I could hear Stan firing up some sort of power tool in the garage and Morgan still hadn't come out of her room, I headed down the hallway to check on her. The bedroom door was open just a crack, and inside the room that was just barely shaded by a pair of curtains, Morgan and Etta were fast asleep on the bed.

The room was kind of messy, and I wrinkled my nose at the smell wafting from the garbage pail in the corner. Without making a sound, I moved toward the stench and realized as soon as I stepped close that the pail was full of dirty diapers waiting to be washed. With Stan's words in my head, I lifted the pail, holding it as far from my face as I could, and carried it into the hallway.

I'd been doing laundry for half my life. Cleaning diapers couldn't be too hard, right? Stan laughed as I carried the diapers toward the washer and dryer against the back wall of the garage.

"Better be careful," he advised, gesturing with the sander in his hand. "She's got some complicated routine she uses to clean those."

"No shit?" I asked, setting the pail down so I could take a step away from it.

"No shit," he confirmed. "Might want to Google it."

I was pretty sure Stan hadn't ever used the internet, but I followed his advice. There were about fifty different links telling me fifty different ways to clean those fucking diapers. Soak them, don't soak them, use half the amount of detergent, use the recommended amount of detergent. Some of the websites even advised to use some special shit made for cloth diapers, but I ignored those, assuming that they were trying to sell their own brand of laundry soap.

"Does she soak these?" I asked Stan finally, yelling over the noise of the sander.

"Nope," he yelled back.

"Well, shit," I mumbled, pulling up another website with a routine that didn't involve soaking.

It took me at least half an hour to find what looked like a reputable cloth-diaper company's diaper-washing recommendations. Pulling the diapers out of the pail was like that Halloween game when you're a kid when they'd blindfold you and then put your hand into a bowl of spaghetti noodles or wet gummy bears. I had no idea what I was going to encounter every time I dipped my hand back into that pail, but I just kept doing it until there wasn't anything left to grab.

"Brave man," Stan said, coming up beside me to peek into the washing machine. "Don't know why she can't buy regular diapers like everyone else."

"I don't know either," I replied, holding my contaminated hand out to the side, careful not to touch anything.

"What are you doing?" Morgan asked suspiciously from behind us, making me and Stan both jump.

"Laundry," I replied, awkwardly holding my hand as far from her as I could as I turned around. "Did you have a good rest?"

"Why are you doing—" She must have caught a whiff of the diapers because her nose wrinkled and her eyes widened. "Please tell me you didn't do anything to Etta's diapers."

I shook my head quickly, scooting the pail behind me with my foot. "I just put them into the machine."

"Oh, thank God," she said in relief. She checked inside the washer, then leaned around me. "Oh, Trev," she said softly, starting to snicker.

"What?" I asked, spinning around, my hand waving wildly in the air. "Is there something on me?"

"No," she choked out, reaching for the pail.

I took a big step back as she pulled the liner out of the plastic pail and tossed it in on top of the dirty diapers.

"All you have to do is pull the liner out and empty the diapers into the machine and then throw the liner in with them," she said, her eyes wide as she tried not to laugh. She kept glancing at my hand as I held it straight out beside me. "Did you—" She giggled, then cleared her throat. "I'm guessing that's the hand you used?"

"You could have told me," I hollered at Stan, who was over at his workbench snickering.

"Thank you," Morgan said, her eyes shining as she reached out and started the washing machine. "Washing diapers was next on my to-do list."

"You're welcome. Uh, I really need to wash my hands," I mumbled.

"Come on." She grabbed my wrist and towed me back into the house

As soon as we reached the sink, she poured soap into my hand and turned on the faucet, making sure the water was the right temperature before she stepped out of the way. "You didn't have to do that," she said, staying close by my side as I scrubbed my hands.

"I know." I looked down at her while I continued to scrub. "But it needed to be done."

"Sorry, I fell asleep. You should have woken me up."

"You obviously needed it," I replied, twisting a little to kiss the top of her head. *I love you*, I thought.

"Yeah, it's been kind of a shit show around here lately," she confessed, leaning against the counter. "I haven't found a new job yet and we've all been tripping over each other. By the time I get to bed at night, I can't fall asleep because my mind is too full of junk."

"You can't stop thinking about my junk, huh?" I teased, reaching for a towel.

"Yes," she replied, deadpan. "That's exactly what I meant."

I laughed and turned to her, smoothing the hair back from her face gently. "It'll all work out, beautiful," I said softly. "You know that, right?"

"Yeah." She sighed. "I can't believe you drove all the way down here."

"I told you," I said. "I missed you."

"Still." She looked past me and twisted her lips a little. "I'm not sure what you were hoping for."

"Yeah you are," I chastised.

"We live in different states," she pointed out, pulling away from me.

"Semantics," I replied immediately. "Come home with me tomorrow. Problem solved."

She started to laugh, but the sound cut off when she realized I wasn't joking.

"I can't just go to Oregon with you," she said, looking at me like I had two heads.

"Why not?" I took a step forward and she took a step back. "You're not working right now."

"Thanks for the reminder."

The more I thought about the idea, the more sense it made. She wasn't sure about me yet. Something was holding her back. I had a feeling if we were in the same place for a while, things might be different. Long-distance relationships could work, but they needed a solid foundation first. Besides, I just really wanted her with me and I needed to get back to work before the company started imploding.

"Etta isn't in school yet," I continued. "And your dad would probably be stoked to have the house to himself again."

"I wouldn't decline the offer," Stan said, moving past us to the sink. "Don't mind me, just need to wash the grease off my hands."

"Jesus, Dad," Morgan griped. "In a hurry to get rid of us?"

"Not at all," he replied, his back to us as he washed up. "But you ain't doing anything here but sitting on your ass. Might as well go for a visit."

"Maybe I don't want to," she said, throwing her hands in the air.

"Or maybe you do," he shot back.

Morgan's mouth snapped shut as she glared at his back, then turned accusing eyes toward me. I didn't let the look bother me, but I filed the fact that she didn't like feeling cornered into my memory. Keeping my expression passive, I returned her stare.

"I'll think about it," she said finally.

"Good."

"That's not a yes," she mumbled.

"Not a no, either," I pointed out.

With a huff, she left the kitchen.

"Damn, son," Stan said as soon as we were alone. "Do I have to help you with everything?"

"What's your stake in this, old man?" I replied, crossing my arms over my chest.

"Just want my girl happy," he said, crossing his own arms. "Think she'll be happy with you."

"Look who's awake," Morgan said just seconds later.

"Twevo!" Etta yelled, galloping toward me.

"Hey," I replied, pulling her into my arms as she flung her little body in my direction. "Did you have a good nap?"

"No," she said easily. She reached up and petted my beard with both hands as she continued. "Me no like naps."

"Sometimes our body just needs a rest," I replied, watching her expressive little face as she parted my beard and smoothed it under her fingertips.

"Me no need west. Me need bananas and hot dogs and fwench fwies," she said seriously.

"That's an odd mix."

"Me like nuggets, too."

"Chicken nuggets?"

"Yeah."

"I like those, too," I said, nodding a little when her eyes rose to meet mine. "I like to dip them in sauce."

"Me no like sauce," she said apologetically, shaking her head from side to side like she thought I was a little crazy but she didn't want to hurt my feelings. "Me just like nuggets."

"Fair enough," I murmured, tilting my head a little as she pulled on one side of my beard. "You like my beard?"

She replied in gibberish, and I had a feeling she'd used up the number of English words she was willing to give me. When I looked up from her sweet face, my eyes immediately caught Morgan's.

"Just a short visit," she said, her eyes soft. "And I'm driving my car."

"Why would we drive two cars?"

"Because I want my own," she said. I opened my mouth to respond, but stayed silent as she walked forward. She kissed Etta on the back when she reached us, then slid her hand along my side as she moved around us. "I should probably pack."

I couldn't stop the grin that pulled at my lips as I turned to follow her down the hallway, ignoring Stan's snort of amusement and the little fingers pulling at my beard. I watched Morgan's ass as she moved in front of me, and could barely contain my excitement. I was going to have her all to myself.

* * *

The drive north completely sucked. I followed behind Morgan most of the way, and the woman drove like a geriatric. I didn't understand how she'd learned to drive in California but refused to drive more than five miles over the speed limit. Between her leisurely pace and the number of times we had to stop to let Etta out of the car, it took us a good three hours longer than it should have.

By the time we pulled into my driveway that night, all of us were cranky, tired, and more than ready to stretch our legs a bit. Etta ran circles in the driveway until she heard the puppy practically howling and took off around the house to find him, her mother following behind at a much slower pace. Koda was going crazy in his dog run because I'd told Ani that we'd be home that night and she hadn't come to take him inside to sleep.

I ran a hand over my face and hit the garage door opener as I followed them. I had a feeling none of us would be getting any rest for a while, even though it was already after midnight.

"Puppy!" Etta yelled over and over until I unlatched his gate.

"Jesus," Morgan mumbled as Koda stumbled into the yard and Etta dropped to her hands and knees to copy him. "I shouldn't have let her sleep for the last couple of hours."

"Debatable," I joked. "Listen to her whine in a confined space, or sit on the back porch and let her wear herself out with a puppy. I'd choose puppy."

"You're probably right," she snickered, smiling as she glanced my way.

Since she'd agreed to come stay for a while, we'd been tip-toeing around each other. I'd sat on her bed and watched her pack, giving tips and generally making a nuisance of myself, but I'd barely touched her again before I'd left for my hotel last night. This morning I'd barely been able to say hello before we'd hit the road, and I hadn't had a minute alone with her since.

She sat down on the back porch steps as Etta chased Koda across the grass, and I smiled at the picture she made. The back porch light was glinting off her blond hair but her face was in shadow, making her look like some sort of phantom.

"You look exhausted," I said, stretching my arms above my head. "I'm going to go open up the house."

As soon as she nodded, I hurried back around front and started carrying all of our bags onto the front porch. I only had the one suitcase, but Etta and Morgan had three, and they were big. I hoped that meant Morgan was planning on staying awhile, but I hadn't asked her when I'd seen them in her car earlier. Part of me wanted to just get it out in the open and tell her that I wanted her to stay indefinitely, but the other part, the smarter part, knew that if I pushed her, she'd push back. I was picking my battles.

"They slowing down yet?" I asked, poking my head out the back door a few minutes later.

"You just scared the crap out of me!" Morgan hissed, laughing breathlessly. "Good grief, it's dark out here in the boonies."

"You've got the porch light," I pointed out, teasing her a little.

"A single lightbulb isn't exactly the same as streetlights every thirty feet," she argued, walking into the yard. She picked up Koda and grabbed Etta's hand, helping her walk up the stairs. "It's franking quiet out here."

"Oh, are we back to *franking*?"

"I'm trying, all right?" she said, shaking her head a little as she handed me the pup. "Sometimes the other ones slip out. It's my dad's influence."

"I'll have a talk with Stan."

"Oh." She laughed, ushering Etta into the house. "Please do. Let me watch."

As soon as I'd shut the door behind them, I turned to see Etta's face scrunched up in the cutest scowl I'd ever seen in my life.

"Me not tired," she said conversationally.

I bit the inside of my cheek to keep from smiling.

"Me awake and me happy." She grinned huge, showing off her mouthful of baby teeth.

"Is that right?" Morgan asked, tilting her head to the side in amusement.

"That right," Etta replied, wrinkling her nose.

"Mama's tired."

Etta shrugged and looked at me.

"Uncle Trev's tired, too," I told her with a nod.

"Koda not tired."

I coughed to cover the laugh that I couldn't hold back. The puppy was already completely limp and snoring in my arms.

"M-O-V-I-E?" I asked Morgan out of the side of my mouth.

She nodded and followed me into the living room, where I was glad to see that Ani really had cleaned up. If I wasn't mistaken, she'd even polished the coffee table.

"Trevor," Morgan said, stopping short of the couch as she stared at the suitcases right inside the door. "You didn't have to bring those in."

"It took two seconds," I replied with a shrug. I didn't want to make a big deal out of it, but I was treating Stan's words like gospel. Surprisingly, it felt really good to step in and help when the other person didn't expect it. At some point Morgan was going to notice what I was doing, and I was sure she'd have plenty to say about it. Until that time came, I was just going to keep doing stuff for her whenever I saw an opportunity.

I sat down on the couch with Koda while Morgan changed Etta into a fresh diaper and some pajamas. A few minutes later, we were lined up on the couch with a princess movie on the TV, and Etta was scooting closer and closer into my side. I wasn't sure if she was trying to get closer to me or to the puppy in my lap. Leaning back a little, I lifted my arm above her and laid it across the back of the couch so I could run my fingers over the back of Morgan's neck.

As the woman I loved relaxed more and more against my hand, I increased the pressure on her neck, massaging it until I was practically holding her head in my palm. Etta fell asleep less than half an hour into the movie, but Morgan and I didn't move from our places on the couch. We just sat there, staring blankly at the TV screen, while the puppy and the baby slept peacefully between us.

"I can't believe you talked me into coming here," she said after a while, her voice low. "I have a million things I should be doing in Sacramento."

"You regretting it already?" I asked, rolling my head to the side to look at her.

"Actually, no," she replied, her lips tipping up at the corners. "I'm really glad we're here."

"Me too," I said, giving the back of her neck a gentle squeeze. "You think you'll stay awhile?"

"At least long enough for your mom to visit Etta," she said, half joking.

The reminder had me holding back a grimace. My mom still hadn't made contact, and Morgan had no idea how bad it actually was. I'd mentioned the argument to her when I'd first shown up at her house, but we hadn't discussed it since. I was dreading Morgan's reaction once she knew that my mom wasn't speaking to me because of our relationship. She didn't need an extra reason to push me away; she'd been doing that just fine on her own.

"If you stay longer than that, I'll make you coffee in the morning," I promised, running my fingers through her hair.

"Breakfast, too?"

"And lunch," I agreed. "Dinner, even."

"That's hard to pass up."

"Then don't." Her face was illuminated blue and green from the light of the TV and I couldn't help but run my thumb over the curve of her cheek. She was so beautiful, even when she was rolling her eyes at me.

"I should probably get her in bed," she whispered, changing the subject like she always did.

It didn't bother me like it had in the past. I wasn't sure if it was the setting, or the way her eyes lingered on my face, but the knot in my belly that usually showed up when she shied away from me was absent.

"I'll carry her in," I replied, letting the moment pass.

That night I didn't even mind going to bed alone. The house felt alive for the first time since I'd moved in. As I stripped down and crawled between the sheets, I could hear Morgan singing softly to Etta across the hall.

"Etta, my baby, you're sleepy and it's time to rest. Tomorrow you can play all day. Koda is sleeping and Uncle Trevor is sleeping, so sleeping would probably be best."

I grinned into the darkness.

Chapter 18

Morgan

It's about time you called me," I said into the phone as I watched Etta splash in a puddle in Trevor's backyard. "After leaving like an asshole."

"I'm sorry," Miranda replied, sighing in exasperation. "But I didn't want to get into it with you."

"You could have at least left a note."

"Well, yeah," she grumbled. "But I didn't think about it."

"Too busy sneaking out with all of your earthly possessions?" I asked.

"I only took a backpack," she replied drily. "The rest of it is stored in Dad's garage."

"I looked!"

"I put it with the Christmas shit so you wouldn't go snooping for clues."

"I've seen everything you own," I shot back. "And I wouldn't have snooped."

"You totally would have," she argued, chuckling a little. "I just needed to get out of that house, you know?"

"Yeah, I get it," I replied. I'd given it a lot of thought on the long drive north, and I couldn't really blame my sister for wanting to escape. But the way she'd gone about it still annoyed me. "You had to go with *Frances*, though?"

"You're the only person he lets get away with that shit," she mumbled back. "You know that, right?"

"Yeah, yeah," I said, rolling my eyes. "He loves me, blah blah."

"He's not quite the monster you make him out to be."

"I don't think he's a monster," I snapped. Etta glanced at me, and I smiled through gritted teeth to reassure her. "I just don't think he's good enough for *you*."

"Yeah, well, you'll just have to deal," she replied.

"Tell me you're joking." The silence on the other end of the line gave me my answer. "I hope you know what you're doing."

"I can handle it," she said finally. "Besides, you have no room to talk."

"What does that mean?"

"Where are you right now?" she asked, chuckling. "Let me guess. Somewhere in the wilds of Oregon?"

"You called Dad first?" I asked indignantly.

"I knew I'd get a better reception," she replied.

"Oh, I bet. He lets you get away with anything."

"And he's so different with you?"

I shrugged, even though she couldn't see me.

"So, you're at Trevor's," she said, humming. "How's that going?"

"We just got here last night," I replied, pulling my knees up so I could pull my oversized hoodie over my legs. "So far, it's been good."

"And where did you sleep?"

"In the guest room, nosy."

"Why the hell would you do that?"

"Because I'm a guest?"

"Don't play stupid."

"Because," I ground out. "He hasn't made a move."

"So?"

"So, I think he's waiting."

"For what, marriage? You guys have already done the deed."

"I don't know." I sighed and leaned my head back against the chair I was sitting in. "He made coffee and pancakes this morning, and then went in to work for a couple hours. He kissed me good-bye, but it was pretty platonic."

"I can't imagine those lips being platonic about anything."

"Don't imagine his lips at all," I ordered.

"Calm down, tiger," she replied. "You know my tastes run a little more toward long-haired bikers."

"Don't remind me."

"So, what?" she asked. "You're just friends?"

"No." That, at least, I was sure about. "He told his family that he wants to marry me."

"Say what?" she practically yelled.

"No kidding."

"Jumping the gun a little, isn't he?"

"I don't think he was completely serious."

"Does Trevor seem like a guy that says stuff he doesn't mean?"

"No."

"Well."

"Yeah."

"What are you going to do?"

"I have no idea," I confessed. The idea of marrying anyone terrified me. Hell, the thought of just living with someone terrified me. Marriage was huge, epic, life altering.

"He loves you," Miranda said softly. "That's big."

"I know."

I watched Etta in the yard, getting muddy as hell and as happy as I'd ever seen her. This could be our life—the man, the house, the dog, the unending yard to play in—it could be our reality if I just reached out and took it.

"Do you love him?" Miranda asked.

"How do I know?"

"You'll know," she replied instantly.

* * *

That afternoon Etta and I rode into town with Trevor to get groceries and some clothes for Etta to wear outside. I'd realized a little too late that her leggings and tennis shoes were not cut out for country living. By the time she'd come inside for a warm bath, both had been stained beyond repair by the clay that was mixed in with the dirt around the house.

According to Trevor, she needed some rain boots and jeans if she was going to be a country girl, and since she only had a pair of sandals left after the mess she'd made earlier, I accepted the idea gracefully. That was how we ended up in the shoe department of the local store, trying shoes on a two-year-old who wanted no part in the process.

"Etta, which ones do you like?"

"Me like cookies," she replied.

"I know," I replied, sitting her on the bench for the fifteenth time. "But you already got a cookie and now it's time for boots. Which boots do you like?"

She didn't bother answering as I shoved her feet into some pink princess boots.

"Me like those," she said, pointing to a different pair as soon as I'd gotten the pink boots on her feet.

"Here you go," Trevor said, handing me the green crocodile boots she was pointing at.

I switched the boots and helped Etta down from the bench, even though she'd proven over and over that she could do it herself. After she'd walked back and forth a few times, she pointed to the pink boots again.

"Me like those."

"I thought you liked the green ones?" I asked, running out of patience. I didn't know why I'd even asked for her opinion. She was two years old, for Pete's sake. She wouldn't care if I dressed her in a monkey suit every day.

"Me like those," she repeated, pointing to the princess boots.

"Okay." I had slipped the green boots off her feet and started to put her sandals back on when all hell broke loose.

"No, me like those," she cried, pointing to the princess boots again. "Me like those!"

"I know," I replied, trying to shush her.

"No these ones." She kicked out her feet, trying to push the sandals back off.

"Henrietta," I hissed, trying in vain to make her stop kicking like a lunatic. "Stop it."

"Me like those!"

"Jesus," I mumbled, standing up. My face was burning with mortification when I met Trevor's eyes.

"Grab the boots," he said calmly.

Then, without fanfare, he picked Etta up and started carrying her out of the shoe department. I grabbed the boots from the shelf and threw them in the cart as I followed. By the time I caught up with them, Etta was completely silent.

"You all done?" Trevor asked, walking toward the checkout lines.

"Yes." I leaned around him, but Etta was facing away from me and I couldn't see her expression.

"I think I startled her," Trevor said, accurately reading my confusion. "She stopped as soon as I started walking."

"I'm so sorry," I mumbled.

He didn't let me pay and he was so gracious about the whole thing that by the time we got to his truck, I was so embarrassed I could have cried. After quickly buckling Etta into her seat, he turned to me but didn't say whatever was on his mind. Instead, he shut Etta's door and took my face in his hands.

"She's two," he said softly, giving me a sweet smile. "Don't stress."

"You still bought her the stupid boots," I choked out.

"She's *two*," he repeated. "And I have a feeling she'll be asleep before we leave the parking lot."

"It's so embarrassing when she does that," I confessed, resting my hands on his sides. "Everyone was staring."

"No one was paying any attention."

"Like, God, what a horrible mother," I continued like he hadn't spoken. "Why can't she control her kid?"

Trevor burst out laughing and leaned down to kiss me

firmly on the lips. "Anyone that thinks that has never had a two-year-old," he said, kissing me again. "Now, hop in the truck and I'll load our bags."

"I can help," I argued.

"Truck, Morgan," he said, ignoring me as he started putting bags into the storage box in the truck bed. "Hurry, it's about to start raining."

He shifted as I tried to reach past him, bumping me deliberately with his ass as he continued to unload the cart. "Go."

* * *

Over the next few days, we fell into a familiar pattern. Trevor made us breakfast in the mornings before he left for work, just like he'd promised, but I was the one who made lunch and dinner. I didn't feel right letting him wait on us, especially when he refused to let me pay for any of the groceries, and, honestly, I enjoyed doing things for him. I'd fallen surprisingly easily into the domestic role, and I couldn't say that I disliked it, even though it felt pretty damn weird.

Etta and I usually spent the day playing with the puppy and taking rainy walks around the property. We never strayed so far that we lost sight of the house, but we still found new areas to explore every time we went out. Trevor's property was gorgeous, and Jesus did it smell good, especially after it rained. Everything felt clean and fresh out there in the middle of nowhere.

Unfortunately, before Trevor had left for work that morning he'd dropped a little bomb into the center of our idyllic break from reality. We hadn't seen anyone else since we'd arrived, and I had a feeling that Trevor had asked them to stay away for a little while. I'd been really thankful for the reprieve as we'd settled in, but it looked like the easy visit was coming to a close and things were about to get a bit more complicated.

Trevor's family always had dinner together on Friday nights. It was some sort of tradition that had been going on for years. He'd been really cool about it, and had made it clear that we didn't have to go, which I appreciated. However, I couldn't really think of a reason to refuse beyond pure selfishness.

So, instead of taking Etta on a nature walk that afternoon, I was busy cleaning us up and making us presentable. I dried and curled my hair for the first time in weeks, put Etta in an outfit that actually matched, packed up the diaper bag with enough supplies to take care of any emergency, and made sure we were ready by the time Trevor pulled in from work that evening.

"Damn," he said, grinning as he caught sight of us sitting on the couch. "How did I get so lucky?"

"I know," I replied, standing up and twirling around. "I actually showered today."

"You did?" he joked, coming in close. He sniffed. "Yeah, you did."

I burst out laughing and pushed at his chest. "I didn't stink."

"Well," he replied, drawing out the word like he didn't agree.

Etta chose that moment to stand up and do a little twirl of her own.

"Me wearing fethah panties," she said proudly.

Trevor looked at me for clarification.

"Feather," I murmured, snorting as Etta did a little dance. "I have no idea why she's so proud of her diapers, but I have a feeling at some point it's going to become a problem."

"As long as we can break her of it before she starts pre-school," Trevor replied in mock seriousness. "I think we're safe."

"From your mouth to God's ears," I said, raising my hands in supplication.

After a quick change out of his work clothes, Trevor led us outside to his truck. The nights had been getting colder since we'd arrived, and I had a feeling it was going to be getting pretty cold before too long. Our days of exploring were going to come to an end if I didn't get us some winter clothes.

"We're eating at my aunt and uncle's place," Trevor said as he pulled out of the driveway. "They're just right down the road."

"I remember," I murmured.

I was nervous about seeing everyone again and I wasn't really looking forward to dinner, but it seemed like Trevor was even tenser than I was. He wasn't outwardly nervous or any-thing, but there was something about the way he held himself that put me on edge. I couldn't describe the vibe I was getting from him so I didn't bother to say anything about it on the short drive, but I continued to watch him closely.

Within minutes, we were walking past a bunch of vehicles to the front door of his aunt and uncle's house. I'd known they had a big family, but walking by all of those cars really drove the point home, no pun intended.

"Hey," Ani greeted the minute Trevor ushered me through the front door. "It's good to see you again."

"You too," I said, following Trevor's lead as he took off his boots. "How's Arielle? Is she sleeping yet?"

"Unfortunately, no," Ani said ruefully. "But we're getting about two more hours than before, so I'm just going to be thankful for that."

"Yikes," I murmured.

Just then, three little boys of varying ages came running down the hallway yelling for Trevor. As soon as they reached him they started wrapping their little bodies around his torso, and with a look of pure horror Etta practically dove out of his arms in an effort to reach me.

Thankfully, I caught her just before she toppled out of his arms.

"Boys," he said firmly, bracing himself on the wall. The boys instantly quieted and looked at him expectantly. "Morgan, this is Keller, Gavin, and Gunner. They're Shane and Kate's boys."

"Hey guys," I said, trying and failing to get Etta to release her death grip on my neck. "This is Etta."

They said their hellos to me and Etta, but lost interest really quickly as they continued to climb on Trevor. I watched quietly as he listened to each of their stories with complete concentration and replied with questions that showed he'd been listening. Slowly, we moved out of the entryway and into the living room, where Ani and Abraham were sitting on the couch across from another woman.

As soon as the woman turned to say something to Trevor, I recognized her.

"Hey Trev—" Her eyes widened when she saw me and Etta. "Holy crap, you're here!"

She jumped off the couch happily and came in for a hug.

There wasn't anything uncomfortable or awkward about it, either. I had only one arm free, but I used it to squeeze her back.

"It's good to see you again," Kate said like we were old friends and it hadn't been over ten years. "You look great."

"You do too," I replied.

"Ha!" She laughed. "I don't think I've washed my hair in a week."

"I only did today because we were coming here," I confessed, making her laugh some more.

"Well, don't feel the need to do it next time," she said, leading me to the little grouping of seats. "Friday night dinner isn't anything fancy."

"One time the guys got back from hunting right before dinner and they all came to the table smelling like complete ass," Ani added with a snicker. "Liz didn't even say a word, she just moved all of their plates to the back porch."

"Oh, God," Kate said with a groan. "I totally remember that."

"We filled the freezer that year," Abraham pointed out.

"Completely irrelevant," Ani replied with a conciliatory pat on his knee.

"Hey, Katie," Trevor said as he finally extracted himself from the little boys.

She stood back up and gave him a big hug, murmuring something I couldn't hear into his ear. He nodded, but when he pulled away I couldn't read anything in his expression.

"Did you guys fly?" he asked, sitting down next to me.

"Of course," she replied. "It's more expensive, but it helps me keep my sanity." Kate looked at me and smiled ruefully. "I have five kids. Road trips are the worst."

I didn't say much as the conversation flowed around me. There was an easy relationship among all of them that was evident in the way they teased and bickered. I liked that. It reminded me of what it was like when Miranda and I hung out with Danny and Lorraine's boys.

"I hear I have a great-niece in here," Trevor's aunt called as she walked into the room. "Morgan, I'm not sure if you remember me. I'm Liz." She reached out and shook my hand warmly.

"Of course I remember you," I replied with a smile. "This is Etta."

"Hi, Etta," Liz said, leaning down a little so she could see Etta's face. "It's kind of overwhelming in here, isn't it? You'll get used to it, though, and when you're ready, there's toys in the other room."

Etta didn't reply, but she smiled a little around the thumb in her mouth.

"It sometimes takes a minute for her to warm up," I said apologetically.

"Aw, I don't blame her," Liz said, grinning as she stood straight again. "We're a noisy bunch."

She left almost as quickly as she'd come, assuring everyone that dinner was almost done and she didn't need any help. As she left the room, a little girl came in and climbed onto Trevor's knee. Etta's entire body stiffened as she watched, then relaxed as she became fascinated with who I assumed was Kate's oldest daughter.

"Hi, I'm Sage," she said, introducing herself to me as soon as she'd sat down.

"I'm Morgan and this is Etta," I replied, bouncing Etta a little on my lap. "She's deciding to play shy at the moment."

"I don't blame you," Sage said conspiratorially to Etta. "It keeps those annoying boys away."

"Boys away," Etta agreed, leaning toward Sage just a little.

"We've got some toys in the other room, though," Sage said, shrugging one shoulder. "If you want to play."

"Me play," Etta replied, sitting up completely.

"Is that okay?" Sage asked me.

"It's just on the other side of that wall," Trevor said, tipping his chin toward the toy room.

"It's okay with me," I replied, letting Etta climb off my lap. She followed Sage out of the room without a single glance backward.

"Kids are weird," Kate said with a laugh. "How is it that easy to make friends?"

"I have no idea," I said, shaking my head.

Conversation started up again, and before long I was a part of it. The Harris and Evans families were easy to be around, just like I remembered from when I was a kid. It was a relief to know that I'd been nervous for no reason.

I was feeling pretty good about the whole situation a half hour later as I used the bathroom and washed my hands. Etta was having a good time, Trevor's family was super welcoming, and I hadn't felt out of place since the initial few minutes inside the house. So I kind of felt like I'd been hit with a two-by-four when I came out of the bathroom and overheard the conversation happening between Trevor and his parents. They must have arrived right after I'd gone to the bathroom.

"You know you're always welcome," Mike said. "Everyone just got a little worked up—"

"I wasn't worked up," Trevor replied flatly. "And Mom was pretty clear."

"I was just frustrated," Ellie said. "I don't know how you can talk about your brother like that."

"Like what? Like he was human? Like he was a deadbeat who left his daughter and didn't look back?"

"Trevor," Mike said in warning.

"I loved him as much as you did, but I'm not going to pretend he was a saint."

"No one's asking you to, son."

"All of this over that woman?" Ellie asked, making my throat tighten. "What has gotten into you?"

"Are we just going to pretend that none of us were pissed at Henry when we found out what he'd done?" Trevor asked tiredly.

"Is that how you're excusing it?" Ellie asked, her voice softening. "Because you're mad at him?"

"Jesus Christ, Mom," Trevor said in disgust. They still hadn't noticed me at the end of the hallway. "I'm in love with Morgan. Saying that has anything to do with Henry is like saying that the Giants are going to win the Super Bowl because Bram decided to wear an orange shirt yesterday."

"I think—"

"No," Trevor cut her off. Ellie's back was to me, so I couldn't see her expression, but I'd never forget the look on Trevor's face as he met her straight on. "This ends now." He glanced at his dad, who was surprisingly silent. "*I'm in love with Morgan.* She's funny and kind and stubborn as all hell, and at some point I want to have a family with her. You can be pissed about it if you want, but I'm telling you right now"—he paused, taking a deep breath—"you won't win this. All you're doing is ensuring the fact that I won't let you anywhere near her or Etta. Henry did enough—this family isn't going to pile any more bullshit on top of her."

I must have made some noise, because as soon as Trevor had finished speaking his eyes rose to meet mine and he lifted his hand in my direction. "You ready to go, baby?" he asked. "Think we'll come back for dinner another time."

He came toward me and wrapped his long fingers around mine, then walked me past his parents, making sure that he was a solid barrier between us. If he'd asked, I would have told him he didn't need to do that. I wasn't afraid of them.

Sometime between him telling them that he loved me and his refusal to listen to a word they said, I seemed to have grown this weird barrier that made it feel like nothing could touch me. I calmly grabbed Etta's bag and shoved my feet into my shoes as Trevor grabbed the baby, and in less than two minutes we were out the front door and walking toward the truck. We climbed in without a word, and instead of driving toward home, Trevor headed to town.

It wasn't until he'd ordered us burgers and french fries from a small drive-up diner that I finally found my voice.

"I love you," I said, just as he'd taken a large bite of his hamburger. "I know it's probably a really shitty time to tell you that, after all that stuff that happened with your parents, but—"

He dropped the burger and wrapped a hand around the back of my neck, and when he kissed me, he tasted like the thousand island dressing they'd put on his hamburger and a little like onions. It didn't matter. His lips were both soft and scratchy when he pressed them against mine and his hand was firm on the back of my neck, providing an anchor I hadn't realized I'd needed until that moment.

"Anytime is a good time to tell me that," he said against my lips.

We pulled apart when Etta started kicking the back of the seat, then ate our dinners quickly. The drive back to the house seemed like it took two hours, and getting Etta to sleep once we got there took another thirty minutes. Eventually, though, I ended up in the middle of Trevor's bedroom, practically shaking as he stripped my shirt over my head.

"We should really talk things through," Trevor said, his hands shaking as he slid them down my arms then up my sides. "That would be the wise thing to do." He was staring at my torso, and I couldn't tell if he was talking to me or himself. "But if I'm not inside you soon, I might completely lose it."

"Well, I wouldn't want you to lose *it*," I teased softly, reaching forward to tug at the hem of his T-shirt.

"See, you're joking," he said, stripping his shirt over his head. "While I stand here, afraid I'm going to pass out."

I laughed at his earnest expression.

"I'm not kidding," he said, yanking open the front of my jeans. "It's been too goddamn long."

"So what are you waiting for?" I asked as I pushed the pants over my hips.

"I'm trying to savor the moment," he replied, ditching his own jeans and boxers all at once.

"Can we savor it afterward?" I asked hopefully.

With a growl he leaned forward and threw me over his shoulder, making me laugh hysterically as he stomped toward the bed and tossed me onto it. Before he could even put a knee to the mattress, I was pulling my underwear off and flinging them away. I reached back to unhook my bra, but by the time I could peel it off, his mouth was already on me through the lace, making me groan.

"I'm going to trace your tattoo with my tongue," he mumbled, his lips tracing a path down my belly. "Eventually."

His lips pressed against me and my legs dropped shamelessly wide as I gasped for breath. The lips that felt so good against my own felt infinitely better when they were manipulating the skin between my thighs. I was racing toward the edge, my fingers digging into the comforter beneath me and my eyes clenched tightly shut when his mouth slid away.

"Someday we won't need these," he said as my eyes popped open. He was rolling a condom on to his erection while his mouth traced patterns on my inner thigh. "But for now, we'll be careful."

"Thank you," I whispered.

He crawled up my body and pressed his lips gently to mine. "And someday you won't thank me for taking care of you," he said seriously, his words so gentle they made my nose sting with unshed tears. "You'll just expect it."

Then, slowly and reverently, he slid inside.

We didn't switch positions or race to the finish line. The first time he was inside me had been frantic, but this time was slow and steady, almost in time to the rain we could hear splashing onto the roof. When I came, it settled over me like a warm blanket, turning my bones to jelly. And when he finished close behind me, I watched through half-closed eyes as his face went slack with pleasure.

Together, we rolled to the side and I snuggled in close as he pulled the blankets up and over us.

"Jesus," he mumbled, sighing as he pulled me even closer. "It actually gets better."

"I didn't think it was possible," I replied in wonder, staring at the ceiling.

"Hell, neither did I."

He started to chuckle and the sound was so infectious that I did, too.

"I love you," he said, pressing his lips against my forehead.

"I love you, too," I replied, a little nervous even though I'd already said it to him before.

"I'm sorry about tonight," he murmured, running his hand lightly up and down my spine. "I just assumed that they'd skip dinner this week since my mom is still pissed at me. I wouldn't have brought you there if I'd known they were going to cause problems."

"It wasn't your fault."

"Still." He paused. "I didn't want you to have to deal with that."

"They're your family, Trev," I said gently. "It was bound to happen at some point."

"Not if I can help it."

I leaned up on my elbow and looked into his eyes, easily reading the worry there. He'd fought with his mom, the person he'd confessed more than once was the closest person to him in the world, and he was worried how I felt. It boggled my mind.

"I'm sorry that you and your mom are fighting," I said, laying my hand on his jaw.

"I meant what I said to her—"

"I know that."

I lay back down and wrapped my arm around his waist as he sighed.

"How are you so sure all of a sudden?" he asked, his voice barely breaking the silence around us.

"Because," I said simply, closing my eyes as I rested my cheek against his chest and listened to his heart beat. "You don't use words to hurt people."

* * *

The next morning, everything felt different. As soon as I heard Etta awake in her portable crib, I climbed out of bed and got dressed quietly, letting Trevor sleep in. He'd tossed and turned and I didn't think he'd slept much.

I hated that I was causing such a problem between him and his mom, but I wasn't about to become a martyr for her cause. I knew better than to think that if I disappeared things would go back to normal for them. Too much had been said, and she'd overstepped too badly for anything to be fixed that easily.

"Please tell me you didn't make the coffee," Trevor said groggily as he came into the kitchen.

"Of course not," I replied, giving Etta her plate of scrambled eggs. "Even I don't like my coffee."

"I can show you how to do it," he said, grinning as he shuffled to the coffeepot.

"But then I'd have to make it," I pointed out, putting the rest of the eggs on two plates. "Why would I want that?"

"Good point," he replied. He walked toward me and kissed me gently. "Good morning."

"Good morning," I whispered back.

He took the plates from me and carried them to the table, kissing the top of Etta's head as he passed her.

"Hi Twevo," Etta said, completely oblivious to the change in dynamics.

We ate breakfast in companionable silence and took the dog out for his morning constitutional, but we didn't make it in to town for a midmorning movie like we'd planned because we had unexpected company.

"Shit," Trevor mumbled as we watched his parents pull up the driveway.

I didn't repeat his sentiment, but I felt it. The cape of invincibility I'd worn the night before had dissipated in the light of day, and I was suddenly feeling very exposed, even with Trevor standing right beside me. Knowing someone doesn't like you is a gross feeling, and knowing that there's nothing you can do to change their mind makes it even worse.

"Etta," I said, calling her back to me when she started venturing toward the driveway. "Bring Koda over to the grass so he doesn't hurt his paws on the gravel."

My excuse for her to move away from her grandparents was flimsy, but thankfully it seemed to make sense to her, and she called Koda impatiently as she moved toward the side of the house.

"If they say anything shitty, take Etta into the house," Trevor said quietly as his parents climbed out of the SUV. "I don't think I can keep my cool."

"Yes, you can," I replied, resting a hand on his back in a quick touch of reassurance.

By the time Mike and Ellie reached us, my arms were crossed over my chest and Trevor had grown so tense I was afraid he would snap.

"I'm sorry," his mom said, not bothering with a greeting. "I don't want to fight with you."

Trevor softened a little—I could tell by the set of his shoulders under the flannel he wore—but he didn't say a word, just nodded.

"I'm having a hard time with all this," Ellie said, chewing the inside of her cheek as she fidgeted.

"What she means to say is that she knows you're an adult and you make your own decisions. And we support you in everything you do," Mike added, his voice firm.

"I don't want to lose another one of my boys," Ellie said, her voice barely a whisper.

"That was never going to happen," Trevor replied.

Everyone went silent then, unsure what was left to say. Ellie had apologized and Trevor had softened, but he didn't make any attempt to continue the conversation. He also didn't invite his parents inside.

"I love you," Ellie said finally, stepping forward to give Trevor a long hug.

"I love you, too, Mom," he said, wrapping his arms around her shoulders.

When he didn't say anything else, she gave him a watery smile and went back to the car, leaving his dad standing in the driveway with us.

"I'm real sorry about last night," Mike said to me.

"It's okay," I replied.

"Well, no," he said, tilting his head. "It's not." He looked at Trevor. "But we're family, and family works through the hard times."

"It might take me a minute," Trevor told him honestly.

"Understandable." Mike looked over at Etta and watched her crouch down to say something to Koda. "But we'd sure like to see you once in a while."

"I'll call Mom later this week," Trevor conceded. "That's the best I can do for now."

"All right." With a nod good-bye, Mike turned and walked back to the car.

I watched them drive away with a sour feeling in my gut that only intensified when Trevor's arm wrapped around my shoulder.

"You should let it go," I said, surprising even myself.

"What?"

"You should let it go," I repeated. "Just...let it go."

"No," he replied. "That's not how it works."

"Maybe it should be," I said, shrugging as he stared at me. "Look, I don't think we'll be best friends"—Trevor scoffed—"but that's your mom. That's Etta's grandma. Life's too short to hold grudges."

I figured I'd regret the words the moment I said them, but I didn't. I was on the winning end of this scenario. My place in Trevor's life wasn't up for debate, and knowing *that* made me crazily calm about the whole situation.

"I'll work on it," Trevor said. He kissed me and walked into the house.

I didn't follow right away, thinking that maybe he needed

a little time to himself, but half an hour later I was freezing my ass off outside and herded Etta and Koda into the living room. I came to an abrupt halt when I found Trevor sitting in the middle of the floor with boxes and a giant green bag spread out around him. I recognized the bag—not specifically, but generally.

"What are you doing?" I asked, scooping up the puppy before he could go prancing through the stuff with his muddy paws.

"I'm—" Trevor went silent as he looked at the stuff he'd spread out. "You're right. Life's too short to hold grudges."

His eyes met mine and we stared at each other for a long moment.

"Come on, Henrietta," I sang quietly. "It's movie time in Uncle Trev's room."

After putting the puppy in his kennel, I cuddled up with Etta in Trevor's bed until she fell asleep halfway through the movie. Thankfully, she was tired and hadn't needed much of my attention, because my mind was still in the living room with that bag that had Henry's name on it. Scooping Etta into my arms, I carried her to her portable crib and tucked her in.

Then I made my way back into the living room.

"The kid had a lot of porn," Trevor said, laughing a little even though his voice was hoarse with tears. "He may have had a problem."

"Oh yeah?" I replied, stepping gingerly around various flotsam as I ventured farther into the room. "Find anything else?"

"Dirty socks," he said, gesturing toward a brown pair of

socks in the corner. "Some letters he got from my parents, bottle caps, clothes, that kind of stuff."

"Did you find what you were looking for?" I asked, letting him pull me onto his lap when I got close enough.

He was silent for a long moment as he rested his forehead in the crook of my neck. "I was hoping for a note or something," he finally said. "There wasn't one."

"I'm sorry," I replied, reaching up to smooth my hand down the back of his head.

"It's okay," he said, sighing heavily into my neck. "I knew there wouldn't be one. The only time Henry thought ahead was the day he put those insurance papers in your name. I'm just going to sort through this shit and then hand it off to my parents without the porn."

"You don't want to keep any of it?" I asked, looking at the little badges and pins that should have been on a uniform. There were tons of the little things, like Henry had just kept losing them and buying new ones. Oddly, when his things had been packed up, they'd all been found again.

It was strange to see Henry's life summed up in a small pile of odds and ends. I thought about the time I'd spent with him, the nights of laughter and drinking, the early mornings when he'd followed me into the shower even though I was running late, his grin and the way he'd thrown his head back when he laughed. My eyes watered. I'd never loved Henry, but he'd been a great friend and he'd given me Etta. I'd always be thankful for that.

"Nah, we can put a few things away for Etta," Trevor said. "But I got what I wanted when Hen's will was read and I came to find you."

"It's weird how things happen, isn't it?" I asked softly, leaning back against Trevor's chest as I looked over the little pieces of Henry's life spread out on the floor.

"Yeah, it is." He kissed the side of my neck, then whispered in my ear. "Are you going to stay with me?"

I swallowed hard and nodded once, immediately feeling relieved instead of the panic I'd expected.

"Good. You still love me?"

"I love you," I confirmed, twisting to look up into Trevor's eyes. "But I need a shower like you would not believe."

His eyes crinkled at the corners when he realized that I was trying to make a joke. "Too late," he said. "You can't hide anymore."

Oddly enough, I didn't even want to.

* * *

We spent the day playing with Etta and the puppy she'd begun to call hers. I couldn't remember the last time I'd felt so settled in one place. Our apartments and houses had always felt like a stopping point, never somewhere we would stay for a long time. Even my dad's house had been temporary until I got on my feet again. Trevor's house was different. It felt like a place we could spend our lives, somewhere Etta could paint her room whatever color she wanted and someday invite her friends for sleepovers.

I was happy. Genuinely content.

That's why, after dinner had been cleared and Trevor had cuddled up with Etta on the couch, I put on my jacket and grabbed my car keys.

"Where do you think you're going?" Trevor asked, teasingly reaching over the back of the couch to grab me.

"We're really low on toilet paper," I said with a grimace, making him laugh.

"I can go," he said, moving like he was going to get off the couch.

"No, it's fine." I set my hand on his shoulder and leaned over to kiss him. "It's kind of exciting to go by myself for once."

"Me go," Etta said, popping up from where she'd been lying.

"Nah, we'll let Mama go while we watch a movie," Trevor replied, pulling her onto his lap.

"No, me go, too."

"I think we have ice cream," Trevor whispered, immediately quieting her protests.

"I'll be back soon," I murmured, sneaking out before Etta started whining again.

My stomach churned as I drove away from the house. I didn't feel good about lying to Trevor, but I knew that if I'd told him where I was going he'd either try to stop me or want to come along. I loved that he felt so protective of us, but this was something I needed to do on my own.

I'd never been to Trevor's parents' house before, but I knew I could find it by process of elimination. There were only three driveways on the stretch of road lining the property, and I'd already been down two of them. It was kind of hard to find my way in the dark, especially since all of the driveways were so long and winding, but eventually I knew I'd found the right place when I saw Ellie's car parked in front of the beautiful one-story house.

I was a little shaky so I hid my hands in my pockets as soon as I'd knocked on the front door. It was so quiet out in the middle of nowhere that I could hear a TV playing inside the house and the thumping of footsteps as they came toward where I was standing. When Mike opened the door, his eyebrows rose in surprise.

"Hey, Morgan," he said, taking a step back to let me inside. "What brings you by?"

"Hi, Mike." I tried to smile at him, but nerves made it more of a grimace. "Is Ellie around?"

"Sure." Mike hesitated, and looked past me. "Trev come with you?"

"No, it's just me," I said quietly.

He closed the door behind me without a word, then reached up to scratch the side of his jaw. After a moment, he nodded.

"She's back in the craft room," he said, nodding his head toward the hallway. "I'll show ya."

Ellie was sitting at a long table covered in scraps of paper and photos. She was so engrossed in what she was working on that she didn't look up right away when we reached the doorway. By the time she stopped what she was doing and lifted her eyes, Mike had slipped away—or run for cover—and I was the only one standing there.

"Yes?" Ellie asked, her voice flat.

I'd had all of these replies prepared for when she asked why I was there, or called me a name, or kicked me out of her house, but I didn't have anything planned for that kind of reception.

"Um." I clenched my fists inside my coat pockets.

"I'm in the middle of something—"

"Why do you hate me?" I asked, her dismissive words

triggering a little attitude of my own. "You don't even know me."

"And whose fault is that?" she asked, throwing the paper in her hand down onto the table.

"You're kidding, right?" I sputtered. "I tried to get to know you. I invited you to my house."

"Then turned my son against me."

"I didn't do that," I ground out.

"Thanks," she said condescendingly.

"If that's what you think happened, I'm sorry." My tone was nothing but nice, even though I wanted to turn around and walk right back out of that house.

"Is that all?"

"I think we got off on the wrong foot here," I tried to say, but stopped when she snorted.

"I've already said that I was sorry and cleared everything up," she replied.

It took everything I had not to snap at her. I'd never done anything to the woman and she seemed to have some major problem with me. I just didn't understand it. I thought about leaving, but only for a second.

"Listen," I said, leaning against the doorjamb like I planned to be there for a while. "I'm here for one reason."

"I don't have any more available sons," she muttered. It was a low blow, but I let her take it.

"I love Trevor," I said, my voice quiet but strong. "And he *adores* you."

She flapped her hand in the air like she didn't care what I was saying, but she didn't reply.

"I don't understand why you're so upset with us, but I hope

that we can move past it. Not for my sake—I can handle anything you want to dish out—but for Trevor and Etta."

"Don't you dare—" she practically growled, getting to her feet.

"Mom," Trevor snapped, startling me. I looked over my shoulder to find him coming down the hallway, his expression dark.

"Trev," I said, putting a hand on his chest as he reached me. "How did you know I was here?"

"Hard to go shopping when you left your purse at home," he said, still looking at his mom. "Good thing Etta's seat is still in my truck, or I would've had to walk, and then I'd be really pissed."

"Go home," I murmured.

"Not a chance in hell."

"I am happy for you, you know," Ellie said to her son, her lips trembling with emotion.

"This is a real good way of showing it," Trevor replied.

"You don't know what it's been like." She lifted a hand to her mouth and shook her head once. "He was my baby."

"I know that," Trevor said softly.

"And suddenly he was gone," she rasped out. "But then we found out he had his own baby. My baby had a baby." She sniffled and my eyes began to water.

It didn't matter how horrible she'd been, or if she didn't like me, or if I didn't like her. In that moment, she was a mother and I was a mother, and I couldn't even fathom the pain she must have been in.

"But that baby was so far away," she said, her voice barely audible. "And with a mother who didn't seem all that interested in us."

I wanted to argue, but I didn't. This was her story to tell.

"I was so worried about Etta, so concerned that she was okay, that I may have seen some things that weren't there," she said, meeting my eyes. "I *am* sorry for that."

I nodded.

"But I thought we worked that out," she said, lifting her hands in an *I don't understand* gesture. "We were in contact after that, and everything seemed okay."

"Everything was okay," I replied quietly.

"So then why didn't you tell me you were in town? Why wouldn't you let us see Etta? Why all the secrecy and sneaking around with my son?" Her eyes went to Trevor. "You knew what you were doing was wrong. That's why you hid it."

"No," Trevor said, cutting her off. "I knew that you wouldn't like it. That's the only reason I didn't talk to you about it. Everyone knew, Ma. Everyone."

"Well," she said, her face paling with shock. "That's good to know."

"I love you," Trevor said. "And I've never wanted you to be hurt or sad. Honest to God, Mom, I have no idea why you have such a problem with Morgan."

"I don't," his mom yelled in frustration. "I never have."

"Then what the fuck?" Trev replied, making me glance at him in shock. I'd never heard him talk to anyone that way.

"I was jealous," Ellie finally said, looking away from us. "That's all it was. Jealous and scared."

"Of what?" Trevor asked in confusion.

"Oh," Ellie hiccupped tearfully. "Everything, I guess." She laughed humorlessly. "I was jealous that she'd spent time with

Henry, probably more time than I had in the past few years, and that she had a small piece of him in Etta."

Her words hit me like a ton of bricks, and if I'd thought she would let me, I would have hugged her. God, I'd been so concerned with how she felt about me from the beginning that I'd ignored the pain she'd been in since Henry died. I'd assumed that she was still dealing with the loss but I'd never really thought of what her pain looked like in real life.

"And then after you met her you started acting different," Ellie said, a rueful smile tugging at her lips as she swiped at the tears on her cheeks. "You stopped coming by as often, stopped telling us about your life. All I could see was you slipping away, and I knew it was because of this relationship that the two of you had started."

"Mom," Trevor said softly. "You know I'd never go far."

"Knowing and believing are two different things," she replied. She looked at me, shame filling her eyes. "It was never about you, Morgan. I think you're great. But...you just seemed to be caught up in the middle of it."

"I've never had the chance to tell you how sorry I was about Henry," I said. Now that I'd seen the pain she was in firsthand, I had to acknowledge it before I could say anything else. "I can't imagine what I'd do if I lost Etta."

Before my eyes, Ellie seemed to wilt. Her hands covered her face and her shoulders rolled forward and a heartbreaking sob split the room.

"I'm so sorry for how horrible I've been," she said into her hands.

Trevor slid past me and wrapped his arms around his mom, his cheek resting on the top of her head as he rocked them back and forth. I watched them for only a moment before I turned and walked back down the hallway.

"You get it all worked out?" Mike asked when I found him on the living room floor playing with Etta. He said the words easily, like he already knew the answer.

"I think so," I said with a small sigh. I sat down on the edge of the couch and smiled when Etta reached past Mike to steal some of his pile of Legos.

"That's good," he said, scooping up the Legos Etta had stolen and putting them back in his pile.

We didn't talk anymore while we waited for Trevor and his mom to come out. Even Etta was quiet while she played. When I finally heard footsteps coming down the hallway, I turned my head just in time to see Trevor wiping his palms over his eyes. When he saw me looking, he smiled.

"All good?" I asked as I stood up to wrap my arms around his waist.

He nodded and leaned down to murmur in my ear. "My mom asked us to stay for dinner and I didn't have the heart to tell her we'd already eaten. Is that okay?"

"I *am* feeling a little hungry," I whispered back.

"I love you," he said, his voice a little louder as he kissed the side of my head.

I stayed in the circle of his arms, not quite ready to disconnect yet. "I love you, too."

"Me love you, too," Etta piped in, not even looking up from her blocks.

Did you miss Kate and Shane's love story?

Please turn the page for an excerpt from

unbreak my
HEART

Prologue

Shane

W hy are we going to this shit again?" I asked my wife as she messed with her makeup in the passenger-side mirror.

"Because it's important to your cousin."

"She's not my cousin," I reminded her, switching lanes.

"Fine. It's important to *Kate*," she answered, losing patience. "I don't understand why you're being a dick about it."

"How often do we get out of the house with no kids, Rach? Rarely. I'd rather not spend our one night alone at some fucking coffeehouse filled with eighteen-year-olds."

"Damn, you're on a roll tonight," she murmured in annoyance. "Kate asked me to this thing weeks ago. I didn't know you'd be home."

"Right, plans change."

"I promised I'd go! I drop everything for you every time you come back from deployment. You know I do. I can't believe you're acting like a jackass because of *one night* that I had plans I couldn't change."

"I highly doubt Kate wants me here," I mumbled back, pulling into the little parking lot that was already filled with cars. "She's going to hate it when I see her crash and burn."

I hopped out of the car and walked around the hood to help Rachel out of the car. I never understood why she insisted on wearing high-as-fuck heels while she was pregnant—it made me nervous. She looked hot as hell, but one day she was going to fall and I was terrified I wouldn't be there to catch her.

"You really have no idea, do you?" she said, laughing, as I took her hand and pulled her gently out of her seat. "How in God's name did you grow up together and you still know so little about Kate?"

"You know I didn't grow up with her." I slammed the door shut and walked her slowly toward the small building. "I moved in when I was seventeen and left town when I was nineteen. She's not family, for Christ's sake. She's the spoiled, *weird* niece of the people who took me in for a very short period of time."

Rachel stopped short at the annoyance in my voice. "She's my *best friend*. My only friend. And she freaking introduced us, in case you've forgotten."

"Not on purpose."

"What's that supposed to mean? What wasn't on purpose?"

"She was pissed as hell when we got together."

"No, she wasn't," Rachel argued. "What are you talking about?"

"Never mind. It's not important."

"Can you please, *please*, just be nice and not act like you're being tortured when we get in there? I don't know what your deal is with her—"

"I don't have a deal with her, I just wanted to take my gorgeous wife out to dinner tonight, and instead we're going to watch her friend sing for a bunch of teenagers. Not exactly what I was hoping for."

I reached out to cup her cheek in my palm and rubbed the

skin below her lips with my finger. I wanted to kiss her, but after all the lipstick she'd applied in the car, I knew she wouldn't thank me for it.

"We'll go somewhere else afterward, okay? I think she's on first, so we won't be here long," she assured me with a small smile, her eyes going soft. She knew I wanted to kiss her; my hand on her face was a familiar gesture.

"Okay, baby." I leaned in and kissed the tip of her nose gently. "You look beautiful. Did I tell you that yet?"

"Nope."

"Well, you do."

She smiled and started walking toward the building again, and I brushed my fingers through the short hair on the back of my head.

It wasn't that I disliked Kate. Quite the opposite, actually. When we were kids, we'd been friends, and I'd thought she was funny as hell. She had a quirky, sometimes weird sense of humor, and she'd been the most genuinely kind person I'd ever met. But for some reason, all those years ago, she'd suddenly focused in on me, and the attention had made me uncomfortable.

I wasn't into her, and her crush had made me feel weird, uncomfortable in my own skin. I didn't want to hurt her feelings, but shit, she just didn't do it for me. She was too clean-cut, too naive and trusting. Even then, I'd been more attracted to women who were a little harder, a little darker, than the girl who still had posters of fairies on her walls at seventeen.

So I began avoiding her as much as I could until she'd brought home a girl wearing red lipstick and covered in tattoos after her first semester in college. I'd ignored the way Kate had watched me with sad eyes as I'd monopolized her friend's time and completely disregarded her hurt feelings. I'd never liked Kate that way, and I hadn't seen anything wrong with going after her new friend.

I'd ended up married to her roommate, and from then on I'd acted like Kate and I had never been friends. It was easier that way.

"Come on, baby," Rachel called, pulling me into the darkened coffeehouse. "I see a table, and my feet are killing me."

Why the fuck did she insist on wearing those damn shoes?

"Can I get you anything to drink?" a small waitress asked us. Like, really small. She was barely taller than the bistro table we were sitting at.

"Can I get a green tea, please?" Rachel asked.

"Sure! The green we've got is incredible. When are you due?"

"Not for a while."

"Well, congratulations!"

"Black coffee," I ordered when the friendly waitress finally looked my way. Her smile fell, and I realized my words had come out shorter than I'd intended.

"Sure thing!" she chirped with a tight smile before walking away.

"Seriously, Shane?" Rachel growled in annoyance.

"What?" I knew exactly what. I'd been a jackass, but I wasn't about to explain that the crowded coffeehouse was making me sweat. People were laughing loudly, jostling and bumping into each other around the room, and I couldn't see the exits from where we sat.

"Hey, San Diego," a familiar voice called out over the speakers. "How you guys doing tonight?"

The room filled with cheers, and Rachel's face lit up as she looked past me toward the stage.

"Aren't you sweet?" Kate rasped with a short chuckle. "I dig you guys, too."

The crowd grew even louder, and my shoulders tightened in response.

"There's a coffee can being passed around, who's got it?" She paused. "Okay, Lola's got it now—back there in the purple shirt with the Mohawk. When you get it, add a couple dollars, if you can, and pass it on."

The crowd clapped, and Kate chuckled again over the sound system. "I better get started before you guys riot."

I still hadn't turned to look at her. Frankly, I didn't want to embarrass her if she sucked. I didn't—

The clear notes of a single guitar came through the speakers, and I froze as the entire room went silent. Completely silent. Even the baristas behind the counter stopped what they were doing to watch the stage as Kate began to sing.

Holy shit. My head whipped around, and I felt like I'd taken a cheap shot to the chest.

Her voice was raspy and full-bodied, and she was cradling her guitar like a baby that she'd held every day of her entire life. She was completely comfortable up there, tapping her foot and smiling at different people in the crowd as they began to sing along with her.

It was incredible. *She* was incredible. I couldn't look away. This wasn't some silly idea she'd had on the spur of the moment. She knew exactly what she was doing, and these kids knew her. They freaking loved her.

And she looked gorgeous.

Shit.

Her hair was rolled up on the sides in something Rachel had attempted a few times. I think they were called victory rolls? I'm pretty sure that's what Rach had called them when she couldn't figure them out. Her skin was smooth, and she wore deep-pink lipstick that made her teeth bright white under the spotlight. She was wearing a T-shirt that hung off her shoulder and ripped jeans that were so tight, I wasn't even sure how she'd managed to sit down.

I blinked slowly, and she was still there.

"I tried to tell you she was good," Rachel said smugly from my side.

"Did she write that song?" I asked, turning to look at my wife.

"Babe, seriously? It's a Taylor Swift song."

"Oh."

"This one's a Kenny Chesney song."

"I know this one," I murmured, looking back toward the stage. "Does she only sing country?"

"Hell no. It's mostly other stuff, but it's usually got a theme. Tonight is obviously about kids...teenagers, since the donations are going to some stop-bullying charity."

I nodded, but my eyes were on the stage again as Kate danced a little in her seat, tapping out the beat of the new song on the front of her guitar. Had Kate been bullied? I didn't remember anything like that, but like I'd told Rachel, I'd only stayed with Kate's aunt and uncle for a little over a year before I left for boot camp. Maybe I'd missed it. The thought made me grind my teeth in anger.

Kate pursed her bright lips then, blowing a kiss with a wink for the crowd.

My breath caught.

Jesus Christ.

I pushed my seat back from the table and grabbed Rachel's hand, pulling her over to sit on my lap.

"What are you doing?" she whispered with a laugh.

"If I've gotta stay here, I'm getting some perks."

"Oh yeah?"

"Yeah." I leaned in and kissed her hard, ignoring the lipstick I could feel smearing over my lips. I slid my tongue into her mouth and felt her nails dig into my shoulder as she tilted her head for a better angle. God, kissing her still felt as good as it had the first time I'd done it. I hadn't known that loving someone so much was even possible before I'd met her.

"Rain check?" she asked against my lips as she reached out blindly and grabbed a couple of napkins to clean off our faces. Her face was flushed, and I wanted nothing more than to leave that fucking coffeehouse and get her alone.

My wife was the most beautiful woman I'd ever known, and it wasn't just her looks. She'd grown up like I had, scrounged and fought for every single thing she'd needed—and I was proud of the family and the life we'd built together. We'd come a long way from our nasty upbringings.

"Can we go home yet?" I replied with a smirk as I wiped my face.

"Hey, you two in the corner!" Kate called into the mike, interrupting the incredibly sexy look Rachel was giving me. "None of that, I've got kids here."

The crowd laughed, and I glanced sharply at the stage.

Kate was smiling so brightly that she looked giddy. "That's my best friend, right there. Isn't she gorgeous?"

The crowd cheered as Rachel laughed softly in my ear and blew a kiss at Kate.

"I wanna know who the guy is!" a girl called out from across the room, making everyone laugh.

"Eh, that's just her husband," Kate answered flatly, making the crowd snicker. She met my eyes and winked, then grinned before looking away and starting in on the next song as if she hadn't just made my stomach drop.

We watched her for almost an hour as she fucking killed it onstage. Then I ushered Rachel out of the building without saying good-bye, making excuses about wanting to beat the rush of kids.

I had the distinct impression that I knew very little about the woman I'd been avoiding for the past ten years, and I wondered how I'd missed it. She wasn't the awkward girl I remembered, or the sloppy woman in sweats and tank tops that Rachel occasionally invited over to the house when I was home.

The Kate I'd seen onstage was a fucking knockout—confident and sassy. I knew then that I'd continue to avoid her, but for an entirely different reason than I had before.

Kate

Two months later

Evans Web Design," I answered my phone as I switched lanes on the freeway. God, traffic was a nightmare.

"Is this Katherine Evans?"

"Yes, who's this?"

"Sorry, this is Tiffany from Laurel Elementary School. I'm calling because you're Sage Anderson's emergency contact number—"

"Is Sage okay?" I interrupted, flipping off the car that honked at me. Why the hell would they call me and not her mother?

"Sage is fine, Ms. Evans. We were just wondering if you knew who was supposed to pick her up from school today? Class ended about thirty minutes ago, and no one was here to get her."

"Her mom picks her up," I replied, looking at the clock on my dash. "She didn't call?"

"No, ma'am. We've been trying to reach her, but haven't been able to."

"That's weird."

"It is," she agreed.

"Okay, well, I'll come get her and try to get ahold of Rachel, but it's going to take me at least half an hour." It looked like my appointment downtown was going to have to be postponed.

"That's totally fine. Sage can just hang with me in the office."

"Okay, tell her Auntie Kate will be there soon."

I hung up and pulled off the freeway so I could turn around. Shit, if I tried to go north I'd be stuck in stop-and-go traffic for the next two hours. I navigated back streets working toward Sage's school, calling Rachel over and over. The longer she didn't answer, the more my stomach tightened.

My best friend wouldn't forget to pick up her child at school. She was a second grader, for Pete's sake. It wasn't like her pickup time was any different than it had been for the last two years. Something was off.

It took me less time than I thought to get to Sage's school, and I whipped into a parking space with shaky hands.

I had an awful feeling in my gut that I couldn't seem to calm.

"Hey, I'm looking for a girl, short, dark hair, goes by some ridiculous plant name..." I said in my most serious voice as I reached the front office.

"Auntie Kate! I'm right here!"

"Ah, yep. That's the one I'm looking for," I teased, smiling as my favorite girl in the whole world wrapped her arms around me.

"You just have to sign her out," the office lady said with a grin.

"No problem."

I signed Sage out and walked her to my car, popping the trunk to pull out the spare booster I kept there.

"Where's my mom?" Sage asked, bouncing around on her toes. The excitement of riding around in my car had obviously eclipsed the trauma she'd endured by being forgotten at school.

"I'm not sure, kiddo," I answered as I got her situated in the backseat.

"Daddy's at the range today!" Sage informed me as we made our way to her house.

"Oh yeah?"

"Yeah, he's been home for a long time."

"It sure seems that way, doesn't it?" I replied cheerfully. She had no idea.

I didn't mind that Rachel wanted to spend time with Shane while he was home. I totally understood it. But it sucked being the friend who was ignored when someone's significant other came home from yet another military deployment. I practically lived with Rachel while Shane was gone—she hated being alone—but the moment her husband stepped foot on American soil, I was persona non grata again.

It had been happening for years. I wasn't sure why it still bothered me.

"Mom's going to have a baby soon," Sage piped up from the backseat as I turned onto their street.

"I know, pretty exciting, right?"

"Yeah. She's having another brother, though."

"What's wrong with brothers? I have two brothers," I reminded her, pulling into their empty driveway.

I climbed out of the car as she started to answer and looked at the quiet house in confusion when no one came to greet us. Where the hell were Rachel and the boys?

Sage continued rambling on as I helped her out of her seat. "—wanted a sister. Boys stink, and they only play with boy stuff—"

"Kate?" someone called from across the street. "Where's Rachel? She was supposed to pick up the boys like two hours ago!"

I turned to see Rachel's neighbor Megan crossing the dead-end street with Gavin on her hip and Keller skipping alongside her.

"No clue," I answered quietly as she reached me. "The school called because she didn't pick Sage up. I've been trying to reach her for the last forty minutes."

"Where's my mom?" Sage asked, looking between us in confusion.

"Hey, sis, take the boys inside for me, would ya?" I handed her my keys as Megan set Gavin on the ground. "I'll be inside in a sec, and we'll make a snack. You guys want to make some cookies?"

"Yeah!" Keller yelled, throwing his fist in the air.

"No hello for your favorite aunt?" I asked him with a raised brow.

"Hi, Auntie Kate! Cookies!" he yelled, racing toward the door with Gavin and Sage trailing behind him.

I watched as Sage unlocked the door, leaving the keys hanging in the lock as she rushed inside.

"What the hell is going on?" I asked, turning to Megan.

"I have no clue. She said she was going to get her nails done and she'd be back in, like, an hour. It's been well over three now," she replied in frustration, wrapping her arms around her waist.

"That's not like her."

"No, I know it's not." She rushed to add, "I'm not mad, I'm worried. She's usually back *before* she says she'll be."

"Auntie Kate, cookies!" Keller screamed at me from the front door.

"I better get in there," I told Megan, looking over my shoulder at Keller swinging on the open door. "Thanks so much for watching them."

"No problem," she answered with a nod. "Let me know when you hear anything, okay?"

"Sure," I said, already walking toward where my little monkey was trying to climb the door frame.

"Let's go make a mess in the kitchen!" I announced loudly, picking Keller up like a football as he giggled. I forced myself not to panic in front of the kids as we pulled ingredients out of the cupboards and began trashing the kitchen. I told myself that Rachel would call soon, but the longer I was there with no word from her, the less I believed it.

* * *

We didn't hear anything, not for hours.

I tried to call Rachel at least a hundred times but she never answered, and after a while I couldn't even leave another message in her full voicemail.

It wasn't until I was making dinner for the kids that my phone rang, and I almost dropped it in my haste to answer.

"Hello?" I said, walking toward the laundry room for a bit of quiet. "Hello?"

"Can I please speak to Katherine Evans?"

"This is Katherine."

"Hello, this is Margie at Tri-City Medical Center. I'm calling about a Rachel Anderson."

My knees felt like water, and I reached out to grip the washing machine to keep me on my feet. "Is she okay?"

"Ma'am, she's been in an accident."

"Is she okay?" I could hear my voice becoming more shrill with every word, and I clenched my teeth to keep myself from yelling.

"Can you come to the hospital, ma'am?"

The woman's voice was unnaturally calm, and I knew that no matter what I said she wasn't going to give me a straight answer. Hell, it was her job to notify people that their family was in the hospital. She didn't give a shit that I was about to lose my mind.

"I'll—" I looked around the laundry room in a panic. What was I supposed to do? "I'm on my way. Tell her I'm on my way."

"Come straight to the emergency entrance when you get here."

"I will."

The minute she hung up, I bent at the waist and braced my hands on my knees, trying to get my shit together.

Rachel was fine. The baby was fine. I was freaking out over nothing. I was getting myself worked up over nothing. It was just an accident.

"Sage!" I yelled as I walked quickly through the house. "Keep an eye on your brothers. I'm walking over to Megan's real quick—I'll be right outside!"

As I reached the front porch, I began to sprint, and by the

time I was at Megan's front door I was out of breath and on the verge of tears.

"Kate? What's up?" Megan asked as she swung the door open.

"Can you take care of the kids? I have to go—the hospital just called." A painful sob burst out of my throat, and I wiped my hand over my face to try to gain some control. "They said Rachel's been in an accident. I need to get over there."

"Sure, honey. No worries," she answered before I was even finished speaking. "Caleb, get your shoes on, bud! We're going over to the Andersons' for a bit."

"Woohoo!" I heard from somewhere in the back of the house.

"Did you call Shane?" she asked, sliding into some sandals by the door.

"I didn't even think to," I replied with a small shake of my head. "He's rarely here. I forgot he was in town." I felt like shit for not calling him, but I was so used to taking care of things while he was gone that it hadn't even dawned on me. I'd driven Rachel to the hospital when she'd had Gavin, taken care of things when Keller broke his arm, and helped with a thousand other little events over the past few years. I stepped in every time he was gone, and I hadn't thought about him for one second as I'd paced around the house that afternoon.

"We'll be over in a minute. I'm sure she's fine," Megan assured me with a nod. "You better go get some shoes on and let the kids know I'm coming over for a visit."

"I'm not telling them—" I shook my head and looked down at my bare feet. I hadn't even noticed the hot pavement as I'd run across it barefoot. Why didn't I put shoes on?

"Come on," she said gently, pushing me away from the door as her kid raced out ahead of us. "We'll walk you over."

* * *

I'm not sure what I said to the kids about the reason I was leaving, and I don't remember the drive to the hospital or even where I parked that afternoon. I can't recall what the nurse looked like as she searched for Rachel's name in their computer system or the walk toward the room where I waited for someone to speak to me.

The first thing I remember clearly is the white-haired doctor's kind face as he sat down across from me, and the young chaplain's small smile as he chose the chair to my left. Their words became a litany that I would hear in my dreams for years.

My Rachel was gone, but her son was alive and in the NICU.

"Is there anyone you'd like for us to call? Any family or friends that you'd like to be here?"

The question jolted me out of the fog that seemed to be getting thicker and thicker around me. *Dear God.*

"I'll make the calls," I answered, looking blankly at the wall. "Can I have some privacy please?"

"Of course. I'll be right outside if you need me," the chaplain answered, reaching out to pat my hand. "I'll take you up to the NICU when you're ready."

The room was silent after they left, and I fought the urge to scream at the top of my lungs just to hear it echo around me. I understood then why people hired mourners to wail at funerals. Sometimes the lack of sound is more painful than the anguished noise of a heart breaking.

My hands shook as I pulled my phone out of my front pocket and rested it on the table in front of me.

It only took a moment before the sound of ringing filled the room, and I rested my head in my hands as I stared at the name across the screen.

"Hello? Kate? What's wrong?"

"Shane—" I said quietly, my voice hitching.

"What? Why are you calling me?" His voice was confused, but I could hear a small thread of panic in the urgency of his words.

"I need you to come to Tri-City hospital," I answered, tears rolling down my face and landing on the glass screen of my phone, distorting the letters and numbers.

"Who?" His voice was frantic, and I could hear him moving around, his breathing heavy.

"Rachel was in an accident." I sobbed, covering my face to try to muffle the noise.

"No," he argued desperately as I heard two car doors shut almost simultaneously. "Is she okay?"

I shook my head, trying to catch my breath.

"Kate! Is she okay?" he screamed at me, his anguished voice filling the room as I'd wanted mine to just minutes before.

"No," I answered through gritted teeth, feeling snot running down my upper lip as I heard him make a noise deep in his throat. "She's gone."

He didn't say a word, and less than a second later the connection was broken.

I could barely force myself to reach across the table for a

tissue as I scrolled down my contact list and pressed SEND again. I wasn't finished.

"Hello!" Her voice made me whimper in both relief and sorrow.

"Mom?" I rasped.

"Katie?"

"I—I—"

"Take a deep breath, baby. Then tell me what's wrong," she ordered.

"I need you and Aunt Ellie to come down here," I cried, straightening my back and wiping the tears from my face. "I'm not—I don't know what to do."

"Okay, we'll find a flight," she answered immediately, like flying from Portland to San Diego was as easy as walking across the street. "Now what's going on?"

"Rachel was in an accident," I ground out, the words like gravel in my throat. "She didn't make it, and I'm worried about Shane."

"Oh, Katie. My sweet girl," she said sadly. "We'll be on the first flight down, okay, baby?" Her voice became muffled as she covered the phone and yelled shrilly for my dad.

"I just, I'm not sure what I'm supposed to be doing," I confessed with a sob. "Shane isn't here yet, and I don't think I can see her, and the baby is in ICU."

"The baby's okay?"

"Yeah, they said they were just keeping him under observation." I rubbed at my forehead, trying to convince myself that it was all just a nightmare. Where was I supposed to be? What was I supposed to do now? My best friend in the entire world was there in that hospital, but not really. I couldn't bear to see her. I couldn't help her. Where the fuck was I supposed to go? "What do I do, Mom?"

"You go see your nephew."

"What?"

"You go to the NICU, and you hold your nephew, and you tell him everything is going to be okay," she told me, tears in her voice. "You go love on that baby. Where are Sage and the boys?"

"They're with a neighbor. They're okay."

"Good. That's good."

"Yeah."

"Dad found some flights. I'm on my way, princess," she told me gently. "We'll be there soon. Now go take care of our new boy."

"I love you, Mom."

"I love you, too. I'm on my way."

I made my way to the NICU as quickly as I could, and within minutes I was holding my new nephew in my arms. The nurses told me that he'd passed all of his tests with flying colors, and I was in awe as I sat down in a rocking chair, cradling him to my chest.

"You sure got a shitty beginning, little man," I murmured against his fuzzy scalp, rocking back and forth gently. "I'm so sorry, buddy. You're probably missing your mama and that warm bubble you've been in for so long. I can't help you there."

I sniffled, closing my eyes as tears rolled down my cheeks. My whole body ached, and even though I had that little boy in my arms, the day seemed like some sort of surreal dream, foggy in some parts and crystal clear in others. I wanted to hop up and take his sleeping little form to Rachel, to tease her about the weird Mohawk thing he was sporting and make joking comments about how men always seem to sleep through the hard parts of life. I wanted to see her smile proudly at the sturdy boy she'd produced and grumble that I was hogging him.

I wanted everything to be different.

I hummed softly with my eyes closed for a long time, holding the baby close to me. It was quiet where we sat, nothing breaking up the stillness of the room until I heard someone open the door.

"There he is," the nurse murmured from the doorway.

My eyes popped open to see Shane's ravaged face just feet from me. He looked like he was barely holding on. I swallowed hard as his red-rimmed eyes took in his son carefully before rising to meet mine.

"Is he okay?" he asked thickly, searching my face. I'd never seen him so frightened.

"He's perfect," I answered, my voice throbbing with emotion. "The nurses said he's a rock star."

He nodded twice, reaching up to cover his mouth with his hand, but before he could say another word, he was stumbling and falling to his knees with an almost inaudible sob.

About the Author

When NICOLE JACQUELYN was eight and people asked what she wanted to be when she grew up, she told them she wanted to be a mom. When she was twelve, her answer changed to author. Her dreams stayed constant. First she became a mom, and then, during her senior year of college—with one daughter in first grade and the other in preschool—she sat down and wrote a story.